TIME'S UNDOING

take the chance that a letter might be used to find you. The p...
you were the man involved in the altercation downtown. The...
suffered no major bodily harm, but his pride was badly injured
apparently he is a man with some influence.

Policemen came to your mother's house demanding to know you
whereabouts. Thank God Mae and I weren't home at the time.
neighbors say three officers, screaming and waving guns, forced you
t onto her porch while they searched the house. They knocked do...
d turned over furniture. They threatened your mother. She wa...
took to her bed for a few days. She is fine now and we are wat...
her. But at Mama's urging, I've moved home to have the pre...
family. We are all okay and I don't want you to worry.

Mae is doing fine. Growing so fast. She has two cousins he...
, and passes her days in good spirits. At night she calls to you
ms and giggles. She misses you. So do I.

'm finally starting to show. Mama thinks the baby is a boy,
carrying it low in my belly. It certainly kicks like a boy. B...
e we're having another girl.

ank you for the money you sent. As you instructed, I shared...
our mother and I was able to buy Mae a pair of shoes she c...
'm glad to hear your work is going so well. Birmingham sou...
exciting city and it just...

TIME'S UNDOING

A NOVEL

CHERYL A. HEAD

DUTTON

DUTTON

An imprint of Penguin Random House LLC
penguinrandomhouse.com

LIBRARY OF CONGRESS CATALOGING-IN-PUBLICATION DATA

Names: Head, Cheryl A., author.
Title: Time's undoing: a novel / Cheryl A. Head.
Description: New York: Dutton, Penguin Random House, [2023]
Identifiers: LCCN 2022031003 (print) | LCCN 2022031004 (ebook) |
ISBN 9780593471821 (hardcover) | ISBN 9780593471838 (ebook)
Subjects: LCGFT: Novels.
Classification: LCC PS3608.E227 T56 2023 (print) |
LCC PS3608.E227 (ebook) | DDC 813/.6—dc23/eng/20220810
LC record available at https://lccn.loc.gov/2022031003
LC ebook record available at https://lccn.loc.gov/2022031004

Printed in the United States of America

1 3 5 7 9 10 8 6 4 2

BOOK DESIGN BY DANIEL BROUNT

This is a work of fiction. Names, characters, places, events, and incidents are either the product of
the author's imagination or are used fictitiously. The author's use of names of historical figures,
places, or events is not intended to change the entirely fictional character of the work.
In all other respects, any resemblance to persons living or dead is entirely coincidental.

To Willie Mae McGarrah,
Mama, this story is infused with your
memories and perseverance.

To Robert Harrington,
I never knew you until I did.

White people are endlessly demanding to be reassured that Birmingham is really on Mars.

—JAMES BALDWIN

Our memory is longer than our lifespan.

—PROFESSOR KRISTIE DOTSON, UNIVERSITY OF MICHIGAN

TIME'S UNDOING

Prologue

1929

Four hours 'til dawn. The single streetlamp at the alleyway splays veiled illumination on the wet pavement. The rumble and squeak of streetcars ended two hours ago, and the in-a-hurry owner of the diner hauls out the last of the garbage, which tumbles onto the slick red bricks as he slams the door.

Cress lifts the collar of his tight-fitting jacket against curly brown hair. Alert. Smoking. Shifting from one leg to the other. Leaning into the shadows every time he hears loud voices from the street.

I can't feel the rain nor smell it, but I sense its fragrance mixed with the relentless forsythia creeping through every patch of dirt. Anna Kate often remarked that the flowers were her favorite part of living in Birmingham.

A car engine's hum grows louder. Cress melts into the darkness when the blue sedan eases forward and idles under the lamp. The sight of it passes a shiver my body doesn't register. Cress steps forward and drops his smoke, grinding the butt under his boot. He shoves both hands deep into the pockets of his dungarees.

The broad-shouldered detective gets out of the car, moves to the front bumper, and stops. His hat cocked back. He stares at Cress in the alley, then swivels his head to take in his surroundings. He nonchalantly swipes a hand down the breast of his coat.

That's where he keeps his revolver.

Cress waits. No longer fidgeting. Squaring his body. He lifts his hands from his pockets and leaves them dangling at his thighs. Finally the big man walks toward him.

"You've been asking for me, boy?"

"Yeah. I owe you money. I got it here." Cress slides a hand into his jacket.

The man tenses.

Cress extends a palm.

Do these two know each other?

The detective closes the gap between them. He's at least four inches taller, but when he draws close, Cress grabs his coat sleeve, yanking the big man forward. The guy slips but doesn't fall, so Cress hits him in the face with his fist—three times—like a sledgehammer on a slab of concrete. The man sinks, fumbling for his inside pocket. Cress thrashes him again and again while the struggling detective claws at his assailant's legs and arms, trying to right himself. Cress slides and pivots like a welterweight, but his opponent's size and strength give him an advantage and Cress loses his footing. Now they're kneeling face-to-face on the wet pavement. The big man snatches Cress by the hair, but he's not expecting the headbutt. Nor the punch to his solar plexus.

For a split second the fight pauses. The two stare at each other with gaping mouths and bared teeth.

When the detective grabs at his coat I think he's after the gun,

2

but his hand comes away covered in blood. He's been knifed. Cress thrusts the blade two more times, until his opponent slumps over.

This man-to-man battle has been quiet. Neither letting out more than a grunt. Cress lifts to his feet, rubbing at his scalp, looking around. He stares at the body, then aims his boot for a rib-shattering kick.

"That's for my sister," he says, then leans over to wipe the knife on the man's overcoat. Cress turns away, hurrying toward the opposite end of the alley. The glow of a match spirals, then extinguishes in a puddle.

The detective lies unmoving on the alley's surface. His left arm stretching to escape. His legs mixing with spilled garbage and soggy cardboard boxes.

ONE

The Decision

1929

It's quitting time and a group of my coworkers are in conversation in the mill parking lot. One casually leans against my brand-new Franklin Victoria sedan. I take offense.

"Get off my car, Arthur. I spent a lot of time on that wax job."

"Boy, nobody's bothering your damn car. You think you're all big and bad just 'cause you got this Franklin, but I ain't studyin' you."

It's been eighty-plus degrees all day and the heat has me on edge. I consider Arthur for a moment. He's a warehouse laborer. One of those redbone dudes who thinks his good hair is his ticket to success.

"Maybe *you* could buy a new car," I spit out, "if you stop spending your money on liquor and cockfights."

I regret the nagging-wife words as soon as they escape my mouth. I got no business telling another man how to spend his money. Arthur raises the stakes.

"I tell you one thing, Harrington, a fine woman like Anna

Kate wouldn't even *think* of marrying a blue-black fool like you if you wasn't driving this new car."

The gathered men whoop and holler at his retort. Hair tingles on my arms and the back of my neck. All my life I've tried to make up for my dark complexion. My expensive clothes, new car, light-skinned wife, and skills as a carpenter are proof I'm as good as, or better than, any other man. People have told me to my face that I'm cocky. Shit, I'm twenty-eight years old and nobody's lackey. I ain't looking for trouble but ain't running away from it either, and on this sticky Florida evening I'm not in the mood to let the comment go unanswered—especially when Arthur's defiant stare becomes a mocking smirk.

Without another word, my knuckles sink into the folds of his belly and the smile falls from his face as breath escapes his body. He's strong so he rocks back but doesn't drop.

"You motherfucker," he yells and swings a fist, glancing my chin.

For what seems like a minute we exchange blows. Our scuffle finally brings us to the ground, where we wrestle and curse until the foreman pulls us apart. He's a smart white man, six four, 220 pounds, and hired because he knows how to handle the temperaments of laborers in a factory environment.

Both of us should be fired, but only Arthur is let go. My carpentry skills have saved me. The grumbling about favoritism is growing, so I'm offered an out-of-state assignment—work on the mansion of a Birmingham, Alabama, millionaire. I don't accept the job right away because Anna Kate doesn't want to be separated from her family, and to tell the truth I don't want to leave St. Petersburg either. People know me here and I don't want to start out in a new city where I'll be just another colored man in the Deep South.

Two weeks after the confrontation at the mill, I'm involved in another incident. This time with a white man in downtown St. Pete. The guy demands I move my car so he doesn't have to park next to a rain puddle. He's drunk and wants to impress the woman in his passenger seat. He shouts the worst insults, then gets out of his vehicle to challenge me. Instead of backing down, I retrieve a polishing rag from under my seat and begin buffing the front bumper of the Franklin. When he spits on my car, I knock him to the pavement. The screams of his lady passenger cause several people to look our way. I'm sure one of them will call the police. I jump behind the wheel of my car and drive away.

The next day I'm on my way out of town. Word has already gotten to me that the police are asking around town about a Negro who drives a fancy car. I have to temporarily abandon my nineteen-year-old pregnant wife and young daughter in Florida. I take the carpentry job in Alabama because it seems, for now, the best thing to do. I sure hope trouble won't follow me to Birmingham.

TWO

2019

It's my fifth funeral in six months and I'm trying not to succumb to the despair I feel. Another Black man. This time in his early thirties. He'd been returning to his university teaching position after an impromptu lunch downtown with his fiancée. Walking fast because he was late for class, and texting the department secretary, he was unaware a patrol car had pulled to the sidewalk behind him. When the siren blared, Phillip Carter turned to look but kept walking. From there things escalated.

He dropped his backpack as ordered but refused to lean spread-eagle against the parking lot fence. A second officer approached with his gun drawn. Carter lifted the lanyard around his neck displaying his Wayne State University faculty ID. "I'm a professor," he pleaded. "I'm on my way to teach a class." The first cop responded with: "What's in the bag?" Carter crouched to retrieve the bundle of graded papers in his backpack. That's when both policemen fired their weapons.

Those are the details. I'm here, against the back wall of the church, to find something beyond the facts to engage our newspaper readers in the human elements of this story. The viewing of the body is still under way. I watch the somber crowd and make notes. I spot Carter's fiancée in the first row, flanked by her parents. I've seen her on the local news—grieving, poised, demanding justice. The shooting has prompted a half dozen protests in Detroit along with campus demonstrations in Ann Arbor and East Lansing. The firing of both officers by the chief of police hasn't appeased anybody.

I've briefly locked eyes a couple of times with an old Black man standing on the other side of the church. He's dressed a bit too stylish for a funeral, in an out-of-date suit with a polka-dot bow tie. He's coming my way.

"You're a reporter?" he asks.

"For the *Detroit Free Press*."

"Nice to meet you." He offers a handshake. Now that he's closer I notice a piece of stained wood hanging from a leather thread around his neck. It's a small whistle.

"Yes, sir. Same here," I reply, grasping his hand.

He stares at the casket in the front of the sanctuary.

"Why do they keep killing us?"

"I don't know."

"We're running out of time to make things right," he says with a pained look. "They can put men into space, but they won't make space for Black men."

It's a great quote, and I flip to a clean page in my notebook to jot it down. Before I can ask the man his full name, he moves away to wait in the viewing line. After the funeral service, I search for him but he's gone.

THREE

◆

A Fresh Start

1929

I'm part of a five-man carpentry crew working on a residential project. We're creating a grand entryway, foyer, and ballroom for a local steel magnate's mansion. The project involves several more months of work at top pay. It's the kind of opportunity not many Black men will ever get.

But after two months alone in the so-called Magic City, longing for the regular company of my wife and daughter, I'm making my second trip from St. Pete to Birmingham. I'm bringing them to live with me. Anna Kate's not all that happy, and it took some convincing for her to agree to leave her people, but the arrangement will work out pretty well for me.

Travel in our Franklin is pleasant enough. Better than the cramped seats in the rear of a bus, and cooler than the sweltering train cars, but the roads are crude and chock-full of holes. I'm lucky when there's gravel or sand filling in the ruts. That's especially true after we leave the Dixie Highway in Florida. Anna Kate is just six months along but already big, and prefers to sit in the back with Mae, where she has more leg room and can rest her swelling ankles. There is another advantage of her rear-seat perch. We're driving through towns that don't want to see Negroes after dark, and on the open road I'm a pretty big target for the Klan. So to the casual observer, with my light-skinned wife as passenger, I could pass for a chauffeur.

My biggest worry right this moment is getting Anna Kate and Mae to a secure place for the night. Normally, I could grab a few hours of sleep here and there, but with my family I need decent sleeping accommodations. I've arranged with Mama's pastor to stay overnight at a tourist house owned by the local AME church just outside of Macon, Georgia. But first things first, I need to keep my full attention on avoiding the ruts that could break the car's axle, and the white people who could take a disliking to us.

It's almost dusk before we reach the tourist house. Thankfully it's next door to the church where I'm to pick up the key. My carpenter's eye registers the door as solidly built pine. I knock a few times before it opens.

"Pastor Swanson?" I ask of the man peering through the crack.

He's tall and bearded. He reminds me of the stained-glass image of John the Baptist at Mama's church. His beefy hand clutches the handle of a lantern and he lifts his arm so he can see my face, and I can better see his. But this man with the cautious squint and one hand out of view is no baptizer. At least not with water.

"I'm Jacob. The church custodian. Are you Harrington?"

I nod. He glances over my shoulder toward my car. The church door briefly closes and opens again, the lantern replaced by a single key.

"The house is already open. But lock yourself in. We've had a few problems round here lately. Good night."

Jacob shuts the door so swiftly my murmured "thank you" is absorbed into the heavy portal. I hear the lock's tumblers engage.

Anna Kate already has the car door open, and I lift her to her feet and grasp her elbow to steady her steps. My other arm is filled with a wriggling Mae, who is tired and fussy. I push open the door to the tourist home. We pause a moment, staring into the dark, listening for intruders, critters, and ghosts before stepping inside.

The house has electricity—one of the reasons I chose it—and I search for the wall switch. The single bulb dangling from a cord wrapped in black tape casts more shadows than light, but the modest one-room structure is clean and welcoming. The front room has a threadbare sofa, a cushioned rocking chair, and a side table with a lamp. A creaking oak floor continues from the parlor area to a roomy kitchen on the left. Two wood-framed paper screens separate the common rooms from the sleeping area. There is only one bed, so I make a pallet for Mae. We're all too tired to care about food, but Anna Kate finds a tin of loose tea in the cupboard. I light and stoke the coal under the single-burner stove, and she puts water in a pot. Even before the water boils Mae is asleep. I'm sprawled in the rocking chair close to sleep myself, but I adjust my slumping shoulders when Anna offers a cup of tea with sugar.

I watch her prepare for bed. Washing her face and brushing her hair. She's a beautiful woman—a girl, really—and a good wife.

"Robert, I'm so tired."

"I know. You go ahead and lie down. I'll be there shortly."

It's only because I had a steady job, and promised to treat Anna Kate gently, that her mother allowed me to marry her youngest daughter. I don't know if she really loves me, but I adore her. She keeps a clean home and is an attentive mother. In the evenings, after a long day of sweating men, reeking varnish, and clinging sawdust, it lifts my spirits to see her. Even after two years of marriage her fair skin under my dark hands still causes a tremble in my spine.

The warm tea mixes with the heat of my thoughts, and I rise from the rocker to lie with my wife in a strange bed.

FOUR

2019

A few other reporters are scattered throughout the bullpen, but the newsroom is quiet. I like it this way so I can order my thoughts. A lot of us work from home now, but today I'm giving a briefing on the Black Lives Matter protests. I've been with the *Detroit Free Press* covering the BLM movement since the Michael Brown shooting in Ferguson. I've built up a solid network of sources, which gives me both street cred with protesters and beat-reporter chops at my job. The editorial meeting is in an hour, but first I need to call Grandma, who lives in an assisted-living facility in Florida.

After a squeal of excitement and a quick hello, she dives right into our competitive political banter. Grandma has a voice and opinions—she likes using both to keep her mind sharp.

"You still writing about them riots?"

It's her opening gambit.

"They're protests, Grandma." I shake my head. A symbolic gesture since she can't see me. Grandma owns a cell phone but has no internet or laptop. She watches no TV and listens to a single Christian radio station.

"My pastor says folks were looting and burning buildings. That's wrong."

"The people looting are not protesters. These are legitimate social justice demonstrations."

There is silence on the other end of the line. My mother's mother, Willie Mae Harrington-McGarrah, has been Black in America a long time. She's ninety-two and wields the number like a waving flag on the crest of a conquered hill. She's had the N-word flung at her as a child and adult, lived through the Depression, moved from the South to find the promised opportunities of the North, and married a soldier returning from World War II. Together they raised children with tough love. Grandma voted for Dwight Eisenhower, then shifted her political allegiances to John F. Kennedy. She wept over the murder of Martin Luther King Jr. and cried for joy at the election of Barack Obama. My grandmother holds fast to the beliefs of her southern upbringing, which include a literal interpretation of the Bible and the power of redemption.

"How are you feeling today?" I finally ask.

"I'm ninety-two years old and so are all my organs. I don't go much on feelings."

"I called for a reason," I say. "I was at a funeral last week and it made me think about what happened to your father."

The story of my great-grandfather's death at the hands of police in 1929 fades in the telling with each passing year. Part fleeting history, part body memory, part family myth, it's a smattering of details carrying equal authenticity and dread. A master carpenter, Robert Lee Harrington's skills garnered him a salary beyond a laborer's wages. Family lore has it he bought a new car every year and dressed like a dandy. In the only photograph Grandma has of her father, taken on his wedding day, his dark skin is radiant. He wears a flashy suit and a cap, and his expression is one of pride and accomplishment. Great-Grandmother sits by his side wearing a lacy flourish of a dress with white stockings and slippers. She's a seventeen-year-old girl who could pass for white. Two years later—in Birmingham, Alabama—Great-Grandpa was murdered by police. Maybe because of his wife's complexion; maybe his pride. Or maybe it was something else.

"You had to go to a funeral?" Grandma asks.

"The police killed another unarmed Black man last week."

"Oh, Meghan." She gives a quick inhale. "I feel so sorry for him . . . and his family."

"I do too, Grandma. But what about *our* family?" I say quietly. "We don't even know where Great-Granddad is buried. All we have is his wedding photo and your snatches of memory. It's as if he never lived."

My grandmother was just shy of two years old when her father was killed. I listen to her labored breathing and wait for her response. When it comes her voice is hoarse with sadness.

"They say he was a man too boastful for his own good. Never shied away from a slight. But he didn't deserve to die before he really had a chance to live."

"I'm planning to write Great-Grandpa's story, and about the trauma police have caused Black families in America for more than a century."

"After all these years, you'd think things would change," Grandma says. "But I guess they haven't."

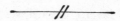

The conference room is abuzz with energy and ideas. There are ten of us around the table, led by our news director, Serina

Sharma, a South Asian woman with kickass reporting credentials and equally good skills as a manager. She's the only other person of color in the room, and, at twenty-eight, I'm the youngest.

I realize, when I start speaking, that the unsettled stomach I've felt for the last couple of hours is butterflies. I take a quick drink of water, swallow my nervousness, and continue with a fifteen-minute briefing.

"Excellent update, Meghan," Serina says. "Is it me? Or do these recent protests seem different than the others?"

"I think it's the makeup of the demonstrators. They're still predominantly young, but there are more white people, more Asian people, more families. The energy is more focused. There's just a lot more outrage."

There are murmurs of agreement and several conversations bounce around the room. Jim Saxby uses his tablet to project a dozen images on the whiteboard. He's the paper's deputy national editor and senior photographer, who cut his photojournalism teeth during the post–civil rights era. He's an old hippie. His gray-haired ponytail is his statement about the activism of his generation and his unwillingness to let it be forgotten. I like Saxby. He's seasoned but not cynical, and he's been an occasional supervisor and mentor to me.

"Look at these images." He stands to point at the board as we scan the earnest faces of protesters in Oklahoma City. "These are kids. From all over. And the protest signs aren't just about their hurt; it's a demand for change." Saxby punches up a new photo. He enlarges it with a spread of his fingers until it fills the whiteboard. A brown teenager with braids swirling like Medusa's snakes brandishes a poster high above her head. It reads: I'M SICK AND TIRED OF BEING SICK AND TIRED.

The room grows noisy again with excited discussion. I take another drink of water.

"I have a pitch," I say, loud enough to get everyone's attention. "I want to write a news piece about my great-grandfather. It has resonance with what's happening in the Black Lives Matter activism, but it's also about the relationship between police and Black people in this country that predates the current social justice movement."

"What's his story?" Saxby asks, returning to his seat.

The din in the room fades to anticipatory quiet. Every gaze is fixed on me. I open my notebook. Pick up a pen. Then push both away. I don't need them. I've overheard this story dozens of times during the tête-à-têtes between my mother and grandmother about life and neighbors and white folks. Most often the conversations occurred during our family trips to Florida when we were kids, or during Grandma's annual visit to Detroit. At night I'd eavesdrop while they sat at the kitchen table and chatted until way past my bedtime. Sometimes I'd hear snatches as they sipped morning coffee on the front porch, or hung clothes on the line under the midday sun. Their gabfests were accompanied by laughter, lofty wisdom, gossip, and occasionally, when they spoke about my great-grandfather, whispered tones. That's when I heard Grandma recount vague cautions about not trusting the police in the South.

"My great-grandfather was murdered by Birmingham, Alabama, police in 1929," I announce. "We believe it may have been because they mistook his wife for a white woman, but we don't know the full story." I place the wedding photo on the table. "This was taken the day they were married. The way I've always heard it, my great-grandparents left St. Petersburg, Florida, where they lived, to go to Birmingham so my great-grandfather could take a temporary job as a master carpenter. There was a housing boom in Birmingham at the time because of the success of the steel industry. We don't know where they lived or how long they were there before he was killed, and we don't know how he ended up being shot by the police. My great-grandmother returned to St. Pete after his death—without his body. We've never known where he's buried, or even if he *was* buried."

After my account Saxby leans toward me with empathy, and Serina closes her laptop. The mood in the room is uncharacteristically muted. A couple of my coworkers look at me with pain in their eyes; others won't make eye contact.

"Do you have any proof your grandmother's story is accurate?" Serina asks.

"The account has a lot of holes, but it's the one I've always been told. Then last weekend I found a news clipping from the September 29, 1929, *St. Petersburg Times*," I say, passing around an enlarged copy of the one-inch news story.

LOCAL NEGRO KILLED BY BIRMINGHAM OFFICER

Robert Harrington, negro of 1403 third avenue South, was shot and killed by a police officer in Birmingham, Ala, Friday morning when he resisted arrest, according to information received by the St. Petersburg Police Chief Saturday. Details of the shooting were not included in the message.

"This is your great-grandfather?" Serina asks.
I nod.
"It's an amazing find," Saxby says.

"I just sat there staring at the article. I don't even understand why a mainstream newspaper of that day would print a report about his death. Maybe it's because St. Pete's police chief was the source. I don't know."

"So after all these years you have proof the rumors about his death were true. It must have felt like a miracle," Saxby says.

"It did. I haven't even told Grandma about it."

"Why?"

"Because when I do I want to give her the details she's never had. If the St. Pete police were told of his death, there must be corroboration."

"Not if we're talking law enforcement of the Jim Crow era," Saxby notes with disdain. "It's odd the Birmingham PD even called this in to another department. Lots of Black people were killed and there were never *any* reports."

"Have you talked to the Birmingham police?" Serina asks.

"I spoke to a woman in the public information office. Apparently their digital archives don't go back that far. She wasn't very cooperative. I want to go to Birmingham. There has to be at least one person who knows the truth about his murder."

Serina isn't convinced. "I don't know." She begins shaking her head. "We have a limited travel budget and it sounds like you'd need to be there a while to shake any facts loose."

But Saxby's on my side.

"Think about it," he pushes. "Our Black Lives Matter coverage has become formulaic. A piece like this, with the historical context and the personal element, could really shake up our readers."

"But why now?" Serina asks. "I get the parallels—it's a great story hook. But for you, personally, Meghan. You've covered this movement for four years and lived with this tragedy all your life.

What's got you so fired up about telling your great-grandfather's story now?"

I certainly know why. Though I'm not sure I want to share the reason with my colleagues. I've worked hard to build my journalist credentials and reputation for maintaining objectivity. But the truth is covering the police shootings of Black men and women, most of them my age, month after month after month, has left me like the teen in Saxby's photograph—sick, tired, and infuriated.

"You know I covered the Carter funeral," I say to Serina. "That's after reporting on the protests following his murder, and interviewing the police chief about the need for reforms in his department. At the funeral this old man came up to me, and he said something that shook me to my core." I pull out my notebook to read his words. "'They can put men into space, but they won't make space for Black men.'"

I shake my head at the recollection. I feel myself getting angry and I don't want to show it. I adjust myself in the chair, sitting upright, and place my palms on the table. I lock eyes with Serina. "I think this could be a very important story. I've uncovered a few solid leads I'd like to track down, and I hope you feel I've earned the right to try."

Serina holds my stare, glances at Saxby, then back at me, and lifts her hands in surrender. "Okay. I'll find the money. How much time do you need?"

"Two weeks?"

Serina scowls. She picks up the copy of the news clipping and looks at it as if she's studying every word. My colleagues are completely silent. I'm holding my breath. "Okay. Get me a budget!"

The newsroom erupts in questions, speculation, and suggestions. One staffer offers to help me with a search of legal documents. Another mentions a contact at the Birmingham Civil Rights Institute who might be helpful.

"What about newspaper archives?" Saxby asks.

"The largest paper at the time had a fire in 1947 that destroyed most of their back issues. But I spoke with a city librarian who put me in touch with the publishers of a couple of Birmingham's African American newspapers."

"What became of your great-grandmother?" Serina asks.

"What I've been told is two of her brothers drove from St. Pete to get her away from Birmingham right after my great-grandfather was killed. She wasn't one to suffer in silence and they worried she'd also be murdered."

"Ninety years ago," Serina says with a wince.

I nod.

"Get me that budget today."

Saxby suggests a coffee at a nearby park, where we sit on a bench at the Detroit River. It's a beautiful early fall morning. The sun reflected in Windsor skyscrapers is bright and hopeful. A Canadian barge makes a slow westbound traverse, and a steady stream of walkers and bicyclists moves in the opposite direction along the five-and-a-half-mile Riverwalk.

"Thanks for standing up for me in the editorial meeting," I say.

"It's a big story, McKenzie. But you own it. Nobody else can do it justice."

I nod. This is a Saxby pep talk. He's given me encouragement before. I was a *Free Press* intern, fresh out of Medill J school, when he showed up at my small desk where I was attempting the almost impossible feat of making wedding announcements sound interesting. He placed his Nikon on top of my pile of notes.

"Know what that is?" he challenged.

"A Nikon D5?"

"Well, I was going to call it a 'truthteller,' but since you know your cameras I'll take a different approach." He extended his hand. "Jim Saxby."

He wore a denim jacket, chinos, and a pair of green Chucks. His ponytail was tied with a rainbow band. My assessment at the time—he was an old-school dude who wouldn't let go of his youthful swagger. I recognized the attitude from my father, who still thought *he* was cool. I eyed Saxby with amused suspicion, hoping he wasn't trying to hit on me.

"I'm Meghan McKenzie. My dad's a photography buff. He has a half dozen really good cameras at home. He likes the Canon but swears by the Nikon." I picked up his camera and looked through the viewfinder. "This is a really nice one." I could tell he was impressed.

"I read your bio, McKenzie. I'm a Medill alum myself. You must be the real deal if you made it through Northwestern."

"It was the best decision I ever made. I was accepted at Columbia too."

"Also a good school." Saxby sat in my side chair looking at a few of the engagement photos strewn around my desk. "At least you're working on beginnings."

"What?"

"Wedding announcements. Most interns start out working on endings—the dreaded obituary files."

That was four years ago. After that, Saxby occasionally lobbied to bring me along on a hard-news story. One of those times, I interviewed residents about the impact of a gang-involved shooting on Detroit's east side. That led to my first byline, a series of follow-ups, and a nomination for a George Polk Award.

"I'm anxious about this assignment," I admit to Saxby as we walk back to the office. "I mean, it's an old story and I have to make it relevant to today's readers. And then there's the family element. I'll be writing about my grandmother's life."

"Well, let's get some focus on the assignment," Saxby says, going into editor mode. "What are your specific goals for writing this story? Do you want to answer the question the old guy at the funeral posed to you about why this country hasn't made space for Black men? Or do you want to pursue the facts around your great-grandfather's murder?"

"Both. I want to illustrate the parallels of today's relationship between police and the Black community, and the one that existed in the Jim Crow South. I also want to know the circumstances of Great-Granddad's death. The news article says he was resisting arrest. But what does that mean? Was there some kind of altercation with the Birmingham police, or did he have the audacity to speak up for himself, and that got him killed?"

"Right," Saxby says.

I pause when I feel tears forming and look away. "Sunny today. I should have worn my sunglasses," I say, cupping a hand at my eyebrows.

I know Saxby's staring at me. Pretending he didn't see the tears. Waiting to see if I have more to say. There *is* more.

"I want to know who my great-grandfather was. He didn't live to be thirty. Same age as me. Did he ever have the chance to accomplish his dreams? Were he and my great-grandmother happy? Was he haughty, as my grandmother describes him, or was he just a proud Black man?"

Saxby smiles. "You'll do fine balancing the professional and the personal and telling a story that intertwines all the elements you mentioned. You're a talented writer, you know how to put people at ease, and you can separate bullshit from the real thing. That's why we're sending you to Birmingham in the first place. You got this, McKenzie."

"Can I call to talk things through when I need to?"

"Absolutely. And use that fancy phone camera of yours to send me a few pics. I haven't been to Birmingham in a while. I hear things have changed."

FIVE

2019

Daddy has dragged Mom's super-large suitcase up from the basement while she cooks pasta and points out the dozen reasons I shouldn't go to a city that has caused our family so much pain. Daddy grew up in Atlanta and feels a strong connection to the South. By contrast, Mom has an almost irrational fear when it comes to crossing the Mason-Dixon Line. It's one of the few things on which my parents fundamentally disagree.

During dinner Mom mentions the 16th Street Church bombing in Birmingham. The tragedy had outraged the world in 1963, and although my mother lived seven hundred miles away, and was nine years old at the time, she's still haunted by the incident.

"I remember Mama crying when those innocent children were murdered," she says, putting her fork aside and focusing her comments on me. "Your grandmother and I watched the news that night and she held me so tight I could barely breathe." Mom's eyes are lowered, re-creating the memory on the table's surface. "She didn't let me go out of the house for a week after that."

"Things have changed since then, baby," my father responds, twirling linguine in the pesto on his plate.

Mom shakes her head. "Not enough. Hate groups are on the rise, and police are shooting Black people like they're on a damn English foxhunt."

"I'm not saying we've turned the corner on racial injustice; all I'm saying is times are changing and there's a *new* South," Daddy argues.

I usually stay out of this modern-day civil war my parents repeatedly wage, but today I enter the fray. "I've seen a study showing more than fifty percent of fatal police shootings of unarmed Black people occur in the South." Daddy aims a look at me that says *I thought we were on the same side.*

"It's research I've done for my Black Lives Matter stories," I explain.

"See? That's what I mean," Mom picks up the argument, and her fork, and runs full of steam again. "There's not been *enough* change. That's why all these kids are out there protesting."

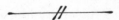

I'm a daddy's girl. We both love music, and cars, and a good adventure. Daddy and I are not great with goodbyes. We both cry every time he drops me off at the airport, so that's why I've asked Mom to drive me this morning. Up until earlier this year she'd been a high school principal juggling the priorities of an inadequate budget, negotiating with the school board and teachers' union, and standing up to belligerent parents. She spent twenty-eight years looking after other people's kids. But she never stopped looking after me.

She's unusually quiet compared to last night's emotional words.

The car radio is tuned to NPR, but I'm listening to the *1619* pod-cast. When we merge onto the airport access road, she finally breaks the silence.

"I guess you know what you're doing," she says, staring out the windshield.

"What?" I remove my earbuds. She shifts in her seat so she can see the road and me.

"I said I guess you know what you're doing going to Bir-mingham."

"I could do a lot of it by phone and online, but nothing beats talking face-to-face. People trust you more when they can look you in the eye and size you up. And vice versa."

"You sound like your father."

"I believe Grandma will be grateful if I can uncover the de-tails of her father's death."

"She's an old woman, Meghan. She's lived without the whole truth all these years. Maybe we should let bygones be bygones."

"You can't really mean that. You're the one who taught me it's important to know the truth about the history of this country. You bought me the books, took me to the Wright Museum, you've even marched for Black Lives Matter. I was really hoping for your blessing to write this story."

WHEN WE ARRIVE AT THE AIRLINE DEPARTURE AREA, MOM RE-leases the trunk to her new Lexus—a retirement gift to herself. She bounds over to the curbside attendant and passes him what I know must be a ten-dollar bill, because he hurriedly tags the bag he's working on, heads to our car to yank out the monstrous suit-case, and carries it to sit near the conveyor belt. Mom grasps my shoulders and pulls me into a long hug.

"Honestly, I'm worried that what you find in Birmingham might put you in danger." She holds me at arm's length and stares at me intently. "But I realized a long time ago that you're braver than me. Call me if you need anything, honey."

Mom strides back to her car. My love for her clutches my throat. She turns and waves.

I'm a calm flyer but still anxious about the work ahead of me. The jitters in my tummy remain by the time I'm done with TSA. I buy a pack of Pepto Bismol from the airport gift shop. It's the same stuff Mom would give me as a kid when I'd eaten too many sweets. Two decades later, she's still worried I've bitten off more than I can chew. I plop the chalky pink tablet on my tongue and fight back the thought that she could be right.

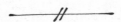

I've rented a car and arranged a stay at an Airbnb in Avondale. A house where I can prepare my own meals is more cost-effective than daily room service or eating out for every meal. I've ordered Uber Eats for tonight, but tomorrow I'll pick up groceries.

My bungalow is cute. A one-bedroom with a spacious, well-equipped kitchen, a separate office nook with reliable wi-fi and a printer, and a driveway for the car. The location is within minutes of downtown with easy access to the crisscross of freeways surrounding Birmingham. Tomorrow I have an early appointment at the main library, and later I'm hoping to meet with the seventy-six-year-old granddaughter of the publisher of *Awaken*, one of the city's now defunct African American newspapers.

I munch on a yummy entrée from a four-and-a-half-star Thai restaurant while watching the evening news on a wall-mounted television. My food is paired with a cool glass of the pinot gris left for me by my Airbnb host. The BBC reports on massive fires in the Amazon rain forest and unrest in Hong Kong. In their US news coverage, they interview witnesses in another mass shooting, this time in Texas, and I watch BLM protesters in Portland being taunted by a group calling itself the Patriot Brothers.

Garrett calls at ten, but I don't answer. We split a month ago, but he still phones at least once a week. It's been a messy untangling and I'm still conflicted in my feelings for him. In bed, I listen to the Spotify smooth jazz playlist Daddy created for me and make a few notes on my phone for the meeting with the city archives librarian. When I'm done, I lean back on the pillow and thumb through the Birmingham almanac left on the nightstand. It's filled with visitor information, statistics, articles, and photographs of a city with a controversial history, a modest skyline, and big ambitions. It was nicknamed "Magic City" in the 1920s because of its prominence in the steel industry. My great-grandparents would have arrived from St. Pete around this time of year, and as I settle into sleep I imagine the awe they must have felt seeing Birmingham for the first time.

———◆———

SIX

The Journey

1929

This pregnancy is easier on Anna Kate than the first. When she carried Mae she had severe morning sickness starting in the fifth month. By the seventh month she was ill-tempered, and coming home wasn't as pleasant as it had been in the honeymoon phase of our marriage. This time, except for occasional swollen ankles and complaints about the heat, Anna is still spritely and able to care for Mae, as well as perform her wifely duties.

We're on the final day of our drive and, God willing, we should arrive in Birmingham well before dinnertime. The late morning sun is blazing hot. Mae sits in the front seat playing the little whistle I've made for her from a piece of birch. Anna Kate is stretched out in back, relying on the open windows and a paper fan to ward off the heat.

On this narrow stretch of dirt road, I'm wrestling hard with the steering wheel to avoid the ruts and furrows as numerous as pockmarks on a teenage boy. Mae thinks the bouncing is fun; she's giggling and squealing as the vehicle swerves and bumps. I follow a sharp turn of the road with tall Georgia pines on either side, and around the bend are two white men walking in the middle of the lane. I smash down on the brakes, but one of the men hollers and leaps sideways to avoid being hit. He slips and slides into the gully below. Mae giggles when the car lurches to a stop.

The man still on his feet gives me a dangerous look. He's carrying a shotgun. He peers into the ravine at his fallen friend, then his glance sweeps over the car, taking in me and Mae in the front seat, and locks on Anna Kate in back. I hear her quick intake of air.

The crickets and birds have fallen silent. The only sounds are Mae's laughter and the grunts of the man in the ditch. The craggy bottom is still wet from last night's rain and the man has difficulty pulling himself up to the road. When he finally does, his overalls and boots are caked in thick red mud. He wipes at his pants leg before raising his head to glare open-jawed at my car and my Black face.

These white men are obviously related. In addition to their matching overalls, they have the same pinched nose, flyaway hair, and weak chin. The older man with the shotgun glances over his shoulder to the younger guy and says something I can't hear.

"Where the hell you get that car, nigger?" the one who looks more teen than man hollers.

I lift Mae over the passenger seat to sit with her mother. When I turn back to the men, I make sure my revolver, which has been tucked into the cushion of my seat, rests on my lap. I think about what I'm going to say in response to the question.

"It's my car. I bought it. Sorry about coming up on you so fast," I say, looking away from the shotgun to the young man. "I didn't see you around that blind curve."

"What you doing around here, boy? Where you going?" shotgun man asks.

I return my attention to him. "My wife and daughter and I are on our way to Birmingham. I work there."

I watch their faces first go blank, then shift to disbelief, then turn angry with unspoken questions: *How can this Negro own this car? And is that a white woman in the back seat?*

The insects and birds have returned to their noisy business. Mae wriggles in her mother's lap, still giggling, while Anna Kate shushes her. The teen moves toward the car squinting at Anna while I keep my eyes on the man with the shotgun. Mae is all the while babbling. She announces she's ready to go and reaches for me in the front seat. As the young guy draws closer to the vehicle, Mae parrots "hi" over and over and waves a pudgy hand at him. The look on the boy's face is one of menace, not cordiality. I grip the pistol with my finger on the trigger.

Then a loud screech of brakes startles us all, and the danger falls away just as quickly as it had risen. My car is blocking the road and a delivery truck has come to a stop right on my bumper. A dancing cow is painted on the hood of the vehicle, and beneath it the name IVANSON'S DAIRY is printed backward so I can read it in my rearview mirror. The driver of the milk truck pumps a short blare of his horn. The two men on the road stare at me and I stare back. The driver prods again. This time he lays on the horn and waggles an arm out of the window for me to move along. I gratefully put the car in gear. The man with the shotgun steps aside as I inch forward, his face contorted in hatred, then I press down hard on the accelerator.

I travel another two or three miles with the milk truck in my wake. When I see a glistening lake running parallel to the road, I signal and pull over. The driver toots his horn as the vehicle roars past. I step out of the car, and only now do I return the revolver to the folds of the seat. Anna Kate watches me. She's still pale and trembling when I open the door. Mae holds out her arms and I scoop her up.

"You feel like sitting next to the water for a minute?" I ask.

Anna Kate shakes her head vigorously. "No. I think we should keep moving, Robert. There's no telling who we might run into on these country roads."

"I can protect us."

She squints her eyes and her full lips press together to form a tight line. "I know you can, but what happens afterward? What happens to all of us if you go and shoot some white men?" she says with tears pushing past her thick brown lashes. "I wish I'd stayed in Florida."

Mae sees her mother crying and wants to return to the back seat, so I walk the few yards to the lakeshore alone and squat to wet my handkerchief. The cold water feels good against the back of my neck and calms my nerves. It was a close call with those two men. Anna Kate is right: I was prepared to kill them both.

When I look over my shoulder I see she has opened the car door for air. Her stockinged legs dangle to the ground, and she massages her slender calves. The sun catches her curly hair, which alternates between a light brown and auburn. With her high cheekbones and pink mouth she reminds me of a princess in a picture book. Anna Kate notices me looking at her and smiles shyly. Mae plays happily at her feet with a ball of yarn.

I dip my handkerchief in the stream once again and take a few more minutes to admire my beautiful family. They are my pride and joy. The Franklin makes me stand out, just like having Anna Kate on my arm makes heads turn. I like attention, but not the kind that brings danger to my family. Once we get settled in, maybe I'll consider selling the car and getting something less flashy.

I know we're close to Birmingham when the packed-dirt roads turn into a smooth surface. Before long we're mixed in with other cars, bicycles, streetcars, and pedestrians. Multistory brick buildings command every corner, and a skyful of electrical wires zigzag overhead. In the distance, the chimneys of factories and steel mills billow smoke hundreds of feet into the air. I've visited Atlanta before, but Anna Kate has never been outside St. Pete. She sits upright in the back seat with Mae on her lap to take in the sights—her anxiety from this morning's incident replaced by amazement.

"Oh, Robert," Anna Kate exclaims. "I never dreamed it'd be anything like this."

SEVEN

——◆——

2019

The desk in the office nook isn't large enough for me to work, so I've spread out my folders, notes, and laptop at the kitchen table of my Airbnb. I check in at nine with Saxby to let him know I'm on the job, then phone the Birmingham Civil Rights Institute and the police department with requests for interviews. I also confirm my meeting, this afternoon, with the daughter of one of the city's former Black newspaper publishers. Then I'm off to the library.

The downtown branch of the Birmingham Public Library is modern, with an abundance of natural light. I pass a mural titled *A New Day in Old Birmingham* celebrating the diversity of the city, then follow the front-desk directions to the research library. The director of the city archive, Kristen Gleason, is maybe thirty—a white woman with jet-black hair, a tunic, and leggings. With her good looks, pale skin, and dark lipstick she could be mistaken for a singer in a Goth band.

"I have to admit you're not what I expected," she says after we've talked, with coffee, about the *Black Panther* movie posters that frame one area of her office. "On the phone I pictured you as kind of, uh, old and stuffy."

I laugh. "Believe it or not, that's a compliment. People used to tell me I sound like a twelve-year-old on the phone."

"How long have you been a reporter?"

"Four years. I graduated from Northwestern with a journalism degree in 2014. I did undergrad at Stanford."

"You got a job right out of college?"

I shake my head. "No. I spent a half year traveling after that. Just to clear my head. Ghana, Brazil, South Africa—anywhere I could spend time around Brown and Black people. I pitched a story about the new Black expatriate experience to *HuffPost* that got the attention of the *Free Press*, and they took me on as an intern. That led to a full-time reporter position. I was lucky, but also prepared."

"I imagine you had to be both."

"And you? I Googled and saw you have a library sciences degree."

Kristen smiles. "Yes. I grew up here, went to the University of Alabama–Birmingham, and I've always loved books. Oddly enough, my undergrad degree is in philosophy. I wanted to understand how I could have a positive impact on the world."

"There's nothing wrong in that," I say.

"Yeah. Well, tell that to my parents," she says, rolling her eyes.

Kristen reminds me of a few of the girls I knew at Stanford. Smart, capable, not eager to walk the lines established by authority. They believed in social justice and truly wanted to be allies, but ultimately most weren't willing to sacrifice their privilege.

"You still live at home?"

"No. I finally moved out a couple of years ago. I have a little house in Southside. So, you're tracking the Black Lives Matter movement and making connections to an old case?"

For a few moments, we stare at each other over our coffee cups. Both Saxby and Daddy have emphasized the importance of family connections in Birmingham. Kristen has those connections. My Google query also revealed her father runs the largest insurance company in the region. She seems cool and might be able to help me cut through some red tape, but I'm not ready to tell her the whole story of why I want to snoop around in her archives. In my experience, no matter how woke someone may seem, they're never prepared to hear about the horrible things that happen in their own backyard.

"I'm investigating a police shooting of a Black man in the late 1920s. I'm hoping to learn more details about the shooting and use it to illustrate an historical context to the current shootings and demonstrate decades of institutional racism."

She nods. "Birmingham is a pretty good place to start."

I can tell Kristen loves her job as she guides me on a tour of the full library and the city archives. She's upbeat, knowledgeable, and thorough.

"We have more than thirty thousand documents in our collection. Pictures, maps, real estate contracts, insurance policies, death and marriage announcements, letters and photographs. Some of them haven't even been digitized yet. Each item has a story behind it, and some, undoubtedly, have horrible secrets attached to them," she says.

"Is that what they teach in library sciences?" I ask. "That it's important to read between the lines?"

Kristen laughs. "Yes. Unless it's poetry."

"Well, that's the same thing you learn in J school. But without the poetry."

At the end of the tour Kristen sets me up with researcher credentials, which include a private carrel, a temporary parking space, and after-hours access. I'm ready to get started.

FOR THE REST OF THE MORNING AND EARLY AFTERNOON I scroll through newspaper archives. There were dozens of papers published in Birmingham in the early twentieth century. Some have digitized archives, some are incomplete, and most have the status I dread: *No online records available.*

I've narrowed my search to Black-owned-and-operated newspapers. It makes sense to me that those publications would report the violent death of a Black man from out of town, and I've already spent a couple of hours in the digital files of one of the largest publications, *The Reporter.* I've had no luck on my story but I've read dozens of accounts of mob lynchings, imprisonments, and beating deaths of Blacks throughout the South.

My phone and my fatigued eyes sound the alarm at about the same time. I didn't take a break for lunch, and I still need to do grocery shopping before my four o'clock appointment. I stop at Kristen's desk to say goodbye and invite her for dinner tomorrow but leave a note when I don't find her.

The grocery store nearest my Airbnb is one of those high-end gourmet marts with more prepared food, wine, deli, and baked goods than standard groceries, but the meat and seafood quality is very good, and the produce is adequate—so I pick up some fish and lamb chops and lots of veggies. I've recently graduated to cooking Middle Eastern dishes, and there is an aisle of the spices, grains, and beans I like to use. I also spring for a fresh bottle of olive oil, a gallon of bottled water, red wine, pasta, eggs, and a package of red velvet cupcakes. A hundred and eighteen dollars later, I have enough supplies to prepare tonight's dinner plus breakfast and dinner for the rest of the week. Some of my purchases, like the olive oil and salmon, wouldn't have been available to my great-grandparents when they were here. They probably cooked with lard and bought simple farm meats—pork, chicken, maybe even goat. Their food would have come from a Black grocer or a local farm. They might have even grown some of their vegetables.

The temperatures are still hovering near eighty degrees, so I shower again, change into a sleeveless summer dress and flats, then head to meet members of the family that published one of Birmingham's now defunct Black newspapers.

It's only a twenty-minute drive to the Tudor-style house that has been in Roberta Banton's family for four generations. It's in need of a paint job and is tucked in the middle of a block with more updated houses. I pull into the driveway, and before I get up the porch steps, a short, plump woman wearing nurse's scrubs gives me a cheerful greeting. "I'm Germaine Rankin. Roberta's niece." She extends her hand to me. "You must be the reporter from Detroit."

"Yes. Meghan McKenzie. Nice to meet you, and thanks for letting me come by. I hope I'm not disrupting your evening."

"No. Not at all. I'm just getting home from work, and I've already put dinner in the oven. Auntie Roberta is waiting to see you."

I follow her through the living and dining rooms, where a dozen or more framed family portraits hang on the walls and cover a large antique sideboard. My grandma has one very similar.

The kitchen wall also has a series of photos—the kind taken annually at school. Two pretty brown-skinned girls start off with pigtails, progress to headbands, smile with braces and bangs, and finally beam in cheerleader uniforms. A couple of backpacks, soccer balls, and a bicycle pump are stacked against the back door. I spot penciled measurement lines on two sides of the door that adjoins the dining room. The last measurement on both doorframes stops at five foot six. Germaine grabs the coffeepot and fills it with water. She points to a door. "Auntie's room is there. Go on in."

Mrs. Banton's bedroom opens onto a lovely patio with more than a dozen flowering potted plants. She uses a cane as she walks, and I follow her outside, where we sit in sturdy high-backed chairs. Next to her, on a metal table, is a ceramic container with potting soil. She ladles dirt into a pot and reminisces about her life as a young Black girl in Birmingham's segregated neighborhoods. Her father was a prominent minister, and her grandfather an educator and publisher of *Awaken* newspaper. She'd been a debutante in 1959, and a leader of the local Jack and Jill organization. When she married she'd moved away from the family home before returning after her husband died, seven years ago, to move in with her niece.

"Birmingham was a wonderful place to raise children. Our community had its own businesses, social and civic groups, and good schools. But, of course, there were always people who were disturbed by segregation. They came to town from all over—the NAACP, the Southern Christian Leadership Conference, the unions. I remember them. They came to the house to speak with Granddad and Daddy about Black people deserving equal rights. There were also well-meaning white folks trying to help. But, in my opinion, the civil rights movement just got people riled up."

I watch her take off her gardening gloves and brush dirt from her apron.

"When I spoke to you earlier you mentioned your grandfather kept some back issues of his paper."

Roberta nods.

"I particularly hope to find archives from 1929 and 1930. I'm following up on a case involving a police shooting."

"That's a really long time ago. Was it a Black man who was shot?" she asks.

"Yes. He moved here from St. Petersburg, Florida, to do some short-term carpentry work. He had a pregnant wife and daughter."

Roberta takes in my last words. Her thoughts furrow her brow and she purses her lips.

"A lot of Black men were shot, and worse, back in those days."

"Many newspapers have digital archives now, and I found copies of *The Reporter*. But I've found none for *Awaken*."

"Oh, *The Reporter*. They were Granddaddy's strongest competitor. They got most of the big advertisers. But Granddaddy's paper focused more on what the people in the city were *really* talking about."

Roberta takes a handkerchief from her pocket and touches it to the sides of her nose. Her tone suggests she's aware that even with her family's stature in the community, she did not grow up in the upper echelons of Birmingham's Black middle class. *The Reporter* catered to families of older lineage and deeper pockets, devoting its space to national business, education news, and issues related to the Black churches and the Masons. *Awaken* leaned toward civil rights stories and community news. I'm hoping the paper's more progressive focus might have spurred the publisher to report on the killing of a Black carpenter.

"*Awaken* folded in early 1945, right after the war," Roberta says, reminiscing. "One of my father's brothers died in the fight. After that they say Granddaddy didn't have the same kind of energy. He got sick, packed up everything, and walked away from the newspaper. But he didn't believe in throwing anything away. He kept a copy of every paper he published. I can't imagine what kind of shape they're in, but they're stored down in the basement. Germaine's husband packed them all up from a storage unit and brought them here when I moved in. You should go ahead and take a look."

I HOLD ON TO THE BANISTER OF THE NARROW STAIRS AS I DE-scend. It's refreshingly cool in the basement. The newspapers are stacked in clear storage bins five high and six abreast. They cover a third of one wall. Someone has carefully organized the containers, placing a masking-tape label on the front of each indicating the publication year, and they're arranged chronologically. The bottom bins contain the issues I need, but I'd have to unstack them to get to those. The later issues are just at my eye level. Nearby, a low wood stool gives me the added inches I need to grasp the handles of the highest bins. I test the weight. Not nearly as heavy as the suitcase I hauled yesterday from my rental car into the Airbnb. I swing the bin to my waist and step down. The blue top has a sheet of paper taped to it that reads: AWAKEN. 1943–45.

There's a table nearby, but an old desktop computer takes up all the surface space, so I perch on the arm of the blue La-Z-Boy recliner in the corner. Across from it is a large TV. The paper on top is dated September 8, 1945. Same time of year as now, almost seventy-five years ago. The newsprint is shiny and the corners brown and curled with age. The masthead is printed in an ornate script, but the motto is in block letters: PROGRESS DOESN'T HAPPEN WHILE YOU SLEEP. The slogan reminds me of the BLM movement's caution to "stay woke."

I lift the first paper and ink smudges my fingers. I quickly return it to the bin. I'll need to wear some kind of gloves. Maybe I can borrow a pair from the library. I'm trying to contain my elation at the treasure that lies before me, but my heart pounds in my chest.

Footsteps sound on the stairs, and Germaine peeks her head over the handrail. "Coffee's ready. You want some?"

I quickly return the plastic bin to its place. The two women are laughing and talking but stop and look at me expectantly when I step into the kitchen. Roberta beckons for me to sit. Germaine has set out a nice snack of cookies, cheese cubes, and a bowl of green grapes. My hand trembles as I add two sugars to my coffee. Both women notice and I give a sheepish grin.

"Maybe you need chamomile tea instead of coffee," Germaine says, smiling.

"I guess you found what you wanted," Roberta says.

"It's wonderful," I say breathlessly. "Amazing. It's just amazing."

Germaine laughs. "You sound like John. He was so excited when I showed him the newspapers in the family storage unit, and I bet he's spent hundreds of hours organizing them. If you ask me he's OCD," Germaine shakes her head. "Once he gets hold of a project it's hard for him to let go. You should talk to him about what's in those boxes down there."

"Can I?"

"Of course. He'll be home soon. You should stay for dinner."

John Rankin is former military. A sergeant who worked in procurement at a base in Arkansas. Now he works for UPS—still managing the flow of packages, mail, equipment, and supplies from order to delivery. He turns out to be just like his wife—warm and generous. He's built solid, burly, and his energy lights up the house. The Rankins' two teenage daughters, who had remained unseen on the upper levels, suddenly appear with smiles and childlike excitement at their dad's homecoming. They give their great-aunt awkward hugs, and me a curious stare when Germaine makes the introductions. Dinner of chicken casserole with a green salad and sweetened iced tea is followed by a banana pudding John made the night before. The banter between the parents and their daughters, about homework, cheerleading, future shopping trips, and the latest on Camila Cabello, makes me nostalgic for my carefree teen days—just a decade ago. After dinner, John, Roberta, and I remain at the dining table and chat.

"Your grandpop was a pioneer newspaperman," John says. "Ambitious too. He saw a need and he filled it. Folks like Marcus Garvey, A. Philip Randolph, and players from the Negro baseball league came here for dinner, didn't they, Auntie?"

"Mama and Daddy did entertain a lot of important visitors. I remember Mama talking about how the paper took up so much of the family's time," says Roberta. "We all lived together right here in this house."

"So the paper carried sports as well as politics?" I ask.

"There were a couple of pages for sports, entertainment, and social news, but most of it was commentary and hard news," John says. "It was a weekly, you know."

I nod. "How about crime?"

"Oh sure. I saw a lot of lynching stories, accounts of race riots and mob beatings, Black men accused of stealing, that kind of thing. White people were killing Blacks every day and, occasionally, vice versa."

"What about police shootings? Like now in the Black Lives Matter movement?"

John sat quietly in thought for a few moments. "No. I don't remember seeing any stories about that, though I'm sure there were. In those days, Black people were probably afraid to go up against the police. And a Black publisher reporting about police brutality might put himself, and his family, in danger."

"Makes sense," I say.

My spirits dip. Secrets and fear are inextricably connected when it comes to uncovering nasty truths. I'm sure I'll encounter resistance as I try to get the facts of my story.

"Is there a particular incident you're interested in?" John asks.

Before I can answer, Roberta responds. "The police shot a Black man from Florida. It would have happened sometime in 1929."

"That doesn't ring any bells," John says, stroking graying whiskers. "But I have a database downstairs with some detail on the contents of the boxes."

"You do?"

John and Roberta are laughing now. Without realizing, I've pushed my chair back and I'm on my feet. I feel my face flush. I apologize and retake my seat.

"Don't sit back down, young lady. I see you're ready to check out what I have. C'mon."

I HADN'T NOTICED THE HALF DOZEN STOOLS IN ONE CORNER OF the basement. John pulls two over to the computer table and powers up the heavy old desktop unit. The database is both rudimentary and brilliant. John could well have been a librarian if procurement and inventory hadn't been his vocation. Each bin contains thirty to fifty newspapers and its contents are notated with the paper's date and volume. John has listed the major stories in each volume and has even highlighted keywords.

"When did you find time to do this?"

"This is my man cave. When the football game is on over there," John says, pointing to the big TV, "sometimes I'm over here inputting information from these boxes. I'm just a nerd, I guess. I've always liked spreadsheets, and tables, and organizing."

"Well, your nerdiness is very much appreciated. This is great!"

"The shooting happened in 1929?" His eyebrows rise.

"Yes. In September."

"Unfortunately, I started the database with the latest papers and so far it only goes back to 1935."

I like John. I find myself telling him even more than I've told Roberta or my new librarian friend. He listens intently and at one point sadly shakes his head.

"I'm very sorry about your great-grandfather, young lady. Every volume of the original paper is in these bins. If the story's here, you'll find it. You'll just have to search through them."

"I've already done that with *The Reporter*. So I know what I'm in for," I say.

John provides me with plastic gloves and I begin my search. When I finally leave the Rankin home, several hours have passed, and I haven't turned up any reports of a police shooting that fit my timeframe, but John, Germaine, and Roberta have invited me to return the day after tomorrow to continue my research.

"I'm glad you think Granddaddy's newspapers are worthwhile," Roberta says. "I sure do hope you find what you're looking for."

EIGHT

———◆———

Arrival

1929

Anna Kate isn't impressed with the boardinghouse I've been calling home. The landlady greets us as we enter the front door weighted down with the suitcases and bags that contain our lives. Mrs. Ardle is a vain woman and a bit of a flirt. Her husband died two years ago, leaving her the boardinghouse, and she takes pride in keeping the place running. She does the bookkeeping and rent collection, jobs that had been hers to begin with, and out of necessity she's added the small maintenance tasks her husband once handled. Today, she's putting new washers into the bathroom faucets, and she wears black galoshes and a piece of red cloth tied around her graying hair.

She immediately whips the rag from her head when I introduce her to Anna Kate. The two stare at each other without a word for ten seconds. Mrs. Ardle then picks up her small pail of washers and returns to her work. I have the feeling the two women have come to some silent understanding about things a man will never know.

At the threshold of our one-room apartment, Anna Kate slowly removes her hat and jacket. She wrinkles her nose in distaste as she walks around the space with its Murphy bed and tiny kitchen. She looks in the cupboards and the icebox. I pay ten dollars a month extra for a room with a separate washroom, and Anna Kate recoils in disgust when she pokes her head inside the door. She turns to give me a look that would stop a feral cat in his tracks. I probably should have paid Mrs. Ardle extra to clean my rooms.

As soon as I release Mae's hand, she runs to the front window and cocoons herself in the lace curtains. She stares down at busy Fourth Avenue and taps on the pane.

"Don't touch those grimy curtains, Mae. I don't want you roaming around this place until I clean it up," Anna Kate says, more for me than Mae. "Come over here and sit on this suitcase and don't move."

Anna Kate has rolled up her sleeves and tied up her long hair with a scarf. She moves first to the kitchen, finds a rag on the counter, and begins scouring the sink with laundry soap. "You have a bucket around here?" she asks.

I keep my bucket in the bathroom. I return with it and also bring a broom, a scrub brush, and two bars of hard soap. Anna Kate seems to approve of my initiative.

"Okay. I need the two of you to keep from underfoot for a couple of hours. I'll make some supper after I get charge of this house. I need you to buy milk, bread, butter, cabbage, and get a good-size ham. Oh, and if you can find some tomatoes that would be good too."

I grab Mae by the hand and head out the door. Anna Kate's scorn is now focused on one of the kitchen cupboards.

I always park the car behind the boardinghouse—that's another three dollars a month—but after two long days on the road,

I'm tired of sitting, so I decide Mae and I will walk to do our shopping. We start out on Fourth Avenue and move in the direction of Eighteenth Street. Mae is tall for her age, and it doesn't take much for her to keep up with my stride. She skips along and swings my arm. She's a happy, outgoing girl and shouts "hi" to everyone we pass. Some folks greet her in return.

Many Blacks, even in the city, grow their own fruits and vegetables. Those lucky enough to have a house also raise chickens and pigs. For people like me who live downtown and work in construction or in one of the steel mills, there are small grocers, produce stands, and a meat market to fill our food needs. That's where we're headed.

At the grocery, I purchase a small sack of flour, sugar, salt, and coffee. I also get a bottle of milk and a pound of butter. I haven't bought much food during my two months in Birmingham. Usually I'll pick up cooked meat and bread to make my lunches, and Mrs. Ardle provides a dinner meal for her boarders for an extra fifty cents. I usually sit at her table with a couple of other residents a few evenings a week. I guess that'll be coming to an end now that Anna Kate is here.

The hunched-over man at the fruit stand has fingers gnarled with arthritis. A few crags of skimpy gray hair poke from the perimeter of his green knit cap, and he strokes a kitten that sits at his knee. Mae asks to pet the cat and the man gives his permission, then offers her a gift of an apple. She eats it to the core within minutes.

"I guess you're hungry, darling," I say.

I buy her a second apple, and one for myself. Then I select a cabbage, tomatoes, and some rhubarb, which I hope Anna Kate will cook down for a pie. The produce gent gives us an extra sack to carry our purchases. We both thank him before moving on to the butcher shop, where the man behind the counter picks out a nice ham for us.

Mae and I hurry home as nightfall flirts with the light in the street. By the time we return to the boardinghouse, our apartment is spick-and-span. Anna Kate has asked Mrs. Ardle for a clean pair of curtains, and Meg twists herself in the lacy fabric until she looks like the mummy I saw in *Ripley's Believe It or Not!* Mrs. Ardle has also provided another set of bedsheets, a blanket, and the loan of a mop, which sits on the now-shiny floor near the front door.

Anna Kate collects the groceries, cuts a couple of pieces of ham to boil, and peels and slices potatoes, which go into the pot with the cabbage and chunks of ham.

"Where'd the potatoes come from?" I ask.

"Harriet."

"Who?"

"Your landlady. She and I both appreciate a clean house."

When Harriet Ardle comes by fifteen minutes later to retrieve her mop, she and Anna Kate seem fast friends. Dinner is a feast, not only because it's delicious, but also because it is eaten with my family. Mae sits atop two books in her chair, her spoon navigating a mix of cabbage and potatoes. Anna Kate's cheeks are blushed with the effort of her cleaning and cooking. She promises a rhubarb pie tomorrow and talks of how she can spruce up our new home.

While Anna Kate washes the dinner dishes and puts food away, I read a story to Mae. Her favorite—*Robinson Crusoe*. She doesn't understand the words, but I believe she likes sitting on my lap, the sound of my voice, and looking at the pictures. Her eyes are already droopy when Anna Kate takes her for a bath, and later I tuck her into a pallet on the couch. I smoke a cigar, read more *Robinson Crusoe,* and peek up at Anna Kate, who is mixing the dough for tomorrow's pies. She covers the flour balls with a damp cloth, then retires to the bathroom with the smaller of her two suitcases. When she exits she is a queen, and I'm her king. I hold her a long time, taking in the smell of her skin, stroking her hair. Tonight we will sleep in our own bed.

NINE

―――――――◆―――――――

2019

I t's my first full day at the library and I've found another half dozen publications targeting Birmingham's Afro-Caribbean and African American readers in the 1920s. Only a few are in digital collections, and I've spent all morning skimming the spotty archives. Several of those papers ambitiously tried to put out a daily—little more than newsletters, really—but most were weeklies that printed a mix of hard news, social events, and commentary. By one o'clock, my stomach is complaining. I secure my laptop in a library locker and head outdoors for lunch and a bit of fresh air.

Downtown Birmingham bustles during midday. Office workers, students, construction workers, and visitors to government buildings mix in the pedestrian swirl. It's a hot day, but after sitting in the air-conditioned library I don't mind the warmth. I walk along the park on Twentieth Street, past Third Avenue North, where I find an outside table at a nearby pizzeria. I order a personal Greek pizza with a salad and lemonade and alternate between people watching, reviewing my calendar, and making phone calls.

Saxby has scored an interview for me with a staffer at the city's Office of Social Justice and Racial Equity. I phone the number he's given me, and the call goes directly to voicemail, where I leave a message. Next I phone the research coordinator at the Birmingham Civil Rights Institute, who has returned my call. I tell her the general focus of my story, and she informs me of the repository of family documents they receive each year in their collection. She knows Kristen and invites me to call when I'm ready to visit.

My final call is to Monique Hendricks, my Black Lives Matter contact here in Birmingham. She's a dynamic young activist—a few years older than me—whom I met covering a rally in Washington, DC, two years ago. When I told her I was coming to Birmingham, she offered a tour of the city and agreed to an interview. I don't reach her but leave a voicemail.

THE PIZZA AND A BIT OF SUN WERE JUST WHAT I NEEDED, BUT it's time to head back to the library. I'll spend the rest of the afternoon in newspaper archives, and tomorrow I'll return to John and Germaine Rankin and the *Awaken* bins in their basement.

I'm feeling the pressure of time. I have only a few days to come up with enough information for the first installment of my reporter's notebook.

Kristen is working with a couple of researchers. Her Goth attire has been substituted with a fitted grayish-blue pantsuit and flats. I want to speak with her, so I hang around her workstation. While I wait I scroll through my text messages. There's one from Garrett. He still thinks we can work out our differences and get back together. We spoke briefly last night and he asked about my assignment, but within a minute of my recounting my first full day in Birmingham, he interrupted to describe what a difficult time he was having preparing for an upcoming trial. I listened and offered encouragement as I always do. The conversation ended with him saying he felt optimistic about our relationship, and me feeling the opposite.

Kristen heads my way. She moves a nice leather briefcase from her chair so she can sit at her desk.

"You look different. Got a muckety-muck meeting today?" I ask, sitting in her side chair. She rolls her eyes.

"I had lunch with Mom and Dad and our family attorney at the City Club. There's a dress code. I guess I shouldn't complain. Ten years ago, I'd have had to wear a dress or skirt," Kristen says, shrugging out of her jacket.

"If you had a fancy lunch, you're probably not interested in grabbing dinner tonight."

"Oh yes, I am. Didn't you see my reply to your note? When you log into the researcher portal, there's a notification icon. I sent you my answer yesterday."

"I didn't even look. Okay. What time works for you?"

"How about seven thirty? There's a new place, a wine bar I've been wanting to try. But I have to go home and get out of this torture garb first. The wine bar is casual."

"Sounds good. I have a few more hours of work, and I want to freshen up too. Meet you there?"

"I was hoping you could pick me up. My place isn't far from the restaurant. I put my address in the message. You have a car, right?"

"I do. I'll plan to be at your place by seven fifteen."

It's a real perk having library researcher status. In addition to the carrel, the locker, and a parking spot, I have access to the special collections not available to the general public. When I log into the portal, I spot the green bell at the top of the screen and click on it. I have two notifications—one a welcome message, and the other from Kristen accepting my dinner invitation, suggesting the wine bar, and providing her address. It'll be nice to have company for dinner and see a bit of Birmingham's nightlife.

About an hour into my scanning I spot an item that gets my attention. It's in a weekly paper called *The Truth*. The headline reads: BODY FOUND IN ALLEY. It's a brief news item about two Negro janitors discovering a dead man behind a downtown building. The men had arrived at work for their late-night shift and stumbled across the body behind the trash receptacles. The dead man was not identified, nor is his race mentioned, notable because race has been front and center in all the news stories I've been reading. What really catches my eye is the date. The story appears in the September 27, 1929, edition, around the time Great-Grandpa died, and just weeks before his wife gave birth to a second child. "A life was taken, and a life was given," is what Grandma always says about the ironic timing of the two events.

I use the print screen button to capture the article, and save it to my research folder. Tomorrow, I'll look through both *The Birmingham Reporter* and *Awaken* in search of further mention of this story. The hair at my neckline prickles. It means I'm on to something, and I trust my intuition. I lean back in my chair, close my eyes, and breathe deeply until my phone vibrates. The caller ID shows a number I don't recognize.

"Hello. Meghan McKenzie," I answer.

"Ms. McKenzie. This is Darius Curren. I'm outreach director at SJRE."

"SJRE?"

"Sorry. The Mayor's Office on Social Justice and Racial Equity. We heard you were in town."

"We?"

He chuckles. "We have a very active grapevine. I was told you reached out to the police information officer, and Saxby called the mayor's office to arrange for you and me to speak. So, yeah. A few people know you're here and are curious about what you're writing. By the way, how's Saxby? Still hipster and irascible?"

"That's our guy," I say, trying to sound lighthearted. But I've been thrown off guard. I lean back in my chair to contain the shiver that zips up my spine. *So some of the power folks in Birmingham already know I'm here and are asking questions about me.* It's unsettling, and I decide to say so.

"Birmingham is just a big little town. You'll figure that out soon enough. So you're working on a Black Lives Matter story, I understand."

"Yes, it's about BLM, but it's more of a historical piece, and a rather complicated story. I'd like to talk to you about it in person if you can spare me an hour."

"Well, I can't do it today. But how about tomorrow?"

"I'm afraid I'll be knee-deep in the archives of the *Awaken* most of the day. Is it possible to meet Thursday morning?"

"Wow. *Awaken.* You're really going back in time. Well, how about first thing tomorrow? Before you start with your research. Say eight o'clock breakfast?"

"I could do that," I say quickly.

"I'm buying," Darius says. "Oh, that's right. If you're on a story you can't accept a free meal, can you? Professional ethics or something."

"Did Saxby tell you that?"

"Him? Oh no. He always lets me buy him food."

"Well, I accept the meal offer. It's a Detroit thing. *Never* turn down food. Where shall we meet?"

"Do you know Birmingham?"

"Not well at all."

"Well, Google the Magic City Grille. I'll meet you there in the morning. It'll be a hearty breakfast, so bring your appetite."

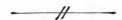

I'm thinking about the hearty appetite I'll need for the morning when I skip dessert at the wine bar in the trendy Five Points South neighborhood. Kristen has ordered a lamb entrée with couscous and a goat cheese salad. I've ordered the three-meat loaf with garlic mash and fried green tomatoes. We've also shared a bottle of a red blend, served in a decanter. The menu is too high-end for casual family-with-kids dining. The clientele is a mixture of hipsters and business types, with a sprinkling of students. Kristen seems to enjoy the place. The food is tasty, but I'm not really into the atmosphere. Feels like it's trying way too hard to be stylish.

Kristen has returned to her black garb tonight, but with more of the flair of her creative side. Her tunic, worn over black leggings, has a touch of purple in the fabric, which matches her fingernails. I'm curious about her Goth persona. It seems incongruous with her job, her family, and her outlook.

"How long have you been Goth?"

"Oh, for a long time. Now it's mostly about the music, but I still like to make a statement at the library, because nobody's turning me into a corporate type."

Kristen is energetic and opinionated. I realized it when we first met at the library, but after three glasses of wine, she's downright gregarious as we talk about books, movies, climate change, and social inequality.

"I'm telling you, McKenzie, it won't be the kids at the university who'll turn this country around. It'll be the kids on the streets. They're already more comfortable with pushing for systemic change than our generation *ever* was. I'm sure you've already seen it."

I nod. She's taken to calling me by my last name. Saxby uses it too. I'm not really enamored of it, but I've also had two and a half glasses of wine and my semi-drunk default is introspection rather than argument.

"I'm skipping dessert," I announce, "just ordering strong coffee."

"Suit yourself. I'm having a crème brûlée." Kristen punches her choice into the electronic tablet the establishment uses for ordering. "I really like this place. It's rad. What about you?"

"The food is really good," I say. "Decadent. I'd love to have the recipe for that meat loaf."

My response seems to mollify Kristen, and she picks up her narrative about social justice. Before grad school, she tromped around Europe, Asia, and South America with a group of fellow students. She thought about joining the Peace Corps but ended up teaching for three years in Paraguay. I listen thinking about how much I need coffee—I have a buzz and I'm driving.

"So, tell me about yourself, McKenzie. Do you have a boyfriend?"

"I was dating a guy for about a year but I'm winding down the relationship."

"Really. Why? Tell me all about it."

I don't mind Kristen's prying. It's actually nice to have someone to talk to about Garrett.

"His name's Garrett Saunders. He's an associate at one of Detroit's big law firms. They're grooming him for partner. We really hit it off right away, and my parents like him—"

"So, what's wrong with him?" Kristen interrupts and plunges her spoon into her just-arrived custard.

"I didn't say anything was wrong with him."

"You said you want to slow things down. Is he boring? Sounds like he might be."

I laugh. "You know, he really kind of *is*. To make partner you have to kiss everybody's ass. Garrett doesn't see it that way, but it's Jimmy Cliff clear to me. This spring we had to postpone our trip to the Virgin Islands to bail out one of the partners. The jerk couldn't finish a brief because his son had a baseball game he wanted to attend. Of course Garrett offered to write it, which took the whole weekend. We'd planned that vacation for months."

"Wow. That's effed up."

"Right." I have coffee now and take a sip. "Well, what about you? Who's *your* boyfriend?"

"Who says I date boys?"

"So you're queer?"

"Couldn't you tell that just by looking at me?" Kristen laughs. "I don't really label myself, and right now there's nobody serious. I was dating this guy off and on for a while, but now it's pretty much off. He works at UAB."

"University of Alabama–Birmingham," I say, and Kristen nods. "Is he a professor?"

"Ha. No. He works in the athletic department."

I raise an eyebrow and take a longer sip of coffee. I hope the cup covers my smirk. "You're dating a jock?"

"My father likes him—and he works for my brother, Scotty, who's an assistant football coach."

I think about Garrett. He seemed a good catch when I met him at a friend's potluck in suburban Detroit. He was handsome, attentive, and employed. He made a good first impression.

"Garrett and I do have a few things in common, but the way we look at the world is really different. Lately, I've realized I'm way more excited about my career than I am about being with him." I lean across the table a bit. "Could I ask you something? How much of your worldview is still influenced by your parents?"

Kristen lays down her dessert spoon. "Hmm. That was delicious, and that's an odd question."

"Yeah. I know. I get like this when I'm drinking."

"I am *so* unlike my family," Kristen says, her eyebrows coming together in concentration. "Like from another planet. They're conservative. But, you know, almost every day I do something that reminds me of Mother. It drives me crazy. I noticed it again today at lunch."

"Does she work?" I ask.

"She's the wife of a prominent businessman. That's her full-time job, and she's very good at it." Kristen scrapes at the bottom of her brûlée bowl, then drops her spoon. "She was groomed for the role by her own mother."

"And she expects the same of you?"

"Not anymore. She finally gave up on the idea. Thankfully, I have a younger sister, Sara, so my mother's ambitions are not totally lost."

"I think I understand that. I'm like my mother in some ways,"

I say. "I really admire her, but I'm more in sync with my dad. He's a musician, writer, photographer, and he's been involved in justice movements all his life. My mom, not as much."

"Does your mother work?"

"She retired last year. She was a high school principal and worked a lot of long hours—nights and weekends—but always had time for me."

"Wow." Kristen looks at me. "You're lucky."

"And *your* father?" I ask.

"I grew up thinking of him as my hero. He treated me like a fairy-tale princess when I was growing up. I mean, I could have anything I asked for, McKenzie," she says, her eyes shifting from happy memory to sadness. "I still love him very much, but we're not the way we used to be. He loves his wealth and status, and there's a thing in the South about families and legacy, and that's important to him." She smiles pensively. "He tries to meddle in my life, so we have lot of conflict. I know he loves me, but I also know I embarrass him."

"Uh, Kristen. Please don't be offended by this question. Do you dress the way you do to piss off your parents?"

"I know you're a reporter, but you're really irritating."

"Sorry. I've been told that before. But do you?"

"I dress Goth to express my independence. It's my personal protest of the things that are wrong in the world—and, like I said, the music. The fact that it pisses off my dad is just a perk."

She laughs half-heartedly, and not knowing what to say next, I smile and change the subject.

"I have a confession. I did more research on you. You didn't just teach in Paraguay, you also set up a school there. That's impressive. You're really making a difference."

Kristen smiles and nods. "Thanks. And I looked you up too."

We both laugh.

"Occupational habits," I add.

"I have a trust fund. I have some more money coming to me soon and I want to use it for more schools in Paraguay. That's what my parents and I discussed over lunch. Daddy freaked. He said he doesn't want me, quote, wasting money on some Brown kids in some third world country." Kristen shakes her head. "Sometimes having money can be a burden."

"As burdens go, that's not such a bad one to bear," I say with a scoff.

Kristen's back stiffens. She avoids eye contact and taps burgundy-lacquered fingernails on her glass before taking a sip of wine.

Uh-oh, too far with my teasing.

"I mean, my grandmother always says it's fine to *have* money, you just can't let the money have you."

Kristen lightens up and smiles. She holds her wineglass aloft. "To Grandma."

I toast with a sip of coffee, and then—because I feel bad about embarrassing Kristen or because I like what I've learned about her, or maybe a bit of both—I confide the full story of my assignment in Birmingham. She's interested and sympathetic, asks a few questions, and promises her full assistance while I'm in town.

On the ride to her house we discuss the pros and cons of Kanye and agree that Taylor Swift and Lizzo are both really talented, but Swift is America's idea of what a pop star should look like. When I drop Kristen at her door I remember to tell her I won't be at the library the next day because of my meetings, and she speaks of her father again.

"By the way, when I mentioned I was having dinner with you, Daddy said he'd heard there was a northern newspaper reporter in town asking about an old police case. His insurance company has connections to the police department, and he said to let you know he'd be happy to help."

HOMESICKNESS KICKS IN ON THE WAY TO MY AIRBNB. AFTER the conversation with Kristen, I'm feeling lucky to have parents who accept me the way I am. I decide to call to say good night.

"How's my girl handling the Deep South?" Daddy's amusement sounds through the car's speakers.

I don't laugh at his wisecrack. "Pretty good," I say.

I tell him about the hospitality I received from John and Germaine, my accommodations at the library, and the convenience of my Airbnb. I also complain a bit about the tediousness of newspaper scanning.

"Sounds like you're off to a good start. Are you having any fun?"

"Tonight I had dinner with my contact from the library. She's really nice. We had a good time, and the meal was quite tasty. Tomorrow I'm meeting someone from the mayor's office who's promised a big southern breakfast."

"I didn't think you'd be disappointed in the food," Daddy says. There are several seconds of silence before he asks, "What else?"

"Today I came across a small item in one of the old newspapers. It's a story about the murder of an unidentified man, and it looks like it occurred about the same time Great-Grandpa died."

"You think it could be him?" Daddy asks.

"Not sure; there weren't any details in the story, but I have a feeling about it."

"That's great, baby girl. You know you've always had a sixth sense about things. How come you don't sound more excited?"

"I am, but there's something else. I've barely started my investigation and already a lot of people seem to be fishing for information about me and what I'm doing."

"Well, that's not so surprising. Birmingham wants to protect its reputation. I believe in the new South, but not every city can easily catch up to the future, and every place has to reckon with its past. No matter how much things change, secrets will bubble up through the ground. One of my jazz pals always used to say, 'The earth holds all the dirt.'"

TEN

—————•—————

2019

Birmingham, like Detroit, is a city of cars. I feel at home with the congestion and rhythm of the traffic and I easily maneuver my rental into the blend of the morning commute. Magic City Grille's address is on Third Avenue North, but the entrance is really on Twenty-second Street on a block with a mix of manufacturing, service businesses, and condos. There's street parking, but I don't know how long I'll be, so I pay for a parking space in a nearby lot.

I step in the door at seven forty-five and wait in a short line. The breakfast atmosphere at MC's is best described as the confluence of an assembly line and a family reunion. The place is small—the opposite of fancy—and operating at full tilt. A diverse mix of folks come in and go out for takeout—office workers, police officers, and neighborhood residents, who all seem to be regulars. Most are greeted by name or called "sugar" or "honey." A buffet area is already being set up for what I learn is the popular

$9.99 lunch, which starts at eleven thirty. I'm finally led to a small booth with blue vinyl seats, paper napkins, and a plastic menu. My server—a middle-aged woman with salt-and-pepper hair and an impressively large cross at her neck—approaches my table.

"Get you something, sugar? You want coffee?"

"Uh. I'm waiting for somebody, but I'll take a Pepsi until he gets here."

The lady looks at me and purses her lips. "We only serve Coke products." She doesn't smile. I guess my sugar has melted.

"Oh. I'm sorry. I didn't know. I'll take a large Diet Coke."

As I peek up from my menu her countenance transforms. She flashes a smile such as I wouldn't have thought her capable of. Then I realize it's not for me. I look over my shoulder for the cause of her metamorphosis. It turns out to be a tall, slender brother in a dark blue shirt. He has thick, shoulder-length locs and beautiful teeth.

"Are you Ms. McKenzie?" he asks, squinting at me.

"Mr. Curren?"

"She with you, Darius?" the server asks with a raised brow.

"She is. An out-of-town guest. I told her she could get the best breakfast in town here."

The woman smiles again, sharing about ten percent of it with me. "Your regular, Darius?"

"Absolutely." He looks at me with light brown eyes. "You like catfish?"

"Sure, but . . ."

"Two regulars, Patience." He points at me. "What is *she* drinking?"

"Diet Coke," Patience says wryly without a glance my way.

"I'll have a regular Coke, and can we have waters?"

"Coming up," she responds energetically.

I watch her walk away. Apparently she lives up to her name only for handsome young men like the one taking a seat across from me.

"You're not what I expected," I say, regretting it immediately.

"Why? Because you thought I was a stuffy old bureaucrat?"

"Busted," I say with a smile.

Darius laughs. "If my father were here, your civil servant meter would be *way* in the red. I came into office with the *new* mayor." He squints again. "So, you're a reporter?"

"Ha. I am. And I'm not what *you* expected."

"Touché." He laughs again. An action that squints his eyes and engages his full, brown face. "I guess we both made assumptions."

I suddenly realize I didn't come here for repartee or flirtation. Darius Curren is a source. Maybe he can point me in the right direction for my story or refer me to someone who can. Certainly, with his position in the mayor's office, he could open a door for me if one happens to be marked "no entry."

Patience has returned with our drinks and two big plates of catfish on top of collards, and grits pooled in butter. The biscuits are the size of softballs. Darius quickly picks up his fork and digs into the grits. I'm right behind him. After a few minutes of cutting catfish, layering grape jelly on biscuits, and mixing butter and grits, we both look up from our plates grinning.

"Told you," he says.

"You did. This is serious. That biscuit is as large as . . ."

"Joe Louis's fist?"

I stare at Darius. Maybe flirting is not in order, but he's so obviously smart, self-confident, and down-to-earth that I can't help but be intrigued.

"You *have* heard of Joe Louis?" he asks, looking smug.

I raise an eyebrow and give him a deadpan glare. He may be good-looking, but he's also a smart-ass.

"Yes, I've heard of Joe Louis," I reply indignantly. "There's a large outdoor statue of his fist in downtown Detroit. It's his hometown. You should look it up."

I take a long draw on my soft drink while staring him down. He looks contrite so I decide to let him off the hook.

"I also know about him because my father is a big boxing fan," I say.

"So is mine," Darius replies.

"Your father works in city government too?"

"He's deputy mayor for economic development."

"Sounds impressive."

"He's an impressive man."

Turns out so is Darius. He has a political science degree from Temple University and a graduate degree from Howard University and has written two books on the impact of systemic racism on income inequality. He's also very connected to the local BLM organization. I tell Darius the full story of my assignment. He listens with those squinted eyes and responds with empathy and complete optimism that I'll be successful in uncovering the truth of my great-grandfather's murder.

After the food is eaten and we sip our refills, we discuss how modern-day police reform might look. He offers to facilitate an interview with the mayor if and when I want one. We end our conversation at a quarter to nine because Darius has a meeting in his office. We exchange cell phone information, and I promise to keep him posted on my progress.

"Oh, by the way," he says as we part in front of the restaurant. "Joe Louis moved to Detroit when he was twelve but he was *born* in Alabama."

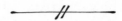

After a few hours of unsuccessful searching in the basement archives of *Awaken*, the lack of light and the dampness topple my spirit. It also doesn't help that paper after paper describes the twentieth-century efforts of southern cities to maintain Jim Crow laws and hold back Black progress in every arena of life. The voluminous news reports of mob riots and Klan marches are demoralizing.

I haven't come across a single clue about my great-grandfather's murder or any additional information about the man found stabbed to death in an alley in late September.

After another half hour with the *Awaken* volumes, I ascend the stairs. Roberta has been picked up by the church van for a senior outing, and Germaine is leaning over her laptop at the dining room table with a pile of papers on either side.

"Hi. I think I'm going to take a drive and find some coffee," I say to her.

"Oh, I can make you coffee."

"I don't want to disturb you from your work, and honestly, I could also use some sun and a walk. It's pretty dim in the basement. I need to get my juices flowing again."

"I know what you mean. John can work for hours on end down there. But it's his man cave, and that's the way he likes it."

"Is there a nearby park?"

"There's an outdoor recreation area a half mile from here. It has a nice walking path. I'd go with you, but I'm studying for my nursing recertifications. That's what I usually do on my day off."

ACROSS FROM THE PARK I SPOT A STRIP MALL WITH A COFFEE shop. After a few sips of chai tea and a few minutes of walking, I'm beginning to feel part of the world again. The square-block neighborhood park is well used by the area's residents. Several people are walking dogs, and I share the path with joggers, bikers, and a couple of inline skaters. In one of the park's half dozen meadows, a young couple have stretched a blanket on the grass for a picnic lunch. I sit on a bench near a fountain and let the warmth of the day seep into my bones.

Two little girls twirl, squeal, and run through the fountain water in their summer togs, getting completely soaked. They wave happily at their watching fathers. A memory of those carefree days sparks inside my chest. These children have the certainty that they are loved and safe. It spreads over them like the picnic blanket covering the grass in the meadow. The scene is a reminder, too, of Grandma's fatherless childhood. I feel the stir of a breeze at the back of my neck. *I need to get back to work.*

I return to the Rankin house with two carryout lunches from the coffee shop. Nothing special, just sandwiches with chips and a pickle, but Germaine is so grateful she leaps from the table to hug me. I trudge down to the basement with my sandwich and more coffee, take a few bites of pastrami on rye, then don my plastic gloves for the next newspaper.

I've read about a labor strike in North Carolina and tornadoes in Arkansas. The paper has ads for local eateries serving home-cooked meals, hair-growth products, and clothing—including women's hats for the price of a dollar. Economic matters take up a lot of space in this volume. I read a commentary condemning the poverty within the sharecropping system, and a sociologist from Howard University forecasts a massive migration of Blacks from the South to northern cities to find jobs. The instability of jobs and financial institutions has definitely fueled racial tensions. An entire half page of this eight-page volume has accounts of Klan rallies, cross burnings, and four lynchings.

Then a headline catches my eye. NO MOTIVE IN ALLEY MURDER. It is a two-column story, in the October 4 edition, about the killing of a policeman, Carl Simenon, who was discovered behind the Carstairs Furniture Company in late September. He succumbed to stab wounds in his belly. The last sentence in the story notes a janitor has been charged in the murder. I'm confused. This isn't the story I hoped to find. The dead man is *not* Black, *and* he's a cop.

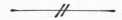

I cook a quick dinner of pasta and salmon, eat a red velvet cupcake for dessert, and, per the instructions of my Airbnb host, take out the trash for the morning's pickup. This house is in a pretty block of freshly painted homes with mature trees and landscaped lawns. I hear the strains of a heavy metal band and look up the street at a white van double-parked near the corner with its windows open and hazard lights blinking. After I've angled the trash container at the curb, the next-door neighbor comes down his driveway with his trash receptacle. He waves. I wave back. He stares at the van. The driver—who is probably making a delivery—rolls up the window.

"This is usually a quiet neighborhood," the neighbor says.

"Yes. I've noticed," I reply, heading up the porch steps. "Good night."

I pull out my research notes and spread them across the kitchen table. Before I left the Rankin house I'd found another news story related to the policeman's murder, published a week later, and now copies of both—plus the original item I found in my library search—are lined up next to one another. I read and reread the three articles, hoping for some insight. The last clipping has the most detail. The dead cop managed to snatch a bit of his assailant's hair, and the sample did not match the janitor, who was subsequently released from custody. In the final paragraph, the police chief—a man named Pruitt—called the crime the act of animals. "Nobody gets away with killing an officer of the law in Birmingham," he's quoted as saying.

With the beginnings of a headache, I scoop my notes into a folder, half fill a glass with red wine, and head off to bed to relax with a romance novel. Within a half hour I abandon the escapism and return to my research file. There's something about the story of the white policeman's death that nags at me. Saxby and I have talked a lot about the value of a reporter's hunches. He calls it his "wait just a damn minute" feeling. I line up the stories on the bed to read again.

I WAKE UP WITH A START. IT'S ALMOST MIDNIGHT. I GATHER the newspaper clippings and handwritten notes strewn around the bed into a manila folder and stuff them into my tote. "Let sleeping dogs lie," Mom said when I told her I was coming to Birmingham. I turn off the lamp on the nightstand and try to settle back into sleep, hoping not to continue the dream of being chased by a rabid barking dog.

ELEVEN

Tradesman

1929

My job at the mansion goes well. Some days there are as many as thirty men—Black and white—doing various jobs on the inside and outside of the structure. Work continues on preparing the ground for a massive wrought-iron fence. It's back-bending work. Toiling in the midday heat is almost unbearable, so the digging crews begin just before daylight. When I arrive, an hour later, the laborers in the trench are already covered in a fine dust, and they pause in their digging to stare at me and my car. Most have smiles; a few glare with envy. One man tips his hat. The white workers are not so generous.

I park my car near the other vehicles. Mostly trucks. The carpentry crew gathers near a pile of lumber at the side of the house, waiting for the supervisor's orders for the day. Three white laborers are mixing cement for a large courtyard at the rear of the mansion. As I walk by one of the men shouts out, "Uppity nigger."

It is a lesson of survival for the Negro race to ignore these insults. Old Black men have been the most vocal teachers. Their very existence gives them credentials. I pause a second but keep walking until something splatters at my feet. I look down at my boots; one is covered in wet cement. I swivel to see the thrower—a scrawny pock-faced man wearing a tilted denim cap that doesn't conceal the scar on his forehead. We stare at each other. He wears raveling coveralls and scuffed brown boots. His arms are unusually long, his fingers stretching beyond his knees. He reaches toward his back pocket. I twitch. My revolver is in my lunch box. The man pulls out a dirty rag and rubs at the cement mixture on his hand.

I'm weighing my odds at successfully tackling the long-armed man without involving his friends in the fight when Pete, one of my white coworkers, appears at my side.

"Harrington, the supervisor is here," he says loudly, then whispers in my ear, "You don't want to find dried cement on the Franklin at the end of your shift."

I return to the car and park it on the other side of the work site.

"Thanks," I say to Pete as we move inside the mansion to begin our shift.

"That's a beautiful automobile. I'd hate to see anything happen to it."

I nod.

"You ever think of selling her?" he asks.

I stare at him. He's not bad for a white guy, and he's an excellent carpenter. He's older than me and I've learned a few things from him—and vice versa.

"Lately, I've been thinking of maybe getting more of a family car. I have another baby on the way."

"Well, if you decide to sell her, let me know," Pete says, looking back at the Franklin. "She's a real beauty all right."

———————

I'VE BEEN TOLD BY WHITE MEN THAT I HAVE A WAY WITH wood. I know it sticks in the craw of some of them to admit it, but I already know it's true. Papa Tico saw it in me as a young boy when I would join him in whittling. He'd learned to carve in Haiti, where he'd free sugarcane of its hull to reveal the succulent pulp. Under his watchful eye I made crosses, animals, and tiny replicas of him and Mama from the chunks of pine I'd find behind our Georgia cabin.

Over the years I learned to make magic with fresh-cut wood. A cut here, a nick there, sanding with the rough surface of discarded bark, smoothing with my fingertips. At first pale like the skin of a white baby, then eventually—as air and handling breathes life, form, and function into it—glowing with natural color.

My job on the interior of this Birmingham mansion is custom carpentry work on an ornate stairwell that will join the upper floor of the residence to a grand ballroom on the first level of the home. The main construction crew had roughed in the stairs even before I arrived in the city. But the detail requires my kind of skills. Though I have not personally seen one, I'm told these types of sweeping staircases are staples in the most elegant of wealthy homes.

Built from a gorgeous oak, the steps will be stained and carpeted, and each step will have an etched border. Last month, my teammate and I carved and assembled the balusters, spindles, newel-posts, and fittings. The banister will have twelve posts and sixty spindles, though we've made extras of each in case they become damaged during the installation. At a temporary workbench we sit outside for hours at a time with our chisels, strap clamps, bevels, and glue. Each banister post will have a finial shaped like a lion's head, and I have drawn with pencil on wax paper a design of the finished product. I'll personally handle that delicate carving work. We are about halfway through the stair assembly, with another three weeks of work ahead of us before we begin the final tasks—engraving the borders of each step and etching the elaborate curlicues on the handrails and footrails. According to the supervisor, the homeowner—an iron-ore industrialist—is thrilled by what he's already seen, and the builder has hinted there may be more work for me when this job is complete.

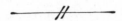

I've put in a full day and as I clean and gather my tools I look up and notice the fellows mixing and pouring cement. Their work has brought them to my side of the mansion, where the ballroom will spill out onto an expansive patio. They watch as I load my tools into the trunk of the Franklin and start up the engine. When I drive past, long arms is leaning on his wood rake. He spits in the dirt as we lock eyes.

TWELVE

———◆———

2019

"Pruitt?" Kristen punches at her keyboard. "There's a Pruitt who was chief during the civil rights years. He came in right after Bull Connor left the scene."

"Nope, that can't be him. My guy was quoted in a 1929 paper. I think he'd be too old to be chief in the sixties."

"Okay. Yep," Kristen says, fingers gliding. "The guy you want is Jeff Pruitt *Jr.* Almost eighty-seven years old. And you're right, his father was also a Birmingham chief of police. All in the family, huh?"

I nod and lean over her shoulder to look at the record she's pulled up. "If I find him I hope he has a clear mind and can tell me if his father kept any records from ninety years ago. For that matter, I hope he's even willing to speak with me."

"And why is it you think this policeman's death is important?"

"It may not be. I found three brief newspaper reports about this cop being killed, with a smattering of details, then no other mention of him—not even in the mainstream papers." I notice the slow wriggle up my back. "I think it's worth a try to look up this Pruitt and see what he knows about the case."

Kristen shrugs. "How'd your meeting go with the guy from the mayor's office?"

"Fine."

"What's his name?"

"Curren. Darius Curren."

Kristen executes a slow smile. "I see him on the local news all the time. He's quite the looker."

"I guess so. I didn't really notice."

"Then you must be losing your eyesight."

USING MY *FREE PRESS* ACCOUNT, I BEGIN A LOCATION SEARCH for Pruitt and within five minutes have an address and telephone number for a home in Gardendale, a northern suburb of Birmingham. There's no answer when I call, but I leave a message.

I jump when my phone vibrates a few minutes later, and hope it's Pruitt returning my call. Instead the phone displays the name of the local Black Lives Matter coordinator.

"Hi. Glad to hear from you, Monique."

"Sorry, would have gotten back sooner. I've been crazy busy. There was another police shooting in Chicago yesterday."

"I hadn't heard."

"It hasn't made the national news yet. The mayor jumped on the situation right away. Fired two officers because they didn't have their bodycams activated. She's trying to get in front of the protests and has already ordered her chief to do an investigation. He has two days to report back to her."

I'm taking notes as Monique Hendricks speaks. "Well, that's a good way to handle things. Look, if you're jammed up we can talk later."

"No, no. I'm happy to make time for you. We really appreciate your reporting. We get lots of calls from newspapers, the networks, and cable news—usually reacting to an officer-involved shooting. That's all the media does. React. They're never doing the stories about the root causes of this madness. You're doing righteous work, sis. I was saying that to Darius this morning."

"You and Darius were talking about *me*?"

Monique laughs. "Yeah, girl. To tell you the truth, he called to remind me to get back to you. Anyway, are you ready for the 'what the tourists don't see' Birmingham tour?"

I laugh. "Sure am. Are you thinking today?"

"No time like the present."

"I'll need a couple of hours to get some notes together. Can we meet after that?"

"You driving?"

"Yep."

"Okay. I'll text the address. Let's meet at one o'clock."

"I'll be there."

At eleven thirty my phone vibrates and the caller ID shows a Gardendale number. The last copy has fallen into the catch bin of the printer and I swoop up the papers and connect the call as I return to my carrel and close the door.

"Meghan McKenzie," I say into the receiver.

"Uh. This is . . . uh, you left a message for me," the woman says tentatively. She sounds white, southern, and wary.

"Yes, ma'am. I'm a reporter with the *Detroit Free Press*. I was wondering if the former chief of police, uh, Mr. Pruitt, might be able to talk to me a few minutes about a case I read about in one of the local newspapers. It's an incident where, unfortunately, a Birmingham officer was killed."

"What newspaper?" the woman asks suspiciously.

"The, uh, *Independent.*"

It's a small lie. I've come across the *Birmingham Independent* during my research. It's touted as a conservative publication and had a good run in the years following the spark of civil rights activity in the city.

There's silence at the other end of the line. I wait. Daddy's advice to me was if I'm talking to southerners of a certain age I should give them time to digest information. "Don't rush people," he said. "If you ask someone a question, give them room to think." Thirteen seconds tick by on my watch. It feels like thirteen minutes.

"The *Independent* was a good paper in its day." The lady speaks louder than before, like someone is listening in the background.

"Yes, ma'am. So I've heard."

"What kind of story you writing?"

"I'm doing research on how dangerous policing can be."

"Ain't that the truth," a voice chimes in from an echoey background.

I must be on speakerphone.

"Daddy really don't take many visitors," the woman says. "He's in a nursing home, you know. He don't get around too good no more."

"If it's no trouble, maybe I can arrange to speak with him by phone. Just ten or fifteen minutes is all I need of his time."

"Well . . . sometimes my grandson visits Daddy, and when he's there we do that Zoom thing. You know, where you can see each other?"

"Yes. Zoom. I use it all the time."

"Give me your number. He might could talk to you tomorrow morning."

"I'd appreciate it, ma'am."

That's more of Daddy's advice. Address older folks as "sir" and "ma'am." Include the word "appreciate" along with phrases like "thank you kindly" and "if it's no trouble." In other words, speak like Laura Ingalls in *Little House on the Prairie*.

"Okay. I'll call you later," the woman says.

"By the way, ma'am, who am I speaking to?"

"I'm his daughter. Velda."

"Thank you kindly."

I disconnect and slump in my chair, exhausted by the interaction. Choosing my words carefully, tiptoeing around the truth, letting silence unfold, is hard work. I stand, stretch, and open my cubbyhole door to get some air flowing. Persuading and making nice on the phone is something I've done numerous times. It's a tactic reporters use to gain the cooperation of a reluctant witness or information source. But this time, as I cajoled and "yes, ma'amed" I was distracted by my angry thoughts of centuries-old conversations in the Deep South where Black people literally had to bargain and plead for their lives.

My phone alarm reminds me of my appointment with Monique, and I gather up folders and notes and stuff them into my backpack. I program the address Monique has sent into my maps app, and I'm on my way. In just a ten-minute drive from downtown to Birmingham's inner city the economic disparities of the haves and have-nots are dramatically revealed.

I grew up in one of Detroit's nearby suburbs where Black professionals raise their children in homes with manicured lawns, summer camps, and college funds. But Detroit still has scores of neighborhoods like this one, with abandoned buildings, over-grown lots where houses once stood, and blocks where poverty and despair cling like sweat on dark skin.

I'm meeting Monique at the church that serves as the local headquarters for BLM. I enter through the basement and follow the security guard. I see two dozen volunteers making prepara-tions for an upcoming rally. They're mapping out a march route, lettering placards, and practicing protest chants. On the other side of the room, in a well-appointed kitchen, three older Black women are wrapping up the remainders of a lunch that has been served. The efficient women wear Evangelical Church name tags. We pass a table stacked with flyers and posters ready to be distributed throughout the city. Upstairs on the choir stage, Monique is con-cluding a training.

She has a commanding presence and a warm energy. I'm five eight and she's taller, maybe ten pounds heavier, with a head of long, beautiful twists. My curly hair, inherited from my mother, doesn't braid well, and I'm always envious of sisters with locs, twists, or braids. Today Monique wears a BLM tee, leggings, and boots. The others are similarly attired, and I feel conspicuously overdressed in my tunic top, slacks, and flats.

I met Monique the year after she and a group of Samford University students had made a six-hour drive from Birmingham to Baton Rouge to protest the police killing of thirty-seven-year-old Alton Sterling. Later that year, she dropped out of school to commit herself to the Black Lives Matter cause. She's been trained in civil disobedience practices and is now passing on her knowl-edge to others.

"You'll be confronted by police, outside agitators, and some-times right-wingers looking to do us harm. The key is to stay calm and unified," Monique says to the volunteers. "We have a *right* to peacefully protest, but the moment there's violence the police can, and will, move in. It's critical for us to focus on what's important. We're exercising our constitutional rights, our First Amendment rights of peaceful protest against police brutality and racial injustice. That's what I keep in mind whenever someone tries to bait me."

"What if someone hits me or throws something at me?" a twentysomething white kid with freckles asks. "I'm not just gonna stand by if someone takes a punch at me or one of my friends."

There are murmurs of agreement and heads nod in the group gathered around Monique. She grabs a folding chair from the side and pulls it close to sit among the trainees.

"Look. I'm not going to tell you not to defend yourself if you feel your life is in danger, but most of the time that won't be the case. Remember, you're not out there alone. If someone starts shoving or punching, our protocol is to tighten our ranks. Most of these bullies who try to incite violence will back down if a group confronts their actions. It's the same for the people who loot. Those folks are opportunists, not activists. I'm not marching for free sneakers, and I'm sure none of you are either."

The trainees nod and a few applaud. Monique spots me in the back of the sanctuary and hands off her clipboard to one of her associates. When she joins me I extend a hand. She brushes it away and pulls me into a hug.

"So those are your new volunteers?"

"Just one group of them. We get thirty or forty new people every month. Our contributions are way up, too. It's amazing how many people want to be engaged in this movement right now."

"I can feel the energy. This is a remarkable operation."

"And it could be bigger. The local paper just asked me for an interview to rate the four major gubernatorial candidates—one of them is really bad news, a state senator. He'd be a train wreck, but as an organization we've decided to stay out of partisan politics. We've also had offers of corporate space, but we're always leery of police spying and infiltrators."

I've read the reports that local BLM organizations are scrutinized by the FBI and other agencies who are not above embedding agents within the social justice groups. It happened fifty years ago with the Black Panthers, and no one is naïve enough to think it's not happening now.

"So, should we sit and talk or get started on our tour?" I ask.

"Let's drive. I've been cooped up inside all morning. You picked the best time of the year to come to our neck of the woods. Fall is really beautiful in Birmingham, and it's not so ungodly humid."

We take my car and Monique is right about the season. The trees on the distant Red Mountain haven't changed yet, but there are yellowroot, climbing hydrangea, and purple blooms, which Monique tells me are Stokes' aster. She's also right that this neighborhood—despite the flora—will never make it into the chamber of commerce promotional brochure.

As we travel block after block we fall into a comfortable silence. I sense Monique looking at me, gauging my reaction to the blight and impoverishment, but I'm concentrating on driving. On the very busy main streets, I can only take in a broad sweep of my surroundings, but as we pass through residential areas I get a good look at houses, people, and living conditions.

"What do you think?" Monique asks.

"It's a lot different from downtown."

"Yep."

"But isn't Birmingham going through a growth spurt? The university is expanding and that's generating other development. Right?"

"You've been reading the newspapers."

I laugh. "Actually I've been reading a shitload of papers. That's what I've spent most of my time on since I got here."

"You ready to do the interview? We can stop at a fast-food place and grab a burger or something. Have you had a meat-n-three yet?"

"Not yet."

"Oh, then I know the place to take you, and this time of the day we can sit and talk and nobody will hassle us."

We drive through an industrial area crisscrossed with railroad tracks, fast-food restaurants, and billboards for ambulance chasers and funeral homes, then head out Finley Avenue, passing by blocks of small businesses and side streets leading to residential areas.

Niki's West, I learn, is a wildly popular restaurant. The eatery has a semi-nautical theme. A cobblestone wall adorned with shark sculptures flanks a small fireplace. Tables and chairs are polished to a sheen that matches the wood paneling, and booths are both roomy and comfortable. Folks queued at the buffet bar are jovial, excited like they're in line to see a Beyoncé concert.

"It's crowded. I don't know how long they'll just let us sit," I say.

"No worries. It's a big place and a lot of people are getting carryouts."

A gracious host seats us at one of the corner booths when Monique informs her we want to sit awhile. We drop sweaters and bags in our seats and queue up. We make small talk in the line, and I aim my writer's eye at the people and the environs. When we return to the table we find napkins and a pitcher of sweet tea. Condiments, including tabasco, steak sauce, and relish, are clustered on the table along with pats of butter, salt, pepper, and sugar. The head buzz I get as soon as I swallow the sweet liquid tells me I won't need the sugar.

My tray has two plates filled with fried shrimp, macaroni and cheese, broccoli, and fried okra. I skipped lunch today, so I'm counting this meal as an early dinner, and it's just what the doctor ordered. I admire Monique's food choices for a few seconds—beef tips with rice, collards, and black-eyed peas—then dive into my food.

The interview starts organically and without note-taking. Monique has put aside her graduate studies in social work to learn on the job and in real time. Her mother, like mine, is an educator. She's also a PK, a preacher's kid. Her father is the pastor of the church we just left. BLM became personal for her when one of her friends—a fellow social worker—was injured in the Ferguson protests.

"Greg's an activist, someone who believes in fighting for the community. He works with young teens in after-school programs. He was marching with his father, who lives in St. Louis," Monique says, remembering. "They were protesting near city hall when police lobbed smoke bombs. Gary has asthma. He was hospitalized for weeks and now has long-term health issues to deal with, including COPD. That's when I got off the sidelines and moved to the front lines."

"He sounds like a good guy," I say.

"He truly is."

Monique is a fourth-generation Birmingham resident. Nimble with details about the city, its residents, and their relationships. She knows all about the history of the restaurant and the neighborhoods we've traversed in the last couple of hours, explaining that many of the communities were their own cities before being annexed in the heyday of the steel industry.

"These neighborhoods were thriving, but when the mills started closing, they began to change. That's code for whites moving out," she says.

I nod. "It happened in Detroit too, after the rebellion of '67."

"So you know. It makes me so angry when people try to diminish the value of Black Lives Matter with the false argument that more Black people are shot by other Black people than the police. It's a simplistic deflection that ignores decades of poverty and disenfranchisement," Monique says with passion. "Sorry. I can get worked up about this stuff. Anger isn't great for digestion."

"You sound like my mother," I say with a smile.

"Then *she* sounds like mine."

We laugh. In tribute to Black mothers, and to keep the rage at bay.

"What's Detroit like?" Monique asks.

"Similar to Birmingham. It's changed. In a lot of ways for the better, but at the same time the soul of the place has been fractured. Downtown Detroit is thriving, getting hipper and more desirable as a place to live and work, but the inner-city neighborhoods are still neglected. You should come visit."

Monique and I spend an hour in conversation. She speaks of the new work of activism, the allies and detractors, the comparisons and differences between the civil rights era and the social justice era. We discuss the urgency of today's protesters and the signs of deep division within the country. I take notes, needing to prompt only a few times for a deeper understanding of her views. She's a dream interviewee.

Her phone has beeped several times during our meal, and she finally looks at her messages. "I have to go soon," she says, rummaging through her bag and pulling out a wallet.

"Put your money away. I'm buying," I say.

"Girl. I guess you wouldn't know how things work in the South. You're a visitor, and that means *we* feed *you*."

"Okay, but let me leave an extra-nice tip for the waitress."

ON THE RIDE BACK, I CONFIDE IN MONIQUE MY PURPOSE FOR coming to Birmingham and what I hope to achieve. She listens without interruption.

"Well, damn, girl. That's serious business. The old-timers at our church talk about how the cops swept into Black neighborhoods like they owned the place. Those months before the Depression were rough-and-tumble days. Everybody was searching for work, and the tensions between Blacks and whites spiraled. If your grandmother's daddy had a good job, a nice car, and a light-bright-damn-near-white wife, he was *definitely* a target. Are you interviewing anybody from the police department?"

"I hope so. I've put in a call to them."

"Darius knows a captain on the force. He attends our church from time to time. I've been in community meetings with him. His name is Masterson. Maybe you should talk to him."

"Can you make an introduction?"

"Nah-uh."

"Why? Don't you trust him?"

Monique raises an eyebrow. "The Birmingham police and BLM have a shaky relationship. You should ask Darius to introduce you."

I drop Monique off at a different church, where she is doing an evening training. When she opens the door I think I hear strains of heavy metal music again. Monique's already late, and pulling her training materials out of the car, so I return my attention to her for our quick goodbye.

"Write that story! It's important to the cause, and let me know if you need any help." She stops at the sidewalk and turns. "Oh, by the way, I think Darius likes you."

I have a quiet evening at the Airbnb. It's just what I need. Time to reflect on the events of the last few days. Monique has inspired and reaffirmed my commitment to my family story. It *is* important, and relevant. A human tragedy of the past too much like the Black family tragedies of our present. I think about the poverty and despair I've seen today. Maybe my story will help at least one reader understand the viciousness of racism. How it props up broken systems and bad policies. Making those who are marginalized mistrustful of authority, and those in authority fearful of, and hateful toward, the people they're supposed to serve.

I have a voicemail message from Velda Pruitt. Her father will speak with me tomorrow at ten, and her son, Zach, will send a Zoom link. Zach's text comes an hour later. He's done a Google search of me and warns that his grandfather probably won't speak to a Black woman. He adds the BLM hashtag at the end of his message. My reply to him is: Thank you. Any ideas?

I'M REVIEWING ALL THE NOTES FROM MY NEWSPAPER RE-search. Again. Looking for context, insight, takeaways. Birmingham's mainstream newspapers of the twenties and thirties have scant reporting about the needs and interests of what was then called the Negro population. Much more common are the stories of uprisings in Black communities where the population is portrayed as rioters rather than as victims of Jim Crow injustice. I remember one of my father's favorite sayings: "Same song. Different tune."

The African American publications try to counter this lopsided coverage with stories about Negro contributions to America, commentary on their second-class status, and glimpses of Black daily life—birth announcements, celebrations, church services, death notices, and comings and goings.

At midnight, I put down my notes and rub my tired eyes. I've written about five hundred words of background copy that I can drop into my story. It was great getting together with Monique. I'll write up and send in my interview in a couple of days, along with the photos I took during her training. I'm sure the editors will love it. Just before I turn out the light, I check my phone. Garrett has sent another text. I don't reply, and scroll through my other messages. The one from Monique is troubling. The guys who look out for me say a white van followed us from the church today. Probably nothing. Comes with the BLM work. But now that you're associating with me some of it might rub off on you. Just thought you should know.

THIRTEEN

◆

Daily Life

1929

Anna Kate has transformed our sparse two-room apartment into a cozy haven. She loves to knit and crochet, making doilies and tablecloths, and shawls and sweaters for Mae. We've added a dresser to our furnishings, and a rocking chair, and I've built a new table that serves as our dining area. It's little more than a movable flat surface, but it's well made and stores easily against the wall when we're not using it. I've also built Mae a little high chair so she can sit at the table with us for meals. She is thriving in our new life in Birmingham, has grown at least another three inches, and has discovered a few children her age among the boardinghouse residents.

I've worked every day but Sundays for the last three weeks and no longer have a predictable schedule, except that I know my shifts will be long. Now only a bit more carving is required before the sanding and staining can begin, and the grand staircase in the ballroom of the Bessemer mansion becomes a one-of-a-kind showpiece. The job has tested my skills as a carpenter, and I'm as proud of this work as of anything I've ever done. I'm hopeful my knowledge and craftsmanship will continue to please the architect and I'll be offered another job soon.

While my work goes well, Anna Kate is making a slower adjustment to the rhythm and personality of a bigger city. She enjoys her new church home, where she has joined the choir and helps to teach Sunday school. Still, too much of her time during the week is spent in solitude. She has not always fit in where she isn't known. Her striking beauty, which gives me so much pride, can be a burden for her, often keeping good friendships at arm's length. She's envied by other women—especially those with husbands whose glances turn into lingering stares. So I'm grateful that she and our landlady have taken to each other. A few times I've returned from work to find Anna Kate and Mrs. Ardle at our table peeling potatoes, snapping peas, and scooping preserves into mason jars.

Despite the uncertainty about finding another job, the constant strain of prejudice I feel from most whites, and Anna Kate's loneliness, I don't regret bringing my family to Birmingham. We are doing pretty well. I get paid every two weeks, and after paying our bills, buying groceries, and sending some money to Mama, Anna Kate is able to squirrel away a few dollars for the savings jar. I also have enough money left to spend on a man's enjoyment. In my case, that means poker. I don't do any heavy gambling, just play for a few hours and have a bit of fun.

Tonight, for the first time in more than a month, I'm going to Griggs Ballroom. It's a place where Negroes gather on Friday and Saturday evenings to eat supper, listen to the latest dance music, and—for those in the know—play some poker and buy a couple of drinks.

Anna Kate has made another wonderful supper of a roast chicken with turnips and sweet potatoes. The other boarders are getting a similar meal since Anna Kate and Mrs. Ardle bought the same food items from a backyard farm. Now Anna Kate sits in our new rocking chair and knits a scarf while I get dressed to go out. I feel her sullen mood pierce the bathroom wall. I'm dressed fine in my brown suit and matching hat with a crisp peach-colored shirt and a polka-dot tie. I've finished grooming and as I apply aftershave she comes to the door.

"Don't know why you need to smell fancy just to gamble away your money."

Anna Kate knows I like to look good, but she's also aware of my premarital reputation. On the day Anna Kate and I married, her mama, who is half Indian, sat me down to warn of what would happen if I hurt her child in any way. I have no real interest in another woman, but I do want them to find me attractive. Just like I want men to envy me.

"If I don't use this, I'll get bumps. You know that," I say, patting the aftershave onto my face. The spicy lotion soothes my stinging face and spirit.

"I don't want bumps too, Daddy," Mae says, grabbing my leg. I lift her and dab a bit of the mixture onto the tip of her nose. She laughs and squirms out of my grip.

Anna Kate is back to her knitting. She doesn't look up at me when I open the front door. I love this woman. I know the overtime has kept me away from home a lot, but a man has to blow off a bit of steam sometimes. To compensate I've agreed to attend church this week.

"I'll be home before too late," I say, looking over my shoulder. "Tomorrow's Saturday. I have to work a half day, then I'll come get you and we'll do our shopping. After that I'll take care of whatever chores you have for me. Sunday we'll all go to church as a family."

Anna Kate doesn't say a word. She just gives me a nod before returning to her knitting.

FOURTEEN

2019

At my request, Darius has passed on my name to his police captain friend and the man's name flashes on my phone.

"This is Meghan McKenzie," I say, answering.

"Joshua Masterson. Darius Curren asked me to give you a call. You're a reporter from Detroit writing a story about the Birmingham police?"

"Not exactly, and thank you for calling, Captain Masterson. My story is a historical piece connecting a specific incident in Birmingham with the Black Lives Matter movement."

"You should be speaking with our public information officer. All our press requests come through her."

"I don't have any particular requests yet, sir. I'm still just working on background, but I do have a couple of general questions."

"Okay, I'll try to answer them."

"Would the department have files that go back to the early twentieth century?"

"I know we have files as old as the department itself. We received a grant two years ago to digitize all our records, but I believe only a small percentage of the files from that far back would be available electronically."

"What about information about homicide investigations?"

"Homicide cases are not available to the public," he says.

"I see." I pause. Darius has told me Masterson is one of the good guys. He's head of the department's Civil Rights Unit and is a second-generation cop.

"I'm aware the new mayor has put an emphasis on improving police-community relationships. I also understand your father is a retired member of the force. In your opinion have things improved?"

"Are we speaking on the record?"

"Yes, sir."

"I'll only answer your question off the record, young lady. If you want to request a formal interview, you'll have to go through channels. Are we clear?"

"We're clear. Starting now we're off the record," I say, writing OTR at the top of this section in my notebook page.

"Relationships between the department and the community have improved. Dramatically. But we have long memories in this city. There are families, neighborhoods, organizations, who don't, and never will, trust the police. That lack of trust is perpetuated by the mindsets of some of the personnel who still work in our department. I, and many others, work every day to rid ourselves of that mindset."

"Thanks, Captain. I don't have any other questions at the moment, but I'd appreciate it if I can be in touch again."

Masterson hesitates. "Like I said, you should speak with our officer in press relations."

"I understand."

"Darius says you're a fair person and a professional," Masterson says after a pause.

"I strive to be. He says the same thing about you."

We disconnect. It was a good call because I understand exactly where I stand with BPD and I'm not surprised. My best bet for getting information on the shooting death of my great-grandfather will be through a FOIA request. I call Saxby and ask him to get the paperwork started.

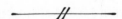

Kristen and I are prepping for my Zoom interview with Mr. Pruitt. She's agreed to substitute for me on the call. It was Zach's idea. We'll do the call from my library carrel and the camera will show white Kristen while Black me sits across the table, out of range of the camera, passing her questions to ask.

At the appointed time I click the Zoom link from my laptop. The screen prompts us to wait for the host. I activate the app that will allow me to record the screen and audio during the call, then duck out of view. I'm using Kristen's laptop to mirror my screen so I can see Pruitt.

In a few seconds, the call is established and the face of a handsome young white man in a knit cap and sports jersey pops up on-screen. I can see him, but he can't see me. He sees Kristen. He's probably in his twenties, with a warm smile and bespectacled eyes. His screen name reads: "Z-man."

"Hello. I'm Kristen. I'm hoping to be able to speak to Mr. Pruitt."

"Well, hello. I'm Zach. Mr. Pruitt's grandson. Where's Miss McKenzie?"

"She was called away on another assignment but she didn't want to have to reschedule. I'm her associate, and she asked me to fill in. Is that okay?"

Zach smiles and winks. "Sure is. Things happen." He winks again. "Let me introduce you to Gramps."

We watch the bouncing view of the laptop camera as it's carried to a table where a grizzled man slumps in a wheelchair. My heart sinks. He looks frail and incapacitated. Zach positions the laptop. He sits next to Pruitt and puts his arm around the old man.

"Gramps. Wake up. I told you I was going to connect the reporter. She's here now and wants to talk to you."

To my surprise Pruitt perks up, squaring his shoulders and sitting upright. He adjusts his eyeglasses and peers into the screen. His face is drawn but comes to life when he sees Kristen.

"Hello there, young lady. Aren't you pretty," he says with leering eyes. "I bet you're real juicy."

"Gramps!" Zach shouts.

Kristen's back stiffens, so I nudge her with my foot. I hope this old lecher doesn't make her change her mind about helping me. "Uh, Mr. Pruitt, thanks for speaking with me today. I won't take up much of your time. My colleague and I are doing a story about policing, and we came across the mention of one of your father's patrolmen. I wondered if you might remember him."

Kristen recites the script just as we rehearsed. When Pruitt realizes Kristen is all business and won't respond to his vulgar flirting, he adjusts his body and his attitude. He looks sullen.

"What's your name?" he asks sourly.

"Kristen. Kristen Gleason."

Pruitt perks up again. "Gleason? Any relation to Gleason Insurance?"

"That's my father."

"And Hiram Gleason is your grandfather?"

"Yes."

"I knew Hiram," Pruitt says. His face fogs with a memory. "Knew him pretty well."

"My family's been in Birmingham a long time," Kristen says.

"I know. So's mine. My grandson here doesn't care much about our family history. He's modern," Pruitt says, looking at Zach with affection. "Like you, I suspect."

"No, sir," Kristen says. "I believe in family and legacy. That's why I have a question about your father's work."

"What do you want to know?"

"There's a case we've run across in some old newspapers. A police officer, one of your father's men, was murdered. We wondered what you might know about that."

"Murdered?"

"That's what the papers say. His name was Simenon. Carl Simenon," Kristen reads from my note.

"Simenon," the old man says, shaking his head. "That doesn't sound familiar. Not at all. Of course, I wasn't chief until twenty years after Dad stepped down."

I pass another note to Kristen. She glances at me and her eyes widen. I nod vigorously. She clears her throat.

"He, uh, might have been a dirty cop. He was found knifed to death downtown."

"What?" Pruitt's eyes narrow, then he turns away from the screen.

"Who is this girl, Zachary?" he says, then returns his suspicious look to Kristen. "What kind of story did you say you're writing?"

I've passed two more notes to Kristen. She looks at them but turns them over and squares her shoulders.

"Sir, I need you to understand that we're trying to write a fair story, and the only way to do that is to have the full truth. I believe most law enforcement officers want to do a good job, but I do know there's always one or two bad apples in the barrel."

Kristen pauses, giving old man Pruitt a chance to noodle over her words. He's pushed his wheelchair away from the table. I watch his mouth twitch and finally his lips tighten into a thin line. He frowns. Kristen waits. It's the same advice Daddy gave me but something she knows intuitively. Zach's head swivels from his grandfather to the screen, where he raises an eyebrow and shrugs.

Finally, Pruitt turns his chair back toward the table. "What did you say his name was?" he asks, scowling.

"Carl Simenon." Kristen looks at the notes. "Mr. Simenon wasn't in uniform when he was killed. We can't find any more information about his murder. We thought maybe your father had mentioned the case."

I'm watching Pruitt's face on-screen. His curiosity about this call has turned to irritation. He fidgets, and curses under his breath. He no longer looks like a vulnerable senior citizen; instead he is a man who can't hide his anger. He leans into the screen sneering, and I instinctively shrink back. I'm imagining how he must have appeared sixty years ago as a street cop, and later in a chief's blazer. He must have been a man who wielded his authority with no room for questions or criticism.

"Young lady, this interview is over," Pruitt announces.

"Gramps, what about that old file cabinet in the garage? Maybe there's something in there about this Simenon dude."

"Turn off that damn computer," he orders. "Why should I help her? We're done."

"Mr. Pruitt. I'm sorry if I've offended you. As you know, my father is an ardent supporter of Birmingham PD and the police pension fund is insured by his company. I know he'd appreciate your cooperation."

Good old Kristen.

"Well, I'll be goddamned," Pruitt says as his face flushes the color of ripened strawberries. Zach reaches out to touch his arm.

Pruitt doesn't like the veiled threat or the reminder that his advanced age gives others power over him. His mouth tightens, and he blinks twice to settle his ire. I bet the nursing home staff is used to his outbursts and bad behavior.

It's evident that Zach really cares about his grandfather, but he's no acorn from the tree. He looks both concerned and embarrassed during the course of the man's meltdown.

"I'm tired now," Pruitt says, slumping in his chair.

I can't tell if it's an act or if the conversation has really zapped his energy.

"I have just a couple more questions," Kristen coaxes.

"I got nothing else to say. Okay, now stop that damn Zoom thing, Zachary. I'm going outside for a smoke."

Pruitt grabs the wheels of his chair and tries to turn it to leave, but he can't quite maneuver it. Zach grabs the handles to help.

"I'll call you back," Zach says into the camera, and waves before he ends the call.

"Well, look at you. You've turned into a reporter," I say to Kristen. "It was brilliant the way you played the 'my daddy insures your pension' card."

Kristen wears a devilish grin. "It just came to me. Daddy's a huge contributor to all these police charities. The cops know him."

"Now we have to hope that Zach comes through for us," I say. "Otherwise we just wasted our time."

We replay the ten-minute interview. The audio is pretty bad, but we can hear Kristen's questions and clearly see the expressions on Pruitt's face shift from lechery to irritation to anger, and then to contrition.

My phone buzzes. I look at the text I've just received from Zach, grin at Kristen, then hand her the phone.

> Sorry. He's an old man. I'll look through the files this
> weekend. Promise. Text me anything else you need.
> Hi to Kristen. #BLM

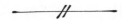

I'm back at the newspaper archives. This time scanning the main-stream *Birmingham News*. It's an old publication but most of its editions are digitized, and I'm focusing on the ones between July and October 1929, just before and after my great-grandfather was killed. I've gotten good at speeding through the world news pretty quickly, then scrutinizing the sections that report on local news, community activities, and crime. The July papers are a bust, but in August I find mention of Patrolman Simenon, credited with stopping a man who had fired shots at officers during a race riot. The riot stemmed from a raid on a restaurant and dance hall. More than sixty Negroes were arrested, and three Black men killed, including the proprietor. Simenon received a citation, and the story concludes with the announcement of his promotion to detective. I copy the article. If Simenon was a detective, that would explain why he wasn't in a uniform when he died.

My phone vibrates, and I smile when I recognize Darius's number. I've thought about him many times since our breakfast a couple of days ago. I take a deep breath and answer with my work voice.

"Meghan McKenzie."

"Hi. It's Darius," His baritone voice punches a hole in my professionalism.

"Hi yourself. How are you?"

"I'm good, and I'm busy, and wondering why I'm taking time out of this hellacious day to check in to see how *your* work is going."

"I don't know what to make of that comment. Why *are* you taking the time to call?"

"I was hoping you might know."

I decide to change the subject. "Thanks for setting up the call with Masterson. He phoned this morning."

"He's a good guy."

"If you say so. He wasn't very helpful."

"He likes to follow protocols," Darius says. "How's the work going?"

"Things could be better. I can't even tell you how many hours I've spent sitting and staring at news archives. I had notions of exercising or doing a spa treatment at some point. So far none of that has happened. Plus I'm running out of time. I'm leaving next week."

"That soon?" Darius says. "Uh, you want to hang out tomorrow? We could go to my gym."

"I have to work tomorrow. Monique called with a lead and I need to follow up on it."

"You want some company while you're doing that?"

"No. That's not necessary."

"Lots of people know me in the inner city. I might be helpful to you on the east side of town."

"How do you know where . . . oh, I see. You spoke to Monique."

The phone is quiet. Darius is giving me the southern pause.

"We can go to my gym after. Get in a workout. I can always bring a guest."

It's a persuasive argument. Although, to tell the truth, I was ready to say yes when he first asked.

"Well, if you want to join me . . ."

"I'd love to," he says quickly.

"Can we manage to wedge a meat-and-three into the schedule?" I ask. "Or maybe we should make it salads."

Darius is still laughing when we disconnect. I like his laugh.

FIFTEEN

Nightlife

1929

Griggs Ballroom is owned by a veteran of the Spanish-American War. Griggs lost his left arm fighting in Manila but found his future wife there, and sent for her as soon as he was discharged and settled in Birmingham. Clarita is a beautiful woman with shining black hair and eyes to match. Twenty years younger than Griggs, she is clearly as much a draw for the dilapidated old dance hall as are the music, gambling, and illegal drinks. Clarita greets me with an appreciative smile and makes a fuss over my bow tie.

"Que guapo," she says with a wink, and leads me, hips swaying, through the smoky front room dimly lit by wall sconces and bare bulbs extended from the rafters. In one corner, a half dozen couples are swaying to a Fats Waller tune from the piano player. The oak floor creaks with the weight of their fancy footwork.

We pass a line of women—Black, Indian, Asian, and some who can pass for white—leaning along the wall as we head to a booth where I am to buy tickets. Three dollars will buy me two tickets. One for a dance, and one for entry to the back room. Griggs mans the booth. He's a big guy, skin the color of mahogany. Tonight he looks older than usual and reeks of cheap booze. He connects his rheumy eyes to mine. I push a five-dollar bill toward him.

"I don't like the way you look at my wife," he says, using the long-fingered hand of his good arm to slide first a green ticket, then a red one through the cash slot, along with my change.

"Clarita is lovely," I say. "But I have a beautiful wife of my own at home."

Griggs squints and exhales an assault of bad breath. "Some folks say your wife is white," he remarks.

I smile and turn my back. I assess the line of women waiting to dance and offer my hand to someone I know. Nedra is a woman with red hair and a slender waist. The red hair comes from her white daddy. Her mother is Creole. She's a favorite in the place and loves the attention. I know she likes me. We move to the dance floor.

"You smell good, Bobby," she says in my ear.

"You *look* good as usual," I reply.

"Why you never ask me for more than one dance anymore?"

"Nedra, I just come to play cards now."

Everyone knows not to mention the liquor sales. A place like Griggs could be shut down permanently if an unfriendly patron or a police informant overhears talk about the availability of liquor. Or if Griggs stops paying the police to look the other way.

"Is that *all* you come for?" she asks, squeezing my hand and pushing her thin hips into mine. "The action behind the back door?"

"I'm afraid so, darling. I'm a married man."

"Didn't matter before," she says, flashing angry eyes.

I stare down at her. "Well, it matters now."

For the right price, and a cut to Clarita, the dancers at Griggs will lead you to one of the small rooms upstairs. I'd danced with Nedra several times before she invited me upstairs. I was lonely for Anna Kate that night and I didn't see any real harm in having my needs met. But after I'd been with Nedra, Clarita had approached me with a warning.

"You're playing with fire, Bobby. Nedra likes to stir up trouble, and she has a jealous new boyfriend."

"I can handle myself," I said to Clarita, who shook her head.

"No entiendes. Él es policía. Un detective."

Clarita always breaks into Spanish when she means business. I don't speak the language, but I picked out enough words to be worried. I decided then and there it was time to bring Anna Kate and Mae to Birmingham.

The dance is finished. Nedra doesn't wait for me to escort her back to the wall, where three other men are already descending upon her. She shoots me a nasty glare. I shrug.

At the far end of the dining room a tuxedoed maître d' takes my red ticket. He leads me to the rear room and raps tonight's knock at the massive maple door with the peephole. The sentry lets me in. The backroom bar and drinking tables are full. A jazz trio is playing on the platform that serves as a stage. With a wave of a George Washington I signal one of the girls for my regular drink and step into the poker room. Two whisky shots, eight dollars lost, and three hours later, I'm ready to leave.

My car is parked around the corner, and I pause in front of the building to light a cigarette. That's when I notice a police car idling across the street. I consider returning to warn Griggs, but before I do Nedra darts out of the entrance. She waves in the direction of the squad car, then notices me. A look I've never seen before crosses her face and she smiles strangely. That's when she steps toward me and attempts to kiss me on the cheek. I pull back as the passenger door of the police car opens. A man who isn't in uniform steps out. He's big, with shoulders that cut a long, straight line. Nedra turns and bounds to the vehicle. He grabs her arm and pushes her roughly into the back seat, then gives me a stare down. I pull up my jacket collar, put my head down, and walk to my car. I glance back. The man has been joined by a patrolman, who leans on the open driver's door. They're both looking my way.

I start the Franklin and ease away from the curb, eye fixed on the rearview mirror. When I'm satisfied the patrol car isn't following me I head in the direction of home. But rather than park in the usual place, behind the boardinghouse, I drive a few more blocks, lock up the Franklin, and hope my vehicle will be safe until I retrieve it for work in the morning.

Anna Kate is waiting up for me, reading in bed, when I step into the apartment. She can always tell when something's wrong, and after a "hello" I quickly look away. In the bathroom I hang up my suit on the back of the door and crack the window so the night air can draw some of the smoke smell from the fabric. I'm staring into the mirror when the door opens.

"What happened?" Anna Kate asks.

"Nothing, woman. Everything's fine."

I run water into my palm, splash it in my eyes, and rub hard. Then I grab a towel. Anna Kate is still staring at me.

"Something's wrong, Robert. What is it?"

"Nothing really. Just some police were watching me when I came out of the dance hall tonight. They were outside, and they kept an eye on me all the way to the car. I thought they might follow me, but they didn't."

Anna Kate's gray eyes fill with worry. "You know you can't

get into trouble here, Robert. If they check with the police in St. Pete they might find out about you hurting that white man."

"I know."

St. Petersburg police officials hadn't much cared about a fight between two Black coworkers, but when someone reported I'd hit a white man two weeks later, they put a warrant out for my arrest. Anna Kate had written to say two detectives came to my mother's house looking for me after I left.

"We can't go back home," Anna Kate says with tears flowing onto her cheeks.

Her tears are not for me. She's crying for the loss of her mama, brothers, and familiar surroundings, and for the misfortune to have married a man whose temper and pride will keep her, and her children, in a city of strangers.

Perhaps my bosses at the woodworks plant haven't told the Florida authorities about my work assignment in Birmingham, or maybe they already have. If so, the police may one day show up at the mansion or the boardinghouse. Then there's Nedra. I ignored her advances and she wants to get even. That's why she made that show of trying to kiss me. She'll tell her police boyfriend everything she knows about me.

I stare into the mirror again, then close my eyes. I'll never be anything but a Black man. And for that I will always be hated. I'm scared, but I don't want Anna Kate to know it.

"Don't worry, darling," I say, taking her into my arms. "Everything will be okay. I promise. I'm selling my car. It draws too much attention, and it's the only way the police will recognize me."

I don't think she believes me, but she wipes at her tears as I lead her to bed. I fall asleep to the sound of her sniffles—my throat parched from alcohol and fear.

SIXTEEN

◆

2019

Monique has suggested I talk to a woman with old and deep ties to Birmingham's residents. The woman's family has managed housing accommodations for southern Blacks for decades, including in the late 1920s, when my great-grandfather would have been in the city.

Darius insists on driving and picks me up early. As we did in my travels with Monique the day before, we avoid the web of freeways, staying on the city streets and finally traveling along First Avenue North toward the airport. He tunes in public radio's *Weekend Edition*, and we drive in comfortable silence. First Avenue is a stew of growth and gentrification. Office buildings, condos, and eateries mix with galleries, furniture outlets, and drugstores. Some of the architecture is magnificent. Occasionally, Darius points to a business, a school, or a church and tells me a story about its claim to fame. But mostly, he's checking the rearview mirror.

"Monique told you somebody was following us yesterday, didn't she?" I ask.

"She mentioned it."

"She says people phone to call her names, and threaten her on social media, all the time," I say.

"Unfortunately, that's true. But Monique has a whole lot of people watching her back."

"And now you're watching mine?"

"Not exactly. I wanted to see you today anyway, and squiring you around is one way to do that."

As we get closer to the airport, the road widens, with fewer buildings and a more industrial feel.

"This street reminds me of Grand River at home," I say. "It goes miles and miles, all the way from the western suburbs of Detroit into downtown. There are sections of blight but many more pockets of enterprise and stable neighborhoods. Yesterday, Monique and I traveled through blocks a lot dicier than these."

"She told me."

"You two seem to talk a lot."

Darius laughs. "I've known her for ages and our work intersects all the time. I'm a big fan of what she's done around social and racial justice in the city."

"Me too. I hope the *Free Press* will publish the profile of her I've just written. Part of a series focusing on the new civil rights leadership in this country."

"She deserves the recognition. She's doing good work."

"But apparently she also has detractors," I say.

"You know how it is. Haters gonna hate," Darius says.

The Harrick Motel is not a five-star establishment. The exterior paint is chipped, the front doors of some rooms appear to have been hit with a battering ram, and one of the *r*'s in the neon sign has been destroyed. Nevertheless, a few cars are parked in the lot of the twelve-unit, single-level, L-shaped building, and a NO VACANCY banner hangs across the office window. In protector mode, Darius scans the lot when we step out of his SUV.

The interior continues the outside's seen-better-days motif. A layer of dust covers the chairs and the counter. An ashtray is not so much overflowing as burdened with ash. The reception area's paneling goes halfway up the wall, where it meets peeling aqua paint. The year 2004 must have been really good for business, because the wall calendar is stuck on that year.

The proprietor comes out of a side door. She's tiny, not more than 120 pounds. Probably in her seventies. Vein lines show on her hands and on the sallow skin of her pale arms. Her coarse silver hair is pulled back in a ponytail. Her mustache, however, is still quite dark. A cigarette dangles from her lips, and one is tucked behind her ear. The gray smock she wears has had a recent run-in with blood.

Monique said she's known Cecile Clarke all her life, and that she is a valued church member at Evangelical. I try to remember that as the woman gives us the once-over.

"We don't have any vacancies," she drawls.

"Cecile, I—"

She gives me the evil eye and interrupts. "You don't know me well enough to call me by my first name."

"I'm sorry."

"It's Mrs. Clarke," she says gruffly, taking a drag on her cigarette.

Darius touches my arm, turns on that smile of his, and takes control. I'm not sure whether I like it or not.

"Mrs. Clarke, we don't want a room. We just want to talk to you."

She looks skeptical but Darius has her attention and curiosity.

"I've seen you someplace before," she says, narrowing her eyes at Darius.

"I'm on TV a lot. I work in the mayor's social justice office."

Clarke sucks her teeth. "Hmm. Hmm. That's it. I didn't vote for that new mayor. He's too young."

She waits to see what reaction she'll get. Darius is still smiling, and his raised eyebrows invite her to speak her mind. Instead, she eyeballs me and I stare back deadpan.

"Ms. McKenzie is a reporter with the *Detroit Free Press*; she's hoping you can give her some advice about a story she's writing."

"What kind of story?" she asks, assessing my pantsuit. "You know, you're kinda young too. You an intern?"

"No, ma'am. I'm doing research on the murder of a Black man here in Birmingham back in the late twenties. Monique Hendricks thought you might . . ."

"Oh, so *you're* the one. Monique mentioned some friend of hers would be coming by to ask me questions about the old days."

The woman's entire demeanor shifts from surly and suspicious to welcoming. She stubs out her cigarette and hangs the disturbing smock on a hook. I suspect she wears it for effect.

"Why don't you come on back with me into my rooms. I live here on the premises. We can talk there. In peace."

She lifts the hinged wing in the dusty countertop that separates her from the motel customers and beckons us through. We follow her to a door at the rear of the office and step into her living quarters—units one and two of the motel. With the wall removed it is a huge space that has been transformed into an amazing luxury apartment. We enter first into a galley kitchen decorated in various tones of gray. The countertops are granite, flanked by subway tiling. There are stainless steel appliances and the flooring is hardwood. The kitchen flows into an open living area with modern furnishings in Scandinavian light woods and chrome. For security and noise abatement, the front windows are covered in patterned drapes, but the apartment is filled with light that comes from two beautiful skylights. Mrs. Clarke (who now asks us to call her Cecile) brags that with the flip of a switch the skylights can be hidden and a dozen recessed spotlights revealed. A door in the side wall opens to a hallway leading to a king-size bedroom with en suite on one end, and a den with a marvelous library, built-in bar, and pool table on the other. Framed and signed photographs of Sammy Davis Jr., Harry Belafonte, Jackie Robinson, and Lena Horne hang on a trophy wall.

Darius and I are blown away by the fancy layout. Cecile circles us back to the kitchen and directs us to sit at the island.

"I always have a cup of tea around this time. Shall I make enough for three?" she asks, filling an electric kettle.

Tea? Shall? What's happened to the small package of rough-and-tumble who manages the motel office? I share a quick look with Darius, who smirks.

"I've only *heard* about this place," Darius says with an admiring look for the woman.

"What do you think you know about this place, young man?"

"Father told me about it. An out-of-the-way roadside motel out First Street North where, back in the day, Black dignitaries and celebrities stayed safe from unwanted limelight and the threats from the Klan."

Cecile nods. "There used to be a dozen places like this throughout the South. We don't get much use out of this apartment these days. Celebrities and politicians and such *want* the media scrutiny now. But sixty years ago, a place like this was a necessity."

"So you live here permanently?" I ask.

CHERYL A. HEAD

"Unless it's needed for a VIP, and that only happens once or twice a year. I have the place upgraded every five years or so. My niece is an interior designer. She did a renovation a couple years ago. It's nice, isn't it?"

We murmur our agreement. While we drink tea Cecile talks about her experience in the hospitality business. She agrees when I ask permission to take notes. "My sisters and I still own eight other hotels and motels in Alabama. It's all family run. We got the nieces and nephews and cousins and grandkids managing the different sites. Before me and my sisters, it was my father and his brothers. Before that *his* daddy and his wife. We've operated hotels in Montgomery, Atlanta, and parts of Mississippi. Some of Dr. King's people stayed here in '63 when he came to do the eulogy for those little girls killed in the 16th Street Church bombing. Coretta stayed right here in this very apartment. It was different then, but it was fit for the first lady of the civil rights movement. I remember Father talking about the tragedy of Martin King's assassination. I was nineteen at the time. Father always used to say if King had stayed in a place like this when he went to Memphis, that crazy white man might not have killed him."

"That's a remarkable story," I say, finishing my tea. "I'd like to tell you one about my family, if you have the time."

"You go ahead while I make more tea."

As I talk Cecile listens intently. When she returns to the island to sit, she pulls a small notebook out of her dress pocket and writes something on a fresh page. Every time I look up at Darius he has this silly half grin on his face. But his eyes tell me to keep going. By the time I get to the conversation with my editors, and my assignment, Cecile's pulling a phone out of her other pocket.

"Wait just a minute. I have to call my nephew."

We listen to her side of a two-minute conversation. She's an animated speaker, clearly excited, and gestures when she talks.

"I want to help this girl, Marvin. She doesn't know where her great-grandfather is buried. If we can figure out what part of town he stayed in, maybe that can help her narrow her search. Are those journals in the back or not? Well, where else could they be? I sure hope you didn't throw out anything that belonged to Grandma Ardle. Okay, okay. Well, I'm going to look for them. If you think of anything else you call me back. Hear me?"

Cecile returns the phone to her pocket and gives me a puzzled look. But she's not really looking at me; she's thinking. Finally, she leans forward and slides the paper she's written on to me. It's a name: Harriet Ardle.

"My grandma Ardle ran a boardinghouse in the twenties in a part of downtown Birmingham. It was where a lot of colored folks lived then. Especially some of the ones who worked in the steel mills." She sees my furrowed eyebrows and waves her hand. "I know. I know. Your great-grandfather wasn't a mill worker, but a lot of other workmen stayed there too. Grandma's place was one of the few that had a radio in those days. If your father was looking for a steady place to live when he came to Birmingham, he would have stayed in one of Grandma Ardle's rooms."

"I did some research about where the Black population stayed in Birmingham in those days, and I thought he might have lived in an area called Tuxedo Junction," I say.

"Well, that's possible. That was a thriving neighborhood in an area called Ensley. We owned a couple of places there. The nightlife at Tuxedo Junction would have been very appealing to a single man, but the way you speak of your great-grandfather it doesn't make sense to me that he'd have brought his wife to a flophouse or someone's farm. He'd have found a room in a board-inghouse that was run for Black people of means. I'm sure of it."

"You hear that," Darius exclaims. "That's a big-time clue."

I'm more measured in my excitement. "How could we confirm that information, Cecile? Would there be records?"

"That's why I called Marvin. We have files on all our proper-ties out back in the storage shed. We have most of Grandma Ar-dle's papers and other documents. She became a very important businesswoman. A member of the Eastern Star social group and deaconess of her church."

Cecile leads Darius and me through a rear door to a loading dock and gravel lot. Thirty yards away, near a tree line, is another structure almost as large as the motel.

"That's the shed you were talking about?" Darius asks. "It's huge."

"We store a whole lot of stuff in there. Furniture, old appli-ances from our other places, signs, landscaping equipment, and documents we don't know what to do with."

We step inside the warehouse. It's true. There is a lot of stuff—beds and dressers, bathtubs, sinks, cleaning supplies, an old neon sign, a golf cart, and the most impressive stack of straight-backed wood chairs I've ever seen—it's almost five feet high. A small truck with a snowplow and two riding lawn mowers is at one side of the building. On the opposite side is an office tucked into a corner. That's where Cecile is headed.

The office is musty. The outer windows are covered in secu-rity screens and cobwebs. Two large wood desks take up most of the space in the middle, and along a side and back wall are a dozen large filing cabinets. Most of the cabinets are the newer kind, metal with locks and keys, but a few are very old, narrower and constructed of wood. I walk toward them. They are definitely antiques, and probably worth a lot of money.

"I see you've already spotted the good stuff," Cecile says.

"These are beautiful," I say, touching the top of one of the cabinets and regretting it when I pull back a finger loaded with dust and a few dead insects. "They could use a good cleaning," I say, brushing my hands together to free the dust, "but they're lovely antiques."

"Oh. Well, that's probably true," Cecile says. "They're old and grimy, and probably antiques as you say, but that's not what I mean about the good stuff," she says, smiling and gesturing. "Those are the ones with Grandma Ardle's papers."

I'm not dressed for combing through old files, and neither is Darius. To explore the documents, I need work clothes, plastic gloves and rags, and a scarf to protect my hair from dust mites and spiderwebs, but I'm not giving up a chance to find a real clue about Great-Grandpa's life in Birmingham. I look at Darius. I know he wants to do a workout.

"You shouldn't pass up this opportunity," he says, reading my mind. "We can change our plans."

"This is *my* task. Why don't you go on to your gym?"

"I'm staying to help you."

"You could come back to pick me up in a few hours."

"Nope. I'm staying. The good news is we have our workout clothes in the car. Let's change and dig into these files."

"Is it all right with you for us to stay?" I ask, turning to the motel owner.

"Fine with me, if it's okay with your young man, here."

"No, no, Mrs. Clarke," I say, flustered. "You have it all wrong. Darius and I just met—"

"I know what I see, young lady. And like I said, you can call me Cecile."

CECILE LETS US USE HER BATHROOM TO CHANGE SO WE CAN handle the dusty files. When I get back to the storage unit, Darius is wearing a sleeveless jersey and baggy shorts. He looks sexy. I stare a few seconds before I realize I'm doing so. He has several rolls of paper towel and a bucket of water and has started wiping down one of the file cabinets.

"I hope you're not putting too much water on that wood," I say, donning the plastic gloves I've carried since exploring the Rankin basement archives. I hand Darius a pair.

"No, I'm not, Meg," he says with a wink. "But a dry cloth would only move the dust around. Besides, is that all you have to say to me? Not, 'Damn, Darius, you must spend a lot of time in the weight room.'"

Some might consider him a bit skinny, but in this dusty room with sunlight filtered through the grime on the windows, he is Adonis. "Sorry," I say, laughing at his silliness and my gawking. "Thanks for staying and helping, and you look like a bona fide gym rat." I decide that's as far as I'll go with a compliment. He already thinks too well of himself. And, if I didn't mishear, he called me Meg, a nickname I had in college. Hearing him use it makes me unsettled.

There are three filing cabinets. Two have folders, registry books, and other documents. The third is completely filled with letters. Business and personal correspondence bundled in rubber bands. I thumb through a few of the bundles. There are scores of letters in envelopes addressed to Harriet Ardle, and letters without envelopes that seem to be copies of her correspondence. Smudged, but readable.

"I don't think we should start with the letters. That could take us days. If we find something, I can come back later to look at them. Let's start with what looks like the business papers."

We each use one of the desks and divide the first drawer of files. Paper towel, dampened a bit, comes in handy to control the dust. The folders are not organized chronologically, but the receipts, lease agreements, checks, loan documents, and maintenance records associated with a single property are filed together.

"I have no idea what place we're looking for, but the important year is 1929, especially for the last half of the year," I say.

"Okay. I'm on it," Darius replies.

These documents reveal the lifetimes of people, businesses, and relationships. I can't help but wonder about those who hauled ice, repaired fences, were presidents of Black-owned insurance companies, sold produce, or toiled in the steel mills. Ardle and Clarke are the signatures I come across most often—fading from the weight of time and forgottenness. The first few folders we peruse are for an establishment named the Freedom Call, a small hotel or boarders' house. There are receipts and ledgers, but I don't see anything relevant. There are four guest books for the Tuxedo Junction Rooming House. Cecile is right. These are visitors staying a day or two, sometimes a week, paying three dollars a night for a bed. Darius and I take two ledgers each, scrolling through sheet after sheet of fading names.

"Any luck?" I ask Darius.

"None. Half these names I can't even read. The bottom two drawers are labeled the Fourth Avenue Inn. Why don't we each take a drawer?"

The files suggest the Fourth Avenue Inn was a boarding-house: an eight-unit brick building, mostly single rooms, but a couple of apartment units with their own baths. A splotchy four-by-six sepia photo in an envelope fits the description. I stare at it a long time. The building has a side yard with large trees, and a four-step stoop. I find receipts for meals. Some initialed, some associated with a date and unit number, most with just first names. Stanley, Joshua, James, Samuel. Men who probably ate together in the dining room of the house. I wonder about them. Were they strangers to one another passing through Birmingham for work or some other reason? Did they have families? Were they lured by the promise of the nickname Magic City? Did they move on to another town, a new boardinghouse, and another meal with different strangers?

Darius and I work in silence for almost forty minutes. Then he gets up and walks to my desk, where he wipes at the corner with a damp paper towel before he sits. "The name of your great-grandfather again?"

I look up from the loan document I'm perusing. His face is solemn. Expectant. He holds a tattered book in his hand. He locks his eyes on mine. My voice catches in my throat when I try to answer.

"Robert Harrington."

"I think I found something. In this ledger book for the Fourth Avenue Inn. It's dated August of 1929." His index finger marks a page in the folded journal.

My hand shakes when I reach for the book. Darius leans over my shoulder. He points to a line on the page where there's a signature pale and thin like worn denim. I touch the line with the fingertip of my disposable glove.

"It says Lee Harrington. You think that's him?"

"Lee was his middle name," I say, following the signature line to the notation: *PAID IN FULL*. It's written in capital letters in a different hand. "I think you've found him," I say quietly, holding back the nervousness roiling in my core.

Darius pulls his chair to my desk and in the next two hours we find five more documents associated with my great-grandfather's stay at the Fourth Avenue Inn. Three receipts for meals, written in the curlicue cursive of the proprietor, and two rental agreements. The first, a one-page contract, is for a month-to-month single occupancy beginning in June of 1929. That one is signed Robert Harrington, but it's the same signature—wide, even lettering with little jiggles for the *r*'s in Harrington. The second rental agreement begins in July for three occupants. *That must be when Grandma and her mother arrived in Birmingham.* I stare at each item, holding my breath. Finally, I lean back in my chair, overcome with emotion. I peel off the gloves and untie my scarf to run fingers through my sweat-drenched hair. I begin to laugh and Darius joins me. Deep, shoulder-shaking, celebratory laughter.

"You found it, Meg. Another piece in the puzzle," Darius says.

I nod. I'm grateful to him and the universe. Tears begin to glide down my cheeks. I have known Darius for four days. I don't want him to see me ugly cry, but I have no choice. Finally, I cup my face in both hands and weep.

SEVENTEEN

──────◆──────

2019

Before we leave the motel, Darius and I change from our gym togs back to our street clothes. Cecile is genuinely pleased about my discovery. She offers to look through the letters in the cabinets and call if she finds anything else related to my search. She brushes off my profuse thanks with a wave of the cigarette in her hand.

Darius has suggested we get dinner since we've missed lunch, and on the ride to the restaurant, I call home.

Daddy answers with a hurried "hello," apparently not looking at the caller ID. I hear music in the background, and the sound of conversation and laughter.

"Daddy. It's me."

"Well, hello, baby girl. Anne, it's your daughter," he shouts to my mother.

"Are you having a party?"

"Your uncle Joe came by, and two of my musician buddies and their wives. Jake and Rudolph, you remember them, don't you?" He talks fast, and as he continues, I can tell he's had a couple of drinks. "The weather was nice enough today to do a little cookout, and we're having cocktails. Wait a minute, you want to speak to your mother? Here she is."

"How are you doing, honey?"

"Mama." My throat catches.

"Is everything all right?" Her voice is louder and concerned.

"I'm okay. Today I learned exactly where Great-Grandpa lived in Birmingham. I found a rent document with his signature on it."

"Oh my," Mama gasps.

"Baby. What's wrong?" I hear my father say.

"Meghan's found something."

"What?" Daddy snatches the phone. "Tell me. No, wait a minute. I'm putting you on speakerphone."

"Great-Grandpa lived in a boardinghouse while he was in Birmingham. I saw his name on the ledger, and I met a relative of someone who actually knew him."

"Well, that's big news, daughter. Big news."

"It's just a first step, Daddy, but now maybe I can piece together a little about his life. We've only ever talked about how he died. Never how he lived."

"Is the boardinghouse still there?" Mama asks.

"I don't know. Probably not. The family who owned the place sold it right after World War II. But I intend to go to the address where it would have been."

My end of the conversation is also on speakerphone, and Darius has been listening quietly while he drives.

"I didn't find this information alone," I say. "I've had lots of help, and today a new friend helped me go through gobs of old documents. He's driving now, and I've got you on speakerphone. John McKenzie, meet Darius Curren."

"Hello, sir," Darius says in his baritone.

"Well, hello yourself," Daddy answers. "Thank you for helping my daughter."

Next I introduce Darius to my mother, then she and I chat another minute about what to tell Grandma. We decide it's too soon to bring her into the loop. We don't want to get her hopes up.

"Are we still on speaker?" Daddy asks. "Take me off."

I disengage the speakerphone and turn toward the window. I give only yes and no answers to my father's string of questions. After I hang up from my parents, I feel Darius's eyes bouncing on my face.

"What?" I ask.

"What was *that* conversation about?"

"It was private."

He's quiet for a moment. "Your parents sound like nice people. I can tell they really love you."

"Yes. I'm very lucky."

THEY KNOW DARIUS AT THE ITALIAN RESTAURANT, AND WE'RE quickly seated in a corner booth near the kitchen with the old-fashioned amenities of a family-run eatery. After plates of spaghetti with meat sauce, a marvelous three-cheese ravioli, and two glasses of a satisfying red blend, we're both feeling relaxed.

Darius tells me of growing up in Birmingham. His mother died when he was thirteen. His father was already a well-known politician, so he spent a lot of evenings at conferences, campaign rallies, and church basement strategy meetings. It was in one of these churches that he met Monique, the preacher's daughter.

"Oh, so you've known each other a *very* long time," I say to cloak the question I really want to ask. *Have the two of you ever been an item?*

"For ages. She's like the sister I've never had, and on occasion she seems to think she's a substitute mother. What about you? Do you have brothers or sisters?"

"Nope. Only child. Like you."

"I would have guessed. Your parents seem really protective of you."

When the check comes we don't linger. I'm super tired, and despite the heavy meal, Darius is still eager to get in a bit of a workout. He pays for the dinner, and I promise to pick up the next meal. When he stops in front of my Airbnb I turn to him.

"I know I've already said it, but I wouldn't have found those documents without you. Thank you."

He smiles. "I like you, and I was glad to help. I do have one question. Did your father say something about me when you took him off the speaker?"

I laugh. "I really shouldn't tell you. You might get a swelled head."

"Aw. C'mon."

"He asked if you were the one who knew about Joe Louis."

Saxby and I have agreed I should do a reporter's notebook blog, a tease of the full story I'm writing. It's due on Tuesday, with a second one by the end of next week. Then it's back to Detroit. The full story with any updates will be in the hard-copy paper.

So far I've uncovered only two clues to corroborate Grandma's story—the news report from the *St. Pete Times* confirming a

Birmingham police officer shot Great-Grandpa, and now I can definitively say where he lived while in the Magic City. But that's not nearly enough to write a decent blog.

I stare at my list of loose ends. It's formidable.

- Death Certificate: I filed a request form with the state of Alabama for Great-Grandpa's death certificate a week ago. But, because all I had was his name and an approximate date of death, the form I mailed was incomplete. I'll count myself lucky to receive it.

- FOIA Request: Saxby confirmed that a Freedom of Information Act letter has been forwarded to Birmingham police requesting any information about my great-grandfather's homicide, and disclosure of public records for Detective Simenon. I'm not holding my breath.

- Police Interview: I need a formal interview with someone in leadership at Birmingham PD. Even a "no comment" or a "homicide records are not public" quote is better than nothing.

- Simenon Follow-up: Hopefully, Zach will find something in his grandfather's papers about Simenon. If not, I'll cross off that line of inquiry. It was a long shot anyway.

- Black Mortuaries: Another long shot. But, like everything else in the Jim Crow South, the handling of bodies was a segregated business. Maybe I can learn where, or if, my great-grandfather was buried by contacting Birmingham funeral homes.

———

I'VE CALLED THE SIX BLACK FUNERAL HOMES LISTED IN THE Birmingham directory. Only one has been in business since the twenties, but I've left messages at all of them.

I've also texted Zach.

At ten p.m. my phone rings. I don't recognize the number on the display. But it could be a return call from one of the mortuaries.

"Hello."

The caller breathes raspingly, then coughs. I hear traffic noise, and something else.

"Hello," I say again. "This is Meghan McKenzie."

"Go back to where you came from. You've been warned." The male caller is calm. His voice gruff. There's another moment of heavy breathing mixed with the cacophony of heavy metal music before the call disconnects.

My heart skips a beat and I look at my phone display with a shaking hand. The Shazam app identifies the song in the background as "Thirteen Knots." I send a text to Kristen to see if she knows the song.

Kristen's reply text comes immediately. Where'd you hear that. It's hate music!

Tell you later. Have a good weekend.

I don't want to worry Kristen about this crank call. It's like Monique said. Black reporter asking questions about white police. Comes with the territory. No biggie.

EIGHTEEN

The Car

1929

The Franklin is parked on a commercial street blocks away from the boardinghouse. Far enough that if the detective who saw me last night comes across the sedan, I'll still be in the clear. But this car always draws attention, and I don't want anyone to tamper with it, so I'm up and out the door as soon as daylight splinters the curtains.

I'm not alone on the sidewalks. Folks are already preparing for the commerce of Saturday. I walk straight to the car and find it secure and gleaming in the sun. I make sure I don't see any idling patrol cars before I get in and start the engine.

I love this automobile. It makes me feel important, successful, and free. Mama once told me it had gone to my head. "No matter how fancy your car is, you have to remember your place in this white world," she'd said. But I have never been content with my place in this society, and I won't be held back by the limitations my skin brings.

I arrive at the mansion an hour before starting time. The security men wave me through the new gate, and I park on the leveled ground that will become the patio. I find the rag and polish I keep in the trunk, roll up my sleeves, and wax the car. I lean my muscles into every circular motion, firmly but gently rubbing the aluminum and steel and wood as if caressing a woman's body. I polish the vehicle from its headlights to the silver plate on the trunk. The next task is to clean the tires. I fill a pail with water from the rain barrel and retrieve the wood box I use to store a tiny jar of oil and a piece of foil containing peroxide. The auto salesman told me these tires are the best you can buy, and I wanted the best. When I'm finished the rubber shines like patent leather, and the whitewalls are as bright as the day I first drove the car home.

When the full crew arrives, there's no time for socializing or drinking coffee. The supervisor points us to our assignments and we work quickly with the goal to make our half day of work garner a full day's results. When we stop at noon, the men gather their tools and head for Saturday activities, but I pull Pete aside and lead him over to the sedan.

"You still want to buy her?" I ask.

"I told you, Harrington, when you're ready to sell her, I'm ready to buy. I'll give you seven hundred dollars for the car. You know that's more than a fair price for a used automobile," Pete begins the negotiations.

"Well, yes, that would be a good price for anything other than a Franklin Victoria," I say, moving to the rear of the car.

Pete and I enjoy working together and have expressed our mutual respect for each other's carpentry skills. Nevertheless, he doesn't want to be taken by a Negro. That's why he undervalues the car. He watches as I move to the luggage compartment and open it wide. The inside of the trunk is pristine, as is the spare tire. I pull out the rag—it still has a residue of wax—and begin walking slowly around the vehicle. Pete keeps step. My wax job is already perfect but I concentrate on rubbing at imaginary streaks on the name plate and the hood.

"You know, Douglas Fairbanks has one of these cars," I say, wiping the hood ornament. "I guess I would take nine hundred for her."

Pete starts shaking his head. I squat to flick a bug away from the whitewalls, then stand and kick the tires to demonstrate their firmness.

"I've taken real good care of her. I ride her gentle, like she was my woman. And she pays me back with her steadfastness. Why don't you get in and turn over the engine," I say.

Pete nestles into the leather seat and pushes the starter button. The engine turns over immediately and purrs. He holds back a smile, but I watch a look of authority transform his face when he grips the steering wheel. He's itching to drive her. I climb into the passenger seat.

"Take her out and around the house," I suggest.

Pete confidently reverses the vehicle and steers her along the broad sweep of the mansion. In the rear they've completed the foundation for the swimming pool, and an area has already been marked off for a tennis court. I wave at the security man at the back of the house, and he steps out of the guard shack to watch us circle the property. When Pete gets back to the front, he stops at the newly paved road leading to the circular drive and main gate. He turns off the engine, quickly exits, then shoves his hands into his pockets. When I get out of the car I make a show of brushing off the passenger seat with the rag, then take my time coming round to the driver's side.

"I'll give you eight hundred for the car, Harrington. Not a dollar more."

I pause to pretend I'm considering the price, staring at my shoe, then shove the rag into my back pocket and cross my arms. I shake my head. "I just can't do it for eight," I say, looking remorseful.

"Okay. Okay. But only because I know you, Harrington, and because you're such a damn good carpenter. I'll give you the nine hundred."

"I'll sell it to you at that price. I'm okay with it because I know you'll take care of her."

Pete takes a handkerchief from his back pocket and wipes his brow. He may feel he's been outsmarted, but he also knows the car is worth more than he's paid.

"I can have the money ready for you on Monday," he says.

"That's fine. It gives me one more chance to take my wife and baby to church in style."

We shake hands and Pete heads to his own vehicle. I slip behind the wheel and put the Franklin on the road to town. I give her a little gas to feel her power beneath me, then ease off. When I get to the boardinghouse, I tuck her into my backyard parking space, under the trees, and cover her with a tarp to protect her from the sap.

Anna Kate is waiting for me at the door. She and Mae are dressed for shopping and I change quickly out of my dirty work pants and boots into my everyday clothes. I grab a few cornmeal sacks, tuck them under my arm, then lift Mae onto my shoulders, where she begins to play her whistle; then we join the parade of shoppers on Fourth Avenue. On Saturday, there are a dozen more vendor carts and stalls on the sidewalks. Anna Kate's worried that with our late start we might not get all the things on her list, but we have no trouble buying everything we need. She wants more knitting yarn and sewing thread, and I tell her to buy enough to last her a couple of weeks. For a treat, I buy us all a flavored ice. When we get home, I work through the list of Saturday chores while Anna Kate prepares dinner. That evening we join a few of the boarders in the downstairs front room to listen to *Amos 'n' Andy* on the radio, and then a music show from Chicago. Anna Kate isn't comfortable when sitting for long periods of time, and after Mae falls asleep on my lap we say our goodbyes and return to our apartment. I tuck Mae in for the night while Anna Kate prepares herself for sleep. As we lie in our Murphy bed, I hold her in my arms and tell her about my conversation with Pete.

"He's going to give me the money on Monday. I'll get another car. Something ordinary."

Anna Kate reaches for my hand and squeezes it. "I know how much you love that car. I'm touched that you would sacrifice it for the good of our family."

"You, Mae, and the new baby are more important than any car. Selling it will give us a chance for peace. I've been thinking about something else, darling. I might start going by my middle name."

"Why would you do that?"

"In case the police are looking for a man named Robert. It will be a new start for me. I'll become another man."

"Lee," Anna Kate says, practicing my new name. "I don't know if I like it."

"They called me that when I was a boy. When Papa Tico was still alive. So we'd both know which 'Robert' Mama was calling."

"I love you," Anna Kate says out of the blue.

It is the first time in our marriage that she's used those words. I stroke her face and kiss her. Her body folds into mine. Car or no car, I know I am a man to be envied.

NINETEEN

2019

I told Monique I might try to attend the eleven o'clock service at her church, but I won't make it. I have too much work to do this morning. I've put last night's phone threat behind me and I'm moving forward.

I pull a fleece top over my pajamas, put on a pair of socks, and move to the kitchen with my laptop and story file. I measure for three cups of coffee and cut into the piece of cheesecake I brought home from the Italian restaurant. I pile my notes and documents on the table and sip coffee. This morning I'm following up with the funeral homes I called last night. Persistence is everything.

On my second cup of coffee, and third call, I hit pay dirt with the oldest Black mortuary in the city. According to the man I talk to they're the only ones who will still have records from 1929. I have an appointment for tomorrow.

I begin outlining my preview blog. Fleshing out the information I know. Speculating about other things. On the third cup I realize I've had one coffee too many. I desperately need to move and think. This would be a good time to take a break and exercise.

I consider calling Darius to take him up on the gym pass, but it's still too early. I stare out the window. According to the forecast it will be another warm day, but right now there's a light breeze. I remember the public bikeshare a few blocks over and don shorts, a tee, and athletic shoes. I grab a fanny pack and stuff it with my wallet, phone, and keys. I can get some exercise *and* do a bit of research.

The map at the bikeshare stand shows two paths, and I take the one toward downtown. The rental bike is heavy. At home, I ride a Fuji hybrid, lightweight and sleek. This bike isn't that, but the seat adjusts easily, and I'm soon on my way.

Birmingham has beautiful green spaces, and one I noticed on the visitors' map is named after one of Detroit's household names. Eddie Kendrick Memorial Park celebrates the lead singer of the Temptations in the Motown group's hit-filled early years. Since arriving in Birmingham I've learned Kendrick is a native son of Birmingham.

I get off the bike to look at a plaque with a very good likeness of Eddie, then walk through the park hearing his iconic falsetto wafting through speakers. The main attraction is an amazing sculpture of the Temps. The five members, etched in granite, execute one of their signature moves, with high-stepping feet and their coattails flipping behind them. People in the park are singing the tunes and some are dancing. I take a selfie to send to Daddy.

I'm near the 16th Street Baptist Church and pedal a few blocks more into what is known as the Civil Rights District. The memorial for the four little girls killed by a white supremacist's bomb in 1963 is diagonal to the place of worship. A beautiful sculpture depicts the young victims of that violent Sunday fifty-six years ago. There are a lot of people in the area, including those entering the church for the regular service. Visitors take pictures and lots of selfies. But the tone here is solemn and respectful.

On the way, I've passed Kelly Ingram Park, which was ground zero for the clashes among civil rights demonstrators and state and national law enforcement in the sixties. The park's new design commemorates those struggles and welcomes all to reflect on peace and justice. Monique says many of the local BLM marches begin at Kelly Park.

The books I've read about Birmingham's history point to two hubs of Black life—Tuxedo Junction and the business district on and around Fourth Avenue North, where Great-Grandpa lived. I pedal with purpose as I think about the boardinghouse he apparently called home in the final days of his life.

As I slowly move up the Fourth Avenue corridor and its side streets, I try to imagine the pulsing energy of this area in the 1920s. Residents would have flocked to these sidewalks to purchase the necessities of everyday life. The streets might have been cobblestone or packed dirt rather than the asphalt I'm traveling on. In the early morning, corner gaslights might have illuminated the predawn hustle and bustle of men and women going to work—clerks, seamstresses, nurses, cooks, the dry cleaner, the doctor, and the dentist. Those with jobs outside the neighborhood would take a short walk to the streetcar, where they'd sit on the rear benches reserved for Black passengers.

The address for the old boardinghouse is now a corner bank with condos on top. The whole area has been gentrified. I get off the bike and stand on the sidewalk, peering into the window. Only the original cornerstone remains on this new, multistory building, and the date is carved in Roman numerals. MCMVI. 1906.

I close my eyes, trying to connect with the ground under my feet. The sidewalk is modern, but the earth beneath is a witness to the stories of this corner. I'm not sure how long I've been planted in front of the bank when a voice startles me.

"What?" I say, opening my eyes and looking into the face of a well-dressed man with gray in his mustache and at his temples.

"I was asking if I can go around you." His dark skin is radiant, reflecting a warm vitality. "Your bike is blocking the ATM."

"Oh, I'm sorry. I was daydreaming," I say, moving aside.

"No worries, young lady. Daydreams are openings to the unknown."

I nod, not really listening, and maneuver the bike to the curb. I cross the street, and when I look back, the man has already gone.

I linger, thinking about the bonds among Black people that must have existed in this neighborhood. Despite incessant racism and life-threatening violence, the people who once lived here managed to thrive, nurtured in the safe spaces they created. The ones we've always had to create.

I lean my bike against a bench and slump into the seat. The visits to 16th Street Baptist and this neighborhood have left me dispirited. I could call Darius and invite him to brunch—it's my turn to buy the meal. But I don't want him to see me in a funk. If I call home, Daddy will ask a bunch of questions and then worry about me. Mom will understand, but she might say "I told you so." Garrett pops into my mind. Perhaps I've been premature in dissolving our nascent relationship, but right this moment I don't have the energy for a negotiation with him.

These are the times I wish I had a gaggle of girlfriends. I

don't. I'm the smart, boring Black girl who is nice but kind of weird and standoffish. Not my self-assessment, but what a class-mate at Stanford actually said to me. I stay in touch with a few women my age, some I went to school with, others from work, but I haven't really cultivated the kind of female friendships you see on TV sitcoms. Ones where you gather with your sister-friends to laugh and cry and commiserate about relationships, work, and life.

My phone vibrates. It's a text from Zach.

Grandpa has a whole drawer from his father's time as Police Chief. I found some stuff on the guy you were asking about. Mom's away. Do you and Kristen want to come and take a look?

I respond with a simple: Yes! Thank you!! Let me check with Kristen on a time.

"You want to do it now?" Kristen asks when I call her about Zach's text.

"Yes. And Zach specifically invited you. But I'll go alone if you can't make it."

"No, I want to go. I'm curious."

"Okay. I have to get home, do a quick change, and then I'll pick you up. Give me an hour."

I'M GLAD KRISTEN'S WITH ME BECAUSE I FOLLOW HER DIREC-tions to Zach's address rather than the GPS.

"Why do you suppose the old man still has files from ninety years ago?" she asks.

"Dunno. Some people never throw anything away. I imagine when his father retired he scooped up his files and took them home and they've been there ever since."

"Well, anyway, it's awesome that Zach's trying to help. Maybe I was wrong not to give him my number."

"He asked for your number?"

"Yeah. In the chat when we were doing the Zoom call. Didn't you see it?"

"I guess I missed that. He seems like a good guy, and definitely cute. Don't you think?"

"Yeah, but . . ."

"You've got so much in common with the boring on-again, off-again jock boyfriend?"

"Oh, you're a comedian *and* a reporter," Kristen responds. "It's just that he's young."

Zach comes out of a side door smiling when we pull into the driveway. He nods at me but can't take his eyes off Kristen. Today he's not wearing a cap and we can see his shock of blue hair. He looks like an American member of BTS, the South Korean boy band.

"The files are in the garage. C'mon in before the neighbors start gawking," Zach says, leading the way.

The space in the two-car garage is primarily taken by a 1994 Pontiac Grand Prix. Its metal is eaten away front and back, but the V-6 engine in this car is still more powerful than those in most modern cars. I push back my curiosity about the mileage and follow Zach to a corner where a beat-up rusting metal file cabinet is sagging under the weight of a stack of crates. Zach yanks open the middle drawer of the three-drawer cabinet and pulls out a skinny hanging folder.

"I found these. They weren't all together so I put them in this folder."

I quickly scan the half dozen pages. They tell of a man who is a product of the Jim Crow era. Born in 1899 in Clayton, Alabama, Carl Simenon dropped out of high school, enlisted, and served in the last year of World War I. After the war, he worked as a laborer for four years before applying to the Birmingham Police Department. He received a citation for bravery eight years later and soon after was promoted to detective.

There are three personnel actions. The first is a partial copy of a citizen's complaint from a thirty-five-year-old woman who accuses Simenon of sexual assault. The name and race information are redacted. On the back of that document is a photocopy of a check from the Policeman's Justice Fund for ten thousand dollars, dated September 30, 1929, made out to Patterson and Arnold, Attorneys-at-Law. The second document is a one-page notice of a two-week suspension—with pay—for flagrant force. It's dated November 1928. The third paper, another citizen complaint, is also a single page, but this time, the complainant's name is listed: George Freeman. After the name, in parentheses, is written *Negro*. There is no indication of an investigation, suspension, or any further action and the date is October 7, 1929. I take photos of the front and back of the documents. They all have missing pages.

I look up at Zach and Kristen. She's staring at me. He's staring at her.

"What are they?" Kristen asks, looking at the folder.

"Pages from personnel documents. Background on the guy, two citizen complaints, and a payout to one of the complainants. He wasn't exactly Officer Friendly. Was there anything else in the files that looked interesting?" I ask Zach.

"I looked through the top drawer and didn't see anything with the guy's name on it, and the bottom drawer is just a bunch of old academy programs, books, and catalogs."

"Can we take a look?"

"Sure. Help yourself. Mom won't be back until tonight," Zach says, grabbing a couple of wood stools from under a workbench. "We can pile the stuff from the bottom drawer over here. It'll be easier to work with."

While Kristen and Zach take the seats at the workbench to look through the binders and books, I pull a pair of plastic gloves from my backpack and focus on the top drawer. It contains police station rosters, policy handbooks, more personnel sheets: promotions, complaints, training scores, dismissals. Most of these records are from the sixties and seventies, when Pruitt Jr. was chief. Only a couple are from his father's term as chief in the late twenties and early thirties. Nothing in the top drawer has a mention of Simenon.

I join Zach and Kristen at the workbench. They've been chatting amiably while thumbing through the binders and books.

"So what is all this stuff?" I ask.

"Old magazines, store catalogs, and *Farmer's Almanacs* dating back to the 1900s, books about firearms and mining, a few police academy yearbooks," Kristen says.

"Do the yearbooks go back to the 1920s?"

"Unfortunately not."

I look at Kristen's fingers smudged with grime. "Sorry, I should have brought another pair of gloves for you."

"I have hand sanitizer inside," Zach says, moving toward the open garage door. "I'll get some, and paper towels."

"So you two seemed pretty chummy over here," I tease Kristen after Zach has left. "I thought you said he was too young."

"Maybe I was wrong about that. He's super smart. We already exchanged numbers."

I'm no longer paying attention to Kristen because I'm staring at a booklet on the workbench. It might be a program for a banquet or awards ceremony. The top half of the cover—a thick piece of parchment paper—has been torn away, removing what was probably the name or title of the event and the date, but something on the bottom of the cover catches my eye. I pick up the five-by-eight-inch booklet. It's glued together. The seven double-sided pages have come loose and contain row after row of alphabetized names. One of the pages is dog-eared and near the bottom is the name Jefferson Pruitt.

"What's that?" Kristen asks.

"Maybe an event program. It's just a list of names. Pruitt's name is here, but I don't see Simenon."

"What got your attention?"

"The numbers on the bottom of the cover," I say, pointing. "Three-one-one is a symbol sometimes used by the Klan."

KRISTEN AND I ARE BACK IN THE CAR. I HAVE PICTURES OF THE Simenon documents and the booklet.

"Do you have time for lunch?" Kristen asks.

"No. I hope you don't mind. The clock is ticking for me. I already had a to-do list, and now researching the two complaints against Simenon is added to it."

"If you want I can assign one of the research staff to look into that booklet and the 311 symbol. We'll put the names into our database and see what comes up."

"That's a great idea. Thanks. I'll text you the photos. So, did I hear Zach ask you out for coffee?"

143

"Yeah. We're meeting one day next week."

The car fills with silence.

"Are we done with that topic?" I ask.

"Yes. For now. What else do you want to talk about? Did Garrett call?"

"He texted. I didn't respond right away. Later I sent him a text calling things off for good. But then I thought about him again this morning."

"Hmm."

"What's that supposed to mean?"

"Did you call things off with Garrett because of Darius?"

"Maybe. I really like Darius."

"You've just met him."

"I've just met *you*, and here we are talking about my love life," I say flippantly.

Kristen dips her head.

"I didn't mean it to come out that way. I'm grateful to have met you," I say. "I've been really emotional today. I thought a bike ride might help, but it only made things worse. All the while I was pedaling, I was thinking of the uphill journey Blacks have always had in America. It made me angry at first, then sad."

At one thirty I drop Kristen at her house. She's helping her brother with an award ceremony tonight at the university, and the effects of my multiple cups of coffee have finally worn off. I'm thinking about a quick nap, but Monique phones.

"I'm returning your call. I was in church."

"Yeah. I forgot. I was restless and wanted to talk. I was going to offer to buy you breakfast or something. But I went for a bike ride instead."

"Darius and I were just talking about food."

"You're with Darius?"

"Yep. You want to get an early dinner? The three of us?" Monique asks.

I'd planned to make a meal in tonight and keep working, but the thought of seeing Darius makes my skin tingle.

"I have a few hours of work to do, but then I can cook something. Can you come at five thirty?"

"That's good for me. I'll check and send you a text," Monique says.

TWENTY

Worship

1929

Anna Kate looks radiant as she pins up her hair for church. She wears a cream-colored dress with green ribbon threaded through her sleeves. Even with her seven-month belly stretching the lacy fabric, she's as beautiful as she was on our wedding day. Mae sits on the couch squirming. With her newly pressed hair, polished shoes, and white anklets, she looks like a little lady.

"Come on, darling," I say to Mae. "Let's go downstairs and wait for Mommy. You look so pretty I want to show you off."

"Don't let her soil her dress," Anna Kate cautions as we close the apartment door.

In the front room of the boardinghouse a few of the male residents are gathered near the radio. They've just finished Mrs. Ardle's famous Sunday breakfast. Mae darts off to play with the daughter of the house's newest boarders.

The Freemans have moved from Shreveport, where he was an experienced chef. Lured by the wages, Freeman has come to work as a cook at one of the diners near the steel mills. His wife is a meek woman. Petite, with a shock of unruly hair, she greets me with a quick curve of her lips and a quicker glance to her feet. Mr. Freeman is just the opposite. Gregarious and friendly, he slaps me on the back and his voice booms through the room.

"Off to church, I see, Mr. Harrington," he says, admiring my tan suit. "My wife's cousin has invited us to her church today. We're Baptists, you know."

"We're grateful to Mrs. Ardle for introducing us to her Pentecostal church," I say.

"Well, I see our girls have hit it off," Freeman says. "Our Carrie Mae is an only child and we're glad she's found a playmate, aren't we, dear?" Freeman looks at his wife. She gazes up at her husband, nods, and drops her head before returning her attention to the girls. Both are sitting on the floor, and Mae has seized Carrie's Raggedy Ann doll. I intercede.

"Okay, darling, you know Mommy will be upset with us if you get your dress dirty." I sweep Mae up in my arms.

"Well, there's your lovely wife now," Freeman says loudly.

As Anna Kate steps into the room, all the men stop talking and stare. Mae reaches out for her mother and tries to wriggle from my arms.

"I'm ready, Lee," Anna Kate says softly.

I say quick goodbyes, and with a squirming Mae in one arm, I envelop Anna Kate with my other. As we leave I notice Mrs. Freeman's head is raised as she looks at Anna Kate with undisguised envy.

I've touched up the polish on the Franklin this morning. It gleams like a regal carriage. I help Anna Kate into the front seat and then place Mae on a folded blanket in the back. It's a quick ride to the Rock of Ages Church, but we turn heads as we roll along the streets where most of the city's Negro population lives.

Anna Kate says Rock of Ages reminds her of the churches at home because its congregants include members from all parts of the community. After her earlier visit to the Baptist church, she'd announced the people there were too snooty.

The one-floor storefront church has folding chairs instead of pews. A gigantic picture of a blue-eyed Jesus dominates the sanctuary. Thanks to an energetic young minister and a soul-stirring choir, the chairs are filled to capacity this morning. The air moving in the building doesn't come from the open doors and back windows but from the flurry of paper fans in the hands of worshippers.

Sunday service is more important to Anna Kate than to me, but I am a believer. Mama and Papa Tico made sure I went to church every week for sixteen years before I rebelled. Four years ago I came back on my own, and that's how I met Anna Kate, sitting with her family at Bethel Missionary Church in St. Petersburg. I'd come to the service with my uncle Johnny Goldwire, my mother's brother, who loved automobiles as much as I did. I'd finally saved up enough money to think about buying a car, but Uncle Johnny was going to first let me try out his new Studebaker. There was one condition. I had to visit his church.

I have a few memories of that visit. I know I put two dollars in the collection plate to make a good impression. I remember the choir was stirring and the sermon was too long. But I didn't mind because it gave me ample opportunity to look at Anna Kate's profile.

When Uncle Johnny introduced me to the Smith family, Anna Kate barely looked at me, but I could hardly take my eyes off her. I know I looked good because I was wearing my new blue suit with a striped tie. Anna Kate's mother asked me a couple of questions that Sunday, and more questions every Sunday after that, until I got up the nerve to ask if I could court her daughter.

This morning the young Birmingham preacher is talking about the enduring value of faith. He's been at it for twenty minutes. Mae has started to squirm, and Anna Kate's fanning has increased. I take a stick of Black Jack gum from my pocket, remove the foil, and break it in half—one half for Mae, the other for me. The sugar appeases her, and she sits back in her chair. Anna Kate doesn't approve of chewing gum in church and she cuts her eyes at me. I give her my fan so she can generate more air and take her mind off the gum.

"The Lord says in the Old Testament: My ways are higher than your ways; and my thoughts higher than your thoughts," shouts the preacher.

"Amen" is chorused around the sticky room.

"You can't do nothing without the Lord's help. And I'll tell you one more thing. *With* his help, you can do things you never thought you could."

On those last words, the organ music begins a steady buildup of volume and speed, until the preacher is high-stepping on the altar, and we all get to our feet. After two full minutes of joyful music and Holy Ghost dancing, the organ shifts to a slow rendition of "What a Friend We Have in Jesus," and the offering plate is passed for the third and final time.

"Have we trials and temptations? Is there trouble anywhere? We should never be discouraged. Take it to the Lord in prayer," the congregation sings.

I give Mae a nickel to put in the plate and add three more dollars for me and Anna Kate.

I squeeze my wife's hand. She squeezes back.

Anna Kate wants to greet the pastor after the service, so I take Mae outside to get some air. The sky is turquoise blue with no cloud in sight. Harriet Ardle exits and we chat a few minutes before she heads back to the boardinghouse to start supper for her lodgers.

When Anna Kate steps out onto the sidewalk, she's flushed both by the heat and by the nourishment of her spirit.

"Why don't we go for a drive," I say. "It'll be hot in the apartment this time of day, and this way we can get some more air."

"I wouldn't mind," Anna Kate replies.

We cruise around parts of the city we don't see every day, with Mae perched on two blankets in the back seat. When we pass the jovial fans lined up at Rickwood Field waiting to see the Birmingham Black Barons play baseball, Mae claps her hands and waves and people wave back. We drive by Miles Memorial College in Fairfield, and through the Smithfield neighborhood to admire the homes of the city's prominent Negro families.

"Maybe we'll have a house here someday," I say to Anna Kate.

We pass through busy Tuxedo Junction, dodging pedestrians, other vehicles, and cable cars. At first, Mae giggles. I peek at her through the rearview mirror. But even she grows quiet as she is overwhelmed by the sights, loud sounds, and pungent odors.

"Is this where you play cards?" Anna Kate asks softly.

"No. Griggs Ballroom, not far from where we live."

"I think we should go home now."

"So do I, my love."

Anna Kate fusses over our Sunday dinner. Most of it has been made the night before, but she warms the greens and chicken and mashes the potatoes. After dinner, I help with the dishes and put Mae into the tub for a bath. When Harriet comes upstairs to work on a tablecloth she and Anna Kate are crocheting, I excuse myself to join the men downstairs in the parlor. I smoke a cigar and listen to the radio for a while, then head outside to polish the car one last time.

I've just unfolded the tarp and oiled my rag when Mr. Freeman joins me. He walks slowly around the car, nodding his endorsement of the vehicle.

"That's a good-looking automobile, Mr. Harrington."

"You can call me Lee," I say.

"How long have you owned it?"

"Not even a year."

"Well, you sure do keep her looking good."

I nod. "I'm selling her tomorrow."

"Is that so."

"Sadly, it is. I'm buying a family car."

"I'll buy it from you," Freeman announces.

I shake my head. "It's already promised."

"I'll give you a hundred more than your offer," he pushes.

"No. Sorry. I've promised another man the car."

"I understand. A man of your word. Just as well, I'm saving up to buy a little restaurant."

"You had your own place in Louisiana?"

"Yes. But the people who own the steel plant here offered me twice what I was earning, so here I am. Magic City is what they're calling Birmingham now, and that's what my cooking tastes like. Magic. You should come by the diner sometime. I'll cook you up a meal on the house."

"Now that my wife is with me, I'm already eating pretty good," I say.

"You're a lucky man. An attractive wife who can cook. That's a pleasant combination. My wife is mighty handy around a kitchen herself. She worked with me at the diner in Shreveport, and she'll be with me when we get our place going here. What I really want is to have a place in a neighborhood like this where I can cook for my own people."

Freeman and I talk a bit more about our professions and about how a man has to make his own opportunities in the Jim Crow South. It's almost dark when we say good night. When he departs I roll the tarp onto the Franklin. I'll miss this car.

ANNA KATE'S COMPANY IS GONE AND SHE HAS MADE A POT OF coffee to go with her sweet potato pie.

"Your dessert is on the table," she says.

"Will you join me?" I ask.

"I'll have a tiny bit more."

We sit at our small dining table sipping coffee. Mae is asleep on the couch. Anna Kate tells me about the tablecloth she's making and the plan she has to sell it to a woman who goes to our church. I tell her about my conversation with Mr. Freeman. "He's a good, steady man," I say.

"I like his wife too," Anna Kate adds. "She's joined Harriet and me for coffee a few times."

We talk of the week ahead and discuss names for our new baby—Robert Jr. if it's a boy. And we both like the name Barbara if it's a girl.

"Do you call your automobile by a name? I've often heard you refer to it as 'her.'"

I laugh. "Well, I sometimes called her Frankie."

She smiles. "I know it's not easy to let her go."

In another hour, I pull down our bed while Anna Kate washes up and twists her hair in bobby pins. When she comes to bed, I lie at her back with my knees tucked under her warm bottom. I caress her bulging belly and the baby kicks.

"I think it's a boy," I say before we both drift off to sleep.

TWENTY-ONE

2019

I hadn't planned to cook a big Sunday meal but I'm excited as I gather the ingredients for a vegetarian lasagna for Darius and Monique. The hardest work for the dish is the prep. Slicing eggplant, mozzarella, red and green peppers, and onion, then mixing the ricotta with diced tomatoes and olive oil. I also add a bit of flaked chili peppers to the layers for an extra zing. I make a pan of corn bread—from scratch—and when my guests arrive I'll toss a green salad.

My cooking skills were acquired over fifteen years, from about four years old to high school, of watching and assisting my mother in the kitchen. She was taught by Grandma. I fell away from the stews, casseroles, soups, and baking when I left home for college, but as soon as I got my own place, I picked them up again. In no time my confidence around a stove top and an oven was renewed.

It's fun to see Darius and Monique interact. I've told them to make themselves at home, and Monique immediately kicks off her boots. She chides Darius for not removing his. "You act like somebody's daddy. Loosen up." They really are like brother and sister, constantly gabbing and teasing each other, one reminding the other of some funny or scary incident they witnessed together. Darius calls her Mo, and I heard her call him Gramps.

The lasagna is a hit, and Monique has brought a pecan pie. We're around the large kitchen table with the food and wine and we're enjoying ourselves.

"This is a really fine meal," Darius says when he accepts another helping of lasagna. "After tasting this corn bread I could mistake you for a southerner."

"Yeah, girl. This food is slamming," Monique agrees.

At eight o'clock, Darius wants to watch football on the oversize living room TV, so Monique helps me with the dishes; then, sipping wine, we join Darius and watch him root for the Eagles. Neither Monique nor I are much into football, but he became a fan when he went to college in Philadelphia. By halftime, Monique has had enough.

"Okay, I'm out," she says, standing and gathering her stuff. "Darius, you can stay; I just can't get into this modern-day gladiator spectacle."

I watch them in amusement as they argue about the cultural and economic dynamics of American football—concussions, drug use, domestic violence, teamwork, and the role of sports in building Black wealth.

"Where else can a young Black kid make a million dollars straight out of college?" Darius argues.

"But what happens to them when they don't have the financial acumen or good judgment to use all that money wisely?" Monique counters. "The NFL doesn't give a damn about these young men except to make the team owners richer."

Monique's Uber arrives. I insist she should take home the pie that's left, and wave her goodbye. Darius smiles when I return to the living room. The third quarter has just started. He pats the seat next to him.

I smile and shake my head.

"Do you want me to leave?"

"No. That's not necessary. You sit and enjoy the game. Really. I've got some work to do, and I have a call later with Saxby," I say, grabbing my bag. "I'll be in the kitchen."

I notice Darius's hurt look, but I'm determined not to let his good looks, my attraction to him, and the fact that he's finally taken off his shoes make me act rashly. I clear the place mats from the table and grab my supplies. I've taped several blank sheets of paper end to end to draw the timeline, and it's spread across the table.

Within a half hour, Darius joins me. "They have software programs for that, you know."

"I know. It's a personal preference. When I really want to connect to the events, I mark them in myself. Sometimes I even tape images to the timeline and post it on a wall where I can see it whenever I walk by."

"I bet no journalism class teaches that," Darius says smiling.

I nod toward the TV. "Is it over already?"

"No. But it's a boring game. I came in for another glass of wine and to watch you work."

"Okay, well, sit. Pour me another too, please."

There are large gaps in the chain of events of 1929. I'm working with a set of colored pencils to fill in information. In red, I enter an estimate of the date when my great-grandfather arrived in Birmingham. I believe it's June or maybe even earlier based on the boardinghouse receipts. For July he switches accommodations to make room for his wife and daughter. Next, I move to September on the timeline and put in an estimate for Great-Grandpa's death.

"I can't pinpoint the exact date he was killed. The *St. Pete Times* news story doesn't say, but the article is published in late September of 1929."

"There has to be a death certificate," Darius says.

"I've made the request but it's a Catch-22. You need the date of death when you request a copy of a certificate. Maybe I'll be lucky and still receive it."

"What happened to his body?" Darius asks.

"We don't know. He may have been buried in a pauper's grave, or he could have been left to rot on the side of some country road. That's one of the saddest parts of this story for Grandma. It would give her amazing peace just to know there's a marker over her father's body."

Darius shifts in his seat, then pulls his chair closer. The hair on my arm tingles. I put down my pencils and look at him across the table. He looks away for a second, then back at me.

"Meg. Are you in a relationship?"

"I just split up with a guy I dated for a year," I say without hesitation.

He smiles, then catches himself, adjusting his face to show concern. "Oh. I'm sorry." He keeps the sober look. Then a beat later says: "Not."

We both laugh.

"Are you seeing anyone?" I ask.

"I've dated a few girls recently, but nothing serious. Before that I was engaged. But it didn't work out."

"Earlier today I was thinking about the fragility of Black relationships. All kinds, not just romantic ones. Relationships are difficult enough to nurture and maintain without all the stressors of racism. How did our ancestors ever do it? Fall in love, build families, have hope?"

"They did it with perseverance, faith in God, and more than a little bit of dysfunction."

"How could there *not* be dysfunction when people who hate you to your face have the power to control your life?"

Darius and I stare at each other.

"That sounds like a good start to your story." He reaches across the table and takes my hand. Our fingers intertwine. "Will you go on a date with me?" he asks.

I *want* to go out with Darius. I want him to swoop me into his arms right now and carry me to my bedroom, where I will melt into his body. But I don't say any of that.

"Darius, I have to go home at the end of the week."

"I know. But I *really* like you, Meg."

"I like you too."

He kisses my hand when he leaves. A nerdy, old-fashioned gesture of southern formality. I didn't answer his question about a date, but I believe he knows the answer will, ultimately, be yes.

"Dr. King once called Birmingham the most segregated city in America. They had a so-called Black Code," I say to Saxby on our Zoom call.

I'm agitated, and maybe I shouldn't be having another glass of wine. Or maybe it's the culmination of a week's worth of reading about the misery this country has imposed on Black folks. I can't get off my high horse.

"There was segregation in all aspects of life—housing, schools, hospitals, churches, even in death. It just infuriates me. These draconian laws fucked with Black people every single day, destroying bodies and damaging psyches."

Saxby gives an amused smile.

"What's so funny?"

"You, McKenzie. You've become a student of civil rights history."

"Maybe I have."

Saxby is laid-back. It's Sunday night, he's at home, and his hair is loose, grazing his shoulders. He fiddles with a camera as I talk. Occasionally he looks up and nods.

"Did you know Birmingham's state constitution made it a crime for Blacks and whites to play checkers and dominoes together?" I say, shaking my head. "Can you believe that bullshit?"

"Unfortunately, I can." Saxby picks up his own drink, a martini, and takes a full swallow. "Who did you speak with today?"

"I was on the phone all morning with funeral home directors. Then I went to the 16th Street Baptist Church memorial."

He leans back in his seat and pushes his hair back from his face. "You ever consider how so much of our work revolves around death and destruction? Know what I mean? You start off your career writing the obits, then the next thing you know you're reporting on assassinations, wars, fires, accidents, tsunamis, hurricanes, murders, and rioting."

"Man bites dog. Not the other way around. That's what I was taught about the Fourth Estate. You don't write about the normal things that happen every day. That's not news. It's not what fills the column inches in the paper, or the five-hundred-word blog on the website, or gets designated as breaking news on the cable stations."

Saxby nods. "But too much news these days is about the

tearing down of things—flags, statues, people's reputations, democracy—"

"A few things may need to be torn down. Like police funding," I say, interrupting and leaning into the camera.

Saxby sighs and his face fills the screen. He looks somber. "I'm feeling old, McKenzie. I've been at this a long time and no matter how many things change for the better, there's still so much that continues in the same old wrong way."

"That's exactly what my story is about," I say.

We both reach for our drinks and partake in our joint pity party. Before too long, Saxby puts down his glass with dramatic emphasis.

"Okay. Enough of this. Let's get back on track. First of all, have you started your piece?"

"The first part is done. Almost a thousand words. I'll send it tonight."

"Great. Second, you have to retain some distance from this story. You're getting too . . . too . . ."

"Emotional?"

"Well, I wasn't going to say that, but yeah."

It's the rusty argument used to suggest women aren't right for certain jobs. It was used five decades ago when unions kept women off police and fire departments, used against Hillary when she ran for president, and Monique says it's a regular challenge to her leadership of Black Lives Matter. Normally, I'd push back. But I can't this time. This investigation has unnerved me. I've already admitted it to myself.

"If I just had more facts, I might be able to be more objective. But I don't. So I'm relying on other things," I say.

"Like what?"

"Intuition."

"Nothing wrong with trusting your gut," Saxby says.

"And listening to the universe."

"What?"

"Trusting this story will reveal itself to me, because it wants to be told," I say.

"Whoa, whoa. What are you talking about?"

"Maybe I should say I'm applying metaphysics. It sounds more scientific."

"Look, I ain't against a little dabbling with mind-over-matter stuff. I took some acid in my day, but you're writing a news story, not fiction."

"I know that."

I don't like being chastised.

"I'm convinced that because of the systemic racism of the 1920s, I'll only be able to shine a partial light on the truth. Information was withheld or destroyed when it didn't suit the narrative the powerful wanted told. I've scanned literally hundreds of newspaper pages from 1929, and I haven't read a single account about a Black person getting a fair deal. Not one."

Saxby rubs his chin. He's been around long enough to know what I'm saying is true, but I don't have him yet.

"Listen. Let me tell you what I have so far."

I give him the full rundown of my activities since arriving in Birmingham seven days ago. The research, the meetings and phone calls, the find at the motel storage building, my impressions of the city, and the hospitality and assistance I've received.

"The support has been incredible. I spent hours in the basement of two strangers who just want to help me with this story. My librarian friend has bent over backward to give me access to the city archives. Darius was with me when I found the information on the boardinghouse. In fact, he spotted it first."

"He's a good guy. The first time I met him his father was a consultant to Coleman Young. That was before they moved back to Birmingham. Darius was a funny little kid. He traveled with his father everywhere." Saxby smiles remembering. "Skinny as a beanpole but could put away food like he was a grown man."

"He still enjoys his food," I say.

"It sounds like you're off to a good start, McKenzie. We'll get your blog on the website Tuesday. Then we expect part two by the end of the week. You still plan on being back in the office next week?"

"I may need a few more days."

"That's not going to happen."

"I was thinking I could take some of my vacation time if necessary."

"You'd have to handle your own expenses."

"I know."

"Look, let me speak to Serina. Maybe she'll extend you a few days."

Saxby pauses. I can tell he has more to say. I wait.

"Just don't get too new agey on me."

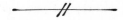

After the call I pace the room. It's almost eleven. But I'm wrought up. When I'm like this I have several coping activities—exercise, listening to music helps, sex gets me right, or I can cook.

I have most of the fixings for a cranberry-pecan bread. I pull up a recipe on my phone, find the jazz playlist Daddy created for me, and I go at it. The recipe's multiple steps keep me focused and busy. I assemble all my ingredients and utensils. The kitchen has a good set of measuring cups and spoons, spatulas, plus the baking soda and vanilla extract I didn't buy at the grocery store. I take my time chopping nuts on the cutting board. I usually mix a majority of finely cut nuts with coarser pieces—it makes for a loaf with an appealing texture. The butter has to be softened, and I use the microwave to do a shortcut. The recipe calls for white chocolate chips to be used for a glaze. I don't have those, but I do have orange juice, which I'll whip with powdered sugar into a wonderful citrus coating. I'm a neat cook, cleaning up after each task, and I only have bowls and spoons to wash by the time the batter goes into the oven.

My phone rings and I smile when I look at the display.

"I didn't want the day to end without saying good night—again," Darius says when I answer. "How was the call with Saxby?"

"So-so. I just baked a cranberry loaf."

"Wow. You know, you're a very good cook."

"A good eater too," I say, laughing. "I've put on five pounds since I got here. Does that invitation to be a guest at your gym still stand?"

"Of course it does. What are your plans for tomorrow evening? We can do a workout and then go out for a light meal."

"Is that the date you mentioned?"

"Oh no. A date means we get dressed up, I pick you up, and we get an extravagant meal with wine."

"I see."

"And when I drop you off at home, I get a good-night kiss."

"Oh, and don't you come in for a nightcap, like they do in the black-and-white movies on TCM?"

"Are you making fun of me?"

"No. Well, sort of. Did anybody ever tell you about your old-school ways?"

"Monique sometimes calls me Gramps," he admits.

"I thought I heard her call you that." I can't keep from laughing, and Darius joins me. He's easy to talk to and we share views on music and sports, politics and books. He volunteers information about his former fiancée—a woman he met in graduate school. They're still friends. I tell him about Garrett and about the boy who broke my heart in college. During our conversation, I add the glaze to the cranberry loaf, cut a slice, and brew a cup of tea. Darius is a year older than Garrett, but light-years ahead in listening and empathy. He understands what I mean when I tell him I'm relying on spiritual guidance to help me write my story. Neither of us is yet thirty, but I think we're both old souls. It's midnight when we hang up after expressing our mutual excitement about seeing each other the next day.

TWENTY-TWO

2019

At just after nine o'clock, I've already called Birmingham PD, again, with a request for an interview, and now I'm at Kristen's desk watching her move around the main room of the city archives. She's unlocking file cabinets, putting paper in the printer, removing dust covers from workstations. I have a moment of déjà vu. There were mornings, if I had a day off from my own school, when I would watch my mother, the school principal, prepare the office in much the same manner.

Kristen returns to her desk and plops into her chair. She looks up at me, exasperated, and grabs her coffee for a huge gulp.

"May I help you, Ms. McKenzie?" She feigns formality.

"Yes, you may. I need a favor."

"Okay. But I'm probably gonna need another cup of coffee before I can help *anybody*."

"Rough night?"

"Scotty had an awards banquet last night. He's separated from his wife and I helped him with host duties. There were twenty-five all-city high school football players and their families for a Sunday dinner and a reception. I had to make a lot of small talk."

"You're a good sister."

"Damn straight. I got home just before midnight and this morning I realized I left my employee badge at the banquet hall." Kristen sighs. "I'm praying the rest of this day is dull and boring."

I slink into the side chair and watch her drink more coffee. She peers at me over the cup. I give her a hopeful smile and raised eyebrows. "Want to hear the favor?"

She puts her cup down. "Not if I'm reading your face right. Did you hear what I said about dull and boring? I think this favor's going to be something hard."

"Depends on whether you're still in your daddy's good graces."

"What's Daddy got to do with it?"

"I need you to call him."

"About what?"

"Remember the complaint charging Detective Simenon with sexual assault? I need the name of the complainant."

"You're talking about information from 1929."

"I know. But your father said he wanted to help, and if his company has always managed the police insurance portfolio, he probably has all kinds of records. Oh, and please don't tell him about how my personal story connects to any of this. At least not yet."

Kristen nods and rubs her fingers through her dyed hair. She snatches up her coffee again but it's empty.

"Meghan, I hope you don't mind my directness, but this Simenon guy probably doesn't have a damn thing to do with your story."

"I've debated the point myself. But it's too much of a coincidence that an unsolved killing of a cop occurs within the same time frame as my great-grandfather's death. Coincidences are troubling things to a journalist. They almost always merit a closer look."

Kristen still looks skeptical. "How do you know it's an unsolved case?"

"All right, think about this. Since those three articles I found I've not discovered a single mention of Simenon's murder in any of the papers I've searched. Not one! A cop gets killed and the story just goes away? That's really odd to me."

"Yeah, I admit that *is* odd. Oh, and I've given that list of names in the booklet you found at Pruitt's to one of our research specialists. He'll scan the names and see if any of them connect to our documents archive. It might take a couple of days to get back the information."

"Terrific. I really appreciate it."

"I hope you're wrong about that number symbol on the booklet."

"I don't think I'm wrong. A lot of police officers were members of the Klan in those days."

Kristen stares at me, then sighs. "Wow. Calling Daddy to snoop into his business. I'll definitely need another coffee."

I've just pulled into the circular driveway of the Maybury Mortuary and I leave the car idling to watch the traffic passing on the street. At one point I thought I was being followed. A van made a couple of the same turns I made, but I don't see it now. *Guess I'm still freaked out by that phone call.*

Two wings have been added to the main structure of Maybury

Mortuary. Ivy grows up the walls, and flowering shrubs line both sides of the main entrance. The newer funeral homes may have eclipsed Maybury in fortune and innovation, but it has elegance and my research indicates there are still those in the Black upper-middle class who trust only this multigenerational family establishment to handle their loved ones.

"Please come in and have a seat in our waiting room. Someone will be right with you." The voice from the video doorbell is female and pleasant. I'm sitting in a stately anteroom among upholstered chairs, paintings of pastoral scenes, wood paneling, and subdued lighting. The experience takes me back to my first visit to a funeral home. I was nine years old and Grandma Rose had died. Daddy was so sad, and he and Mom deposited me in a room that looked very much like this one to wait while they arranged her funeral. Then, like now, quiet music was playing, and everyone whispered like they were in the library. When Mom tucked me into bed that night, I'd asked if the place we'd left Grandma Rose was heaven.

The lobby may be a throwback, but the man who comes to greet me is anything but. Jameson Maybury is movie-star handsome, I'd guess in his early forties, with a neatly trimmed beard, wavy, salon-cut hair, wearing a tan suit with a cream tie and matching pocket square. His leather portfolio is Gucci. Everything about him says quality. Not conservative.

"Hello, Ms. McKenzie. I'm glad you could come by," he says, extending his hand.

"Mr. Maybury, thank you for taking the time to look through your records."

"Well, it's my job. I'm director of communications, and you can call me Jameson."

"Just to confirm for my story, your father is the president and owner?"

"He is."

"Is that him?" I ask, pointing to one of the formal portraits flanking the door marked OFFICES AND CHAPELS.

"Oh no, that's Grandfather. The other portrait is of my grandmother. They're both deceased. He ran the mortuary for fifty years. My father's been at the helm almost that long. We've come a long way since then."

"It looks as though you've kept the traditional feel," I say, scanning the décor.

He nods. "But don't be fooled by our staid surroundings. It's true we don't have all the video presentations, theme funerals, that kind of thing. We believe in a bit more decorum. But our infrastructure and processes are sounder than most and our records are all electronic."

It's my turn to nod.

"I've found a set of records that fit the search criteria you mentioned over the phone. Unfortunately, we don't have a record for a Robert Lee Harrington, but I've made a full list of our shooting victims from the time period, and it includes quite a few John Does," Jameson says, pulling a single sheet from his folder. "If you like, you can look through the records over here." He leads the way to a corner table and chair, then leaves me on my own.

THE COMPUTER PRINTOUT IS FROM A DATABASE QUERY. A LIST of bodies prepared by Maybury Mortuary for September through December of 1929 who died of gunshot wounds. There are eighteen records. The filters at the top read: CONTROL #; DATE; NAME;

F/M; COD; BURIAL; BILLING; NOTES. I settle into the chair and pull my highlighter, pen, and notebook from my tote. I stare at the printout for a few minutes to take in the scope and meaning of the information. COD probably means cause of death, and for each of the bodies there is the number 3 in that column. I put a check next to the category to verify with Jameson what that means. The other categories are self-explanatory. The notes column references a key or legend that I don't have, and I highlight that column.

I immediately cross out six of the eighteen records because the deceased are listed as female. I stare at the remaining twelve entries. Four are listed as John Does, and the other eight names don't mean a thing to me.

A man and two women are huddled together in a seating area I must step through to access the administration office. The older woman, wearing a small black hat with a sheer veil, is being comforted by the others. A second man, as old as the woman, stands cap in hand away from the group and almost in my path. He nods with a grimacing face as I pass on my way to the office. He looks vaguely familiar.

The office has a frosted glass door and another security doorbell, which I press. Within a few seconds, a buzzer sounds. A young woman, dressed in a tasteful dark suit, sits at a desk. She smiles as I step inside.

"I was hoping to speak with Mr. Maybury, if he has a moment."

"Mr. Maybury *Jr.*?" she asks.

"Yes. Uh, Jameson. I spoke with him in the lobby. He gave me some information and I have a few follow-up questions."

"Of course. Would you mind signing in here?" She points to an electronic tablet at the edge of her desk then at a door across from her. "Jameson will be with you very soon."

The modern conference room has a sleek oval table and six comfortable Herman Miller Aeron chairs. There is a large whiteboard with the controls of a high-tech monitor. We have similar ones at the *Free Press*. The speakerphone on the credenza is shaped like the starship *Enterprise*. While I wait, I peruse the reading offerings—magazines and single-page reprints of newspaper articles on home funerals, cremation, and industry trends. Some of the glossy reprints are from *The New York Times*, *The Washington Post*, and *O* magazine.

"Coffee?" Jameson asks as he strolls into the conference room. He's carrying a mug and an iPad. He's now wearing designer tortoiseshell eyeglasses. He sits at the head of the table.

"I'd love a cup."

"Your coffee's on the way," he says after tapping into his tablet. "Did you find what you were looking for in the printout?"

"I'm not sure. First, I'm impressed with your record keeping."

"Thanks. We try to keep things shipshape."

"How come Maybury has been involved with so many John Does?"

Jameson shrugs. "It's a public service. My grandfather started taking in the unclaimed dead right after he opened the mortuary. He was the only one doing it at the time. The city regulates and monitors the work, and occasionally community groups or civic associations will offset the costs."

"I see. And where are these people buried?"

"There used to be a potter's field. But that area is now an arboretum. Others were buried in private cemeteries or ended up in a mass grave. Developers often built right over large cemetery plots. There's a lot more regulation about those things these days. Now unclaimed bodies are primarily cremated."

I take notes as he speaks. I hadn't ever really thought about the fate of people who die homeless without family, friends, or identity. It causes a swirl of hollowness in my core.

THE CONFERENCE ROOM DOOR OPENS, AND A YOUNG MAN wearing black pants and a white shirt enters with a tray containing a small pot of coffee, cup and saucer, spoon, and containers of half-and-half and sugar. He places the silver tray in front of me with a smile, nods to Jameson, and exits. I pour the steaming-hot coffee, add cream and stir, then take a sip. It warms the empty space in my belly. The cup and saucer are some kind of very nice porcelain. I admire the cup before I return it to the saucer. Jameson notices.

"Blue Willow china. Our clients expect this kind of quality."

"Very nice," I say, taking a few more sips. "I feel pampered, and special. Thank you."

"That's what we intend."

"It's hard for me to think about people dying without connections to loved ones or people who care about them." He agrees with a nod. I'm tempted to ask him how he gets through days of talking about death and dying. My expression gives me away, and he answers without a prompt.

"I almost didn't follow in the family business. I thought the job would be a 24-7 downer."

"What changed your mind?"

"I made a deal with my father, right around the time I was finishing college. If I'd accompany him to a month's worth of meetings, he'd buy me a car. He was a shrewd old dude even then. He started taking me on home visits. That's something Maybury still does that the other mortuaries don't do. We don't make families come to us unless they want to."

I pour the last bit of hot coffee and listen.

"I saw how much comfort Dad gave to grieving people. We went into the homes of those who were under stress and Dad took some of the weight off their shoulders. He always says we're not in the death business, we're in the lifeline business. I got my new car, but I also got the calling," Jameson says with a sincere smile.

"I see you did. Wise fathers are a good thing." I switch into work mode by positioning my notebook in front of me. "There are twelve people on the list you provided that I'd like to know more about."

"Okay."

We go over the individual records for each man. Two of the unidentified males are over sixty, and five of the named males are juveniles, so they're all off my list. That leaves me with five people. Two John Does and three identified as Ocie Bain, Albert Griggs, and Joshua Brewster. Jameson provides more physical detail about the five remaining men—height, tattoos, missing limbs and appendages, weight. But I have only my great-grandfather's wedding photo to help me sort the physical descriptions, and I'll do that later.

"I also have questions about three codes on the printout you gave me." I open my notebook. "I'm assuming COD is cause of death?"

"Correct."

"And the numeral 3 means the person was shot?"

"Correct."

Jameson taps his tablet. He stands and slides back the door on the mounted whiteboard and taps the tablet again. I watch as he scrolls to a page labeled TABLE KEYS. "There are seven identifiers," Jameson says, expanding the view with his fingertips. "One indicates natural death; two is strangulation/asphyxia; three, gunshot;

four, stabbing; five, drowning; six, blunt force; seven means the cause of death is undetermined."

"Thank you," I say, jotting notes. I turn the page to read my next scribble. "In the notes column are two abbreviations, or maybe they're initials. What does MUN mean?"

Jameson again swipes and taps on his tablet while I follow along on the whiteboard. I think he knows all this information but wants to show off the fancy technology.

"MUN is municipal. It suggests that either the body came from one of the city agencies or the city paid for the burial."

"Would there be a death certificate associated with each body?"

"Yes. Usually. That's where the control number comes from."

"A couple of these men have an *X* in that column."

"That means there's no certificate, and it's not unusual. Back in those days a dead Black person could just be lying on the side of the road. A Good Samaritan might bury the person where he, or she, fell, but often unidentified bodies would be delivered to a church or a funeral home wrapped in a blanket. Everybody knew Granddad wouldn't turn anyone away."

"Final question. EB also shows up in the notes column. Can you check that one, please?"

"Sure."

I watch again as Jameson navigates the whiteboard. When he zooms in I gasp. "Is Evangelist Baptist Church the same as Evangelical Church?" I ask.

"Yes. They changed their name about the time Dad took over the mortuary from *his* father. You know them?"

"I was there just the other day. So why is the church listed in the notes?"

"It means either they brought us the body, paid for the burial services, or both."

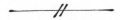

Notes, documents, and copies of newspaper articles cover my carrel desk. One stack is the limited information I have about Detective Simenon. I'll look at that later, and hope to add more after Kristen talks to her father.

I've been doing additional research on the five records from the mortuary. Their deaths fit the general timeframe of my great-grandfather's shooting, and all are between twenty and fifty years old. One of the John Does has a prominent facial scar. Great-Grandpa isn't scarred in his wedding photo, but it could have happened later. The other has no death certificate but has the Evangelist Baptist Church notation. They both stay on my list. Ocie Bain is described as a mulatto in Jameson's records; my great-grandfather had very dark skin. Bain comes off the list. I find an obituary for Joshua Brewster. His burial was paid for by his sister at another local church. He's off my list. Albert Griggs has the Evangelist Baptist connection but had only one arm and weighed 250 pounds. The physical characteristics don't mesh with what I've heard of my great-grandfather. He's off the list.

Now I have only the two John Does. I call Jameson and leave a message with my questions.

I've already texted Monique, and Googled Evangelical Church to peruse their website. There is a photo of the sanctuary where I watched Monique conduct her training, and photographs of the pastor and first lady of the church—Monique's parents. Her minister-father looks beatific, with a round face, salt-and-pepper hair, and a thin mustache. The photo of her mother is like seeing Monique in thirty years. The church's Black Lives Matter statement is front and center on the home page and was probably written by Monique.

There is a church history section with an extensive chronology of Evangelical's engagement with Birmingham's African American community. The church has been around since the 1890s, and changed its name from Evangelist Baptist Church to Evangelical Church in the sixties. The board of directors and governing council have familiar names, including Jameson Maybury Sr. and Raymond Curren—Darius's father. As I peruse the photos, I spot something that makes me lean into the screen. In the rear of the church is a small cemetery. I hadn't noticed it when I picked up Monique.

Clicking through the pull-down menus, I search for more information about the burial site. The 1.4 acres were consecrated in 1891 and registered as a private Negro cemetery for the use of the church. The graveyard holds the remains of nearly two hundred people.

KRISTEN COMES BY TO LET ME KNOW SHE'S TEXTED HER FAther about the name on the complaint against Simenon. "He texted back with a question mark and said he'll call me after three," Kristen says, standing in the doorway.

"Thanks. You're the best, but I may not be here when he calls, I'm leaving today around three thirty to meet Darius at his gym."

Kristen steps inside the tiny carrel and leans against the glass wall. "Are things getting serious between you two?"

"I don't know about serious. He and Monique Hendricks

came by for dinner last night. Then later he called and we talked a long time. I *am* attracted to him."

"That's hardly news. Is tonight a date?"

"He says it isn't."

"So you've talked about having a date?"

"Yes. But tonight is just hanging out."

"Does hanging out mean the same thing in Detroit as it does in Birmingham?"

"Probably," I reply. Then I shrug and my face gets warm.

Kristen's lips curl into a smile. "He's hot."

I'm about to agree but my phone rings, and it's Monique.

"Sorry, I have to take this."

Kristen heads for the door. "No probs. I've got work to do. Catch up later."

"Hi, Monique. Thanks for getting back to me. I was at Maybury Mortuary earlier today. They have burial records from the period when my great-grandfather died."

"I'm not surprised. They're old-school and old-money. Did you talk to Jameson?"

"Yeah."

"Gorgeous, ain't he?"

I laugh. "He's got it all pulled together, that's for sure. A little too old for me."

"Not for me," Monique says, laughing. "So your message mentioned our cemetery. What *about* it?"

"Several records from Maybury referenced Evangelical—well, actually the old church name, Evangelist Baptist. One of them is a John Doe, and that got me to thinking maybe my great-grandfather is buried in your cemetery."

"That would be some coincidence."

"I know, but I'm relying a lot on that kind of thing," I say somberly.

"Well, okay, maybe it's not such a wild idea. Our church goes back as far as Maybury. A lot of Black people didn't have funerals at the turn of the century. Family and friends would just say some prayers over a loved one and put them in the ground. But if they had the means to have a formal burial, it's likely they used our church because of the cemetery. It was the only private site for Black burials back in the day," Monique says. "I know there are ledgers associated with the cemetery. The church secretary would have them."

"What's the best way to reach her?"

"I'll send an email introducing you two. You can call her."

"That's perfect."

"Her name is Mattie Robinson." I hear the tapping of Monique's keyboard. "She's ancient, but sharp as a tack. Don't let her scare you, and don't underestimate her. Okay. Done."

My phone pings, and I see the message is already in my inbox.

"You are a marvel."

"Anytime. Bye, girl."

Within the next half hour, I'm speaking with Mrs. Robinson and explaining the nature of my inquiry. Monique's right. Robinson exudes no warmth over the phone, but she does mention her brother who lives in Detroit. We chat a bit about where he lives, and my town house in the city. That connection may have helped to secure my visit with her the next day.

When Jameson returns my call, I ask him about the two John Does. The additional notes he has are about the conditions of the bodies when they came into the mortuary.

"The man with the scar had suffered a bad burn. An old injury to his face, hands, and torso. Had the man you're looking for survived a burn in his childhood?"

"No," I say, looking at my great-grandfather's wedding picture. His face and hands are dark and smooth. I cross this man from my list. "What about the other John Doe? The one with the EBC connection."

"Let's see. Well, he'd been shot several times. And beaten. He had broken ribs."

"Is there anything about his complexion? Was he a dark-skinned man?"

"It doesn't say."

I STOP BY THE CITY ROOM TO SAY GOODBYE TO KRISTEN. A MAN is sitting in her side chair, so I hesitate, but she waves me over.

"This is my brother, Scotty. I've told you about him. He came to drop off my staff ID."

Scotty nods a hello but doesn't stand or smile. His red hair is in a buzz cut, and his shoulders are narrow under his short-sleeved plaid shirt. He might have been a jock at one time, but those days are far behind him.

"Kristen tells me you're an assistant football coach," I say to be friendly. "That's a big deal in the heart of football country."

He gives me an odd look. "Yeah. We're not the Crimson Tide, but the Blazers won the division title last year. You a football fan?"

"Not really. But my father follows college ball."

"Hmm," he says, standing now. Kristen stands too. He's a couple of inches taller than her. My assessment of his athlete status is affirmed when he smooths his shirt over a noticeable gut. "I'm outta here, sis," he says, resting his hand momentarily on Kristen's shoulder. "Appreciate you helping me with the banquet last night. Gotta get back to campus."

He doesn't say goodbye or acknowledge me in any way as he turns and walks down the hall. Kristen and I watch his exit.

"So that's your brother. Not too warm and fuzzy, is he?"

"Sorry if he was rude. He's been through a lot this year. His wife left him a few months ago. They'll probably get a divorce."

I shrug.

"So you're headed out?" Kristen asks.

"Yep. I had a good day of research. Your father didn't call?"

"Nope. Not yet. I expect he will, though. Oh, I spoke to Zach. One of the neighbors saw us hanging around the garage and told his mother. Zach had to admit that he'd shown us his grandfather's files."

"Damn. I hope he didn't get into trouble. Is he okay?"

"Apparently Pruitt's so pissed he wants Zach thrown out of the house."

"I'm sorry."

"Yeah. But he makes a good salary working IT. He says it's time for him to move anyway."

"Well, I gotta go. We can catch each other up tomorrow. I'll bring you a Starbucks."

"That would be great. Oh, and good luck with Darius tonight."

Darius's gym is full-service. That means machines, a weight room, and classes, plus a swimming pool, whirlpool, gift shop, and juice bar.

The after-work crowd hasn't arrived, so we're able to exercise side by side for twenty minutes on the ellipticals, and then twenty on the treadmill. We're both wearing the kind of exercise gear that says we're fit and proud of it. Darius has tweaked the Bluetooth settings on his phone so we can both listen to his workout playlist, which includes Khalid, Ciara, Childish Gambino, Justin Timberlake, and Kendrick Lamar. I chide him for not having the Jonas Brothers or Taylor Swift. He accuses me of letting Stanford dial down my soul-music meter. It's a fun time and we are companionable without feeling competitive. Then we go our separate ways. Me to thirty minutes of circuit training, and Darius to the free weights. After the circuit I peek into the weight room. It reeks of testosterone, so I pass it by and head to the pool. I didn't pack a swimsuit, so I buy an expensive Speedo and a cap. I do fifteen laps, then move to the steam room. At six thirty, as agreed, I meet Darius at the juice bar.

"I feel great," I say, sipping an electrolyte drink. "Thanks for inviting me."

"You *look* good, too. Relaxed. Happy. Are you ready to eat?"

"Always."

"I know a place with terrific dinner salads. It's not far from here."

"Great. You want me to follow you?"

"Let's just take one car. I can leave mine parked in the garage as long as I like. Do you mind driving? I want to see if it's true Detroit drivers are better than the rest of us."

I laugh. "It's true. We learn about cars and driving in elementary school, right along with the names of the Great Lakes."

THE CRIMSON BOWL OFFERS ASIAN-FUSION FARE AND SALADS with lots of delectable options. I order a salad with plum tomatoes, bean sprouts, snow peas, cucumbers, and artichoke and add a skewer of grilled shrimp. Darius's salad is basically surf and turf on a bed of greens.

"I bet vegetarians are stunned when they see this menu," I say, staring at his six-ounce medium-well filet mignon next to a crab leg and surrounded by onion rings.

"It's a salad. It's healthy," Darius announces, shoving a chunk of meat in his mouth.

"Right. Is that a lonely cucumber I see peeking out from under the crab?"

We share a bottle of Riesling, and our salad comes with a personal-size loaf of bread. The place is filled to capacity, and a few people are waiting outside the door. The dining room is decorated in white and citrus colors, giving it a fresh, modern look, plus the food is delicious. It's easy to see why the place is so popular.

I tell Darius about my visit to the funeral home, my appointment tomorrow with the secretary of Monique's church, my interview request with the police chief, and Kristen's intercession with her father. He seems interested, but he's quieter tonight and doesn't ask a lot of questions. He agrees that reaching out to Kristen's father is a shrewd strategy and offers to ask the mayor to intercede with the police department if I need another way in.

"You seem tired. Did you overdo it with the weights?" I ask, putting a tiny pat of butter onto my sourdough bread.

"Naw. I have a regular routine. I'm following it until my trainer says I need to do something else."

Darius wears a cream-colored zip-up sweater, but earlier—on the elliptical, when he was wearing shorts and a sleeveless tee—I couldn't help but notice his sculpted arms, thighs, and calves.

"Penny for your thoughts," he says.

I look up from my bread, smile, then avert my eyes. "Well, I was thinking that since you have such great arms and legs, whatever you're doing seems to be working just fine."

He smiles and grabs his napkin to wipe it across his mouth, then leans toward me.

"And I was impressed with your parking and driving. You do Detroit proud."

"I thought you hadn't noticed."

"You do a lot of things well. You did that flip thing at the wall while you were swimming," he says twirling his finger.

So he had been watching me.

"I was on the swim team at Stanford. Not a standout, but I held my own."

"I'm sure you did. You're an intriguing woman in many ways. I've been thinking a lot about you. It's time to set that date."

The night is mild, slightly muggy, and a full moon hovers so low over downtown Birmingham it looks like one of those man-made cityscapes at Disney World. Darius has suggested a drive to Vulcan Park—one of the city's main tourist attractions.

The park and adjacent museum on top of Red Mountain are still open, and visitors pour into and out of the site. The view of lights from buildings and homes in the distance is spectacular, and romantic. Casually, Darius takes my hand and we stroll along the lighted grounds. He provides a tour, explaining that the Vulcan statue—looming almost two hundred feet high on an observation tower—depicts the Roman god of iron and commemorates Birmingham's twentieth-century preeminence in the iron and steel industries.

Fifteen minutes later we're on a bench watching the sky and lights and breathing in the mountain air.

"It's beautiful," I say.

"I like coming here at night," Darius says. "It's a good place to think and remind myself of the importance of the work I do. Red Mountain is sort of a demarcation line between the city and its richer suburbs. For those with money and clout, the goal is to move 'over the mountain.' That's changing somewhat, and we're trying to make the city better for everyone. People are moving back downtown."

Darius suggests we leave to avoid the rush when the park closes in a half hour. In the car, we listen to a jazz channel on satellite radio, and as I drive I let my mind wander with thoughts of the day. I pull up next to the garage entrance and put the car in park. I turn down the radio and face Darius.

"So we have an official date tomorrow. What time should I be ready?" I ask.

"Six thirty. Will that give you enough time to finish your work?"

"I'm sure it will."

"Until tomorrow," Darius says. "But I can't wait that long to do this."

His kiss is tender. Probing, but not urgent. When he finally pulls away. I place my hand on the back of his neck and draw him close for another.

TWENTY-THREE

2019

My blog was published this morning on the newspaper website. I checked and it already had thirty-four likes. I have a date with Darius tonight, and I'm feeling pretty good. I've bought Kristen a Starbucks venti half white and am in her side chair. She's texted she's finishing up a senior staff meeting and is on her way to the city room. There are already a half dozen visitors spread across the library research area. One guy, pudgy and bespectacled, I've seen several times in the main reading room. Another guy, wearing a baseball cap, sits alone at the corner table hovering over a book. I notice him because it's a Detroit Tigers cap.

"Hi," Kristen says, swooping in from behind me and scooping the coffee from her blotter. She takes a few quick sips and salutes with the cup. "Thank you for this." She shoves her laptop into her top drawer and pulls out a manila folder.

"What's that?"

"Info I wrote down when Daddy called."

"He came through?"

"I'm his firstborn, no matter what."

I pull a sheet of paper from the envelope and read. The Birmingham Police Justice Fund paid ten thousand dollars in 1929 to Clarita Elana Alvarez. The note includes a case number.

"Wow. This is super helpful. Thank you."

"Daddy asked a lot of questions about your story, and about you. He's worried about what you're writing. I bet he's already had one of his people work up a dossier on you."

"He does that kind of thing?"

"That's what insurance companies do. Check the veracity of people's stories."

"That's not what they say on the late-night commercials," I say facetiously.

Kristen rolls her eyes.

I stand and wave the envelope. "Thank you! I'll see what more I can find about this Alvarez woman."

"I'm sure Daddy's already doing that too. His curiosity was piqued."

"Maybe I should meet with him. What do you think?"

Kristen downs the rest of her coffee. "How did your date go with Darius?"

I sit again. "It wasn't a date. That's tonight."

"Well, how was the hanging out?"

"Great. His gym has all the amenities—including a pool."

"You swam?"

"I did."

Kristen stares for a couple of seconds, blinks, then busies herself by powering up her desktop PC before she looks at me again. I give a knowing squint.

"Go ahead. Say it."

"Say what?" she asks with faked innocence.

"Black girls don't swim."

Kristen gives an awkward grin.

"That's a stereotype." I feign indignity.

"The other Black women I'm friendly with never want to get their hair wet."

"I'll have you know I was on the college swim team."

"No shit!" Kristen says wide-eyed.

"You didn't answer my question about meeting your dad."

"I know."

"He has an in with the police. I called the chief's office yesterday to request an interview, but no one has returned my call. Maybe your dad can set me up with an appointment."

"I just get an uneasy feeling about the two of you meeting. You're my friend and I'd want you both to like each other. What if you don't?"

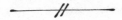

The office at Evangelical is in the administrative wing—well lit and inviting, with comfortable furniture. One wouldn't recognize it as a place for church business except for the large cross hanging in full view of visitors entering the door.

A young woman at the reception desk greets me and points to a chair where I'm to wait. There are four doors with stenciled names. One for the pastor, another for the assistant pastor. There's also a conference room, and one marked OFFICE OF THE CHURCH SECRETARY. The woman who exits *that* door, carrying an armful of papers, glances at me, then leans over the receptionist with instructions on how to handle the correspondence she's just piled on the woman's desk. Five minutes later she looks my way. I raise my eyebrows and the corners of my mouth, offering a friendly face.

She reenters her office without a word but immediately returns with a laptop, a folder, a thermos, and a cell phone.

"Miss McKenzie, follow me," she orders.

Mattie Robinson is a woman who runs a tight ship. I'm guessing even the pastor, on occasion, shrivels under her glare. She looks to be in her mid-seventies, attractively dressed in blue slacks with a cream blouse and a navy cardigan. She's wearing black loafer-type shoes, and a pair of glasses hangs around her neck. She leads me to the conference room, gestures to a seat across from her, and takes me in as I sit. She continues to stare for a few uncomfortable moments. I decide to act like the professional I am and take control of this meeting.

"Thank you for seeing me, Ms. Robinson."

"That's Mrs. Robinson. My husband's passed on but I'm still his wife."

So much for the control. "Yes, ma'am."

"You didn't give me the full story over the phone, Miss McKenzie," she says, glowering.

"Full story?"

"That you're searching for information about your great-grandfather who was murdered here in Birmingham in 1929. You think he's buried in our cemetery?"

I don't know what to say. I guess Monique has already filled her in on my assignment.

"I'm sorry. I'd planned on telling you more when I met with you today. Yes, I *am* researching a story about my great-grandfather, and looking for leads about his death. My family doesn't know where he's buried, and that prompted me to call the Black mortuaries in town. My visit to Maybury Mortuary led me to you."

I've given this explanation in one long, breathless statement. I inhale slowly and entwine my hands on the table, just like I did when Mrs. Pinter took attendance in fourth grade. Robinson and I hold each other's gaze until she turns her laptop toward me.

"This is what you're looking for," she says.

The laptop shows a diagram of the cemetery with a section highlighted. The diagram appears to be hand drawn with an amazing amount of detail.

"How large is this plot of land?" I ask.

"About a half acre."

The grave markings are numbered. Robinson tells me each corresponds to an identifier in her database. There are 180 notations. The area of the cemetery she has highlighted is labeled: GOD'S UNKNOWN CHILDREN. I look up and she gestures for me to hand over the laptop. She punches a couple of keys and turns it to me again with a larger view.

"That's where we buried poor souls our church took in who didn't have families, or for some reason couldn't be identified. I've looked at the records since your call, and I also spoke with Jameson. It turns out we have information on two of the men you're interested in."

Robinson removes a paper from the folder in front of her and slides it across the table. It's a copy of a ledger notation with two ID numbers and dates carefully hand printed. I stare at the ledger for a moment, then shake my head. I fall back against the chair with a sigh.

"I'm pretty sure neither of these men is my great-grandfather."

"How do you know?"

"I've already crossed Mr. Griggs off my list because one of his arms was amputated and he weighed over two hundred pounds. His physical description just doesn't fit. This John Doe's burial date is off. This man was buried in November. My great-grandfather died in September."

"Might your great-grandfather have used another name?"

"His name was Robert Harrington. He may have used the name Lee Harrington while he was in Birmingham."

"How old was he when he died?"

"Twenty-eight years old.

"He died much too young," Robinson says somberly.

When Robinson suggests she'll escort me to the cemetery, I think it's a waste of time, plus I think it might be too strenuous for her, but for this, like everything else, she has a plan. I wait only a few minutes for her to grab a windbreaker and a pair of boots.

"Let's go," she says, whizzing by me. I steal a look at the receptionist, still elbows-deep in correspondence, who gives me a toothy smile.

Robinson walks with purpose, and I have to step briskly to keep up with her. Mature trees with full branches keep the air chilly and the ground soggy in the cemetery yard. The cobblestone is uneven. Wet grass pushes through the footpaths. Robinson was right to get a jacket and boots—my flats are already muddy. She weaves through the headstones and suddenly stops to consult the paper map she carries. I almost plow into her. She points to her left and continues, this time at a slower pace. She pauses at a marker, a rectangular slab flush with the ground.

"This is the John Doe marker."

I squat next to it. A pine tree is etched into the stone above the date, which is obscured by mildew.

"It's a nice engraving."

Robinson nods solemnly, and I think she's about to say something when a man approaches us along the muddy path. I hadn't noticed him. He's old and walks with a cane. His striped suit and red-and-gray tie are dated. As he passes, Mrs. Robinson turns to look at him, and he tips his cap. The man smiles at me, and when he does the lines around his mouth reach up to the dark wrinkles near his eyes.

"Be careful, young lady, the way is slippery. Sometimes you have to retrace your steps," he says, then gracefully meanders through the headstones.

Mrs. Robinson and I watch him for a few seconds.

"Is that someone you know?" I ask.

"I've never seen him before, but the cemetery is open to the public on weekdays and we get visitors in here all the time."

"It's a nice place."

"Ms. McKenzie, I know you've crossed Mr. Griggs off your list, but he's buried just over there if you'd like to see his marker," she says, pointing toward an area of the cemetery we already passed.

"Sure. Why not?"

"Follow me."

We walk the path the visitor has just taken. Instead of a granite slab, there is a pink marble pillar. The column is about three feet high, faded from decades of weather, but the structure is still beautiful, and the subdued light piercing the canopy of trees reveals veins of gold in the stone.

"This is quite fancy," I say, looking around at the rows of thin gray stones. "Especially for this section of the cemetery."

"I see Mr. Griggs was originally buried with a simple headstone," Robinson says, looking at her tablet. "Normally, with a headstone of this size, we would have chosen another area for the plot. But Mrs. Alvarez had this monument delivered later."

My body jerks. "Did you say Alvarez? Clarita Alvarez?"

"You recognize the name?"

"Yes, ma'am." My hands begin to tremble, so I shove them into my sweater pockets. "What was her relationship to Griggs?"

"His wife. Didn't I say that? She was a longtime member of the church before she died. Oh, that must have been almost forty years ago." Robinson looks at me another long moment. "Cel said you were an intense young woman."

"Cel?"

"Cecile Clarke. We grew up together in this neighborhood. She called to tell me about your visit right after you left her place. So when you telephoned, well, it was like I was supposed to help you."

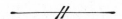

"What are you working on?" Kristen asks, sticking her head in the carrel door.

"Following up on one of the men buried at the Evangelical Church cemetery. That's where I was earlier."

"Do you think it's your great-grandfather?"

"No. It's not him. But guess who the man's wife is."

"Who?"

"Clarita Alvarez."

"That's the name my father gave you!" Kristen says excitedly. "The one who filed a complaint against your detective," she says, leaning over the desk.

"Bingo," I say, smiling smugly.

Kristen's eyebrows bunch together. "But that still doesn't connect the detective to your great-grandfather, does it?"

I stop smiling. "No."

"I stopped by because I spoke with Daddy again. He wants to meet you right away."

"Great. I'd like to speak with him."

"He wants to come to the library this afternoon. I told him I didn't even know if you'd be around. He's waiting for me to call back."

"If we could meet before three, I can do it. I want to leave a little early to get ready for my date."

For the next couple of hours, I lean into my laptop, staring at the digital archives of two more newspapers. So far no mention of Clarita Alvarez or her husband, Albert Griggs. At two forty-five, a message pops up on my screen. Kristen's father is downstairs in the second-floor conference room. I check myself in the mirror and grab my laptop, portfolio, and the folder I've organized on Simenon.

Stan Gleason rises from his seat when I come into the room. He's very tall. Maybe six four or six five. Handsome. He looks to be in his late fifties with a full head of brown hair starting to gray at the temples. He extends his hand and I meet his grip.

"Nice to meet you, young lady. I've heard good things about you from my daughter," he says with a glance at Kristen, who's slouched in her chair, her arms wrapped tightly around her and her face pinched.

"Kristen's been a great help to me and runs a top-notch operation here at the library," I say, sitting across from Gleason.

"So you're writing a news story? A historical piece that connects to the Black Lives Matter protests?"

"That's right."

"How did you come to focus on Birmingham?"

"I thought it was a good place to start because I know some of the movement leaders here." I'm omitting more than fibbing.

"Ms. Hendricks?" Gleason asks.

"Yes. She's one of the people I know."

"Well, that's why I thought we should meet. Perhaps I can be of assistance to you as you write your story. My company insures the police union and manages some of the city's liability accounts. I have very good relationships within the department."

"Kristen mentioned your offer of help, and I really appreciate it."

"What started you looking at Detective Simenon?" Gleason asks.

"I've been researching old newspapers, and his name is mentioned in a shooting incident. That led me to look at his record."

"Uh, where'd you get his record?"

All of a sudden I feel uneasy about this conversation. I stare at Gleason with his squared chin and ice-blue eyes. Kristen's eyes are the same, but they hold more curiosity and less intimidation. I want to slow things down.

"I'd rather not say. It's a confidential source. I'm sure you understand."

Gleason winces. He may understand but he doesn't like it. I decide to test his offer of help.

"Thanks for the information you passed on through Kristen about the police department's payment to Clarita Alvarez."

"Sure. Here's the documentation I found."

Gleason reaches into his inside jacket pocket and unfolds a paper. He lays it on the table and slides it toward me. It's a copy of the check I saw in Zach's garage.

"Ten thousand dollars. That was a lot of money in those days. Do you have any idea about the nature of the complaint?"

"I didn't find out much," Gleason says, "but it appears to be connected to an unlawful arrest."

I nod. That's not what it says on the personnel record. I wonder why he's lying. I glance at Kristen. She's shifted in her chair. She also knows the complaint charges Simenon with a sexual assault. I hope she gets it that my look means we're not arguing the point.

"I realize I'm asking about things that happened a long time ago, but part of my research involves examining the history of police shootings in this country. To that end, do you know if Detective Simenon was involved in other complaints, like citizen shootings?"

"I'd have to investigate," Gleason says. "Have you tried doing a legal search?"

"I have. So far, nothing's turned up. I was hoping Birmingham PD might allow me to look through their records," I say.

"There's not much incentive for them to let you go digging up cases of police shootings, is there?"

"But, Daddy, it should be public information," Kristen says with irritation. She'd been quiet up to now. Slumped in her chair, her energy seemingly drained from her body. Now she's leaning forward and banging her hand on the table. "McKenzie has a *right* to see those records!" She has her father's attention, and mine.

"It doesn't work like that, dear. You know that. The chief isn't going to open his files to some . . . northern reporter." He returns his attention to me. "I'm not sure I can help you with that, Miss McKenzie," he says ruefully.

"I'll just have to wait on the reply to our Freedom of Information Act request," I say.

"That's your best bet, especially if you're looking for something in particular," Gleason says with slightly raised brows.

Kristen's dad has returned to his fishing expedition, but I'm still not ready to reveal the purpose for my inquiries to someone who, frankly, makes me feel uneasy.

"I understand your father was also in the insurance business," I say.

"He started when he was only twenty years old," Gleason

195

responds with pride. "We've grown from an office of three people to employing almost six hundred people around the state." He stands abruptly. "I'm afraid I have to go. Good to meet you. I'll look further into this Alvarez payment and let you know what I learn."

Gleason has a firm grip and unflinching eyes. He's a forceful man. He scares me. As Kristen escorts her father out, I head for the stairs, longing for the comfort and safety of my small carrel. Fifteen minutes later she stands at my door.

"I bet your father almost always gets what he wants," I say.

"He usually does. My heart dropped when you told him you wouldn't divulge your source."

"What do you make of him saying the complaint against Simenon was for a false arrest?"

"I'm not sure. Maybe he doesn't know."

"How could he not know? I gotta tell you, I didn't exactly believe everything he said."

"Yeah, and that doesn't offend me. He keeps family affairs and business affairs very compartmentalized. He won't stand for Mother questioning him about his work."

"Wow. That sounds so 1950s."

TWENTY-FOUR

Black Love

1929

In many ways, the last few weeks have been the best of my life.

Fall has come early to Birmingham. Anna Kate points out the asters and marigolds wherever we go, and we have roses all over the house. She brings one or two home at a time and puts them in water, where they thrive before she transfers the plants to dirt. She's also received a dozen other cuttings from a neighbor's flower garden, and our windowsills are crowded with colorful pansies, camellias, and chrysanthemums.

Mama knew flowers too. So did Papa Tico. He would always tease that maybe Georgia had the best peaches in the world, but they would have to wait a long time to beat Haiti when it came to flowers. "Ayiti son bel peyi," he'd say in his Creole, before switching to English to make his point. "Our wildflowers are as luscious as de women." Then he'd throw back his head for a long, gummy laugh with his thick nappy hair and black skin gleaming in the sun.

Anna Kate sings while she separates the blooms, rotating the stalks, arranging bouquets in glass jars and tin cans. She has a good eye for symmetry and scale and the details of color and texture. She's creating beauty just as I do when I work at the wood. It's another reason to love her.

As promised, the architect of the mansion has found a full-time job for me at a small woodworks shop on the outskirts of town. I'm doing piecework, and I'm the only Negro employed there. The white man who owns the shop has set me up in a small shack away from the main building. That's all right with me. Carving is a solitary task. Last week, I designed and carved six beautiful doorknobs. The owner told me the client was quite pleased with the results. This week I've molded finials to top a magnificent four-post chestnut bed. I've already finished the four pieces, each a work of art, and today I spent the day rubbing stain into the wood. I work fast and I'm good at what I do, so I hope to keep this job a long time.

I also have a new car—a 1928 Ford Roadster. It's a solid family car, with a rumble seat for Mae. It draws little attention from the police or anyone else. I purchased it from a car dealer in town with the cash from the sale of the Franklin. With the money I had left over, I bought Mae a new dress for church, and Anna Kate a new hat and gloves.

It's only eight weeks before Anna Kate is due. She's furiously knitting tiny sweaters and booties, and I've taken on more of the home chores. She can't be on her feet long because her ankles are swollen, so we drive to do our shopping, using the list she puts together. Often she stays in the car with Mae while I negotiate with the butcher over the cost of a cut of meat, and select the fruits and vegetables at the produce stand. In the evening, after dinner, I help with preparations for the next evening's meal and my box lunch.

"I'm ready for bed, Robert," Anna Kate says. It's my signal to pull down the Murphy bed. She retires early these days, soon after Mae is asleep.

The use of a new first name to foil the police detective hasn't worked for her, but others have adopted it easily. My new boss and the man I bought the car from know me as Lee. Even our landlady didn't think twice when I paid this month's rent using my new name.

Anna Kate is large, and waddles, and I help her to the bed. She says she feels ugly, but she could never be anything but beautiful. She leans back on several pillows—it's the only position that allows her to sleep at night—and complains she can't moisturize her feet anymore or paint her toes. So almost every night I rub her feet, and once a week I paint her nails. "It makes me feel like a movie star." She giggles as I dab the bright red color onto the tips of her toes. It has become our substitute for marital relations. That's not been easy for me, but it's the best thing to do for now.

Anna Kate and Mae are sleeping peacefully while I carve a cradle for the new baby. I'm making it out of a wonderful piece of maple. My employer took thirty cents out of my pay for the flawless wood left over from a chest of drawers. When I finish the cradle I'll begin on a small dresser.

I pursued the joys of being single as much as any man could, and I knew what I was trading when I married. I pause in my sanding to listen to the sounds of my family sleeping. Sometimes I'm restless, but the easy and satisfying comfort and connection to my wife, daughter, and our expected baby are what really makes life worth living.

TWENTY-FIVE

———◆———

2019

Darius picks me up at six thirty on the dot. I left the library early to get my eyebrows waxed, and I've washed my naturally curly hair with a lavender-scented shampoo. I'm glad I had the foresight to pack my peach-colored dress. I know it shows off my curves. I'm wearing flat sandals but the dress is short enough, and my legs long enough, to give the outfit a good line. To accessorize I've chosen a simple gold chain with a small cross. It was an impulse. But I believe God is watching over me in Birmingham, and I don't take that for granted.

Darius wears a gray suit that clings to his athletic body and makes him look like John Legend with locs. His brown shoes complement his peach tie. He is deliciously handsome and I'm having trouble holding back lascivious thoughts. I hope he doesn't notice.

"We look color coordinated," he says, smiling.

"I thought you drove an SUV," I say when he opens the door to an Audi convertible.

"That's my work car. The city leases it for me because I have to be in the field all the time. This is my personal car. You like it?"

"I do. The A3, right?"

"Do you know something about everything?"

"No. But, you know. Detroit. The auto show," I say, laughing.

"I left the top down. Will that mess with your hair?"

"Well, let's put it up for now, and put it down on the way back?"

Darius raises an eyebrow slightly and smiles. "Sounds like a plan."

Our first stop is a casino. Neither of us is much of a gambler, it turns out, but it's fun to walk around as a couple, and we sit side by side to play the dollar slots for about twenty minutes. We order a couple of scotches at one of the bars and stand with a small group that is watching a poker game on a video board.

"You know the game?" he asks.

"I can't play poker. I don't have the face for it."

He laughs. "I actually think you hold your cards pretty close to the chest."

"I'd have to count more on luck than skills when it comes to poker."

"I'll give you a tutorial."

As we watch a game of Texas Hold'em, Darius explains the sequence of play and the possible scenario of each player's bet.

"How come you know so much about poker? Are you a down-low card shark?"

He laughs. "No. I like cards, but I don't get to play very often. I learned in college. I didn't do sports. I wasn't good enough, but I'm good at poker."

"I'll keep that in mind."

We stay at the casino for an hour. Combined we've lost thirty dollars. Then we're back in the car to make our eight-thirty dinner reservation.

Darius has reserved space at a restaurant offering a unique private dining experience. The maître d' greets us warmly and personally escorts us to the patio. "We call these dining cocoons," he says. "We have only four of them and they're very popular. You have complete privacy but can still enjoy the night air."

I look up again at the brilliant full moon and feel a shiver of excitement before stepping into the tent-like structure enclosed by semiopaque material at the entrance. A crescent table sits in front of a luxurious high-backed oval sofa. Soft music wafts from two tiny speakers mounted on side posts, soft lights line the crossbeam above, and flickering floor candles give the cocoon a cozy, sexy vibe. There is already a bottle of champagne cooling on a small side table. The maître d' pours the first glass of bubbly.

"Your menu is here." He presents a tablet device. "Press this button when you want an attendant. Otherwise, you will not be disturbed," he says and exits.

"This is magnificent," I say. "Especially after the casino. It's peaceful, beautiful, and romantic, and it's nice to be outside."

"I wanted the evening to be special," Darius says.

"You've exceeded my expectations."

He holds his champagne flute aloft. I hold my glass high too.

"The end is in the beginning and lies far ahead," he toasts.

We clink our flutes and drink.

"Did you make that up?" I ask.

"It's a quote from Ralph Ellison. He's a personal hero of mine."

"What does it mean?"

"To me it means everything has a beginning and an end, but it's the in-between that counts."

"Then here's to new beginnings," I add.

Darius is attentive and thoughtful, and our conversation flows free and easy. We've ordered appetizers and when the attendant departs, Darius leans over to kiss me. Heat starts in my tummy and spreads in all directions. Our lips and tongue explore, and before we separate, he cups my hair and strokes my face. I'm breathless as I lean back. "See," he says, taking my hand. "*This* is a date."

Over appetizers, we select our main course, chat, and drink more bubbly. Darius kisses me again. This time we both lean into the sofa and he slips his arm around my waist. I encourage him by wrapping my arms around his neck. When the string of overhead lights begins to flicker, we pull apart and adjust our clothes. It's the signal our attendant is approaching.

Dinner is superb. I've ordered a trout fillet topped with shrimp scampi. Darius digs into a Cajun chicken and pasta dish. We share a carafe of prosecco. It's crisp and light. We talk more about our previous relationships. Darius asks about Garrett and tells me why he broke off his engagement. He offers a forkful of pasta, I accept, and he lifts the fork to my mouth. He watches me chew and smiles. "You have beautiful lips," he says.

When we've finished our meal, Darius orders a cognac for himself.

"What would you like?" he asks.

"Maybe something nonalcoholic now, like a sparkling water with lime."

"Okay. And let's split a dessert. Do you like bread pudding? They make a really good one. It does have a bit of bourbon in it."

"That'll be fine."

The attendant clears our dishes. "Would you like a cigar, sir? For after dessert," she asks.

Darius looks at me, then shakes his head. "No, not tonight."

The bread pudding is divine. The mix of champagne and wine and rich food puts me in a mellow mood. Darius takes off his jacket and I've removed my sandals. Our kissing leads to petting, and I can feel the warmth of his hands through my dress. Suddenly he pulls back. I'm surprised.

"Why don't I give you a foot rub?"

"A foot rub? You mean like Eddie Murphy in *Boomerang*?" I ask.

Darius laughs. "That's an old-school classic. No, I just think it's safer for both of us if I focus on your feet."

"How do you know my toes aren't my erogenous zone?" I ask playfully.

"Are they?" he responds with raised eyebrows.

"Why don't you take me to my place and find out."

THE RIDE HOME WITH THE TOP DOWN ADDS TO MY RUSH. I RE-cline against the headrest to take in the moon's glow. Darius tunes the radio to the Aretha Franklin channel and we both sing as we speed along the freeway. Darius has a good voice, and he even belts out "A Natural Woman" in a falsetto, which makes me laugh. Soon we are both giggling, and I reach over to rub his leg. His mirth ends and he looks at me with lust in his eyes.

"Don't do that or I'll veer off the road," he warns.

When we get to my rental house we begin awkwardly. In the quiet of the living room, alone with him in the semidarkness, I remind myself that I've only known Darius for seven days. He asks for a glass of water, and during the few seconds of separation I give myself a pep talk. *You know you want to do this. Trust your instincts.* After a few sips of water, we're soon kissing again, and the urgency I feel for him catches me off guard. I totally abandon any doubt and give into his musky scent and strength as he lifts me in his arms and carries me to the bedroom.

Darius leaves my bed a few hours later, excusing himself to the bathroom, while I don a robe and pick up our discarded clothes. We each have early morning meetings, and though we both admitted to envisioning the evening ending in sex, we hadn't intended to spend the night together. When he returns to the bedroom I hold out his suit jacket.

"I couldn't find your tie," I say.

"I stuffed it into my pocket. I had a good time tonight, Meg. You know what I mean. Even before the sex."

"I wanted to be with you. I know we've just met each other, but . . ."

There isn't much more I can say. I could let myself fall for Darius, but that's not why I've come to Birmingham. I have a job to do. I'm more determined than ever to see where my investigation leads, then I'm returning home to Detroit.

"I know what you mean. I'll call you." He turns to leave, then stops and turns back. He takes my hand and kisses my palm. "Tomorrow, I mean, or rather later today. I'll be in touch. Promise."

TWENTY-SIX

A Night Out

1929

The latest letter from Anna Kate's mother says the police have not come around again to ask about my whereabouts. The report of a young white man seriously injured following a Saturday night altercation with a Negro on Central Avenue hasn't been mentioned in the papers for weeks. My mother-in-law writes that maybe the threat of discovery is over.

I've stayed home every evening for three weeks straight. Tonight I'm antsy, and I need to scratch the itch with a bit of nightlife. Anna Kate pouts when I tell her I'm going out to play cards and maybe shoot a game of pool. But after I help her into bed, give her a long foot rub, and make her a cup of tea, she offers a kiss.

I step into the backyard of the boardinghouse. It feels good out tonight, and I don't have to work tomorrow. The air smells of blooming shrubs and trees, and the moon is close to full. I'm wearing a gray-striped suit, a white shirt, and my gray tie with red stripes. I've polished my black shoes to such a shine that I see the reflection of moonlight when I look at my feet. My new car might not be a luxury model but I take good care of her, as I did the Franklin. When I remove the tarp the wax job still looks good. The tires aren't whitewalls, but the wheels and spokes are polished, and all the chrome on the car gleams. I turn over the engine and steer into the heart of Fourth Avenue North feeling a wave of excitement. I'm lucky to find a parking space right in front of Griggs Ballroom. It's still early, just nine o'clock, but there will already be a card game under way.

Clarita greets me at the door, admonishes me for my absence, and admires my suit. "Expensive," she says, touching the fabric on my lapel. The front room is busy. Most of the dining tables are occupied, and there is the unmistakable smell of chitlings coming from the kitchen. A few couples are dancing to a ragtime tune on the player piano, and there is a pool game in progress at one of the two tables. Griggs is in his normal sullen mood. I buy the required red and green tickets, then move toward the back room and my poker game. Before I get halfway, Nedra grabs me by the arm.

"No dance tonight, Bobby?"

"No time for a dance tonight, beautiful, I have money to lose in the back room."

"Why don't you like me anymore?"

"I like you, it's just that I have a baby on the way, a wife, and a new job, and all three of them get most of my attention these days."

She forms her bright red lips into a pout, then slowly strokes my tie, moving her hand from my throat all the way to my belt buckle, where she leaves it. I cup her shoulders and give her a gentle push back.

"I'm not interested, Nedra."

207

In an instant her eyes turn wicked mean and her lips curve into a sneer.

"You'll be sorry for that, Bobby. Who do you think you are, you uppity peacock?"

She spits out the words and I want to slap her for what she's said, but I know better. I've never seen her so angry. I'm angry too. She spins and walks away. Her hips swivel like the valve gear on a steam locomotive moving twenty miles per hour.

I enter the back room and stop to take it in. Despite Nedra's outburst, it's good to be out on the town. Eight bare bulbs hanging from the rafters give just enough light to reflect the stale smoke swirling through the air. The bar area takes up two-thirds of the space—the bar itself made up of four eight-foot pieces of pine nailed to five wood barrels. Each end of the bar holds a kerosene lantern. Behind it, two wood tubs are stocked with blocks of ice and drink glasses. The room's center holds eight barrel-top tables with candles, forming a semicircle that faces a makeshift stage. The straight-backed chairs are really just carved tree trunks. Only half the tables are occupied. A trumpet player is warming up with some slow tunes, but before the night is out he'll be playing hot. One bartender is at work, and a girl in satiny shorts and top, wearing ankle-strap heels, is serving the table guests. Another similarly dressed girl approaches me for my drink order—a scotch. I head to the rear. Before I step through the beaded curtains of the poker room I look over my shoulder. By the time I leave, in a few hours, this place will be elbow to elbow with high-lifers.

The game room has been walled into a rear corner. Only the back table has action tonight, and heads turn as I rattle the curtain with my entrance. The two octagon-shaped card tables are well-made, in pine, but the felt surfaces are worn, puckered, and covered in cigarette burns and drink stains in some places. The chairs are similar to the ones in the bar.

The dealer is a regular. Honest. Nimble hands. With a good memory for cards, people, and names.

"Harrington," he says as I sit.

"Mr. Colt," I reply. His name—the only one I know—refers to the .44 revolver he keeps stashed under the table. I've seen him brandish it just once, quickly ending a disagreement between two players that might have become dangerous.

This is not a high-rollers game. The men, and occasional women, who play cards in Griggs's back room are working people—most without the obligations of family or indebtedness. But these poker games host a cross section of Birmingham's Negro population. The banker has been known to play cards here, as has the butcher, and the man who runs the numbers in Tuxedo Junction. Sometimes the stakes get expensive, but even then I've rarely seen anyone lose more than twenty dollars. That's the cost of a month's worth of groceries.

Tonight's game is five-card draw. It's an easy game for beginners, and good to start off with for the night. There are five of us at the table, and to my mind three players seem ripe for the taking.

A man who thinks himself a dandy appraises my suit. His is a handsome brown tweed, which he wears with a round-collared shirt fastened with a stick pin. It's a good look, but the tie is too cheap to fit the quality of his jacket. Across the table from me is a man I know as the farmer. He's a regular. When he picks up his cards they disappear in his beefy grip. He always wears a cap and a blue kerchief around his neck. He's never picked up the tricks of the game and I always win money from him. The third player is a thin, light-skinned dude. He's a fidgeter. A silver toothpick dangles from his mouth, and he wears a signet ring on each pinky. He seems to me better suited to dice, or the dog races, because he can't seem to sit still. The fourth man is middle-aged, wearing a short-sleeved shirt under a vest. He has bulging biceps and a head too small for his shoulders. He introduces himself as Sam. I can't read Sam. He may be my only rival tonight.

We've all agreed to a fifty-cent ante, and after every four games, a quarter tip for the dealer. For the first three hands my cards are shit, and I'm down two dollars. So I sit out the next two hands, sip on my scotch and water, and hope my luck will change. On the next game in, I'm dealt two queens, and I bet a buck. Everyone else follows suit. I ask for three cards, the farmer takes three, the twitchy dude and the dandy draw two, and Sam asks for a single card. I eye him and he stares back. He could be trying to represent more than he has. I have the pair of queens and a king kicker. I bet another buck. The farmer calls my bet; the dandy folds. Sam calls and raises another dollar. I'm guessing the farmer has a low pair, but he bets anyway. The fidgeter can't keep his fingers from shaking. He has either a good hand or nothing at all. After a couple of moments of fitful thinking, he folds. I'm still staring at Sam. He's averted his eyes and hasn't moved a muscle. I paid attention while I sat out the game. He's been a conservative player up to now. I think he has at least a strong pair, maybe even three of a kind. I won't know unless I call. When I do, he lays down triple eights. I shake my head and throw in my cards.

On the next two hands, I win a seven-dollar pot and an eight-dollar pot. I'm on a roll. I buy a round of drinks for the table. Then the fun is over.

When the gunshots sound they are followed by a split second of heart-stopping quiet. Then the thunderous screech of the back-room door being shattered by a battering ram propels us all to our feet. There are screams from bar patrons in the neighboring room, and another barrage of gunfire.

The main door doesn't give on the first hit, allowing those of us with experience time to exit through the chaos. Colt grabs his gun, scoops up his tips, and heads to a back door. I snatch my winnings from the table and follow him; the farmer slips in line behind me. The door on the back wall leads to a hallway and, beyond that, an alley, which both Colt and I know is already guarded by police. Colt reaches to his waistband to free his long-barreled revolver, and I remove mine from my ankle holster. When the farmer sees our guns he shakes his head and bolts for the alley exit. Colt turns the other way, dashing up a set of rickety wood stairs with me on his heels. The stairs lead to an unsteady catwalk and we inch our way along the wall, careful to avoid the gaping holes and the thirty-foot drop to the floor. Gunfire still rattles inside the ballroom, and there are shouts and screams from outside. Suddenly the alley door slams open. Night air, spotlights, and a squad of policemen rush through. Colt and I drop to our knees on the wobbly catwalk and hold our breath. The cops below us are cackling, stomping, hyped-up on adrenaline.

"Let's get them niggers," one of them screams.

"Shit," Colt whispers.

A flashlight beam bounces along the wall behind us and we lie flat, pressing ourselves against the rough-hewn floor of the scaffolding and burying our faces in our extended arms. I feel the cold surface against my cheek and sniff at the dank, rotting wood. It smells like a knotty pine. I had no idea Colt was a religious man, but he's muttering the twenty-third psalm and I add my whispered recitation. Finally, after what seems like fifteen minutes, the lights and voices subside. Colt lifts to his knees. I follow suit. We slow crawl the last ten yards to a door that opens onto the upper floor of the adjacent building and push through. We sit for a couple of minutes to catch our breath and listen for movement.

This corner warehouse is a dry cleaner, laundry, and tailor shop. I believe the man who owns the place sleeps on the premises. "We have to be quiet," I say. Colt and I creep along the floorboards past boxes of buttons, paper bags, detergent, pallets of fabric, and a dozen sewing machines. When we reach the steel door that leads to the fire escape Colt inches it open and pauses. He extends his gun through the crack, then waits a full minute before he pokes his head beyond the opening. He signals an all clear. We cautiously descend the stairs to Seventeenth Street, still hearing shouts from the alley and seeing the flashing lights of patrol cars on busy Fourth Avenue. At street level, Colt returns his revolver to his back waistband and turns to me.

"That was close, man."

"Yeah. It was," I say. "Thanks for leading the way out."

"Well, I'm breaking off here."

"Yeah. I'm headed home as soon as I can get to my car."

"Stay safe, Harrington," Colt says. He walks across the street and disappears into the shadows.

I brush off my jacket and pants and use my handkerchief to wipe my brow. The Lord has been with me tonight, and I'm counting on him to get me the rest of the way home.

TWENTY-SEVEN

2019

The names Clarita Alvarez and Albert Griggs didn't show up at all in my LexisNexis query, so I'm going through the painstaking work of another online newspaper search. After a straight two and a half hours I have a low-grade headache. I know some of it is eye strain, but the rest is my worry about Darius's reaction to last night.

I stand a discreet distance from Kristen's desk while she finishes up a phone call. The city room is empty this morning except for the same man I saw yesterday, in the Tigers cap, sitting at the corner. Kristen looks up at me and I silently mouth, "I need to talk to you," pointing to my chest and then her for emphasis. She raises a "wait just a minute" finger. She's mostly been listening to the person on the other end of her call, but now she's whispering, scowling, and gesturing. She disconnects with a push of a button and drops the phone on her desk.

"I could use some fresh air," I say to Kristen.

"Me too," she says, glancing at the lone visitor. "Let me get someone to staff the room."

"Okay. Meet you outside."

It's a brilliant fall day. The sun feels good and my headache is already subsiding. Kristen joins me on the sidewalk in full Goth regalia, and she's added a floppy black hat to her outfit.

"Let's go," I say, walking.

"Hey, hold on a minute, McKenzie. Where are we going?"

"Starbucks. I'm buying."

I pause to let Kristen catch up. The people we pass on the sidewalk stare brazenly at her clothing, and she seems to enjoy the attention.

"God, I really needed to get out of there," I say. "If I have to look at one more old newspaper I'll stand on the desk and scream."

"In that case, I'd have to call security to escort you from the library," Kristen deadpans.

I give her a smirk.

Now with coffees, and sharing a two-pack of madeleines, we sit on a bench in Linn Park watching the pedestrian and foot traffic.

"That was my father on the phone before we left," she says sourly.

"You seemed pretty upset."

"Yeah. I'll tell you about it, but first I'd rather talk about something pleasant. How was your date with Darius?"

My headache returns. I take another long sip of coffee before I answer.

"It was magical."

"Magical? Damn."

"First we went to a casino, gambled a bit and had a drink,

then we went to a place called Mélange for dinner. Have you heard of it?"

"No. It must be new."

"I think it is. They have these private outside dining tents. Romantic furnishings, soft lights and music, and no one interrupts you unless you ring a buzzer. We had prosecco, a wonderful dinner and dessert, and wine."

"And?"

"And we kissed a lot, and drove home with the top down on his car, and the moon was full."

"Hmm-hmm. And?"

"I wanted him and he wanted me. And now I hope he doesn't think I'm too easy," I say, tugging at my hair.

"Wow," Kristen says.

We quietly chew our madeleines. I believe Kristen's trying to imagine the sex, but I'm remembering it vividly.

"Did he stay over?"

"He didn't. When he left he kissed my hand and said he'd call me today."

"Have you heard from him yet?"

I shake my head.

"Well, he'll call. Probably."

Across the street I see a guy staring in our direction. I can't really see his face, but he looks like the man in the baseball cap back at the library.

"Isn't that the guy who was sitting in the city room?" I say pointing. "He was staring at us just now."

"Really?" Kristen twists to look, but the man has turned away. She shrugs. "So you want to know what my father said?"

I look at her scowl. "Maybe not. He didn't like me, did he?"

"He called you a troublemaker. Says you're trying to make Birmingham look bad, and he doesn't want me to give you any more library resources."

"Guess that means he won't be calling the chief on my behalf," I say sarcastically. "Are you kicking me out of my carrel?"

"Of course not. Daddy is not the boss of me."

I've almost finished my coffee, and the sun has done worlds for my headache, but I can't put off all the work on my desk. "We should probably head back so I can peer into a monitor some more," I say resignedly.

Kristen and I are walking slowly, neither of us eager to leave the low humidity and autumn sky for air-conditioning and fluorescent lights—nor to sit with our worries.

"Thinking about your investigation or Darius?"

"Both."

"Darius will call."

"What if now that we've slept together, he's lost interest?"

"I doubt that's the case, but even if it were you didn't come here to fall in love."

"I'm *not* in love."

"So you say."

Neither of us is paying much attention as we cross the street in the middle of the block. I look up at the sound of a speeding vehicle heading toward us. It takes only a heartbeat to realize the driver isn't going to stop. Panic thumps my chest and I drop the coffee.

"Quick!" I scream to Kristen and shove her, a split second ahead of me, between two parked cars, where we both trip over the curb, cringing in disbelief.

A white van sideswipes the parked car in front of us with the sickening sound of metal scraping on metal, then doesn't even slow as it careens up the street.

"What the hell!" Kristen shouts. I jump to my feet and run up the sidewalk trying to see the license plate number, but there is no plate. The van lurches around the next corner, barely missing another pedestrian.

I turn back to Kristen. Several people are leaning over her on the pavement, and others are inspecting the damaged car. Two moms pushing baby carriages help Kristen to her feet. I rush to her.

"Are you okay?"

"I think I've twisted my ankle."

In a couple of minutes Kristen can put her full weight on her ankle without too much pain. The mail carrier, who was making his rounds and saw the whole thing, inches closer.

"What was that all about?" he asks.

"I have no idea. Some crazy driver."

"He seemed to purposely aim the van at you two," he says with outrage.

"Maybe a drunk driver," I say.

The postman shakes his head in disgust. He points at Kristen. "I've seen you before. You work at the library. You okay?"

We assure the mailman and the small group of onlookers gathered around us that we're both fine and for a few minutes join them in denouncing a morally lapsed culture in which callous and self-centered drivers won't even stop at the scene of an accident. Then we all disperse.

"You sure that ankle doesn't need medical attention?" I ask Kristen as we slow walk the two blocks to the library.

"No, it's all right. But I'm switching into tennis shoes when I get back."

"I've seen a van like that before," I confess to Kristen.

"What do you mean?"

"I've noticed it a couple of times when I've been out. I think it followed me when I drove to the mortuary, and it might have been parked down the street from the Airbnb."

Kristen looks concerned. "Don't you think you should call the police?"

I shrug.

"I meant to ask why you texted me about that neo-Nazi song. What was that all about?"

I shake my head. "Nothing really, just a crank call. The guy basically told me to get out of town," I say, laughing.

Kristen doesn't laugh. She stops on the sidewalk and stares at me open-mouthed. "You need to call the police."

"What would I tell them? That I got a crank call, and now I think a white van is following me. I didn't see the driver's face, and I don't even have a plate number."

"Well, at least tell Darius. When he phones. He'll know what to do."

TWENTY-EIGHT

Wake-Up Call

1929

I've finally caught my breath after the lucky escape from the poker room. I back into the shadow of a doorway and return my pistol to my ankle holster. Colt has already retreated from the noisy scene of the police raid, but I can't. My car is parked in front of Griggs Ballroom.

Lights from a half dozen patrol cars flood the front of the building and the street. Drawn by the gunfire and the police presence, a crowd has gathered and I mix in with the bystanders. The diners and dancers who were questioned before being released are among the group outside. Six policemen carrying billy clubs hold back the growing crowd. Two paddy wagons idle on the street with headlights on and doors wide open. Those vehicles are soon joined by two ambulances. I can't move the car for a while.

I listen as some of the onlookers describe the moment a dozen cops stormed through the front door, pushing Clarita and others aside, and advancing to the back room. The scene was chaotic, with staff scrambling, customers scattering, and police upending tables. Everyone was shouting. The cops used their batons on anyone who dared step into their path as they rushed to the rear door they knew separated the legitimate business from the illegal liquor sales and gambling on the other side.

"Someone must have tipped them off," one fellow says.

"Yeah, man," a second guy agrees. "They sure knew what they were looking for."

"I can't stand a goddamned snitch," the first man replies.

According to these eyewitnesses, Griggs left the ticket booth with his sawed-off shotgun raised and shouting Clarita's name. When he saw two policemen fling his wife to the floor, he fired both barrels into the advancing line of blue uniforms. The police returned fire, striking Griggs and several other patrons. That assault prompted more gunfire from dance-hall security.

"Bullets were flying everywhere," one of the girl dancers says, crying. A man in a tuxedo jacket tries to comfort her.

"I saw three cops go down, so you know there will be hell to pay," another man says.

The rumor among the people nearest me is that three people are dead and six have been badly wounded. The dead include Albert Griggs.

One by one, officers exit the building with those who have been arrested. The cops shove them roughly through the crowd and into to the waiting paddy wagons. I recognize two of those being detained as ballroom security guards. The backroom bartender is brought out next and then the two bar waitresses. Sam, the new cardplayer, along with the dandy, are pushed into one of the vehicles. I don't see the others. I wonder about the twitchy, light-skinned guy. My money is on him as the informer.

Next Clarita appears in the doorway in handcuffs. Her dress

is torn and her hair disheveled. She's being manhandled by two officers. One slams her knuckles with a billy club, and she screams. She's hysterical. Thrashing, struggling, digging in her heels, and shouting "murderers" at the officers on the scene. The crowd grows restless at the sight of Clarita's passion, and when she is finally dragged to a paddy wagon, several men in the crowd are hollering at the police. I shout too. I'm livid about Clarita being treated so roughly, and despite Griggs's hard feelings toward me, I'm angry he's been killed.

Movement at the front of the building catches my eye and I turn to see Nedra stepping out the door—without handcuffs—followed by a uniformed officer. Rather than being placed in the wagon or a patrol car, she's escorted beyond the restless swarm of onlookers. I squirm my way to the rear of the crowd, hovering near the fringes, to see where she's being taken. A dark blue Chevy is parked under the streetlamp across the street. I recognize the large man in the overcoat and fedora standing at the car's back door. He's the plainclothes cop who was with Nedra three weeks ago and watched as I drove away in the Franklin.

She greets the big man with a touch on the arm, then just before she enters the sedan, she casually looks back and catches my eye. She locks onto me, and in that moment I know this half-white female devil is the informant. Not the twitchy man. By the time her face contorts and she points in my direction, I recede into what is now a mob of angry colored people. I've been fortunate so far—escaped the back room unseen, and with my winnings—luckier than the others who have been arrested and those who have lost their lives.

I watch Nedra and the man confer, then he grips her arm and they recross the street. He says something to one of the officers controlling the agitated crowd, then the three of them begin walking through the throng. Panic rises in my chest. They're looking for me. Nedra said I'd be sorry by the night's end. I'll do everything in my power to make sure she's wrong.

I keep my eye on Nedra and her law enforcement companions as they search for me. In this dense gathering I'll be difficult to spot, and I shuffle and sidewind through the boisterous mob to escape their attention.

Someone yells, "No. Don't do it!" and I turn in time to see a man who had earlier been shouting and cursing at the police throw a rock. His missile hits home and one of the cops guarding the entrance of the ballroom drops to the pavement. Without hesitation, the fallen officer's partner draws his gun and shoots into the crowd, striking the rock thrower. He lies unmoving on the cobblestones.

The next seconds tick in slow motion. First there is an eerie stillness as every Black person inhales a frightened breath, then a roar of mayhem that engulfs the block. The massive mob divides into two swarms of Black humanity running in opposite directions. Angry officers outside are joined by police who were inside the club. They all converge on the sidewalk and street. Some of them, screaming and bellowing, give chase after those fleeing and whale away with their billy clubs on those who fall or are too slow. I've lost track of Nedra and the detective, and I'm being pushed away from the ballroom by the panicked mob. At an intersection I manage to dart to the sidewalk and duck into a doorway to avoid the jostle of those fleeing. It's darker here and the evasion works, as I go unnoticed by the police rushing past my hiding place. After a few minutes I move—hugging the brick buildings—and return to the side street where I'd earlier escaped from the poker room.

I kneel behind a parked truck, my heart beating in my throat. From this vantage point I can see the activity outside the ballroom.

Patrol cars now barricade Fourth Avenue from both ends. Police are circled around the injured cop, who is on his feet and talking. Nedra and her detective boyfriend are among them.

I watch as two medics exit with Griggs's body on a stretcher. I recognize his girth under the bloodstained sheet that covers him. He's placed in the first ambulance. Two other covered bodies are extracted from the building and carried to the second ambulance. Finally, the rock thrower's body is lifted from the street and onto a stretcher and placed alongside Griggs. I stay put until both ambulances have driven away and the menacing detective has returned to his vehicle with Nedra in tow.

The crowd is fully dispersed, but several people are still in conversation near my car. Two men are writing in notebooks; another man is taking pictures of the scene. The flash of lightbulbs repeatedly flares and slowly fades. Patrol cars still block Fourth Avenue, but a work crew has been brought in to board up the windows of the ballroom, and street sweepers are hosing down the street. I don't dare go back for my car. Fortunately, other vehicles are parked on the street, and it won't stand out. I'll retrieve it tomorrow.

I remember Clarita being dragged, and Griggs covered in a bloody sheet. I shudder. I wonder if my fellow cardplayers, especially the farmer, managed to escape through the alley. I hope so.

I shudder again thinking of what I'll say to Anna Kate. She'll know something's happened as soon as she sees my face, and I'll have to tell her about tonight's trouble. It seems to follow me wherever I go.

I pull my collar up and my cap down. The moon lights my walk to the boardinghouse.

TWENTY-NINE

2019

The ball-capped visitor isn't around when we return to the city room, but he's left his book on the table. Kristen limps to her locker for sneakers. I'm curious about what the man has been reading. It's a volume of Birmingham photographs from the turn of the century.

I thumb through the pages. Mining scenes dominate the book but there are also pictures of schools, homes, cityscapes, and workers. The sepia prints show busy cobblestoned streets crammed with pedestrians and various modes of transportation. Birmingham was never more vibrant than when its dominance in the steel industry gave the city license to dub itself the "Pittsburgh of the South."

The segregated Birmingham depicted in this book provides an insight into not only race relations but also class differences. Black and white working poor—itinerant farmers, laborers, and mill workers—lived in similar conditions. Photo after photo portrays farm families in front of dilapidated clapboard structures and dirt yards. Negro and white steelworkers, dressed alike in worn denim and dirt-smeared undershirts, have the same wearied look and slumped shoulders. Sadly, some of these workers are children. Only the faces of the youngest on these pages—Black and white—show any joy or expectancy.

I close my eyes for a moment, transporting myself to these earlier times. I imagine Grandma looking like the little girl wearing white anklet socks and braided hair. Great-Grandpa's rooming house might have had windows looking out at the busy streets shown in this book, and he would certainly have dressed in similar work clothes. As a carpenter he might have avoided the dirt and grime of the quarry or foundry, but he would have returned home each night with paint- and varnish-stained fingers, and sawdust sticking to his skin.

"Can I borrow this book?"

Kristen's sitting sideways at her desk, her ankle elevated on a plastic crate. She's wearing sneakers.

"Should I just check it out online?"

She turns to the back cover. "Is this the book the man had at the corner table?"

"I believe so."

"This volume isn't part of the city collection. But I can still check it out for you."

I watch Kristen's nimble fingers on her keyboard. "Okay. You're all set, but it's only an overnight checkout."

"Got it. Thanks. How's the ankle feel?"

Kristen wags her hand like a waddling duck. "So-so."

I take the stairs up to my carrel and through the glass I see a vase of long-stemmed yellow roses on the desk. The mailroom staff must have delivered them while I was away. I hold my breath as I open the door and sit searching for the bouquet's accompanying card. The sentiment isn't offered in a lot of words; it's simply signed: *Yours, Darius.*

That's more than enough for me.

I want to thank him for the flowers, but he doesn't pick up his phone or respond to my text. I text Kristen with a flowers emoticon followed by a happy face. The bouquet's fragrance wafts through the carrel and I take in a very deep breath. Then I force myself back to the archives. It's a day I can't really stop and smell the roses.

I get a hit on the Griggs search in the *Alabama Reporter. Finally!*

It's an eighth-page advertisement for a nightclub—a hand-drawn depiction of a two-story building with a large striped awning. The ballroom promotes a full-service restaurant and dance hall. Albert Griggs is listed as the proprietor, and the business isn't far from the boardinghouse where my great-grandparents lived. Once I know what I'm looking for, I find ads for Griggs Ballroom going back as far as 1924. And later find a report of a police raid on the ballroom in August of 1929. The story quotes an unnamed police official who says the raid was the result of a tip about illegal gambling and alcohol sales. Dozens were arrested and four people were killed—including Griggs.

I pull out the article I've found in the Rankins' basement archives, which connects Simenon's promotion to a nightclub raid. *This has got to be the same* .

The Birmingham white pages online directory shows zero results on a current listing for Griggs.

I stand and stretch and lean on the edge of the desk next to my roses. I think of Darius for a moment, then turn my focus to the second citizen complaint against Simenon, one made by George Freeman, identified as a Black man. There's an address for Freeman on the complaint form, and it's dated October 7, 1929.

I count eighty-five George Freemans in the Birmingham directory. I include the North Birmingham address from the complaint and get a listing for Carrie Freeman. *Date of Birth: 11/24/ 1927.* There's a lengthy list of relatives associated with the listing, including two named George. I pay extra for a full search, which results in a credit report for Carrie Freeman and two legal documents. In 1959, an Ellis G. Freeman was sentenced to five years at the Draper Correctional Facility. The other record is a property sale, in 1944, made in the name of Esther Freeman. I call the most recent telephone number in the records, and an older woman answers.

"Hello, I'm a reporter with the *Detroit Free Press*. May I speak to Mrs. Carrie Freeman?"

"This is Mrs. Freeman," the elderly woman replies. "Who am I speaking to?"

"My name is Meghan McKenzie. I'm doing research for a story about the police in Birmingham. I'd like to talk with you a few minutes if you have time."

"We don't have much to do with the police," she says. "Can you hold on a minute?"

I hear two voices conversing in the background. Mrs. Freeman is trying to explain my call, and an angrier voice is protesting. The phone is exchanging hands and another person comes on the line.

"Who is this?" the no-nonsense female asks.

"My name is Meghan McKenzie. I work for the *Detroit Free Press* newspaper. I'm doing research on the Birmingham police for a story I'm writing about Black Lives Matter."

"Did Monique tell you to call us?"

After a moment's hesitation I lie. "Yes. Ms. Hendricks has been giving me assistance with my story."

"Well, what do you want to know?"

"May I ask your name?"

"I'm Keisha."

"Keisha, I'm looking for information about a George Free-man who filed a police complaint a long time ago."

"You mean Ellis Freeman?" Keisha asks.

"No. George. Are you a relative?"

"Uncle Ellis died a long time ago," the woman says, not an-swering my question.

This back-and-forth is getting me nowhere, and my experi-ence is that after a half dozen questions the person on the other end is ready to hang up.

"Is it possible I could meet with you and ask a few questions?"

There is a long, untrusting pause on the other side of the conversation.

"Maybe I could buy you a cup of coffee at MC Grille," I add.

"The grille? Well, *maybe* that could work." Keisha covers the phone and I hear muffled voices. I wait less than a minute. "We think you should just do a dinner pickup at the grille and bring it over to the house."

I hesitate. I'd prefer an early meeting. I'd imagined making dinner plans with Darius, but I still haven't spoken to him. I let my fingertips graze over one of the blooms on my desk as I think. I can't afford to pass on the possibility of getting more information on my mystery detective, so I go along with the request from the ballsy Miss Keisha, who has commandeered the phone call and my plans.

"Sure. I'd be happy to pick up some food and bring it over.

Let me get a pen and tell me what you want. Oh, and let me confirm your address."

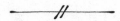

I've arranged to meet both Carrie Freeman and her great-niece, Keisha, at six. I've compiled my limited notes on George Freeman on a separate sheet and jot down a few questions. Sometimes a piece of paper is less threatening than a laptop. The police complaint is short on details, including any resolution, but maybe Mrs. Freeman will have some distant memory about the incident. To complete my meeting preparations, I put in a call to Monique.

"What's up, Meghan? You feeling the afterglow?"

"Is there *anything* you and Darius *don't* talk about?" I ask with embarrassment.

"The answer is no," she says, laughing.

"Well, I called about something else. Do you know Keisha Freeman?"

"I know a Keisha Bradley. Oh, that's right. Her mother's maiden name was Freeman. Why? Did you run into her?"

"No, but I have an appointment to talk to her aunt. I'm taking some food over to their house tonight."

"You going by yourself?"

"I'd planned to."

"Hmm. Keisha's people don't live in the best neighborhood."

"I looked up the address on Google Maps. I'll be okay."

"I'm coming with you."

"You're not busy tonight?"

"I am. But I'm not letting you go into that area at night by yourself. What time are you meeting them?"

"Six."

"Okay. I'll make some arrangements."

"I appreciate it, Monique. I'm ordering food from MC Grille. You want me to order something for you?"

"Of course I do. Get me one of their fish sandwiches. You should try one, too—you'll like it. Nice portions and good-quality haddock. And order me an iced tea, please. After you pick up the food, swing by and get me at the church. It's on the way."

"Okay. I can do all that. Uh. What did Darius say about our date?"

"He sent you flowers, didn't he? That says it all, girl."

THIRTY

Sowing the Seeds

1929

I've been staying to myself at work. Keeping my head down. My new car, which I retrieved from the front of the ballroom the day after the raid, is perfect for maintaining a low profile.

It's been a week since the raid on Griggs Ballroom and a sadness hangs over the neighborhood. Many folks feel the loss of this valued establishment and the man who owned it. Griggs employed a lot of people—waiters, musicians, cooks, dishwashers—and did business with a score of other Black entrepreneurs whose products supplied the restaurant and ballroom. The people killed in the raid had loved ones and friends who are mourning them, and everyone is outraged by the treatment Griggs's wife received. Clarita has not been allowed visitors while in prison, and people say she's been beaten.

We all feel the loathing of the police. They're watching us. Their heads swivel in slow motion as they drive their patrol cars through our neighborhoods. Their eyes flash with unconcealed hatred. We know some of the police trade their blue uniforms for white hoods at night.

Rumors are on the wind about a rogue police detective going house to house threatening witnesses identified the night of the raid. Several prominent clergymen, including the minister at our Pentecostal church, have met with the mayor to express their concern that an overzealous detective has set back the city's race relations. But the backlash toward the police has not come from Negroes alone. Apparently, Griggs's illegal activities were protected by relationships he had in high places. Some of Birmingham's power brokers who benefited from Griggs's supply of distilled spirits are unhappy and the chief of police is said to be under fire. Meanwhile, the ballroom is closed and boarded, and everyone is on edge.

Anna Kate doesn't like to hear me speak of the danger and racial strife close to us. She worries my anger will put us in harm's way. She prefers me to stay home, help her with the chores she can no longer do, and prepare for the baby. With Griggs closed, there's no particular place I want to go.

ON SATURDAY, WE VENTURE OUT TO THE MARKET AS USUAL. Anna Kate insists on walking rather than taking the car. She says it's better for the baby, but it really slows us down. Because of the increased police presence, the sidewalks are only half-full. Several of the food carts we buy from, including the vegetable man, are not in their usual places. We greet our neighbors as we pass along, but residents of the area are tense and cautious.

A patrol car rolls up Fourth Avenue and the action on the block comes to a standstill. I, like everyone else, keep an eye on the vehicle. Anna Kate clings to my arm and Mae waves to the cops. They give the three of us a good long look. I turn away and hurry Anna Kate and Mae along the sidewalk and into the butcher shop.

After lunch, Mrs. Ardle, Esther Freeman, and her daughter, Carrie Mae, come up to our apartment for a visit. I excuse myself to the downstairs parlor to share conversation, and cigars, with Freeman and three other longtime male boarders. One of them, an overweight man who always carries a flask of liquor, offers a drink and we all take a pull or two. The talk starts off with baseball, moves to cars, returns to baseball and the Negro leagues, then finally settles on the police action at Griggs Ballroom.

Everyone has a theory about the real purpose of the raid. Some believe one of the prominent club owners in Tuxedo Junction, concerned with the competition, might have blown the whistle on Griggs's illegal gambling and liquor sales. Others think Griggs may have balked at continuing to pay the police to look the other way. George Freeman, who has experience in the restaurant business, even suggested the Klan might be behind the raid. I think it might be all these things—plus Nedra whispering in the ear of her detective boyfriend.

"Those men who deliver ice and liquor are all Klan," Freeman says. "After work they come out of those company shirts with the names on the pocket and trade 'em for a sheet."

"That's possible," I say. "Some of the crackers working around that mansion project can't stand it when a Black man has something."

"I tell you, Harrington, I know about these things."

The latest news on the raid comes from the flask man. He reports that a new detective is responsible—the same one who's been seen around the neighborhood asking questions. The flask man got that information from one of the security guards at the ballroom.

"This detective told his police bosses that women were whoring at the ballroom and Griggs was selling liquor in the back room. Claimed some white girl told him the whole story."

Mrs. Ardle has just come into the room across the hallway, and the storyteller pauses while we murmur and cuss under our breath. I'm thinking about the last time I saw Nedra walking through the crowd with that big plainclothes cop.

"I think I know her," I say with a lowered voice.

"What?" one of the men asks. "You know the white girl?"

"She's half-white. Worked as one of the dancers. Her name is Nedra." I don't want to answer any more questions, so I change the subject. "How's Clarita doing?"

"She's out of jail on bail," flask man says. "They trumped up a charge about disorderly conduct, and somebody beat her up bad while she was locked up. But some church paid her bail and she's home now."

I return to the apartment to tell Anna Kate that I'm going for a walk and a little fresh air. She, Mrs. Ardle, and Esther Freeman are seated at our new table crocheting a massive tablecloth. Mae and Carrie are playing with dolls on the floor. The women look content, and Anna Kate only raises one eyebrow when I say I'll be back in a couple of hours.

I walk the five blocks past Griggs's boarded building, where locals have left candles, homemade crosses, and a variety of flowers in a makeshift memorial. I'm headed to the streetcar, because I think it's the easiest way for me to pay a visit to Clarita and get back home without raising Anna Kate's ire. At the Wylam platform, I have only ten minutes to wait before the trolley arrives.

Because I've always had a car, I never ride the streetcar and the man ahead of me in line tells me how much to pay for a round-trip fare. The car is filled with passengers and I follow the other Negro riders to the back. The women and children sit with purses and packages on their laps, while the men, holding on to the leather straps suspended from the ceiling, bob and weave with the movement of the car. Up in front, only three white passengers share six rows of empty seats.

Tuxedo Junction isn't in mourning like the Fourth Avenue business district. Pedestrians are crisscrossing the streets, and vendors are doing a brisk Saturday afternoon business even though it's hours before the area's nightlife begins. I hear music wafting through the open front windows of one of the nightclubs. I buy a bouquet of daisies from a vendor and only have to approach a few people—with the lie that I am Griggs's cousin from Florida—before someone points me in the direction of Clarita's house.

The home is a simple wood structure with a porch and a paved walkway. The wood is painted a muted purple that looks rich and warm in the sunlight. Flowers are planted in front of the house and fill the boxes attached to the front windows. I look at my bouquet, wishing I had brought a bag of fruit instead. There is a long delay between my knock at the door and its opening. In between, I see the rustling of curtains.

A young boy, perhaps four or five, appears at the portal and looks me up and down before someone from inside orders him to let me in. Clarita is lying on a large couch in the darkened front room. I can smell, more than see, the flowers crowded into the space.

"Bobby," Clarita says with a muffled voice. "Thank you for coming."

I move toward her with my inadequate bouquet extended,

and it is only then I see the damage to her face and upper body. I inhale sharply. She's covered in ugly bruises. Her left eye is swollen shut and encircled by a blue ring of injured skin. Her jaw and neck are puckered and streaked with dark welts.

"Oh, Clarita," I say, kneeling before her. "What have they done to you?"

She begins to sob and grips my hand with viselike strength until the tears subside.

"They killed my man, Bobby," she says between clenched teeth. "¡Alberto está muerto!

"And I will make them pay!"

———◆———

THIRTY-ONE

2019

W hat the fuck!" Monique shouts when I tell her about the close call with the white van. I'm driving us to Carrie Free-man's house. "Why didn't you tell me before? Did you call the police?"

"The van sideswiped a couple of cars, so I think the neighbors probably reported it to the police. I didn't get a look at the license plate or the driver, and I can't say for sure the van was aiming for me and Kristen. It might have just been a drunk driver."

Monique looks skeptical. "None of the folks that follow me around have ever been that brazen. I got a bad feeling about this."

The Freemans' North Birmingham neighborhood is scarred with depression and resignation. Trash and weeds share the empty lots, and the houses reflect the poverty in the area. At the corner, a ragged circle of young men teeming with restlessness are talk-ing, smoking weed, and drinking from giant bottles of some white liquor. They watch our car's slow approach as Monique points out the house and I pull to the curb. The teens fix menacing glares at our vehicle. I don't think they can actually see us through the windshield, but their stares demand to know our business in their no-man's-land.

"Let's get the food in the house before it gets cold," Monique says, gathering her bag and reaching for the door.

As soon as the corner guys see Monique, they drop their posturing. One of them smiles and waves, while the others resume their smoking and drinking. The smiling kid looks maybe thirteen, and when he comes to the car he embraces Monique.

"What you doing up here, Miss Hendricks?" he asks.

"We're visiting Keisha and her aunt. How you doing, Freddie?"

"Still living."

"Some days that's the best thing we can do. This is Miss McKenzie," Monique says, grabbing my arm and pushing me toward the house.

Freddie's prepubescent eyes light up, and he keeps pace with our trek to the door. "How you doing?" he says to me in his baby mack-daddy voice.

"She's fine," Monique answers for me. "Look, Freddie, make sure the car is okay while we're visiting, will you?"

"I got you, Miss Hendricks."

"Also, keep your eye out for a white van. Some guys have been tailing us."

Freddie's eyes squint and his face turns grave. "You want us to take care of 'em?"

"No, no. Nothing like that. But if you see the van, knock on Mrs. Freeman's door."

"Okay. You got any extra fries I can have?" His face has softened again and he's focused on the bag from the grille I'm carrying.

Monique reaches in the plastic bag and takes out one of the aluminum-wrapped packages.

"Here. Keep an eye on the car."

As we move up to the porch, Monique leans toward me to whisper.

"Freddie's father was shot by the Birmingham police five years ago when they stopped him for a traffic violation. He's paralyzed now. We got the family a lawyer and they received a small settlement from the city."

I nod.

The thirtysomething woman who opens the door is tall, buxom, and intense. She squeals at the sight of Monique and reaches out her arms for a hug.

"I didn't know you were coming. Auntie, Monique is here," the woman shouts over her shoulder.

"You must be Keisha," I say, stepping forward. "I'm the one who called."

Keisha starts to give me the once-over but she spots the two bags of food and that ends her scrutiny. "Come on in," she says and leaves us to close the door.

"Auntie, that reporter is here, and she brought Monique!"

Ninety-two-year-old Carrie Freeman is a small woman, a wheelchair user, her back curved from the weight of too many disappointments. She gives a weak smile as we step into the house. Keisha bounds to the dining room to clear an area for the food, then moves back to the front room to push her aunt to the table. In between, she moves papers from the chairs and turns on the overhead ceiling fan light.

"Did you bring paper plates?" she asks.

"Yes," I say, pulling out the plates, the sealed packets of plastic utensils, and napkins.

239

"Okay, why don't you and Monique sit there." Keisha points to chairs on the side. She puts her aunt's wheelchair at the head of the table.

Monique and I begin to unbag the food. I distribute iced teas and stack three packages of fries on a layer of napkins just in case their oil has escaped the foil.

"What's this?" Monique points.

"That's the pulled pork platter," I say, placing it on a plate in front of Keisha's chair. "Here's the chicken club sandwich for Mrs. Freeman, and these are our fish sandwiches," I say, putting one in front of Monique.

"Where are my fries?" Keisha asks.

"You take one," Monique says, distributing the containers of fries, "and these are for Miss Carrie. Meghan and I will share this one."

The Freeman dining room is filled with large dark-wood furniture, doilies, photographs, and dozens of ceramic Black angels. I've seen similar rooms in the homes of Black seniors in Detroit, and Saxby often speaks of the photographs of Martin Luther King Jr. and the Kennedy brothers on the walls of the Black homes he visited during his heyday covering civil rights in the South. A special place on the Freeman wall is saved for the forty-fourth president and his family, and from my vantage point I'm staring into the face of a smiling Barack Obama.

Monique is right. The fried haddock sandwich is awesome. The breading is light and crispy, and it's served with a secret sauce that I think is little more than a mixture of ketchup, mayo, and a dash of horseradish. Mrs. Freeman and Keisha seem to be enjoying their meals, and I'm surprised at the older woman's appetite. She finishes her sandwich and starts in on the fries. As she eats her mood picks up and she becomes more animated. She's a longtime member of Monique's church and they talk about the up-coming Founder's Day celebration. I'm listening, eating, and very aware that Keisha is staring at me. A couple of times I look up and give her a quick smile before returning to my fish.

When the food is eaten and we're sipping our drinks, Monique brings us to the business at hand. "Miss Carrie, my friend here has some questions about a story she's doing for her newspaper in Detroit."

"You say you're a reporter?" Keisha asks, sipping sweet tea.

"Yes. For the *Detroit Free Press*."

"Well, I don't think we want our names in the newspaper," she says matter-of-factly.

"The information I need is only for background."

Keisha stares at me, puzzled and skeptical.

"That means I want to ask your aunt about something that happened a long time ago."

My initial phone chat with Keisha, listening to Mrs. Freeman's conversation with Monique, and the framed pictures I see on the buffet and bookcases lead me to believe ninety-two-year-old Carrie is likely the daughter of the George Freeman listed on the complaint against Detective Carl Simenon.

"What is it you want to know, baby?" Mrs. Freeman asks.

I give the woman a grateful smile and shift in my seat toward her. She has inquisitive eyes and a hint of energy I hadn't seen when we arrived. I pull my sheet of paper from my bag and smooth it out on the table. Keisha leans across the table trying to read it.

"Did your father ever file a complaint against the Birmingham Police Department?"

"Well, I know he had some kind of trouble with the police when he first moved here."

"Do you know what the trouble was?"

"No. I was just a little girl."

"Your father never told you about it?" I push.

"No. No. Mama told me about it, later. After Daddy died."

"And what year did he die?"

"Nineteen forty-four. Just before the war ended."

"Do you remember *anything* your mother might have said about your father and the police?"

Carrie stares down at her lap. "Well, let me see."

She sits still for a very long time. Monique sips her tea while we wait. Keisha's eyes still swarm over me. My leg twitches. I'm wringing my hands under the table and wondering why my interviews in Birmingham have surfaced all my insecurities about being a good reporter. I'm sure it must be my competing desires to provide some answers for Grandma and write an objective story. I stare at Mrs. Freeman. I hope she hasn't fallen asleep. After an interminable three minutes, she lifts her head.

"Well, best as I can recall, Daddy had a couple of friends who had a run-in with the police. You know them cops back then was out-and-out prejudice. Even worse than it is today," she says, including Monique in her glance. "Anyway, I think one of his friends was killed—or maybe it was two people. I don't quite remember. Daddy spoke up for them is what Mama said."

"Do you remember who his friends were?" I ask with my stomach churning.

"No. That was such a long time ago. Daddy was a cook, you know, and he had his own restaurant downtown."

"I see," I say, leaning back and finally releasing my fingers for the flow of blood.

"Miss Carrie, you think we could see some of your daddy's pictures?" Monique asks.

"Well, I guess that would be all right. Keisha, go get that picture album upstairs in my bureau drawer. It's that big green one with a rubber band around it."

Keisha had pretty much checked out of our conversation and is scrolling through her phone. But she finally looks up at me and Monique with a quick eye roll.

"Go on and get the book, girl," Carrie says. "Stop your dilly-dallying."

Keisha flashes an annoyed look at her aunt, pushes her chair back loudly, and leaves the dining room.

"Is that your father?" I ask, pointing at a framed black-and-white photo on the sideboard.

"Yes, that's him and the one next to it is him and Mama."

"Do you mind if I have a closer look?"

George Freeman looks distinguished in this photo. Even in his seated pose you can see he was tall and strong. In the second photo, of Freeman and his wife, they stand side by side. He has a confident smile. She is small with her gaze cast down as if trying to hide from the camera. The photo was taken outdoors in front of a small building. Mr. Freeman wears a chef's coat and his wife has on a housedress with a half apron.

"What was your mother's name?" I ask.

"Esther," she says.

Keisha returns with the album, and Carrie passes several photos around. There are more pictures of her parents, and her as a child. She shows us one of her father in front of his restaurant, perhaps at the grand opening; he beams proudly in his white coat and hat.

"What year did your father open his restaurant?"

"I'm not sure. Isn't there a date of that back of that one?" Carrie asks.

I flip over the picture and there is no date.

"Here's one with a date," Monique says. "Nineteen thirty-one."

"That makes sense. Daddy opened his restaurant a couple of years after he and Mama got here from Shreveport."

"So that would mean your parents arrived in Birmingham the same year my great-grandfather and his family got here."

"Your people used to live in Birmingham?" Keisha asks, looking up from her phone.

"They moved here from Florida. This is a picture of my great-grandparents," I say, pulling the photo from my bag. "It was taken on their wedding day."

"Oh, they are a striking couple," Monique says, passing the photo. "I remember you saying your great-grandpa was a snappy dresser, and your great-grandmother is gorgeous."

"Oh my," Mrs. Freeman exclaims. She drops the picture and pushes her chair back from the table, gripping the arms with arthritic fingers. She grimaces. "Oh my."

"What's wrong, Auntie?" Keisha is suddenly attentive, squatting next to the wheelchair. Carrie's breathing is shallow and the color in her face has drained.

"Mae," Carrie pronounces with her eyes closed. We're gathered around her. She opens her eyes and peers at me. "Was that your great-grandmother's name?"

"No, ma'am. But that's my grandma's name. Willie Mae."

Carrie smiles. "Yes! We had the same name. I'm Carrie Mae. She and I used to play together. Can I see the picture again?" She reaches out her weathered hand.

Carrie stares at the photo with concentration, and I hug my bag to my chest. Waiting. Conscious of my breathing. Trying to slow my pounding heart. I watch as her jaw slackens and a smile teases at her lips.

"I was just a little girl, but I remember Mae's mama because of her light skin and her gray eyes. I had never seen anyone with eyes like that before."

I try to catch my breath. I now have a connection between my great-grandfather and Detective Simenon. George Freeman.

Carrie Mae sifts through the green album and shows me another photo. "This is where we all lived."

Her parents stand in front of a three-story brick building with lots of windows, a big porch and trees, and a car parked along the side.

"Yes, yes. I've seen another photograph of this building. It was a boardinghouse called the Fourth Avenue Inn. My great-grandparents stayed there also."

Now Carrie Mae's memories about conversations with her mother are surfacing in quick succession. She moves her hands animatedly and her eyes have a spark.

"One of Daddy's friends owned a business. Him and his Spanish wife," Carrie says. "Mama talked about how Daddy spoke up for this man when he was killed. Or maybe it was another man. I can't quite remember. But she always told me Daddy had a limp because he spoke up for his friends."

I can barely sit still now because of the buzz in my head and my racing heart.

"Mrs. Freeman," I say, leaning across the table to get her attention. "You mentioned a Spanish woman. Was Clarita the woman's name?"

Carrie Mae shakes her head, "I don't know. That doesn't sound right. But, like I said, I remember Mae and her pretty mama. Your great-grandma, I guess."

"Yes, ma'am," I say, tears blurring my eyes.

"Whatever happened to them?" she asks.

Between tears I tell my family story. Keisha even sets aside her phone to listen. When I'm done Carrie Mae shakes her head and seems lost in thought. "I'm so glad to hear Mae is alive and doing well, young lady. We old people seen a lot and been through a lot, but I guess you young ones are going through some stuff, too. Monique here is trying to help make things right."

"Yes, ma'am. She is."

"You know, I just remembered one more thing. When we finally had to put Mama in a nursing home she told me that Spanish woman's son was there. She said he didn't seem too sick to her, and wasn't even that old, but for some reason he couldn't take care of himself."

"The woman had a son?"

"That's what Mama said. But I guess if he's still alive he must be even older than me."

—————◆—————

THIRTY-TWO

Skin-Deep

1929

"A re you from Africa?" the boy asks me.

"Naw, boy. I'm from Florida."

"Then why your face so blue?"

"¡Basta! Paolo. Don't be rude!" Clarita demands with slurred speech.

Her jaw is wired shut, the work of a Negro doctor called to the prison to repair her broken body after the savage beating she received from that plainclothes cop. When she says my name it sounds like "Bubby."

I've made a cup of tea for Clarita. She can only take in liquids through a straw, and I adjust the pillows on the couch so she can sit up.

"You gonna need some help, Clarita," I say.

"Oh, I got help. The girls from the club come in the morning, and again at night to make Pauli some dinner and put him to bed."

I have to lean in close and watch her puffy lips to understand what she says.

"Bobby, can you take Pauli to get some candy? He's been stuck in this house with me all day."

The boy asks a lot of questions and speaks with a lazy sway of words. I can see Clarita in his face, but his body, his brusqueness, and the way he moves come directly from Griggs. He won't let me hold his hand as we cross the busy corners in the Junction, and he tries to resist my guide hand on his shoulder as we walk along.

"You sure you not from Africa?" he asks again.

"Boy, what do you know about Africa?"

"My daddy told me about it. He's been to Africa, and a lot of places. In a boat. Do you have a boat?"

"No. I'm a carpenter," I say.

The boy looks puzzled, so I explain that I make things out of wood. I tell him about the stairs I've made for a big mansion, and the dresser and table and crib. I point to the wood structure where I'm going to buy candy.

"You see that man's candy stand? I could build that."

Pauli's eyes grow wide for a minute, then he squints. "Jesus was a carpenter. Mami told me. You not like Jesus. Jesus had long hair and he was white."

I buy a bag and a half of jelly beans, plus an Oh Henry! bar. We sit on a bench in front of the building where the music is playing. I turn the full bag of jelly beans over to Pauli and tuck the half bag into my pocket. While we're sitting, I point out all the things that I could build.

"You see that sign? I can make that, and that door over there with the big window, and that steering wheel on that car, and this bench we're sitting on."

Pauli turns to look at the back of the bench and leans forward to look under it.

"Wood is made out of trees," he announces.

"That's right, but there are a lot of different kinds of trees. Oaks and pines and maples and mahogany, and a whole bunch more."

By the time I walk Pauli back home I'm exhausted by his questions. The door opens as we climb to the porch. One of the dance girls from Griggs steps out and reaches for Pauli.

"Boy, get in here. It's almost time for your bath," she says. "And your mama is looking for you. How you doing, Lee?" she says, smiling at me and grabbing the boy by the hand.

"Lee?" Pauli shouts, looking over his shoulder with a suspicious sneer. "Your name is . . ."

I shake my head. "You can just call me Mr. Bubby. Tell your mama I'll see her again," I say before the door slams shut. I've forgotten to give the boy the Oh Henry!, so I lay the candy bar at the front door and turn away.

As I walk back to the streetcar I wonder if my baby will be a boy, and be as talkative as Pauli. It's nice to have a little girl, like Mae, who's sweet and doesn't ask so many questions.

The image of Clarita's bruised face remains with me. I can't stand the thought of a man doing that to her. She's always reminded me of Anna Kate because of her smooth skin and bright complexion.

When I open the door of our apartment, Mae runs into my arms and I swoop her up. "Daddy, Daddy, Daddy," she says, and I toss her into the air and catch her a few times until her giggles make it difficult for her to breathe.

"That's enough now," Anna Kate says. "She's getting too excited." She looks at me. "What's wrong?"

"Nothing's wrong. I'm glad I took a walk, but I couldn't wait to get back."

"That's good," Anna Kate says with a smile. "I'm getting kind of tired. Dinner's ready and you should wash up."

"What are we having?"

"Your favorite, chicken and dumplings. What's that in the bag?"

"Jelly beans. *Your* favorite."

THIRTY-THREE

———◆———

2019

When I returned from Carrie Freeman's house to the Airbnb I was too excited to work or return calls, even from Darius. Instead, I made two loaves of carrot cake, and right after I got in bed I texted him a "good night." He responded with a van and worry-face emojis. I replied with an "A-OK," which he followed with "night" and a rose emoji. Then I fell into a sleep where I dreamed of being a happy little girl, playing with my friends, until a menacing boogeyman shows up to pursue me. Some variation of that nightmare kept me restless throughout the night.

This morning I have a headache and uneasiness about two calls I have to make. I take a couple of aspirin, then head to the kitchen to put on coffee. By the time I have a shower and put on jeans and an oversize tee, it's only seven o'clock.

The first call turns out to be easy. The owner of my Airbnb has the house available for a few more days at the same price, and without any additional paperwork. That's a relief. It would be a pain to add moving to the list of things I have to do. The second call is trickier.

"It's early, McKenzie," Saxby says.

"I know. I need to stay a few more days. I'm getting close."

"Close to what? Is it the same story you started out with?"

"Not sure. Not exactly."

"You're due back Sunday. Serina wouldn't extend your time."

"I've got a line on this bad cop, from the era when my great-grandfather was killed. He had multiple citizen complaints against him and was later found dead with stab wounds."

"And how does he connect to your great-grandfather?"

"Through someone I met last night. A woman who actually knew my grandmother when she was here. I'm getting close, Saxby, I can feel it."

"So, you're still working more on feelings than facts," he says.

I have to do some fancy talking to move him in my direction. But I know his buttons, and I push them hard. I describe the melting-pot vibe at Niki's West restaurant, and the discovery of the 311 booklet at the home of the former chief of police that I believe points to his involvement in the Ku Klux Klan. I recount my meeting with Kristen's father and his company's longtime connection to Birmingham PD.

I describe Cecile Clarke and her family's work, dating back to the turn of the century, of housing Blacks in the segregated South.

"People have heard about the Green Book, but this woman's family lived it," I say. "Coretta Scott King even stayed at the motel she runs now. Roberta Banton's family still owns the home where all these civil rights icons came for dinner."

I describe the chronic poverty in the neighborhoods of North Birmingham, the impressive organizing work at Evangelical for Black Lives Matter, the creepy cemetery that is the final resting place for dozens of nameless Black souls who died in Birmingham at the beginning of the twentieth century.

"That's good stuff," Saxby agrees.

"A cadre of Black folks have opened doors, documents, photo albums, and graveyards for me. These people hold the collective memory of the city's Black history," I say. "Most of our national consciousness about Birmingham centers on its violent role in America's civil rights history, but there's more to Birmingham than its legacy of racial bigotry. There's the courage and creativity it took for Black people to thrive in the midst of all that hatred."

"That's your lead, McKenzie. Part two of your reporter's notebook. I'll work on Serina again about extending your stay. How many more days do you need?"

"A week?"

"That's pushing it. Anyway, write me up something. We'll run it on the website this weekend, and under your byline in Monday's paper. But don't get your hopes up about staying on."

I decide not to mention the white van to Saxby because I don't want to give him another reason to insist I come home immediately. I also don't tell him that whether the paper gives me an extension or not, I'm staying.

"What's my deadline?"

"Today's Thursday. So, close of business tomorrow."

"I probably won't have any police comment by then."

"That's okay. We'll update later. Good luck."

The deadline adds to my anxiety. I have a shitload of things to accomplish. I do a mental triage of the priorities. In my notebook, I've written:

1. Get help setting up an appointment with someone in the police department.

2. Follow up on Carrie Mae's lead about the nursing
   facility where Clarita's son might live.
3. Research the background of Stan Gleason.

This last item has been on my mind since meeting Kristen's father. I don't trust him. If Kristen's right that he's digging into my background, then I want to dig around a bit in his.

There's no reason to go into the library today. Every task I have I can do from here. I clear the kitchen table to set up as my workstation. First I look at my 1929 timeline and fill in a few dates and notes.

I'm not sure when my great-grandfather arrived in Birmingham, but he was here in June and was joined by his family in July, at which point they lived in the same boardinghouse as George Freeman and his family. In late August 1929, Albert Griggs was killed in a police raid on his establishment. Simenon was involved in the raid and soon after was promoted to detective. In September, my great-grandfather was murdered by an unnamed police officer. Also in September, Griggs's widow, Clarita Alvarez, received a ten-thousand-dollar police settlement in a case that was connected to Simenon, and weeks after that Freeman filed his own police complaint, which was also somehow connected to Simenon. However, that complaint is filed *after* the detective was discovered stabbed to death in a downtown alley.

Simenon's murder is still a puzzle. Was it retaliation for the raid at Griggs Ballroom, or for the assault of Alvarez, or some other reason? The questions remind me to check in with Kristen.

"I won't be in today."

"You okay?"

"I had nightmares last night, I'm swamped with research, and

I have a thousand-word blog to write. How about you? How's the ankle?"

"Oh, it's fine. I'm wearing boots to support it. Did you tell Darius about the white van?"

"No, but Monique did. Don't worry. I'll be alert from now on. Guess what! Last night I met a woman who remembers my grandmother, and I have another lead to follow."

"That's great, and you changed the subject."

We both let the silence take its course.

"Go ahead and get to all that work you have. Oh, and I'll extend you a day on that book you checked out."

"Oh, right. Sorry, I forgot about it. I'll be sure to bring it in tomorrow. Speaking of books, did your researcher find anything in that roster of names we got from Zach?"

"Dammit. He called me about it just before I left yesterday and I was so busy I never got back to him. I'll do that now. Phone you back if there's anything of note."

Next I call Darius. He picks up on the second ring.

"Hold on a minute, I need to step out of a meeting," he whispers.

I pull the library book out of my backpack while I wait. The downtown scenes show a populous city bustling with enterprise. It's only when the camera captures home and work life that the dichotomies of this city—Black and white, and rich and poor—stand out in stark contrast.

"Hi, Meg," Darius's voice snaps me back to the immediate. "Glad to hear from you."

"Sorry to disturb your workday," I say. "I didn't think I should call too early."

"You can call anytime."

"I have two things to discuss with you." I am in business

mode. "I need your help with something—a meeting with police leadership. Someone who can answer questions about the current state of things, but also who can gain me access to historical records. My paper has a FOIA request in to Birmingham PD but I've only heard crickets. I need a quote from the police sooner rather than later."

"Okay. Let me check in with a few people and figure out who that would be. Can I call you in a couple of hours?"

"That would be perfect."

"What's the other thing?" Darius asks.

I pause to acknowledge the excitement I have at remembering his touch. My voice takes a different tone. "Thank you for the very beautiful flowers. They were a nice surprise, and the arrangement is gorgeous. I wish I had them with me, but I'm working from home today."

"I got a kick out of sending them."

"I missed not speaking with you yesterday," I say.

"Same here. And I'm worried about you. Did a van really try to run you down?"

"I don't know for sure. Maybe the guy was just drunk."

"It was a guy?"

"I didn't really see the driver. It all happened fast."

To stop his questions, I begin talking about my meeting with Carrie Freeman, but then I pause. "Oh, that's right, I guess Monique already told you about that too."

"I'm glad she was with you," Darius says. "Rough neighborhood."

"You two are being overprotective. I'm from Detroit. That means I'm no fish out of water."

"Yes, ma'am," Darius says teasingly. "Okay, I gotta get back to my meeting. I'll be in touch before noon. Don't work too hard."

I Google the Caregiver's Nursing Home. Carrie Mae's memory of a son of Clarita Alvarez at the facility where her mother had lived is a hopeful lead. She didn't know anything specific about the son, and there's always the possibility she was mistaken, or that he moved elsewhere or has died. But she was clear about the facility's name.

The closest listing is Caregiver's Residential Living, and I call the number and listen to a message with a lengthy menu of service areas and corresponding numbers to press for connection. The last option is to access an operator, and the phone rings thirty times before I disconnect. Then I call the main number again and select the one service area I know will answer calls during business hours.

"Accounting," the woman answers.

"Hi. I'm calling about the account status of one of our clients at your facility. The payments are made from an estate."

"What's the client's name?"

"Alvarez. It's a male resident."

I hear the clicking of a keypad. "We don't have a resident by that name at our facility."

I have no idea when Clarita's son was born, what his first name is, or if he's the son of Albert Griggs.

"Well, this would be a client with a long-term disability. He might be in the nursing home portion of the facility."

"We handle the accounts receivable for the entire company," the woman says tersely.

"I'm sorry to be so uncertain, but I just got this job and I don't want to have to go back to my boss and tell him I couldn't get the information he wanted." I take a calculated risk. "He's a lawyer, and you know how they can be."

There is silence on the other end of the line. I wait, and breathe.

"My ex-husband is a lawyer, and I can count the days on one hand when he wasn't a complete asshole," the woman says.

We share a laugh.

"Any chance the patient has a different name?" the woman asks.

"Uh. He might be listed by his father's name, which is Griggs."

I hear clicking for a few seconds. "I have a Paul Griggs. Yes, his mother's maiden name *is* Alvarez."

"That's him," I say excitedly. "Is his account in arrears?"

"Nope. He's paid up. For six months in advance. His next payment isn't due until January."

"Well, that's great," I say. "Uh, do you know if he's allowed visitors?"

"You'd have to check with the medical services staff on that. I'd be happy to transfer you."

"I'd appreciate that, and thanks for your help."

THE MEDICAL STAFF ISN'T HELPFUL. THEY WON'T GIVE ANY DE-tails of Paul's condition, but I do find out he's in the memory-care division of their facility, and visitors are allowed only by appointment. I lie, saying I'm Paul's niece, in town for only a couple of days, and I obtain an appointment for tomorrow.

The rest of the morning moves along in a series of starts and pauses. I do a quick Google search of Kristen's father. I'm surprised at how many results I get, and I bookmark more than a dozen of them to look at later.

I begin to write out the questions for when, and if, I get an official police interview. I troll the Birmingham Police website, reviewing the department's org chart and the responsibilities of the command staff—Masterson looks younger in the photo, but as spit-and-polish as always. I scroll through the crime stats and press releases and then click the link for a website showing the department's fallen officers. Four dozen officers are memorialized. The cause of their deaths ranges from gunfire to motorcycle accidents. Simenon is not listed among them. I finish my interview notes, then look at my to-do list. So far, so good. I might as well start on the blog.

When I write, I do sprints, writing for a focused half hour to an hour and then rewarding myself with a short workout or a walk, or a break to grab a bite or cook something. Today my prize will be another cup of coffee and a piece of carrot cake.

The writing flows, partly because I'd already organized it in my head for my conversation with Saxby. I don't worry about structure, dates, and quotes on this first pass; I can always go back and include details. I allow the images, the feelings and reactions, to pour onto the page. Today's readers want more than the facts. They want background, context, and the human elements of a story. In a half hour I stop. I won't look back on what I've written until I start up again. I take a deep breath, drink a glass of water, and thumb through the library book while my coffee is brewing.

I look at the clock—11:20. I start writing again, and I've laid a flurry of words on the page when a knock on the front door startles me. I peek around the kitchen column tentatively, then beam. I open the door to Darius, who holds out a pizza and flashes his marvelous smile.

"Since you're working at home I thought you might need lunch. I'm not staying. I just wanted to bring you the pizza, and this." He holds out a note. "It's the time of your appointment tomorrow with the chief of police."

"Are you kidding? You arranged a meeting with the chief? You're the best! Come on in for a minute. I have fresh coffee and carrot cake."

"Okay, but *really* I can only stay fifteen minutes; I have a community meeting."

I push my notes aside, pour coffee, and cut Darius a generous slice of cake. He takes a bite and closes his eyes in delight.

"You really are an excellent cook," he says, and smiles. "If the journalism thing doesn't work out, you definitely have something to fall back on."

"I know you're joking, but if I don't get this story right, I'll *need* another gig."

"How's it going?"

As I recount my progress on the to-do list I feel anxiety rising again.

"To be honest I'm kind of stressed-out."

At the door, I thank him again for his help securing the interview.

"I'll call you tomorrow to let you know how it went," I say. "Oh, and thanks for the pizza. It'll be my dinner. Oh, and I almost forgot, I'm probably staying a few more days." I smile.

"Well, that's the best news of all," he says.

Darius touches my face and leans in to kiss me. I lean in too. He turns and I watch him until his car rolls up the street and out of view.

AT TWO O'CLOCK I'M UP TO EIGHT HUNDRED WORDS ON THE blog and I've run out of steam.

I need exercise, and I walk over the few blocks to the bike-share. Since it's a weekday, there's a lot more traffic on the route to the Fourth Avenue business district. The photo book has me curious to search for any landmarks that might remain. I start off for the place where my further research shows Griggs Ballroom did business for five years before the raid closed them down. The address is now a building of loft condos with retail on the street level. The multistory structure has a beautiful brick façade and an ornate cornice that is probably original to the building, but I believe the windows have been upgraded. An Uber pickup location is marked by a sign, and one of the drivers, a Black man wearing sunglasses and a hat pulled low over his forehead, has noticed me staring at the building from across the street. He waves me over. I'm irritated by his attention but his car is a pristine vintage Ford Thunderbird and I want to get a closer look at it. When he waves again, I wait for a break in the traffic to push my bike to the window of his collector's car.

"You looking for somebody who lives there?" he asks.

My instinct is to say: "That's none of your business." Instead I peer into his window to look at the dashboard.

"No. Not really. I saw an old picture of the building recently, and I was just curious about it. Is this a '63 T-Bird?"

"I see you know your cars, young lady."

"I'm from Detroit," I say. "She's in really good shape."

"I believe in taking care of my automobiles. Detroit, you say." He removes his sunglasses. "I always wanted to go to Detroit."

I watch distant memories crowd his irises. I'm about to tell him it's not too late to visit, when a young blond woman bounds from the building and onto the sidewalk. We both turn to look at her. She's wearing torn jeans with a short pink denim jacket and an oversize designer bag. Her boots look like Jimmy Choo. She glances our way as she flips her hair outside her collar and steps into the first Uber car in line. The man turns over the engine of the T-Bird and inches it up to the first position. With his hands on the steering wheel, I finally notice his skin is deeply wrinkled. He's a lot older than I thought.

"You know, this neighborhood used to be different," he states.

"Gentrification is happening everywhere," I respond.

He flashes white teeth against dark skin. I decide he's handsome—and somewhat familiar. "Sometimes change is only on the surface. Inside, things don't change that much. People can be like that. Time too," he adds.

The front door of the building opens again, and a redheaded teen with a patchy beard and carrying a guitar case does a double take on the antique car.

"You for hire?" the kid asks.

"Get in," the man says to the teen, then turns to me. "You take care, young lady."

I watch his car pull away, trying to recall something nagging at me, but I can't hold on to the thought. I turn toward the building. I can't see much through the massive brass door, so I lock my bike to the Uber sign and pull on the heavy door. Maybe the old man is right about things not changing.

He isn't. The lobby is modern with marble floors, silver fabric wallpaper, and brass fixtures. A framed black-and-white photograph of the building's original façade hangs over a tiled fireplace. They've added at least six floors to this building. I stand close to the photo and squint while the uniformed man at the reception desk peers at me. The brick and cornice are the same, but the building was definitely smaller and the front entrance used to have an awning. I use my phone to snap a picture of the wall photo, then turn toward the man at the front desk. He watches my approach.

"Hi," I say.

"Hello," he says with more suspicion than friendliness.

"I'm interested in old architecture. Do you know anything about this building? Do you have any brochures about its history?"

"Nope."

"Do you think the leasing office would have information?"

"Maybe. But you have to make an appointment to see them." Before I ask another question he adds, "And you have to do that by phone or online."

I don't thank the white security guard, and I don't look back as I exit.

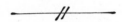

I dock the bike and walk the two blocks to the Airbnb. I'm excited by the prospect of a hot shower and refining the blog over pizza and maybe a glass of wine.

When I turn onto my block I can see the front door of the house. I pause. There's something on the porch. At first I think maybe Darius has had more flowers delivered. I can't make out what's there, but it's not flowers and there's also something attached to the door. It doesn't feel right. I look around for the white van and don't see it. I pull my phone from my pocket and start videotaping from across the street. After a minute, on shaking knees, I tentatively approach the porch and move up the steps. I stop, and gasp.

Nailed to the front door is a noose. A pool of blood spreads across the porch, and a pencil-scrawled note tied to the noose reads: *Questions Get You Killed.*

THIRTY-FOUR

The Warning

1929

What does this woman mean to you?"

It's a fair question for Anna Kate to ask. I've visited Clarita and her son a half dozen times in their little purple house in Tuxedo Junction. The women are taking care of her healing and her house, but she needs someone to share her outrage, and she wants her fatherless boy to spend time with a man.

"She's just a friend. She's been beaten up and is grieving the loss of her husband. She has a young son who doesn't understand what's happening to his world."

"I'm sorry about the boy and his mother, but you have a daughter, and a baby on the way, Robert. I need you too."

"And you have me, woman. I'm here every night, and I work every day. Except for a measly amount I keep for myself, all my money is for us. I won't be gone long."

I'm not fully aware why I feel an obligation to be there for Clarita and her son. I never even liked Griggs, but Clarita always treated me sweetly, and I know how hard it is to be a boy, alone.

This evening, I'm taking Pauli to buy shoes. I won't accept the three dollars from his mother. She's not able to work now, and she's had to pay funeral expenses. She seems embarrassed but grateful. Her body is healing, and she no longer has the restraint on her jaw, but her smile is lopsided because of some permanent paralysis of her face.

"Don't have him out too long, Bobby; he still needs his bath," Clarita says as I shut the door.

The boy's questions start before we get off the porch. He's begun letting me hold his hand, and I lift him as he leaps from the bottom step.

"What did you make out of wood today?" he asks.

"I finished up some doorknobs and started work on a book-case."

"We have a bookcase," Pauli says.

I don't answer him right away, because I'm looking at a late-model sedan idling across the street. I saw this car, or one like it, the last time I came by.

"I know you have a bookcase. I saw it, and you're gonna need a new one soon. Yours is starting to sag because of all the books and magazines."

"Can you make a new bookcase, Mr. Bubby?"

"Maybe I can."

"Daddy used to read me the Nashville Geography. That's why I know about Africa, and icebergs, and gravity."

"I think it's called *National Geographic*," I say, pronouncing each syllable. "That's a good magazine. They have it at the barber shop."

"Daddy got killed, but Mama says he's still looking out for us."

"Yes. I believe that's true, Pauli."

Clarita has instructed me to shop at one of the department stores downtown, so when we get to the busy intersections of the

Junction, I guide the boy, hand on shoulder, to the streetcar platform, and we ride to Loveman's. As in most of the department
stores, our money is good for buying, but there are no Negroes
behind the counters. We have to wait a few minutes until the shoe
salesman serves all the white customers, but when he comes to
where we sit in the corner, he greets Pauli and asks me about his
mother. "She's a little under the weather. I'll tell her you asked
about her. She wants the boy to have new Buster Browns, and she
asked that you please measure his foot and leave him a little room
to grow."

The salesman pulls out the wood shoe measure and writes the
size on a piece of paper. He goes behind the hanging curtain and
returns with a box of new shoes. He then laces up the left shoe.
"Okay, sit still, young man, and let's see how these fit." The man
uses a shoehorn to get Pauli's foot in the high top, and when Pauli
stands the man depresses the shoe tip with his thumb. There is
still an inch of toe space. When the other shoe is laced and fitted,
Pauli struts like a peacock.

"We'll take these," I say.

"I'll throw in a pair of brown socks," the salesman says, accepting my five-dollar bill.

He returns in two minutes with my change and a box containing the boy's old shoes and a new pair of socks.

"Do you sell baby clothes?" I ask.

"Yes, we do. You can find them over there," the man says,
pointing. "Uh, is Miss Clarita expecting?" he asks.

"No. My wife and I have a baby due pretty soon."

The salesman nods and stares as if he's about to paint my
portrait.

"What's expecting?" Pauli asks as he follows behind me in the
store.

When I return home, Anna Kate is still upset and doesn't look up from her knitting. Mae has thrown herself into my arms and is pulling at my cap. I remove it and put it on her head, to her delight.

"We didn't wait dinner," Anna Kate says. "It's important for Mae to eat on time. But I put a plate in the oven for you."

"Thank you. I'll do up the dishes when I'm finished."

"Thank you," Anna Kate responds coldly and with focus on the movement of the knitting needles.

"Thank you," Mae parrots.

I lift her into the high chair and give her a picture book, then take my dish to the table and say a silent prayer over my food. I dig into the green beans, potatoes, and neckbones. Anna Kate has also made corn bread.

"Uhm. Good," I say, and give a green bean to Mae, who is reaching for my plate.

After a few minutes, Anna Kate peers at me. "Did you find your friends well?"

"Yes. Clarita is doing much better. Her jaw's no longer wired shut. Her son, Pauli, is a bright boy, and he asks questions all the time. Clarita asked me to take the boy to get some shoes. She wanted to pay for them, but I didn't let her," I say with a direct look at Anna Kate.

Anna Kate resumes her knitting. A few more minutes of silence come between us.

"I'm going to get a glass of milk. Would you like a glass?" I ask.

"No. But Mae might want milk."

"What do you say, baby girl? You want some milk?"

"Milk, Daddy. Milk," Mae chants, smiling.

"Oh, and I got this for the baby. At Loveman's," I say, taking the blue baby shawl out of my jacket pocket.

Anna Kate unwraps it, looking closely at the ribbon detail on the garment, then lays the shawl aside.

"I'm knitting my own shawl," she says, still peeved at me. "Mr. Freeman knocked on the door a while ago. It's okay with me if you want to go downstairs and visit with him. Esther and Harriet are coming by soon."

"You don't want my company?" I ask, tweaking her cheek.

"You stop that, Robert. I want to stay mad at you."

"But you can't, can you, because I'm such a good husband, and a great father, and I'm also a mighty fine-looking man."

I pull my wife from her chair and move her slowly around the kitchen while I whistle "Ain't Misbehavin'." Mae claps her hands and twirls. "Dance, Daddy. I dance, too."

"You're a mess," Anna Kate says, laughing and pulling away. "Let me sit down and catch my breath. You go on now. I'll finish the dishes. I've done most of them already anyway."

Before I leave, I look over my shoulder. Anna Kate has picked up the store-bought shawl to examine it.

FREEMAN IS PLAYING DOMINOES AT THE DINING ROOM TABLE with two other lodgers. I wave to Mrs. Ardle, who is mopping the kitchen floor. She closes the door when I light my cigar.

"C'mon, Harrington. Jump in here. We can play partners after this game."

I watch the men play and accept the drink that's offered. The men are talking trash and the fat man passes the flask every fifteen minutes before returning it to his inside pocket.

"I heard you came looking for me, George," I say.

"I was just coming to get you for dominoes."

"I had a chore to take care of."

"Esther's going up to your place sometime this evening, and I thought you'd want to get away. I don't know what those women gab about in the evening, since they spend so much time together during the day—shopping and making those doilies and things."

"Women need their friendships," I say. "Just like we enjoy the company of men."

"Well, I know one thing. We coloreds have to stick together. The whites sure do that. The Jews stick together, and the Italians," Freeman says. "Sometimes I think we don't stick up for each other enough."

I look at Freeman and nod.

"Well, I never met a woman yet that I could just be friends with," the man with the flask says. "Not even the ugly ones."

The other men laugh. I don't join in, but they don't notice.

Freeman and I make good dominoes partners, and we've become friends of sorts. He's a thoughtful man, and like me he's respected for his skills. He's a cook, and he cares about his work and family. Over the next hour and a half, we win two games and split our dollar winnings.

"Well, gentlemen, I'm going upstairs to my wife," I say.

"Lucky man," the flask drinker says.

"You're right about that," I say.

Freeman catches up to me before I get to the stairs. "Talk to you a minute, man?" he asks.

"Sure."

"Outside, I mean," Freeman says, heading to the back door.

The boardinghouse has a large backyard, with grass and flowers bordering one side of the fence. On the opposite side are trees and a hard dirt patch where I park my car and where Mrs. Ardle has a shed, four clotheslines, and a small vegetable garden. Free-man walks to the clothesline and stops.

"A man came around earlier tonight looking for you. It was just before dinner, and I was out front watching Carrie Mae play."

"What'd he say?"

"He asked if there was a man named Robert living here. I told him no. He said the man he was looking for drove a Franklin. I told him nobody had anything that fancy here."

"Was he a policeman?"

"Maybe. He was a big man. Had a hard look. He wanted to know who I was, and he seemed satisfied when I told him I was the cook at the mill diner. Then he came back here and looked under the tarp at your car. I watched him from the back door."

"Thanks, Freeman. I appreciate you looking out for me."

"You in some kind of trouble, man?"

"Not really. A detective saw me at Griggs a couple of times. I think that woman who tipped the police off to the booze in the back room pointed me out to him."

"The white woman?"

"Yeah. She's only half-white, but yeah. Her."

"Hmm. If I was you, I'd just keep looking over my shoulder. Something wasn't right about that guy. He made my blood run cold."

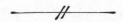

Two days later, the woodworks foreman comes out to my shed and stands in the doorway. I'm shirtless and covered in sawdust because I've spent all morning wood-turning spindles using a pole lathe. Now I'm sanding the first of twenty-four chair legs for the home of a minister in Smithfield.

"You're a fast worker, Harrington."

"Yes, sir. There are no distractions out here, and I can really get a lot done when I'm focused."

"I need to interrupt you for a minute. Mr. Owens wants to see you."

"Okay."

I put down the sandpaper and put on my shirt. As we walk to the main factory I try to brush off as much of the wood particles from my pants as I can. The foreman leads me across the shop floor, and I feel a dozen eyeballs on my back. He knocks and then opens the door for me and beckons me into the office. Owens is behind his desk and points to a chair.

"Mr. Harrington. I make it my business to know as much as I can about the men who work for me. Obviously, the strong recommendation from your last work site went a long way toward me hiring you."

My stomach begins to turn flips. What has Owens found out about me? This kind of speech usually ends in a firing or a promotion. I know I'm not about to be promoted.

"Yes, sir. Mr. Campbell was the architect on the mansion job, and I appreciate his recommendation."

"A policeman came by the office this morning asking about you. He wanted to know if you were a good worker, and he asked what kind of car you drive."

Mr. Owens looks nervous. I glance at the foreman, who gives me a weak smile. Owens clears his throat before he continues.

"Mr. Atterbury here says you're one of the best carpenters he's ever seen. He says you keep to yourself, finish your projects on time, and you're never late to work."

"No, sir."

"Are you in trouble with the police, Harrington? Because if

you are, I don't care how good a worker you are, I'll have to let you go."

"No, sir. I'm not in any trouble. I've never had any run-in with the police. But this detective has his eye on me."

"The uniformed officer who came today works for this detective, I think. I've heard about this man," Owens said. "He has a reputation for associating with questionable people. I'm from Ohio, so I'm not caught up in groups that go about threatening and hurting people. But I don't want the attention of those people either."

"Yes, sir. I understand."

"I need a man like you. Your work gives our company good word-of-mouth references, and that's everything in our line of business. Stay away from these men. Don't give them any reason to be interested in you."

He stands and to my surprise extends his hand to shake mine. Atterbury walks me back to my workshop, and again I feel the stares of the white workers. Before we get to the shed, he stops me.

"Some of us don't condone the acts of the Klan, Harrington. Owens is a Quaker—so am I. We believe every man has a right to live free and make his way in the world. But these groups are dangerous because their hatred comes out of fear. Mr. Owens and I will try to keep you safe, but you should know a lot of the men on the shop floor don't feel the same way we do."

"Mr. Atterbury, I understand and I thank you for speaking up for me."

"Watch your back." He pauses a moment. "Why don't you work an extra hour tonight to make up the time. At the overtime rate, of course."

THIRTY-FIVE

━━━━◆━━━━

2019

I'm in Kristen's car across the street from my Airbnb. It's now a crime scene. Monique is in the back seat. Darius is on his way.

I was so unnerved I called all three of them even before the police. I sat on the curb, hands shaking, and texted a photo of the noose and the warning. Then I began to cry. The gray-haired white couple who live next door came outside when they saw my distress, the lady made me a cup of tea, and they both sat with me on their porch until Kristen arrived.

A police car came next. The two officers—a white male paired with an African American female—were skeptical about my report, nonchalant, until they saw the noose and the blood for themselves. That really got them moving. Within fifteen minutes three patrol cars and a lab vehicle were on the scene. Neighbors gathered to watch the action and the friendly couple moved through the crowd explaining the situation.

When Monique arrived in an Uber I waved her over to Kristen's car, where I introduced the two.

"I'll get in back," Monique said. "The cops don't always react well to me. I don't want to be a distraction. Darius isn't here yet?"

"No. I haven't seen him," I say.

"He'll be here. Tell me what happened."

I repeat the story I've already told the police and Kristen and it brings the tears again.

"Who does that kind of shit?" Kristen says angrily. "This is fucking 2019, for God's sake."

"There's been a resurgence in hate groups ever since Obama," Monique says. "These snakes have been waiting to come up from underground."

Darius arrives in the company of a police muckety-muck whose presence sends the rank and file into higher gear. Kristen toots the horn and I wave.

"I see you brought the cavalry," Monique quips to Darius.

He rolls his eyes and squats at the passenger window, staring intently at me. "You all right?" he asks through clenched teeth.

"She's shaken up," Kristen replies.

"You must be Kristen," Darius says, leaning into the car. "Thanks for being here."

"I live only ten minutes away," she says.

"What the hell is this, Darius?" Monique asks. "What asshole would do this?"

"Let me in," he says cramming his six-foot frame next to Monique in the small back seat. "It hasn't been in the media, but there's been several of these incidents in the last month or so."

"You mean leaving nooses on someone's doorstep?" I ask.

"Nooses, cross burnings, phone threats, anitsemitic graffiti," Darius lists.

"That's some bullshit," Kristen says.

"That's some *throwback* bullshit," Monique adds. "Don't Black people have enough going on without the Klan resurfacing?"

"They never went away," Darius say dourly.

"Look, I need to get back in the house," I say. "One of the officers took my phone and keys. I need my laptop and bag. I have work to do tonight, and I have interviews tomorrow."

"You're still writing this story?" Kristen asks.

"Damn straight. I had my cry. Now I get back to work."

"Okay, okay," Darius says in a calm voice. "Look, Meg. The police aren't going to let you stay in the house tonight. The investigators are being methodical. They're taking prints, talking to neighbors, looking for security camera footage; they'll need to keep your phone, and they want to check for bombs."

"Bombs?"

"One of the recent incidents involved a vehicle bomb. The police want to sweep your car before you drive it again."

"Darius, I need my stuff!"

"I'll talk to the captain. Do you have someplace you can stay tonight?"

I look at him, unsure of what to say. I have important interviews tomorrow, and a story deadline. I don't have time to find another place to stay.

"I guess I could get a hotel room for tonight. But I need my phone. I have notes in my phone. Names and addresses. My schedule. And I need my laptop, my folders, work clothes, *and* my car."

"Okay. Let's talk to Masterson," Darius says.

"*That's* Captain Masterson? He's not going to help me. He's a by-the-book guy."

"These right-wing hate groups are aided and abetted by law enforcement," Monique announces. "I've read the FBI report.

Blue uniform by day. White hood by night. I don't think we can trust any of them."

"We can trust this one," Darius says.

Joshua Masterson and Darius are obviously friends because it's agreed I can keep my laptop for now but I have to bring it to police headquarters tomorrow, and that's when the keys to the car and my phone will be returned.

Darius and I are allowed to enter the Airbnb accompanied by the female officer who was first on the scene. While Darius chats with the woman, I put my laptop and files into my backpack and gather some clothes for the next few days. As we leave I look at the dozen people swarming around the porch and yard. A man dressed in bombproof gear is peering under my car.

Kristen informs me that I'm staying in her guest room tonight. The four of us are gathering at her place now to eat and talk. Darius runs back to the house to see if he can take the pizza and carrot cake. I need to contact the Airbnb host—if the neighbors haven't already done so. I also need to call home.

I'm grateful for the friendships I've made in Birmingham, and it's good to be surrounded by this tribe of kindred spirits after feeling the ground fall from underneath me. Kristen's cat, Biblioteca, circles around us as we drink wine and decry the state of the world that would cause some sicko to come after me. We also speculate on who the culprit or culprits could be. Of course, the police are high on Monique's list.

"I'm meeting with the chief tomorrow and I plan to ask him very direct questions."

"What about old man Pruitt?" Kristen asks, then shakes her head. "No. I guess if he was up to something, Zach would warn us."

"Who's Pruitt?" Monique asks.

"*Former* chief of police," I say. "He's a crotchety old guy but I don't know if he'd still have juice with the people who'd hang a noose on my door.'

"Who's Zach?" Darius asks.

"Pruitt's grandson. He's cool," I say. "Kristen, what about one of the investigators at your father's insurance company? They're cozy with the police and they know I'm asking questions about police misconduct. Plus, the company has funded a few of these alt-right patriot groups."

"You've been investigating my father?" Kristen squints at me.

"Well, I—"

"You're getting too close," Monique interrupts.

"Too close to what?" I ask.

Monique shrugs. "The truth. You stepped on somebody's toes hard enough for them take offense."

"But how could the truth about a decades-old police shooting threaten anyone now?" I ask. "Everyone involved is long gone."

"I believe it has something to do with the Klan," Kristen says. "You were right about that old booklet you spotted in Pruitt's files, McKenzie. It was for a thirties Klan gathering—a convocation of sorts—they were held every year. The attendees were a Who's Who of Birmingham. My researcher connected some of the names in the booklet to old court cases involving racial violence, and now we're checking names against documents donated to the library, the Civil Rights Institute, and the historical society."

"That's why Simenon isn't listed. He was already dead."

"But I bet more than a few of the men, and women, listed in that booklet have children and grandchildren living in Birmingham today who would be horrified to have people learn their ancestors wore white sheets and terrorized Black people," Monique says. "People never want to look bad, and what you're writing might reveal secrets about some very important people."

Darius sits on the arm of my chair. "Have you called your parents yet?"

"No. I still need to do that."

"There's a landline in the spare bedroom," Kristen says. "Follow me. You can make your calls from there." As we step into the room, she stops and turns to me. "Why are you investigating Daddy?"

"You know me. I Google everybody."

"Have you . . . found anything?"

"Just what I said. Gleason Insurance has been a corporate sponsor for several right-wing conferences."

"I didn't know," Kristen says dolefully.

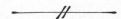

I'm on speakerphone with both my parents. Mom gives an audible intake of air when I describe the noose, but other than asking if I'm okay she's been surprisingly quiet. Daddy insists on either flying to Birmingham to get me, or me boarding a plane for home tomorrow morning. I decline both ideas.

"I'm not in harm's way. I'm staying with Kristen, the librarian-friend I've told you about, and other friends are here too."

"Is that Darius boy with you?" Daddy asks.

"Yes."

"Good. I like that boy."

"When *are* you coming home?" Mom asks.

"Early next week. I've asked the paper for a few days' extension."

"You do what you have to do. You use your head and call us if you need *anything*. You got that, Meghan?"

"I got it, Mom."

When I return to the living room, the conversation stops. Kristen and Darius glance at me, then look away. Monique gives me the full, unblinking Black-woman stare.

"What?" I ask.

Darius answers with a question: "What did your parents say?"

"Daddy says he likes you."

"No. Really? What did they say?" Darius asks, stifling a smile.

"Daddy thinks I should leave."

"You need to go home, girl," Monique states. "That's what we've decided."

"You have, have you?"

I reach for my wineglass, holding it out to Kristen for a top-off. "I have no intention of leaving."

"McKenzie, that's crazy," Kristen says. "Someone's been watching you, they have your phone number, know what kind of car you drive. They knew you were away from the house."

"Well, whoever *they* is, are not scaring me off this story. I've thought about it. If someone really wanted to kill me, I'd be dead. If it's the police, they could just chalk it up to inner-city violence and pretend to investigate. No. This is something else. Someone's trying to make a point."

All three are staring at me now. Darius folds me into a hug. I squeeze him back. "And what point are *you* making by staying?" he asks.

"That we are not the same Black people they terrorized ninety years ago."

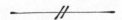

Kristen's guest room also functions as her den. There are mementoes of her travels displayed on the shelves and walls—framed photos of a young Kristen wearing a poncho, surrounded by two dozen kids, and posing with brown-skinned men carrying seed sacks. There are also plaques and certificates of gratitude for her philanthropic work in Paraguay.

I use the guest bathroom across the hall to take a long, hot bath and let my pores release some of the fear and anger that have permeated my skin. When I return to my temporary bedroom, Kristen has unfolded the sleeper sofa and laid out pillows and linens. There's a knock at the door.

"You want help to make the bed?" Kristen asks, poking in her head.

"Sure. Thanks."

"You're only the second person to use this sofa bed," Kristen says. "My sister slept on it a while ago when she was mad at Mom and Dad."

"I'm so grateful to you for letting me sleep here tonight. I really didn't want to be by myself."

"Feel free to use the room for the rest of your stay, McKenzie. It'll be nice having someone around the house. That is, if you can put up with me and the cat."

I drop my end of the sheet and give Kristen a quick hug. "I am indebted to you," I say.

Kristen wipes at a tear, then points to the bed. "Get back to your end of the fitted sheet."

"What's wrong?"

Kristen shakes her head.

"Are you still worried for me?"

"Yes."

We finish making the bed in silence. The cat pushes open the door, her white tail high as she investigates the sleeper sofa. Maybe she's thinking of joining me on the bed tonight. Kristen pulls a blanket wrapped in a plastic covering from the closet shelf.

"It gets cool in here with the air-conditioning. Do you think you can sleep? I have pills if you need them."

"No, thanks. I'm polishing my blog tonight. I'll be up a few more hours."

"I guess you'll have quite the story now," Kristen says glumly.

"Kristen, what's wrong? Tell me."

She dips her gaze. "I'm embarrassed. For my city and for my people."

"Your people?"

"White people. We can be such assholes."

I laugh. But Kristen doesn't. I nudge her a couple of times with my elbow until she gives a weak smile. Biblioteca purrs and she picks her up. "Are you coming into the library in the morning?"

"Darius is taking me to breakfast, then driving me to police headquarters. It might be after eleven before I see you."

"Okay."

"Oh, and here's the library book I borrowed," I say, handing over the photo volume. "I don't need it anymore. I'm pretty sure I have the full picture now."

THIRTY-SIX

⸺◆⸺

2019

Darius picks me up at eight, but there's been a change of plans. I'm not meeting the police chief.

"Masterson called late last night. They were going to pass you off to the public information officer. They're stonewalling you, Meg. I'm sorry."

"It's not your fault. I'm pissed, but I always figured I'd have to go the legal route."

"Masterson wants to see you, though—at the church. He wants to return your personal items and talk to you about a couple of other things. Since we've got the time, let's get breakfast first."

We're back at the MC Grille, where Darius's favorite waitress serves us French toast and Canadian bacon, and I tell him about a soon-to-be-published Northeastern University study I've discovered in my research.

"It's a report about the Birmingham Police Department from 1930 to about 1970. It shows a pattern of police-involved shootings of Black residents, and an equally clear pattern of not disciplining the white police officers involved. The findings miss my great-granddad's shooting by only a year."

Darius shakes his head. "We'll never live down 1963. I should just accept that."

"I know you and a lot of others have worked hard to change the way Birmingham is viewed. But more than a hundred years of civil rights suppression can't possibly be undone in a few decades."

Darius glances at me. "Is that what you say in your blog?"

"Yes. Pretty much. Sorry to be on my soapbox."

"I like you up there."

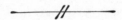

Masterson looks tired when Darius and I walk into the empty classroom at Evangelical Church. The kitchen ladies have fed the captain a late breakfast. The steam wafting from his coffee makes me long for a cup. I'm not sure of the purpose of this impromptu meeting, except to get back my belongings, but I trust Darius and I settle into a seat.

Masterson hands me an envelope. It contains my phone and keys. A kitchen volunteer brings in another tray with coffee and pastries.

"Why aren't we talking at police headquarters?" I ask.

Masterson gives a sardonic smile. "I'm sorry you couldn't get in with the chief. He was advised not to meet with you."

"By whom?"

"People with influence."

"Are we on the record?" I ask.

Masterson and Darius look at each other. The chief has passed on an interview, and protocol would dictate the captain should too. I'm surprised when he says yes.

"Are you sure about this, Josh?" Darius asks.

Masterson nods. He pulls out a handkerchief to wipe his brow. "This Black Lives Matter story you're writing has people on edge, Ms. McKenzie. I don't know what kind of cover-up somebody's trying to orchestrate, but I won't be a part of it."

Masterson's a policeman, but he hasn't been severed from his roots or his race. I decide to trust him, and I give him the details of my family story. He listens and takes notes. I show him the 1929 clipping from the *St. Petersburg Times* confirming the police shooting of my great-grandfather.

"This was called in to the paper by St. Pete's chief of police," I say. "Why do you suppose Birmingham PD would call the chief in another city to report they'd shot a Black man?"

"I have no idea. Unless they feared some kind of backlash. It says your great-grandfather resisted arrest."

He and I stare at each other. We both know under Jim Crow laws a Black man resisting arrest might have been as little as looking sideways at a white police officer.

"You've made inquiries about a detective who was on the force in the twenties. Is that the man you think killed your great-grandfather?"

"I don't know. His name's Carl Simenon. Not a good cop. He was on the job when murdered by an unknown assailant, and as far as I can tell died within days or weeks of my great-grandfather's shooting."

"When an officer is killed there's always a thorough investigation."

"That's what I thought. And the chief of police at the time vowed to find the killer. But the news coverage about this detective's death drops off the face of the earth. And why isn't Simenon listed in the department's roster of fallen officers?" I ask, handing him a copy of the page I found on the department's website. "There are policemen listed here going back to 1900. Simenon's not among them. My paper sent a FOIA request to the department early last week naming my great-grandfather and this detective. No one's gotten back to us."

"I'll find out what I can," Masterson says, jotting down a note.

"I'd like to be allowed to review Simenon's personnel file."

"I'm not sure that will be possible. Personnel files are internal documents—"

I interrupt Masterson. "I already have three pages from his file. Copies of citizen complaints, and some of the information has been redacted."

"And where'd you get hold of those?"

"I'd rather not say, but I'd like to see the rest of the file. At the very least any documents from the file that should be public information."

Again, Masterson and I hold a stare. His resolve comes from being by the book. Mine is fueled by my growing irritation at the Birmingham Police Department's foot-dragging on both the FOIA request and my attempts to get an official interview.

"I'll have to get back to you on that, Ms. McKenzie. Meanwhile, I also want to give you an update on the investigation of your case. We found a fingerprint, and it's in the FBI's database. It belongs to a man who is not a Birmingham resident but is a known member of a domestic hate group implicated in crimes across the South."

"Can you give me his name?" I ask, turning to a fresh page in my notebook.

"No. We don't want this man identified to the public just now.

He's been underground for a long time, and if there's even a small chance we can get our hands on him we want to keep that advantage. I hope you understand."

"I do, but I've included details of the vandalism at the Airbnb in a blog I'm sending to my paper tonight."

"If you'll agree to give me twenty-four hours before you report on this hate crime, we may be able to get this guy."

I aim a skeptical look at Masterson, and then at Darius, who raises an eyebrow. Saxby might not go along with a delay on the blog, and I'm not sure I want to either.

"Darius told you there've been other incidents?" Masterson asks.

"Yes."

"Some have been more violent, but your case is included as among the more serious."

"Should I be worried?"

"We're providing you a protection detail. Nothing invasive, just a surveillance car nearby."

Masterson and Darius wait for my response, but all I can process is the rush of blood to my cheeks and my quickening pulse. *I told Mama and Daddy I wasn't in danger.* I reach for my coffee mug, quickly returning it to the table when I realize my hand is shaking hard enough to be noticed.

"It's just a precaution," Masterson adds when he sees my reaction.

I nod and slip my hands below the table.

"When do you return to Detroit?"

"Three or four days."

Masterson agrees to answer a few more questions but falls into bureaucratic mode on the subjects of Black Lives Matter and hate crimes. He's more forthcoming when I bring up the 1979 case of

Bonita Carter, an unarmed twenty-year-old Black woman shot in the back by a Birmingham police officer as she sat alone in a car.

"You've done your homework," he says.

"The white officer who shot Miss Carter had numerous excessive force complaints in his file. Police leadership knew he was a problem, yet he remained on the job. Why?"

"That case was the impetus for change in our department. We speak of our community policing protocols as before or after BC, meaning Bonita Carter. Once those initials might have stood for Bull Conner."

Masterson departs with a promise to inquire on the status of the FOIA request and the whereabouts of the Simenon file, and with my agreement to wait twenty-four hours before posting my blog.

Darius and I are about to leave when Mattie Robinson, the church secretary, comes into the classroom with a canvas bag. She looks even more stern than the first time I saw her. She places the bag on the table.

"I hear you've had some trouble, Ms. McKenzie. Those kinds of actions belong to a dark time in our history and they can't belong to us anymore."

"Yes, ma'am."

"Here are a few letters and whatnot from Cecile Clarke. I've sorted through them and I know you'll be interested in them." Her stern look becomes somber. "There is also a bundle of letters from Carrie Freeman. She found them this morning and sent them over. I don't know what's in them. Let me know if you have any questions."

"Thank you."

She flashes an exasperated look and seems about to say more when she turns and leaves.

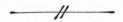

I'm on my way to Caregiver's Residential Living, where Clarita Alvarez's son lives. It's nice to be driving again, and to have my phone. I've missed a call from Saxby, so I toggle between the Maps app and the speakerphone.

"Call Saxby mobile," I order the app.

"How's the piece going, McKenzie?" he asks without a hello.

"Fine. Twice as long as we agreed, but I figured that was all right, given what's happened."

"It is."

"There's one catch. I have a few on-the-record comments from a police official—mostly boring—but they have new information on the noose investigation. They want another day before I publish so they can flush out the guy they think is responsible."

"They have an identity?"

"Yep. From a fingerprint."

"Is he a bad guy?"

"Known hate-group member. He may be connected to other incidents in the city."

"Are you in danger?"

"No," I lie.

"Damn, you're getting yourself quite a story. Yes, we can hold for a day, but I don't want to delay it beyond that. And you're approved to stay an additional week if you need it," Saxby says.

"Thank you, but I may not need the whole time."

"What's on today's agenda?"

"Still trying to connect more dots. I'm on my way to visit someone else who might have known my great-grandfather, and I have new documents—photos and letters—to look through. I'm also waiting for records on the dirty detective. And get this, Saxby, I now have confirmation that the man who was chief of police when my great-grandfather was murdered was a member of the Klan. Not surprising, really, but I saw his name on a roster of Klansmen. My library friend is still running that list of names through her database. Even if none of it lays a trail directly to my great-grandfather's murder, I still have enough to tell a story of systemic police violence against Blacks in Birmingham dating back to the early 1900s."

"Go get 'em, tiger," he says and hangs up without a goodbye.

What I haven't told Saxby is Masterson has already texted to say he can't find Simenon's file. It was checked out by someone in the criminal division, and the records clerk couldn't say who it was.

I pull into the parking lot of Paul Griggs's nursing facility followed by the unmarked police vehicle. The driver gives me a nod before I go inside. The front-desk lady takes my name and asks me to sit until someone can come for me. The waiting area is clean and the décor modest, but it's been my experience that these facilities can have the nicest lobbies yet provide the poorest clinical and therapeutic services. I suspend my judgment until I can get beyond the main floor.

The long-term-care unit is in an adjacent building, and the friendly lady in the green scrubs and beige sweater leading the way chats first about the beautiful weather of the last few days, then, in response to my questions, her fifteen-year history as a floor nurse. She pauses before entering the semiprivate room where Paul has been a patient for more than thirty years.

"Pauli has dementia. He's not going to recognize you," she warns. "It says here you're a niece, but you seem too young," she says, looking at the visitor form.

"I'm a great-niece," I say, continuing my deception. "He hasn't seen me since I was a little girl, so he probably wouldn't have known me anyway. Can he still speak?"

"Oh yes. Quite well when he wants to. He's not ambulatory, but he likes to sit in the sun when the weather permits, and he listens to music. He also still has a pretty good appetite."

"You call him Pauli?"

"Yes. That's what his mother used to call him. He read me some of her letters. But that was a long time ago. He doesn't read now. That's him sitting near the window. I'll introduce you."

"Pauli, this is your great-niece, Meghan," the nurse says.

"Hello," he says without looking at me. He rubs the nurse's hand when she touches his arm.

Pauli is ninety-five years old. His watery eyes are sunken into brown, mottled skin and his lips form a permanent pout. A few strands of gray hair reach across his head from two directions and he has a yellowing beard. Liver spots stretch across his forearms and hands.

"This is Meghan, and she's come to visit you," the nurse tries again.

This time he sweeps his eyes across me before turning back to the window. The nurse signals that I should sit, and I adjust my chair next to Pauli's so I can see what he's staring at. I say hi again. He doesn't respond.

It's a glorious morning. I was too distracted to notice on the drive over. Just outside the window is a beautiful oak, maybe forty feet high with leaves beginning to color, and a magnet for birds and squirrels. I don't know much about birds, but I spot a bright red male cardinal and his duller mate. Birds with a yellow underbelly and black birds with a splotch of orange on the tufts of their heads flit from limb to limb. The grounds are immaculate and the front yard with its arboreal playground makes for an entertaining view.

I reach into my bag and get a packet of gum—the old-fashioned kind individually wrapped in foil and a paper sleeve. I picked up the habit from my visits with Grandma. I begin chewing the gum and the sweet smell drifts between us.

"Juicy Fruit?" I say, offering him a stick.

He looks down at the gum and holds out his hand. When he has trouble manipulating the wrapper, I open it for him and he gives me a crooked-teeth smile as saliva slides through his lips. We both chew in silence for a moment staring out the window. I pull three photographs from my bag. One by one, I place the images on the table between us. A photo of Mrs. Freeman's parents, the image of boarders outside the Fourth Avenue Inn, and finally my great-grandparents' wedding photo.

Pauli doesn't look at the photographs straightaway, but when his eyes finally flick away from the vibrant birds to the black-and-white stills he seems to show interest. He reaches a shaking hand toward the table but can't complete the action. I lift each photo so he has a closer view of the images and stare at his face. When I hold up the wedding photo, wetness springs to his eyes so quickly it startles me. A tear trickles halfway down his sunken cheek and hangs there.

"Mr. Bubby," Pauli says softly.

"Bobby?" I ask excitedly. "Like short for Robert?"

Pauli points a trembling finger at the photo. "Mr. Bubby."

THIRTY-SEVEN

Biding My Time

1929

For the next few days, I'm constantly looking over my shoulder. Only when I'm cutting or carving wood, manipulating it, sanding the grain, brushing it free of dust, do I have a semblance of peace. Otherwise I'm waiting—for Anna Kate to have the baby, for the detective to show his hand, and for a time when I can allow myself a deep breath.

I suspect these shadow men who seem so interested in my comings and goings are members of the Klan and are not to be underestimated. I've heard tales of their danger and destruction all my life, and I've seen tears form in my mother's eyes at their mention. They are a hateful force throughout the South, including Alabama.

I've stopped my visits to Clarita's house. It's safer for me, and her, to stay away. She's better now, anyway, and has other friends to take care of her. But I'll miss young Pauli.

At home, we pass the time in our routines. Anna Kate still takes care of our apartment and our child, cooks our meals, sews, knits, and grows flowers. Mae is a happy, carefree child and often plays with the Freemans' little girl downstairs. She's also become her mother's helper and has learned to put my noon meal in the cloth bag I carry to work.

We still shop together on Saturdays, walking for the exercise it gives Anna Kate, and I feel safe and anonymous on these sidewalks chock-full with other Black folks. Once we purchase our meats, vegetables, and staples, I usually buy ice cream cones for the three of us. I've been putting away an extra ten dollars per paycheck for a while, and we'll use our savings to move to another place across town as soon as the baby is born. We'll need the extra room, and I'll feel better if the police don't know where I live. That means more meals of less expensive meat like pig feet and chicken rather than ham or beef, but Anna Kate can work wonders in the kitchen, and the way she cooks her pig feet—with potatoes, string beans, and applesauce, tastes as good as, or better than, ham.

On Sundays we drive to church for worship, then return home for our meal and our projects. I'm working on more home carpentry pieces—a bookshelf for Mae's books and toys, and windowsill boxes for Anna Kate's blooms. The sewing bees at our apartment have been cut back to once a week, but Anna Kate has crocheted and knitted a dozen sweaters and caps for the baby. We both read Mae stories from her picture books, and I've bought a radio.

Occasionally, I sit out in the backyard with Freeman and have a smoke, but I don't spend much time in the public areas of the boardinghouse anymore. I've come to trust Freeman. He's a steady man, but the others who play cards and dominoes and listen to the parlor radio are men I don't really know. Over the years I've learned that people will usually act in their own interest, and the people who laugh and drink with you one day can have their reasons to talk to the police about you the next.

My workplace environment has also changed. The white workers never said much to me anyway, but since the police visited my employer to ask about me, the friendliness of three recently hired colored workers has ebbed. I always pretty much stay to myself, but a few times, during the half-hour lunch break, I've joined these men to sit on the sawhorses and talk about sports and such. Yesterday, and the time before, I noticed the conversation went silent when I moved into their circle. When it picked up again, it was to talk only of work. So today I'm eating my lunch in the car.

Anna Kate has packed a square of peach cobbler to go with my fried-fish sandwich, and I'm dabbing at the crumbs on my lap when I see a dark Chevy pull off the road near the side of the sawmill. From my vantage point I can see two men in the front seats. The car idles there for five minutes before it turns and moves back down the paved road that leads to town.

I really don't know how to change my situation with the police. I'm not sure I have any other choice but to sit tight. Anna Kate is due in a month. I could drive her back to St. Pete to the safety of her mother, but in her condition the trip would be too difficult. I also can't be certain the police won't arrest me as soon as I return. But one thing I am sure of is that my rejection of Nedra has set my current predicament in motion.

The work whistle blows the end of lunch. I take a last drink of water and head to my makeshift carpentry shop, where I'm carving the inlays for two china-cabinet doors. The afternoon sun pulses sharp and direct on my exposed skin. An occasional breeze flirts with the air, transporting honeysuckle and pine, but it's no reprieve from the heat.

I pick up my paring chisel and return to my task of chipping a raised eight-inch border on the beechwood cabinet door. The carving carries me away from my present troubles, and only as I lift my head to brush away curling tendrils of wood do I take note of the beads of sweat sliding down my neck, or the shiver up my spine.

THIRTY-EIGHT

2019

It's been an intense morning by the time I arrive at the library with a chicken and quinoa protein bowl, a madeleines packet, my tote, and the bag from Mattie Robinson. I don't see Kristen around, and I'm dragging, so I go to my carrel, dump everything into the side chair, and sit on the edge of the desk to smell my roses and, for a moment, visualize myself in Darius's arms. I peer at the bag in my side chair. It taunts me. But I'm not settled enough to glean a stack of letters, so I call Monique to tell her about my run-in with Mrs. Robinson at the church, and the stash I've received.

"Congratulations," Monique says. "You've been officially adopted by the Old Folks Power Network," she says.

"What?" I say laughing.

"Mrs. Robinson was livid when I told her what happened to you at your rental house, and she's been rallying her forces. Everybody wants to help."

DESPITE THE MISSING POLICE FOLDER, THINGS ARE LOOKING up. I mull it all over as I gobble down my lunch and a bottle of water. Just as it had with Carrie Freeman, the wedding photo triggered a memory for Pauli. I don't know what relationship he had with Great-Grandpa, but he knew him. Now I can connect both Simenon complainants—Carrie Mae's father, George, and Clarita Alvarez—to my great-grandfather.

I start writing. The second installment of my blog is on hold but I can begin part three, where I introduce Simenon, detail the Bonita Carter story, and point to a historic pattern of race-based police misconduct. I'm writing easily, not with any syntax or organization, but just creating massive paragraphs of facts, observations, and quotes. Later I'll insert the details and blocks of information within my timeline and polish the language with active verbs and colorful adjectives to make the story really come alive.

After an hour of writing, I'm focused, no longer hungry, and ready to tackle the bag's contents—letters and photographs. I grab the photos. The first images are blueprints, designs of the boardinghouse and the grounds from 1906. The lodging started as only two floors. Later, an additional two stories were added. There is a photo of a couple standing in front of what I believe is the finished four-story building—the handwritten scrawl on back identifies the couple as W. & H. ARDLE. It's Harriet Ardle and her husband.

There are other photos of people I presume are boarders. In one, Mrs. Ardle stands outside flanked by a group of eight Black men. Another shows a group similarly posed, but this time everyone is seated inside a parlor and dressed more formally. There are three women and two children in this grainy black-and-white photo and although one of the women is pale enough to be my great-grandmother, she doesn't look like the young girl in the wedding photo I have.

At three o'clock I'm craving a coffee. Kristen is too busy to leave, so I promise to bring her a latte and head to Starbucks. A black Ford Explorer follows my path, and when I exit the coffee shop the SUV is parked across the street. A bearded blond guy wearing jeans and a navy UAB hoodie is leaning on the door. He gives me a smile and a two-fingered salute and gets behind the wheel as I head back to the library.

"I have police protection now," I say to Kristen and plop into her side chair.

Her eyes widen and she grips her cup in both hands. "Seriously?"

"Yep. I had to give them your address, so I expect they'll be parked outside your house at night. It's a black SUV."

"Wow," Kristen says.

"I brought something for you to look at. Photographs of the old boardinghouse where my great-grandpa lived," I say, placing them on Kristen's desk. "I didn't find him in the pictures, but they're interesting. Similar to the photos in the library book. There's a dignity in the way all the people pose. They seem to realize they're being captured in a moment of time for others to see in the future. Not like the goofy things we do in selfies."

"Selfies also capture a moment in time," Kristen says, flipping through the photos, "a time where we're driven by vanity and the need for instant gratification."

"Well, aren't we in a good mood," I tease.

"I started researching Dad's company. I saw the sponsorship stuff you told me about, and found some of their business newsletters about things like property values and personal safety with barely veiled race-baiting language."

I decide no response is the best response and sip coffee.

"Wow. Some of these are awesome," Kristen says more cheerily. "I wish we had them in our collection. You think Mrs. Clarke would donate them to us, or allow us to make copies?"

"We can ask."

"I see you looked through the old Birmingham book, too," I say, pointing to it in her inbox, where a few pages are bookmarked with purple strips.

"I did. It's glaring how little there is showing Black life—only a dozen or so images. But take a look at that first photo of the men working on a mansion in Mountain Brook."

I stare at the photograph of maybe thirty men, a few of them Black, who are the construction crew for a steel magnate's home.

"What am I supposed to see?" I ask.

Kristen goes to the closet behind her and rolls out a stand magnifier. She opens the book on her desk and positions the magnifier over the page.

"Look at the man in the second row on the right side."

I stand and peer through the magnifier at the dark-skinned man with a mustache, goggles perched on his forehead. He's of medium height, his shoulders just above the men standing in the first row, and unlike most of the others in the photo, he's smiling.

I glance up at Kristen with a puzzled look.

"Don't you see it? Doesn't he look like the guy who had this book over at the corner table? The one you saw later when we went for coffee?"

I lean over the magnifier again. He *does* look a bit like the man who wore the Tigers cap. But then my heart skips a beat.

"Oh God, Kristen. I've seen him before," I say, shaken.

"That's what I'm saying. But it couldn't be him in this old book."

"No. No. You don't understand. I've seen this man at least three times since I've been in Birmingham. Once at an ATM downtown that was once the site of my great-grandfather's boardinghouse. Then walking at the cemetery in back of Monique's church. He was driving a rideshare in front of a building that in 1929 was the nightclub owned by Clarita Alvarez's husband." I run my fingers through my hair and sink wide-eyed into Kristen's side chair. "And now that I think of it, he looks a lot like a man I spoke to at a funeral in Detroit."

Kristen stares at me. "What? I don't understand."

"Neither do I." I shake my head to clear it, and bounce up from the chair. "But I can't figure it out now. I'm on deadline. I better get back to writing."

I do have to write, but that's not the reason I hurry away, leaving Kristen with a stunned look on her face. I don't want to tell her what I'm thinking. But I know who I *can* tell.

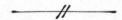

"Well, if it isn't my favorite grand," Grandma says with a smile in her voice.

"You say that to all your grandchildren."

"I know. You're each special to me." Suddenly Grandma's voice breaks. "Is anything wrong? Your mama told me you were still in Birmingham."

I've made my parents promise not to tell Grandma about my trouble in Birmingham, or the clues I've found about Great-

Granddad. I don't want to worry her or get her hopes too high. But now I need her counsel.

"Grandma, I still don't know where your father is buried, or what became of him, but I've found some things. I have pictures of a boardinghouse where Great-Grandpa stayed in Birmingham, receipts with his name on it, and I've seen his signature. I also met a couple of people who remember your mother and father, and one of them remembers you."

"Oh my." I hear her long intake of air.

"A woman called Carrie Mae says you and she used to play together here in Birmingham."

"Oh." She pauses. "Meghan, I just don't remember."

"It's okay, Grandma, you don't have to remember. I'm learning more every day," I say, looking at the bag of letters next to me. "And I'll call again so we can talk all of it over, but I need to tell you something. I know this sounds completely crazy, but I think Great-Grandpa's trying to help me solve his murder. I keep crossing paths with an old man. I've seen him three or four times. He's even spoken to me."

"What did he say?"

I think back. "Well, it's always something encouraging. I was walking through a churchyard and he said to be careful not to slip and fall. Another time he said something about daydreams being useful; we were standing outside of the place where Great-Granddad used to live. It's a bank now. I saw this man again in an antique automobile. We talked about cars, Detroit, and how much things had changed on the surface in Birmingham. Each time I've seen this old man he looks a little different, but also the same. It's hard to explain."

"Go on, Meghan, I want to hear this."

"Okay, so at the bank the man had gray hair and a mustache. The man at the cemetery was even older, maybe in his late seventies—and clean-shaven. I remember the hands of the man in the car. They looked old, but his hat was pulled so low I couldn't get a good look at him. I also think I've seen him at the library where I'm doing most of my research. He was wearing casual clothes and a baseball cap, so he seemed younger. And, Grandma, I think he was the old man I spoke to a few weeks ago in Detroit. At the funeral. Remember? I told you about it. That's the day I decided to write Great-Grandpa's story."

She is still quiet, listening. "What else do you remember about this man?"

"He had a very nice smile and a kind face. He was polite and well-dressed."

Grandma doesn't say anything right away, and when she does her voice is hoarse. She and I have talked about the existence of spirits before. She believes in them. I haven't up to now.

"I used to dream about Daddy even after I became school-age," Grandma says. "He was always merry. We'd dance, and he'd throw me into the air and catch me until I was dizzy with laughter. Mama said she'd hear me laughing in my sleep. It was as if I was undoing time to bring him back into my life."

She laughs now. A deep, throaty giggle. It heartens me. I want to give her peace, relief, not sadness.

"Your great-grandfather was a determined man. I've always heard that. So if there's a way now he could help you find the truth, I know he would."

THIRTY-NINE

If I Should Die

1929

We've decided we can't remain in Birmingham. I've done nothing wrong, committed no crime, but Nedra's detective boyfriend seems to have a personal vendetta against me. Even though my work is going well, and the baby is due shortly, we're moving back to St. Pete. The trip will not be easy on Anna Kate, but now it's just too dangerous to stay.

I'm going to work early today. Anna Kate and I have argued many times about having to work half days on Saturdays. It delays the food shopping, and by the time I return home her energy is low. But we're leaving next week and I need the overtime pay. Anna Kate gets up with me before daybreak and makes me a bag lunch, but she doesn't kiss me or even say goodbye when I head out the door.

It's a short drive to the mill, and the first light cracks across the horizon. I'm on one of the main roads out of town. It's two lanes, mostly soft paved, with long stretches of packed dirt. I'm about halfway to the job, on a remote part of the road, when I see a blue

Chevy ahead pulled to the side. As I get near the car, it veers into the lane to block me. I hadn't noticed the truck behind me, and soon I'm boxed in by the two vehicles. The driver of the sedan doesn't move, but his dark piercing eyes send a chill of fear right down to my feet. The passenger door swings open and the big-shouldered detective steps out and leans against the car, glaring. Behind me the truck's occupants are moving toward me carrying clubs. Three white men in coveralls—one of them the long-armed man from the mansion cement crew. My heart pounds in my chest, and my head swivels between the trouble approaching from behind and the menace in front of me. I reach under the seat for my pistol.

"Get out of the car, boy," the cement man yells from behind.

I don't move except to cock my pistol.

Soon the three men are at my car. Cement man yanks open the door. I point the gun at him and fire. He falls back with a burning hole in his chest. The other two men scatter. I frantically work the gear shift, moving the car into reverse, then into drive, and jam on the accelerator to ram the sedan. The detective moves quickly for a man his size. He extends his arm. I hear an explosion and am pushed against my seat. I'm hit, and hurting. Pain blurs my eyes for a moment, but when they clear I see an escape through the barrier of vehicles. I grip the steering wheel in one hand and the gun in the other. Then a second bullet splits into the flesh and bone of my right shoulder, and the pistol drops to the floorboard. I fall onto the steering column bleeding and gasping for air. The sun gleams on my black fingers as I watch them loosen on the wheel. The cop is at my car. He reaches in and drags me out. I have no strength to resist. The butt of his gun connects with my ear and I collapse to the ground. The detective kicks me. Now the two laborers and the other policeman have joined him. I feel more kicks. To my arms, back, head, each hurting less and less.

My blurring vision mixes with dreams of Mama and Papa Tico. I'm whittling a soft piece of rosewood on the back porch— birds chirping in the peach tree. Then Mae is in her Sunday clothes reaching out with open arms. Her mother stands behind her smiling. "Anna Kate," I scream through bloody, swollen lips. Then there's the rush of another explosion. And everything is dark.

FORTY

─────────◆─────────

2019

The canvas bag falls to the floor, spilling letters next to the desk. It startles me and I jerk upright in my chair. My head is pounding. I rub at my eyes and look at my phone. It's six thirty. The library is quiet. *I must have fallen asleep.*

Kristen appears at the carrel door. "I'm going home. I can't stand to be at my desk a minute more." She eyes the canvas bag and the letters strewn across the floor. "You know we closed a half hour ago."

"I think I dozed for a few minutes. I had some weird dream," I say, trying to remember it. "I'm tired. I didn't sleep well last night."

"Understandably."

"The draft of my latest blog is done, but I still have a rewrite to do," I say, holding my head.

"Look, let's go. You can finish your work at my house. I'll order in some food."

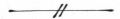

Kristen orders Chinese and as we eat I quickly catch her up on my long and eventful day. She has to work tomorrow and leaves me to my writing. By ten o'clock the blog is done. I've promised Masterson an extra day, so I'll file my story tomorrow.

I stare at the bag of letters, thinking about Mattie Robinson's last indecipherable look and her words when she handed them to me: "I've sorted through them and I think they'll be useful to you." I carry the bag to my room and sit cross-legged on the open sleeper sofa. But instead of reading I call Darius to say good night. We talk until my eyelids droop. I'll read the letters tomorrow. *I'm dead tired.*

FORTY-ONE

Death

1929

The searing lead tearing through my chest is like the distress of wood when split by metal. The bullet an axe separating a member from its source. The sensation begins as excruciating pain but quickly subsides to a state of nothingness and returns as something new.

I sense grunts and shouted curses, the pummel of pounding fists, and steel-toed kicks against muscle, but the impact is a puff of wind. From some panoramic view I witness these hateful men, their life threads drawn together in a common cord of dispatch, beat me mercilessly, then roll my shattered body into the gulley. Discarded like a fallen tree limb. They exit my death scene in a cacophony of gleeful shouts, squealing tires, and swirling dust.

It's almost dusk when a car stops abruptly, sending more dust into the air.

"Did you see that glint of light?" Freeman shouts.

"Where?" the flask man from the boardinghouse asks.

"There in the undergrowth. Near the side of the road."

I watch them carefully climb down the ragged embankment, knee-deep in the brush, clinging to exposed vines and embedded rock. When they finally discover my crumpled body, Freeman lifts the chain of my pocket watch and it catches the sun's last rays.

The men return me to the boardinghouse in the back seat of the car, smothered in blankets, but it is not suffocating. I am neither here in this world nor yet joined with the next. Like those hours when I have surrendered to the wood—yielding to its vision, existing in the same plane, guiding my cuts, directing just the right pressure in the right spots. I sense things around me but I am absorbed into the wood's particles.

Now I'm aware of a rush of activity—hurried feet and frightened voices. Mrs. Ardle orders Freeman to carry me to the shed, then enters the house and returns with my wife.

Anna Kate's wail fills the night with the sorrow of a thousand women. I am almost snatched back to the world—ripped from the earth's womb.

But it is not to be. Those mourning me hide my mangled body in a shallow grave whose dirt is still red from the blood of slaves.

FORTY-TWO

———◆———

2019

It's Saturday and I've slept in. It's the most restful night I've had
in several days. Kristen's already gone to work and I peek out
the window. My protection detail is in place in front of the house.
I make coffee, text Mom that I'm good, and dump the letters on
the kitchen table. There are four written by Harriet Ardle, the
landlady at the boardinghouse, and a bundle of twenty letters
from Carrie Mae's mother, Esther.

The first couple of letters—from Mrs. Ardle to her sister,
Gussie, in Atlanta—are interesting, but not helpful. The sisters
have, obviously, kept duplicates of all their correspondence, and
these are newsy accounts of family, business, and current affairs.
Mrs. Ardle tells of the work she and her husband put into the
boardinghouse, and her plans for expansion. But she also longs for
a different life where she isn't responsible for a houseful of lodgers.
The letters also mention individual boarders, and in one, dated in
late June 1929, Ardle speaks of my great-grandfather.

*There is an interesting gentleman who has come to live at my
house. He hails from Florida. He is young and somewhat brash,*

but very handy and an extraordinary craftsman of wood. He repaired one of the steps on the staircase, and has also carved a new facing for the parlor mantel. With William gone, he's been a big help.

I set the letter aside, wriggling in my chair and dabbing my palms on my sweatpants. This is what I'd hoped for—a way to learn more about my great-grandfather. I pour a tall glass of water, down it, and take a few deep breaths. My hands are shaking when I pick up the last letter from Mrs. Ardle and begin to read.

September 24, 1929

Dear Gussie,

I hope this letter finds you well.

I have sorrowful news. I have mentioned to you before a Mr. Harrington, the tenant who has been so helpful to me with repairs to our mantel and doors. I am saddened to tell you that Mr. Harrington has been brutally murdered, and we are certain he has fallen at the hands of a belligerent and terrifying police detective who has been menacing our community for months. The Harringtons had become so afraid of this policeman that they were preparing to return to Florida. They were only three weeks away from the birth of their child, but they didn't get away in time.

We learned of this tragedy when Mr. Harrington hadn't returned from work and his wife, Anna, asked another tenant to look for her husband. Mr. Freeman found him beaten and shot to death in a ditch on a county road.

Anna has become a friend of mine. She is despondent, and has complained to her minister and directly to the police. This attention has put us all in danger. I've even been warned that the Klan might burn down the boardinghouse.

Mr. Freeman recovered Mr. Harrington's body, but we were afraid the policeman might think twice and decide to cover up his misdeed, so we hid it in a shallow grave at the boardinghouse until we can find a permanent place for his remains.

I have sent a letter to Anna's family asking them to come for her and her toddler before all of us face a fate similar to her husband. We are all afraid, and angry, and on guard.

Finally, I end with a request that you will keep me, and all of us, in your prayers.

Affectionately yours, Harriet

I sit not breathing, not moving. This letter has almost all the information I'd hoped to discover in Birmingham. I rest my arms on the table, drop my head onto them, and cry nine decades of tears.

I haven't told anyone about Mrs. Ardle's letter. Not yet. My mood is a curious mixture of lethargy and elation. Sluggish from the weight of responsibility I feel to tell this story right—for my family and for all Black people. At the same time excited by the revelation this letter has brought. My brain bounces as if I'd downed three cups of coffee. I've only had one.

I have to update my blog, and I'm driven now to have as many facts as the emotions that still threaten to overwhelm me.

I unwrap the rubber bands from Carrie Freeman's letters. They're accompanied by a handwritten note, and with her arthritis it must have caused her some pain to write it. *Daddy never wrote any letters, but Mama did all the time. These are from a long way back.*

Esther Freeman was a prolific letter writer. There are twenty in all—duplicates of her outgoing correspondence. Some in envelopes, some not—and in no particular order. The first one I pick up is postmarked in 1928, outside the timeframe I'm interested in; I discard that one and grab another.

Her cursive is small and precise. The kind she'd have received a star for in school, and she writes on only one side of her stationery. Each letter has pages and pages of description of her surroundings and the people and places she's seen. I've been reading for almost a half hour—there are still a dozen to read. And then. I find two that turn out to be precious documents.

On October 11, 1929, Esther Freeman writes her husband, George, in care of his sister in Waverly, Tennessee, where he'd been hiding and healing after the police beat him. Her letter gives details of their daughter's activities, the work at the diner, and her adjustment to living in a new house. Then on page five she writes:

> *I had a visit from Harriet Ardle today. The police have come around the boardinghouse several times searching for you and demanding to know your whereabouts. She has kept our secret, and protects you, me, and Carrie Mae like we are her own. The pastor has been in touch with me about Anna Kate's citizen complaint, and he, the Black Businessmen's Coalition, and several other pastors—including some white ones—have gone to the mayor with their concerns about the backlash from police following the murder of the rogue detective. The police board is investigating your suspicions that he killed Mr. Harrington. They are also seeking information about those responsible for your vicious beating.*

I hope you are staying well, and following the doctor's orders to give that leg as much rest as it needs. I've written to Anna Kate at the address her brother gave you, but I've not heard from her. I pray that she is well, with her children, and is able to move on with her life after the tragedy that has befallen her.

Five months later there is a reply to Esther Freeman from Anna Kate Harrington. It is a single sheet of white, lined paper—not in an envelope—and is inconspicuous among the thick, folded correspondence written by Esther. I read Great-Grandma's letter three times before losing it, again.

Handling them with trembling hands, I copy the four letters—two written by Harriet Ardle, one by Carrie's mother, and the other from my great-grandmother—and place the originals into separate folders.

I've sent a summary of my story to Saxby with a note that I'll call later. He replies: *Wow!* Masterson has phoned, so has Kristen, but I haven't taken their calls. I have more immediate business.

I arrive at the Freeman house just after two o'clock followed by the police vehicle. The ubiquitous corner loiterers disperse when they see the telltale black SUV trailing behind me.

Carrie Mae sits in her wheelchair at the head of the table. I'm across from her. Her mother's stack of letters lies between us, and Keisha has retrieved the green photo album at my request.

"Thank you for the letters. I'm very grateful to you. I want to tell you about another one I read today written by the lady who ran the boardinghouse where your father and mother lived. I made a copy for you. It was *your* father who found my great-grandpa on the day he was killed. My great-grandma talked him into going out to look for her husband, and when he did he brought his body back to where they all lived. I believe your father helped my great-grandmother file a complaint against the man who killed my great-grandfather—a police detective."

Carrie Mae's face shades in sadness, and she reaches across the table for my hand.

"When the police found out about your father's involvement in the complaint they attacked him at the diner where he cooked. He might have been killed, too, except several of the miners stepped in to save him. Your father then filed his own complaint against the police. He was a very brave man."

The old woman is crying now. Keisha rises to stand behind Carrie. "Maybe you better go," she says. "You're upsetting Auntie."

I ignore Keisha and look into Carrie's teary eyes. "May I look in the album again? I remember seeing an envelope."

I quickly sort through the papers stuffed in the album's back sleeve. Among the property deeds, social security notices, and nursing home invoices I find the official-looking white envelope. The enclosed letter announces the payment of six thousand dollars to George Freeman as a settlement of a complaint. It's from the Police Insurance Fund and is signed by Hiram Gleason Jr.—Kristen's grandfather.

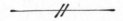

The driver in my security detail fires up the engine when I descend Carrie's porch steps. I wave. Masterson has left another message, but I want to call Kristen first. I have to talk her down from runaway guilt when I tell her of the letter connected to her family's insurance company.

"It was your grandfather's job to make these types of payments," I say. "It doesn't mean he was involved in any wrongdoing. Besides, you are *not* your grandfather."

I suggest cooking dinner for her and inviting Darius and she agrees. The follow car stays with me on the drive to the grocer to pick up eggs, veggies, and fruit for omelets and fried potatoes.

Masterson's message says he's collected some items from the Simenon file and they'll be delivered to Kristen's house this evening. He also tells me I'll lose my police protection tomorrow or the next day.

Kristen isn't around when I return to her place, so I refrigerate the groceries and put the treasure trove of letters and photographs in my temporary bedroom. Then I take a shower. A long one. I'm stunned by the details that have been unearthed in the letters, angry about the murder of my great-grandfather, and heartbroken at the pain my great-grandparents had to endure. I'm relieved, too. Above all, I'm grateful to God for all the help, in person and in spirit, that has shed light on my story. I stand under the showerhead and let the water mix with my tears.

THE MUSHROOMS, ONIONS, AND CHEESE ARE CHOPPED, AND I'M whisking balsamic and herbs for the potatoes when Kristen comes home.

"I thought you were home when I called," I say.

"I was, but I needed a walk." She flops into a kitchen chair.

"Darius is on his way. Want some wine?" I ask, holding up my own glass.

"Desperately."

"You okay?" I ask.

"I called Daddy."

Uh-oh. "You told him about the letter signed by his father?"

"Yes, and I told him you were close to getting the answers you needed about the detective. I was shocked by his reaction." Kristen's hand trembles as she sips her wine. "We argued, McKenzie. Like we've never argued before. He was screaming. He said you have no business dragging people through the dirt just to satisfy your own curiosity."

"He can't think I'm intentionally trying to cause your family harm. I'm following leads."

Kristen shakes her head in exasperation and downs the wine.

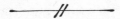

We're halfway into a bottle of Shiraz, the potatoes are done, and I've finished preparing a quick dessert—a peach cobbler made from canned peaches and ready-made crust. Kristen is feeling better and Darius is telling her about a new project he's working on—an oral history of steelworkers' families. That's when Kristen brings up the man in the Birmingham photo book and shows him the picture of the construction crew. I haven't confided to her that I think it's my great-grandfather.

"He looks just like the man at the library," she says, pointing. "And Meghan thinks she's seen him a few times before."

Darius holds the photograph, staring at it. "You think you've seen *this* man?"

"All I know is he looks like the one who was at the library," Kristen repeats. "But McKenzie says she's seen him in front of the bank, where the boardinghouse used to be, and at the church cemetery."

Darius gives me a hard gaze. I look away to load the dishwasher. He's still staring when I look up again.

"You know that's impossible, right?" he says, opening a second bottle. This time a rioja. "This guy is dead and gone."

"Maybe the man in the library is his grandson," Kristen offers.

"Nope. These are photos from the twenties and thirties. He'd have to be his great-grandson," Darius says.

"That still doesn't explain why I keep seeing this man," I say, sitting. Darius fills my wineglass.

"How do you explain it?" he asks.

I decide not to share the conclusion Grandma and I have reached. It's our secret; and our truth.

"All the men were similar. They all sort of look like the man in the photo, and each other, but I guess they *are* different men," I say to put the matter to rest.

"That's what I mean," Darius says. "It's just a coincidence."

I'VE WAITED UNTIL DINNER'S ALMOST COMPLETED TO TELL Darius and Kristen about the letters. I'm cooking the omelets, keeping my mind on the tasks at hand, to keep my emotions at bay.

"I found the whole story behind my great-grandfather's death today," I announce with my back to them.

Darius and Kristen stop talking. I can feel their eyes. I turn around and they both lower their wineglasses.

"The letters?" Kristen asks.

I nod. "I have two sets of them. They're amazing."

Kristen covers her face with her hands. Darius comes to me at the stove and wraps his arms around me.

While we eat I summarize the content of the Ardle and Freeman letters. They both reach out to comfort me when I begin to tear up again. I don't tell them about the Anna Kate letter. I want Grandma to know about it before I tell anyone else.

Like me they're disturbed and angered about the information surrounding my great-grandfather's murder, but when I remind them how fortunate I feel to have found the answers I've been searching for, we all try to adjust our moods. Over dessert we discuss the loose ends of my story—I don't know why my great-grandfather was targeted by Simenon in the first place. I don't know if the claims that he resisted arrest are true. I don't know why Simenon was murdered, or by whom. And I don't know why my attempts to uncover these details have rattled someone to the point of threats and attempts to injure me. Could protecting a city's reputation be that important?

Darius and Kristen listen to my theories, ask questions at the appropriate times, and disagree when something doesn't make sense to them. It's like having a focus group, and the conversation will help with the story revisions I need to make.

Before Darius leaves, he and I sit together on Kristen's porch bench.

"Masterson never sent over the package he promised to send," I say.

"Something must have come up. You still giving him the extra day before you publish the blog?"

"He's had his day, plus some. I'm making some tweaks tonight and sending it in tomorrow."

"You're a tough lady," Darius says, putting his arm around me. "Ten days ago I didn't even know you, and now I can't imagine *not* knowing you, or not seeing you every day," he says.

"You really mean that?"

He answers with a kiss, which leads to a half dozen more. A small truck with white stripes on the side and blackened windows moves slowly up Kristen's quiet street with just enough engine rumble to get our attention. As it nears the front of the house one of the men in the security detail steps out of the unmarked car. The truck takes off up the street and I follow its trek to the corner, where it turns. The officer waves, and I wave back.

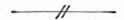

Kristen insisted on finishing the dinner cleanup, and now she's at the kitchen table with a cup of tea and a small sliver of cobbler. "Busted," she says as I move into the room.

I laugh and reach for a napkin. "I'm having another piece too. It turned out pretty good, if I do say so myself."

"You can stay here as long as you like if you promise to cook dinner three times a week," Kristen jokes. "The security guys out front?"

"Yep. Some truck came down the street too slowly and they reacted right away."

"It must make you feel better having someone guarding you."

A shiver racks my torso. "I *am* being guarded, aren't I? I hadn't thought of it exactly that way."

"Have you called your parents again?"

"Uh-huh. Just to assure them I'm okay. They're still worried about me, but they're relieved I have a great place to sleep, and that the police car is outside."

"Have you told them about the letters?"

"Not yet."

"What are you waiting for?"

I shake my head. "We've waited so long to know the truth. I want to do it right. Maybe I'll do a three-way call with Mom and Grandmother. I'll figure it out tonight. But I need time to think about it."

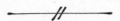

I've been writing for almost two hours. Pausing only to reread the other letter. The personal one. It's dated in March of 1930.

Dear Esther and George, I am sorry to hear of George's recent trouble, but I hope this letter now finds you well. I am forever indebted to you both. It has been a difficult time since returning home to St. Pete. My family had to move almost immediately to avoid the police who were looking for me, and my brothers. I have caused a great upset to my mother.

My daughter, Barbara Ann, was born twelve days after I arrived in St. Petersburg. She is an even-keeled baby, quiet, and so different from her big sister. Mae is doing well, but misses her father so much, I am sometimes afraid for her. At night I hear her giggling and calling out for her Daddy.

Esther, I can hardly believe it. I'm not yet 20 years old, and am already a widow. I still cry myself to sleep sometimes. But I can't afford to cry during the day. I must work to take care of my two children and myself. I do day work, and take in washing. My sister watches the two girls when I must go out to clean or deliver laundry.

I want you to know that I am so thankful to you both, and to Mrs. Alvarez, for making sure that Robert Lee has a resting place. I plan to write to Harriet very soon, but please give her

*my regards when you speak to her. She was a great friend to me
and Robert. Right to the end.*

I remain, yours very truly,
Anna Kate Harrington

My heart shudders. I've discovered the key to a mystery
Grandma's carried all her life.

It's after midnight before I finish what two days ago was a
blog but is now a full-fledged story. I zip it off to Saxby immediately. I open my bedroom door and step into the hallway. I notice
a line of light showing under Kristen's bedroom door, and I hear
her feverishly typing over the background banter of *Saturday
Night Live.*

FORTY-THREE

2019

I find Kristen's note when I patter to the kitchen in my warm socks. She's back at the library again this morning. Unusual. Because it's Sunday.

She's left a pot of coffee and I pour a cup and take the pot to the front porch, where I wave it as an offer to the cops in the unmarked car. They wave back holding aloft their own cups of java.

I'VE SHOWERED, DRESSED, AND TUCKED THE LETTERS INTO MY backpack along with my laptop. I also have a shoulder bag. Kristen's given me a house key and I lock up and signal my protectors. I'm headed to Evangelical Church, and they pull in behind me. I arrive just as the second service begins, and slip into a back pew. I don't attend church. But today I have an ulterior motive—I need another look at the cemetery.

This Sunday the mass choir is performing. I've heard a few of these songs before, but the one I really recognize is "Abide with

Me." It's a punctuation to the pastor's message, which is about faith. I see Monique sitting near the front of the church, and after scanning the room for a few minutes, I spot Darius near the end of a middle pew. He's sitting next to an attractive woman wearing a hat. *Who under thirty wears a hat unless they have an audience with the queen?* When he called last night to invite me to church I told him I didn't think I could make it, so I guess he found someone else to accompany him. While the second offering plate is passed around, I slip out of the sanctuary.

The church office door is ajar and I step inside. The anteroom is empty, but I can hear Mattie Robinson on the phone. I wait until she hangs up to call out a hello. She appears at her office door, pulls her glasses to the tip of her nose, and gives me the up and down.

"Miss McKenzie," she says. "Were you at the service?"

"Yes."

"Marvelous. How can I help you today?"

"I have a few more questions."

"You're persistent. That's a good quality. Come in."

I take a seat across from Robinson's formidable desk. It's full of topsy-turvy mounds of paper, folders, and food containers. She has two landline phones on the credenza behind her, and two mobile phones sit atop a folder pile. Although I try to contain my shock at the chaos, she reads my face. *Note to self. Never play poker with Mattie Robinson.*

"Believe me, Miss McKenzie, I can tell you what's in every one of the files on my desk."

"Yes, ma'am."

"What is it you want to speak with me about? The letters I gave you?"

"Yes."

"Go on."

"Esther Freeman was an avid letter writer."

"That she was," Robinson says, interrupting. "I'm sure I have a few in my own files. So you were saying? There's a letter?"

"Two really. One was written by Cecile Clarke's relative, Harriet Ardle." I pause to get a read on Robinson, who gives away nothing. "It speaks of burying my great-grandfather's body in a temporary grave until it could be safely relocated. The other was written by my great-grandmother," I say, unexpectedly choking up.

"So you've found what you were looking for," Robinson says, gleaming. "I'm so happy for you."

"I'm still piecing it together, but Great-Grandma's letter is a reply to Esther, thanking her and Clarita Alvarez for making sure my great-grandfather had a place to rest. Clarita Alvarez was the woman who paid for the fancy marker for her husband—Albert Griggs." I lean toward Mrs. Robinson. "I think the small marker at the back corner of your cemetery is my great-grandfather's grave."

"Are you asking me?"

"Well, it's speculation, but—"

"Let me see the letters."

"I left them in my backpack in the car."

"Well, go get them!"

Church has let out, and Darius and others are gathered in the basement for cake, coffee, and punch. The hat-wearing diva still hovers around Darius and I don't want him to see me, so I hug the wall and slip out the side exit, which runs parallel to the cemetery gate.

My car is parked at the sidewalk and my backpack is in the trunk. I'm reaching in when a vehicle pulls too close to my car. I look up to protest but I sense someone at my other side, and I pivot, coming face-to-face with a man wearing a black ski mask.

Our eyes lock for only a second before I let out a scream. He pushes me hard against the car and tugs at the strap of my shoulder bag. My heart races as I struggle with the man, gripping my purse strap in both hands and holding on. And I'm shouting for help. I can't believe I'm being mugged, in front of a church, in broad daylight. *Where's my security detail?*

When I hear Darius bellow, "Hey, stop!" I swivel my head in his direction, but someone grabs me from behind, lifts me off my feet, and clasps a gloved hand across my mouth. I'm kicking at the ski-mask man in front of me, who is now holding my bag and my backpack, and squirming in the second man's grip as he slides open the van's side door. Then they both throw me into the cargo space, where my face grazes the metal floor. One of the thugs lands on top of me as the door panel closes. I think I can still hear Darius's shouts as the vehicle lurches away at high velocity. I'm pinned to the floor, and the hand covering my mouth is replaced with a rag smelling of chemicals. I struggle for several seconds before the odor overcomes me, and the interior of the van shades from gray to black.

FORTY-FOUR

———— ◆ ————

2019

The old man at the ATM laughs and beckons me to follow him through a narrow walkway between the bank and the boutique dress shop. The path leads to a courtyard. The gate opens with a squeak as he pushes. Rosebushes and forsythia are planted at the perimeter. Mums and pansies accent the half dozen seating areas. Saplings grow symmetrically in tree beds.

"My wife used to fill our house with forsythia," he says.

"They're lovely. I could sit here all day."

"No, you can't. You can't rest now. Not enough light here. No good for flowers or stories."

"What?" I say and sit in a chair that rocks and swivels. "I'll just rest for a little while."

"No!" He grabs my wrist.

The man's hand is cold. I look at the deep wrinkles on his dark skin. He's pulling me across the courtyard and suddenly stops. He points to a white birch.

"I used to be buried there. Now everything's changed."

"But not on the inside. You told me that. Change takes more than time."

"I'm trying to help you."

"I don't need your help. I'm a journalist."

"What does that mean?" the man asks, now wearing coveralls and boots. He uses a thin knife with a long blade to carve a design in the arm of the bench where we now sit.

"It means I reveal the truth. Dig for the facts. That's what makes a journalist."

"I have a story, and *you* have to tell it. You can't rest now."

I shake my head. But before I can disagree with him, he's moving away, dressed in a pin-striped suit and an old-fashioned cap.

The bench sways and leans and starts to sink as if being engulfed by an earthquake's jagged, hungry mouth. I reach for something to grasp onto but can't stop my fall.

I JERK TO CONSCIOUSNESS. MY EYES ARE OPEN BUT I'M IN COMPLETE darkness. A hood covers my eyes, and my hands are tied behind my back. I'm dizzy, trying to keep from vomiting, and I'm hurt.

I manage to free myself of the hood and I feel blood trickling down my face. I don't know how long I was out but it's still daylight. The van's well is empty but the floor isn't carpeted and it's moving too fast for me to keep my balance. Every time I fall or roll my body slams into metal.

I stare at the white cloth they'd placed on my head. Sprinkles of my blood dot the fabric and are also clotted on my pants. I begin to cry. *Oh, Mama, I should have listened to you.*

"Don't lose your head," the old man's voice sounds in my ear. "There are people ready to help you."

I look around for the source of the raspy whisper, but I'm alone.

My abductors are in the vehicle's cab, and I can hear their muffled voices. "We have her. And we're on the way. Yes. We have her bags, too."

I can hear only one side of the conversation. The growly voice from the phone's speaker is urgent. The men in front speak rapidly—two, maybe three of them—swearing and laughing. Hyped-up.

"Yes, sir. We're almost there. Blood and soil!"

Oh fuck. These are neo-Nazis. They're going to kill me.

When the van comes to a stop I get to my knees and waddle quickly to the rear door. The floor well snags at the thin fabric of my slacks. The van abruptly moves again, slinging me hard against the metal floor. I stifle my scream. I don't want them to know I've regained consciousness. I need to keep my head, listen, and be alert for a way to escape.

I begin to scoot, getting as far away from the cab as possible, and that's when I feel the phone. In my back pocket. They didn't find it. The van is speeding again, moving over paved roads, railroad tracks, not even slowing for what feels like speed bumps. I'm bouncing around the back like a rag doll, and because my hands are bound there's nothing I can do to protect my head.

I lift onto my knees again, trying to reach my phone. I have both hands in my pocket, my fingers wriggling and reaching like the legs of a spider. It takes three tries before I can lift the phone from my pocket, and when it clears it slips through my fingers and clatters loudly to the floor. My heart catches in my throat as I wait for my captors' response to the loud noise. *Thank God. They didn't hear it.* Finally, I lie on my side and grasp the phone, holding down the keys that will activate 911. When I hear the operator's voice I cover the phone with my body to muffle the sound. When the operator stops talking I lean my mouth over the phone to whisper. "Please, I have to be very quiet. My name is Meghan McKenzie, and I'm in trouble. Please call Captain Masterson."

FORTY-FIVE

◆

2019

The van brakes to a stop so fast it wobbles a few seconds. The cargo door slides open and I'm pressed against the corner. I've wedged my phone behind the spare tire. The three men who were in the cab are now staring at me. They're no longer wearing their masks. Two of the men, scroungy-looking white guys, could be twins. I've never seen them before. The third man I recognize. He's one of the officers in my security detail. His sneer is filled with hatred.

"She took off the hood," one of the scroungy guys says.

"It doesn't matter now," the cop says. "Let's get her."

He's big. Moves and acts like a soldier. He orders the others to open the rear door, then steps into the van and grabs me by my hair. I scream and struggle against his efforts, but someone is also pushing me, and they fling me out of the van and onto the ground, where my face meets the pavement.

"Get her in here. Quick," a voice hollers from somewhere ahead of us.

I lift my head, but I can't see the man who now seems to be in charge. The cop removes the binding on my hands and grabs my arm. I try to drag my feet, but he and one of the others lift me off the ground. I take in my surroundings quickly—an empty loading dock. I recognize the UAB seal on the building. While I'm struggling I squint to see the man ordering the others to hurry up.

"Don't forget the backpack," he shouts. "Go back and get it!"

Oh my God, it's Kristen's brother, Scotty!

I manage to land a kick in the family jewels of one of the twins, and he slams a fist into my nose. I feel blood spurt onto my lip, and I fight to keep from passing out. I believe I'm losing the battle when I hear the high screech of seagulls.

No! It's squealing tires behind me.

"Stop now. Drop the bags. Get on the ground," a male voice sounds through a loudspeaker.

The only thing the abductors drop is me. I'm facedown on the pavement again. The scroungy brother darts to one side of the loading dock. I don't know where his look-alike is, but the cop tries to lift me and I kick and thrash at him. My backpack is slung over his arm, and when I see it I struggle all the harder. He finally pushes me away and I land on my knees. He runs toward the building where Scotty is beckoning, shouting, and holding open the door.

I'm dizzy again, bleeding, trying to make sense of the cacophonous scene around me. There's shouting and screaming, more vehicles screeching into the loading dock, cops flinging open the doors of patrol cars, sirens, heavy boots on pavement. And then gunfire. I instinctively flatten myself and bury my head in my arms.

"Police. Drop your weapons," the loudspeaker voice orders. But the shooting intensifies.

I'M NOT SURE HOW LONG I'VE LAIN ON THE GROUND. THE PAVE-ment is cold against my cheek. I wipe at my nose. It's stopped bleeding. There's no more gunfire but I still hear footsteps, the squawking of police radios, and groans. I'm groaning also, still too afraid to lift my head. Then someone kneels beside me and tries to turn me over. I resist.

"It's okay, Ms. McKenzie. You're safe now."

I roll over to see a young female officer squatting next to me. Her blue eyes are filled with empathy, and she's holding my hand.

"An ambulance is on the way. Captain Masterson says I'm to ride with you to the hospital. It's all over. Are you okay?"

I can't speak. I just press my face into the policewoman's shoulder and bawl.

FORTY-SIX

———◆———

2019

I'm a patient in a private hospital room with an IV tube connected to my arm—for dehydration, they tell me. I don't feel sick. The doctor says I have some bruises, and my nose has a small bandage but, thankfully, it's not broken. I have a dull sensation of pain in my back and on my left side. I'm sure it's from flailing around in the van and being dropped on the ground before all the shooting started. I'm just beginning to realize the extent of the danger, and how lucky I am to be alive.

The television is on in my room and I'm watching live coverage of the shootout at the UAB athletic building and my attempted kidnapping. It's a spectacle. It didn't take long for the media to realize that the abduction reported near the Evangelical Church was *not* just another inner-city crime. A news helicopter shows a live shot of a large crowd gathered in front of the church, and media satellite trucks flank both ends of the block.

The reporter announces that the kidnapping of a young parishioner of the church occurred just before noon. A white van was seen speeding away from the scene but was later intercepted at UAB's athletic building, where the young woman had been held hostage. The media must not have my name yet.

The reporter quotes unnamed sources saying the chief has already called in the FBI and the state's Department of Homeland Security. He then intros a taped interview with Monique's father, who decries the violence in the city and says the kidnapping has nothing to do with his church. When the reporter hands off to his colleague who stands in front of the UAB loading dock, I grab the remote and mute the TV.

The campus police officer who helped me from the ground and rode with me in the ambulance said it was my call to 911 that saved me.

"Why didn't they take your phone?" she asked.

"I don't know. It was in my back pocket. Not in my bag, and it was muted because I'd been in church."

"That's how we tracked you," she said. "We got to you as soon as we could."

There is a police guard outside my hospital room. It's caused quite a stir. The doctors and nurses have been kind to me, but I don't want to be here. I have a story to file. I need the things in my backpack. I'm relieved when I finally see Captain Masterson speaking with the officer through the glass sliver in the door. He looks grim when he enters the room but manages a tiny smile.

"Glad to see you well, Ms. McKenzie."

"Thanks for sending someone to the rescue."

Masterson doesn't respond. He just removes his cap and sits in the chair next to my bed. I'd say he's about forty years old, but today he looks older. Just like the last two times we met, he's wearing a crisp white shirt and creased pants.

"I'm sorry for what's happened to you. How are you feeling?"

"A bit achy but not enough to be in the hospital. You should give this bed to someone who needs it."

"I'd like to keep you here at least overnight."

I begin to protest and Masterson lays his hand on my arm. "You're safer here."

"Captain, how did those men get to me? What about the protection detail?"

"One officer is dead. Gordon. Ten years on the job."

"Oh." Suddenly tears spring to my eyes. "I'm so sorry."

"The other officer was one of those who attempted to kidnap you."

"I know. I recognized him. I also saw Scotty Gleason."

Masterson fills me in on what he describes as a conspiracy of hate within the Birmingham Police Department. It's wider spread than even he thought. I can tell he's distraught by the shame that's come to his department.

"The rogue cop is telling all to avoid a death sentence and to receive protection from others who want to quiet him. The FBI's already investigating."

"What about Scotty? He seemed to be in charge."

"It's his father who's in charge," Masterson says.

"Stan Gleason?"

"Yes. But that information is completely off-the-record for now. I have to insist on it. I'm only telling you because you recognized his son. Gleason was the mastermind of your abduction and the earlier threat at your rental house. But we don't know how deep this conspiracy reaches, and if Gleason knows we're on to him we could lose evidence."

I think of Kristen and wipe at my eyes. She'll be devastated. "What happened to Scotty?"

"He was severely wounded. Two others were killed. The man

we identified through the fingerprints at your rental house was one of them."

"Who *are* these people?"

"I thought you knew, Ms. McKenzie. A very sophisticated white nationalist group. They've infiltrated city government, Birmingham's corporate sector, even some unions. They may not call themselves the Klan, but that's who they are. They've been growing in strength for years, planning to counter what they think is a radically progressive agenda for Birmingham. They've kept a pretty tight lid on their growing influence, but your story threatened to expose them."

"How is that?"

"Your detective. Simenon. He's the grandfather of one of our state senators who is considered a front-runner for the governor's office. The senator also has connections to these white nationalists."

"People have to know."

"They will. But first there's the business of lining up the subpoenas we need, and we're not sure which judges we can trust."

"Do you have my phone?"

"Here it is," Masterson says, retrieving it from his pocket. "And your friends have your laptop and workpapers. They're waiting to visit with you."

"Darius?" I ask.

Masterson nods. "Also Pastor Hendricks and his daughter. They all insisted on coming. But, Ms. McKenzie, I must caution you not to reveal to anyone—not your paper, your family, not even Ms. Gleason—what we know about her father."

Masterson and I stare at each other. I don't want to lie to my friends—especially Kristen.

I know the police can detain me under so-called special needs protection rules and I won't be allowed to speak to anyone. Masterson wants to do his job. I want to do mine. But I also know what's right in this moment.

"I'll do as you say."

"I'll get your friends."

As soon as Masterson exits, Darius appears in the door gap peeking in at me.

"Come on in."

He enters with none of the swagger that is his default. He stops at the foot of the bed and we lock eyes. His melt with concern. I know in that moment I'm in love with this man.

Before either of us can speak, Monique storms into the room, overpowering the mood and the quiet. She's carrying my tote and backpack and drops them in the side chair.

"Are you guys through making goo-goo eyes at each other? How you feeling, girl? We're here to take you home."

Darius, Monique, and Masterson stand at the foot of my bed. The pastor pulls up another chair to sit next to me.

"What kind of injuries do you have?" Darius asks.

"Scratches, bruises. A laceration to my nose. I'm okay."

Darius doesn't look convinced. "What happened to the guys who took her, Joshua?"

"Two of the four men are dead," Masterson says. "Another is seriously injured. The fourth man, a police officer, is under arrest."

"Lord have mercy," Pastor Hendricks says, shaking his head. Monique sucks her teeth.

"The officer we've arrested is providing information on the others involved."

"What were they after?" Darius asks.

"The letters and other documents they thought Ms. McKenzie had."

"Why would they be interested in old letters?" the pastor asks.

"These men thought they might prove a connection to a new influx of the Klan. It's a pretty broad conspiracy that we're still gathering information about." Masterson gives me a "don't forget you promised to keep the secret" look.

"Joshua, what do you plan to do about all this? I can't have my parishioners feel unsafe coming to church."

"Daddy, this isn't about our church," Monique shouts. "It's about corruption and white supremacy. This is the sixties all over again."

"No, Ms. Hendricks. This is *not* the sixties," Masterson says, looking around the room. "We are *not* going backward. I promise you that."

"Meghan, come on. We're taking you home," Monique announces, moving to my side.

Masterson glowers at me. "I can't guarantee your protection if you leave this room."

"Captain, I'm not staying unless you're detaining me or I'm under arrest."

"Well, of course you're not under arrest, but—"

"Then I'll be signing myself out today."

"Okay. I'll go get the nurse," Monique says and barrels out of the room to move things along with my discharge. The pastor gives my hand a reassuring pat before saying his goodbye. Masterson leaves with him.

Darius sits on the edge of my bed. "I was so worried about you, I couldn't take a deep breath. The only other time I've felt that way was in high school when this crazy dude punched me in the stomach. Meg, I saw them take you. I ran after the van."

"I know. I remember you shouting before they dragged me in the van. Then I was unconscious for a while, and I had a hood over my eyes."

He leans over me, touches my face and the bandage on my nose. "Did they hurt you?"

"I got most of these injuries banging around inside the van. But one guy hit me when I fought back."

I watch Darius's gentle eyes turn cold and fierce. I feel his hand tense, and he moves it from my face. I reach for it again.

"I'm okay," I assure him. "By the way, who was that hat-wearing woman you were sitting next to at church?"

I hold a look of fake jealousy until he allows himself to smile. I squeeze his hand.

"My cousin. On my mother's side."

"She better be," I say.

"Have you talked to your father?"

"No. I don't want to tell him about any of this until I get home."

Darius nods at the TV. "It's all over the news. It's just a matter of time until they identify you. I talked to Saxby. When he couldn't reach you he called. I told him what's happened. He's on his way. His plane gets in at five."

"Darius . . . I . . ."

"We all believe in you, Meg, and we're all going to support you in getting your story told. The whole story. We talked about it at the church. Mrs. Robinson has something for you. Proof."

"Proof? Of what?"

"I'm not sure. There's a document. Part of an estate left to the church. She wouldn't give me the details; she said there's a nondisclosure agreement. She wants you to come to the church as soon as you can."

"Tomorrow," I say, sitting up and swinging my legs off the bed. "I need to get out of here, Darius. Now."

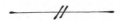

"Another meeting of the Meghan Squad," Kristen quips when she opens her front door, ushering in Monique and Darius and pulling me into a hug. I can tell she's been crying. Maybe she already knows about her father. She fights back tears as she listens to me recount the ordeal, and when I'm finished she hugs me again.

"Saxby's on his way from the airport," I say. "I hope you don't mind him coming over. Oh, and another police car is outside. Masterson insisted. But this time with men handpicked by him. He's promised to call later with an update on the church incident."

"Church incident? Is that what you're calling it? You could have been killed," Kristen says, shaking with outrage and still on the verge of tears.

While Monique and Darius help Kristen pull some food together, I take a quick shower. It's the first time I've really examined the damage to my face. I have a small cut on my right cheek and three on the left, which also has a bluish-pink bruise that wasn't there a half hour ago when I took a peek in the vanity mirror of Darius's car. I also have a bandage over the bridge of my nose. I hear Kristen's front doorbell, and Saxby's voice, and finish dressing in sweatpants and a large pullover.

Saxby's eyes grow wide when he sees my face. I watch him debate if it's appropriate to hug me. He finally does. I assure him I'm okay, and he regains his supervisor distance. Kristen pours him wine and tops off our three glasses, and I go over the story again. As I speak, Saxby takes a few photographs—of me, Monique, and Darius. Kristen turns away when she realizes what he's doing.

The three of them have made a huge meal. Grits, scrambled eggs, waffles, corned-beef hash, and biscuits—the kind that come out of the tube with the doughboy. I hadn't realized how hungry I was until I scooped hash into my mouth. I finish the story, leaving out what I know about Stan Gleason. Saxby asks some of the same questions I've already heard but adds a couple of new ones. He doesn't know how close he is to the truth.

"How do the missing folder of your police detective and the shooting of one of your security detail connect?" he asks.

"Masterson says these hate-group members are infiltrating Birmingham PD," I say.

"You think?" Monique asks sarcastically.

"Also, how did this Simenon guy end up dead?"

"I've been thinking about that. And I don't know how, or why." I squint at Saxby. "So what are you getting at?"

"Maybe that ninety-year-old police file that's been missing for a week has more than just a record of his misconduct. Maybe it points fingers at others in power. Ones who are still connected to Birmingham's upper crust. The Klan, city and state government, and the police force were all interconnected in those days. Klansmen ran legitimate businesses and were judges and doctors and teachers. They were a secret society. That's why they wore hoods."

"I believe Simenon probably was a Klan member. I just don't have proof. From what I saw of his record he was golden for a while. He received a citation for bravery, and then a quick promotion to detective."

"But maybe he got too cocky," Saxby speculates. "Caused too

many problems. Businesses like that nightclub he's credited with shutting down were probably a cash flow for a lot of people— Black and white. And think about the payoffs you've uncovered. Ten thousand dollars to Clarita Alvarez and six thousand to George Freeman. That's a hell of a lot of money to dole out on the eve of the Great Depression."

"If he was on the outs with the department, that would explain why coverage of his murder dropped out of the news. Maybe they dropped *him*. He sure isn't listed as one of their fallen officers."

"You'll know more when Masterson gets you the Simenon file," Darius says.

"If you ever get it," Monique quips. "I just had a thought. What if this detective was killed by one of his own?"

"That's exactly what happened today, isn't it? One officer killed another," Saxby says. "So Simenon being killed by his own is not beyond the realms of possibility, especially if his actions were drawing too much attention to the powers that be. We don't really know, do we?" Saxby punctuates his point by eating another huge forkful of grits and scrambled eggs.

"Everyone's keeping secrets," Kristen says, standing abruptly. Her chair scrapes loudly, and I see her tears before she turns toward the stove.

"You still need to get your hands on the official file," Darius says.

I don't respond because I'm watching Kristen. She's gripping the edge of the stove. I walk over to her. Her face is whiter than when she applies her Goth makeup. I touch her arm, and she turns and buries her face on my shoulder.

"Uh, I think we need a break," I say to the group.

"Yeah. Sure," Saxby says. "I need to check in at home. They'll be worried."

"Take your girl to the back and have a chat," Monique says, standing and removing dishes. "Darius and I will take care of the dishes. Won't we, Darius?"

"Sure we will." He looks at me with a raised brow. "It was a great meal, Kristen. Thank you."

Kristen sobs another five minutes after we sit on my bed, and I wait patiently while she composes herself.

"I have something to tell you," she begins. "It's awful. And, Meghan, I'm so scared."

Kristen never calls me by my first name. I think she already knows about her father and I feel so disloyal. She cries again for a few minutes, and I take her hand. Watching her, and feeling her hand shake, I realize I could easily lose it myself.

"Whatever it is, I'll help you," I finally say.

Kristen grips my hand harder, then speaks fast. "Mom called tonight to tell me Scotty was in the hospital, in critical condition, but she wouldn't tell me what happened and wouldn't let me come to the hospital. Then Daddy called. But I just couldn't speak to him. Meghan, I hate him. He's been lying to me all my life."

"What do you mean?" I say with guilt building in my chest.

Kristen nods, wiping at her eyes and cheeks. "He's part of a hate group, and so is Scotty," Kristen says, sobbing again. "They're white supremacists."

Kristen leans over as if she can't get a full breath of air. Her despair is causing me pain. I want to tell her I already know about her father, and her hate-mongering brother who damn near had me killed, but I've made a promise to Masterson. I'm flashing on scenes from the last ten hours. I've never been hit before, and never felt as vulnerable or afraid as I did sitting in the back of that van. I really could have died today. My injured nose begins to throb, and my tongue feels thick.

"How do you know?"

"That booklet we found in Zach's garage."

"There were no Gleasons on that list of names."

"No. But there was an Aldridge. That's my mother's maiden name. So I kept digging and came across a business document. I found Mom's grandfather listed in incorporation papers for a group called Knights of the South. Meghan, this group has been around since the fifties, and they're still operating. They're online. They call themselves the KNOTS. I found Pruitt's name listed in some of their old newsletters. And . . . and Daddy's now one of their leaders."

Suddenly, Kristen releases my hand and sprints to the bathroom. I hear her vomiting. I can't imagine what it must feel like to learn people you love, and have known all your life, have kept horrible secrets.

When we return to the kitchen, Darius, Monique, and Saxby listen to Kristen's disclosure about her father and brother with wide-eyed amazement. They don't ask any questions. We can all see her suffering. Kristen's trying to reconcile the idea of the father she's grown up with—the man she thought of as her hero—with the man she now considers a monster.

And she only knows the half of it.

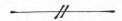

It's almost two a.m. I've sent Saxby my updated reporter's notebook, and an outline for my investigative report, which I'm pitching as a three-part exposé. Masterson hasn't gotten back to me, so the Gleason Insurance connection, any additional Simenon info, and the Klan documents aren't in my story. Neither is my speculation about the whereabouts of my great-grandfather's grave.

I leave my bedroom, tiptoe to the living room, and peer around the corner. Darius is asleep on the couch, snoring gently. He insisted on staying. I'm glad he's here. As I return to my room, I see light under Kristen's bedroom door. I want to knock and check on her, but I don't. I don't trust myself not to tell her everything I know about her father.

FORTY-SEVEN

Retribution

1929

I appear to Anna Kate. Me standing at the door in that gray suit she likes, and she lying on the bed, her full belly stretched to the max. It is a gift, one handed down to me from Mama, the ability to stand between the two worlds, guiding and protecting my family.

Anna Kate doesn't seem surprised to see me, but she is inconsolable. I try to calm her but she's angry, fearful, and grieving. A terrible combination.

Mae misses me. I come to her in her dreams and toss her into the air the way she likes. I also spoke to the new baby. It's another girl. I regret I will not be a father to my babies, nor have more time with my wife.

In my twenty-eight years on earth I've had a lot of good come my way. I married a beautiful woman. I did a man's work every day, and was one of the best at my craft. Not every man can say that. But I guess I always knew I would die early. It's hard to imagine growing old in a place where people hate your very existence.

One feeling still clings to me like withered flesh on brittle bones. The agony of injustice. It tethers me to this place that is no longer my home.

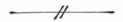

Anna Kate's brothers have come for her. They drove in a Model T along the same route I took four months ago when I first arrived in Birmingham. But they traveled with the urgency of a rescue, and fueled by a baby sister's grief.

Cress and W.M. stumble into the rear door of the boarding-house on Tuesday in the middle of the night, awakening Mrs. Ardle and others. They're both handsome men with skin more white than black, and gray eyes like their sister. Cress's hair is light brown, curly, and worn long—he could be Clark Gable's darker brother. W.M. has thick, wavy hair and a broader nose. He's a couple of inches shorter than his older brother, and his manner is more relaxed.

George Freeman joins the group, and he and Mrs. Ardle pull the two brothers into the night air to whisper before entering the shed. For a few minutes they look at the stained spot where I lay lifeless a week before. Ardle hurries into the kitchen to set two plates of cold chicken and corn bread and pour two big glasses of buttermilk.

Freeman, his wife, Esther, the flask man who accompanied Freeman when they found my body, and Ardle sit at the table with Anna Kate's kin exchanging their views on the situation with the detective and Anna Kate's state of mind. The brothers are intent on driving their sister and niece straightaway to St. Pete, but the fire in the eyes of Cress grows intense as he listens.

"You sure it was this detective that killed Bobby?" Cress asks.

Freeman answers. "He came around here maybe three or four times looking for him when he was alive, and he's come around since asking if we know where he's buried."

"He's a bad man," Mrs. Ardle adds. "My blood ran cold when he laid his beady eyes on me. His tongue flicks like a lizard when he talks," she says, shivering at the thought.

"He's the same fellow people say beat up on Griggs's wife after the ballroom raid," the man sipping from his flask says.

"I hadn't heard that," Freeman says with raised brows.

"It's true," the man replies.

"Robert Lee was worried. That detective had come around to his job at the sawmill once or twice," Mrs. Ardle reports. "He and Anna Kate and little Mae were moving away next week just to be out of sight of the man."

"What'd you say his name is?" Cress asked.

"Simon, or something like that," the flask man answers.

"No. It's Simenon," Freeman says. "Anna Kate asked me and the pastor to make a complaint to the police chief about him."

"Oh Lord," Esther Freeman cries out, expressing her disapproval.

"Well, we're taking Anna Kate and Mae home tonight," Cress said. "But I want a few words with this detective."

"He works nights. Downtown. It wouldn't be that hard to get word to him," the flask man says.

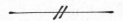

Anna Kate is relieved to see her brothers and collapses sobbing into Cress's arms. He holds her to keep her from dropping to the floor. He seeks help from his little brother, and they lead her back to the bed. I don't know the brothers well. But they have a reputation of being tough boys. Their father, a white man who lived on the other side of the tracks in St. Pete, was more absent than present, and Cress became the surrogate father to the other siblings.

"W.M. is going to stay with you and get you packed up," he says to his sister. "We're leaving before dawn. Only pack the things you absolutely need, Anna Kate. Mama expects to see us late to-morrow. It's going to be a long ride, and we're not going to be able to stop."

Cress pulls his brother to the door to speak out of earshot of Anna Kate, but I hear every word. He's not about to let his sister's pain go unanswered.

It didn't take much to lure the detective to the alley behind the furniture store. Simenon only has a couple of hours left on his graveyard shift, and when he sees the light-skinned man who has told a few people he's looking for the detective to pay him protection money, Simenon gets careless. Cress is at the opening of the alley smoking a cigarette; the detective leaves his car idling and walks into the alley to talk to him.

"Who you representing, boy?" Simenon asks after getting a good look at Cress in the streetlight.

"Lee Harrington," Cress replies, holding out his hand.

Simenon squints. Finally he shakes his head. "Who?"

"The Negro you killed out on the road last Saturday. You re-member, don't you?" Cress hollers, grabbing the detective's arm and punching him. "You remember. He had a wife, a little girl, and a baby on the way."

The two men tussle. Punching, grabbing, slipping, until they're both on the wet pavement. Cress plunges a knife into the man's stomach. Simenon fights back, knocking Cress's cap off and grasping a handful of hair. On the third strike of the knife, Simenon crumples and falls on his side.

Cress looks around, retrieves his cap, and wipes his knife on the detective's coat. I watch him disappear into the dark alley and light another smoke.

FORTY-EIGHT

———•———

2019

Kristen takes the morning off from the library. She's agreed to go along with Masterson's plan. I know she's angry at her father. She's told me of the revulsion she feels for him after learning of his role in my abduction, but her next act will estrange her from her entire family.

I sent Darius on his way to work and spoke with Saxby before he boarded a flight back to Detroit. Monique called to check on us this morning, and at ten o'clock Kristen and I leave her house. The patrol car pulls away from the curb to follow.

Kristen has asked to meet her father for coffee. A public space will make the confrontation safer and quieter. The scheme is to get Gleason to implicate himself in my abduction. The coffee shop rendezvous also pulls Gleason out of his office, where the FBI will arrive soon with subpoenas. I'm here to provide Kristen with moral support.

She sits facing the front door. I'm at a nearby table. There are only four other customers in the establishment during the post–

morning rush hour. I watch Gleason enter the door with a smile for his daughter, until he sees me.

"What is this?" he asks, glaring at me.

"Daddy. Please sit down. I want to talk to you."

Gleason hesitates. He looks like he might turn and run, and then a sneer plays at his lips. He sits across from his daughter. I sit next to Kristen.

"What's going on? I'm really busy, you know."

Kristen looks at her father, and then at me, unable to respond.

"It was my idea," I say. "I believe there are some things you want to tell us, Mr. Gleason."

"I'm sure I don't know what you're talking about," he says, crossing his arms.

"Daddy. I know about you and Scotty," Kristen gets up the nerve to say.

"What do you think you know?"

"I know about your involvement in this Klan group, about you hiding that detective's information from Meghan, and . . ." Kristen begins crying. Her father reaches for her hand and she pulls it away. "And I know you tried to have Meghan killed. What I don't know is why?"

Stan Gleason's face turns to granite. He doesn't move for almost ten seconds, then a vein at his temple begins to pulse, and his face colors. I hold my breath. Suddenly, Kristen pounds the table and shouts.

"I asked you a question, Daddy. Why?"

The man behind the counter and the customers look our way. I touch Kristen's arm. As I do, Gleason grips mine and leans across the table.

"You meddlesome Black bitch," he hisses.

I hadn't noticed one of the officers in my new protection unit slip into the coffee shop to sit in the corner. He's standing over us in a flash.

"Sir, I need you to remove your hand from the lady's arm," the six-foot-two undercover officer says, meaning business.

Gleason looks startled and embarrassed. He stands for a moment at the table looking down at Kristen, then moves to the door. When he opens it, another officer, in uniform, blocks his way. A moment later, Masterson steps in the door and whispers something in Gleason's ear, and the two men glare at each other. The two policemen grab Gleason by the arms and push him out of the coffee shop. Gleason looks back at his daughter, who stares back through tear-filled eyes.

"I didn't get him to confess, Meghan," Kristen says in distress. "He didn't take responsibility for anything."

Every eye in the coffee shop is focused on our table, where this morning drama has unfolded. I gather our things and put my arm through Kristen's to pull her to her feet.

"You did just fine. You were very brave," I say, leading her to the door.

Masterson speaks with us for a few minutes outside the coffee shop. They won't need Gleason's confession because the rogue cop now has a deal from the local prosecutor and has already implicated Kristen's father in the hate crime against me and a dozen others. Masterson gives me a thumb drive that contains the full Simenon personnel folder. "Sorry I couldn't get this to you earlier. There have been, uh, more complications. I'll need to speak with you later. I'll give you a call," he says before leaving.

We're still sitting in my car outside the coffee shop. Kristen waves off the remark when I tell her I'm sorry about the pain she feels. She says she doesn't feel like talking. A few minutes later, Kristen's mother calls. The one-sided conversation is brief, with Mrs. Gleason shouting and Kristen crying. Her mother demanding that Kristen meet her at the office of their family lawyer, and Kristen refusing. The call ends when she accuses her mother of knowing all about her father's dark activities and covering them up.

I look over at Kristen. Her sweater's pulled tight around her midriff and she's trembling. I wonder if she regrets the day, two weeks ago, that I walked into her library.

Monique phones to remind me that Mattie Robinson expects to see me this afternoon. Kristen's coming with me to the church meeting because I won't leave her alone today.

Pastor Hendricks greets us at the door. He's been called to the bedside of a sick parishioner. He pats my arm and predicts I'll be happy with the results of the meeting. Kristen and I descend the church stairs to the basement. Mrs. Robinson and Monique are already seated at a long table, along with a white man in a gray business suit.

Robinson raises an eyebrow when she sees Kristen. I explain that I've invited her to this meeting. Monique takes one look at Kristen, then stands and wraps her arms around her. Robinson introduces the man as Mr. Hazen, one of the church's lawyers.

"Ms. McKenzie, we were interrupted in our last meeting," Robinson says. "You were going to share a letter with me."

"Oh. Is that what this is about? I have two letters."

"May I see them, please?" Robinson asks, extending her palm.

I'm confused. I thought Darius said Robinson had something to show *me*. I pull two folders from my backpack and pass them to her. She takes a few minutes to scan the letters, then hands them to the lawyer, who spends more time scrutinizing the correspondence.

"You have the original letters?" Hazen asks.

"Yes, but I don't carry them with me. I think you can understand why."

The lawyer looks at Robinson with a shrug. She dismisses him with one of her imperious looks and clears her throat.

"Ms. McKenzie, I have a document to give you. It's part of the will of the late Clarita Alvarez. Evangelical is the trustee of her estate. Mr. Hazen here manages the trust."

"I understand you're the great-granddaughter of Robert Lee Harrington. Do you have proof of that relationship?" Hazen asks.

"Well, not with me, but—"

"I think we're prepared to accept Ms. McKenzie's relationship to Mr. Harrington, Wilford," Robinson says, shutting down the attorney's challenge.

Hazen nods. "Your great-grandfather is buried in the church cemetery. Mrs. Alvarez arranged that a grave marker should be made for your great-grandfather's plot. Her directive outlines the markings on the grave site and the secrecy of the plot unless a disclosure is requested by a member of Mr. Harrington's family. Mrs. Alvarez also prepared an affidavit to be presented to the family member requesting information about Mr. Harrington's grave. The entire arrangement is controlled by a nondisclosure agreement. Mrs. Robinson was not at liberty to provide any of this information to you. Only a representative of my firm could do that. I believe presenting these two letters, and your earlier meeting with Mrs. Robinson, constitutes such a request."

I look at Monique, who is smiling widely. Kristen puts her hand on my shoulder. "Oh, you've found your great-grandfather's grave," she says, crying. Mrs. Robinson looks quite pleased with herself.

I've confronted so much emotion in the last seventy hours I can only sit in disbelief.

Hazen removes a sealed envelope from his briefcase. "Young lady," the lawyer says, "here's the affidavit." He places it in front of me.

In a beautiful cursive, the words *To Whom It May Concern* are written on the yellowing envelope. Everyone at the table watches as I carefully remove the seal.

The document is a two-page memorandum of sorts. It describes a two-month span of time, from August through September 1929, when Clarita Alvarez suffered great loss in her life. She writes of a police raid at the business she owned with her husband, his death by police gunfire during the raid, and the sexual assault she suffered at the hands of Police Detective Carl Simenon while she was locked in a jail cell. Then Alvarez describes her friendship with my great-grandfather.

> *Bobby was a frequent visitor to the ballroom. Clean and always well dressed, he was a favorite among the staff—especially the ladies. He always had a kind word and a sophisticated manner about him, but he also had a mind of his own. It was one of our girls—a mulatto hussy I should have fired long ago—that brought the detective's ill attention to our enterprise, and to Bobby. She was angry with him for rejecting her.*

The affidavit describes how, following Alvarez's incarceration and assault, my great-grandfather visited her home many times with offers of money and to spend time with her young son. She writes of the sadness she felt at the news of his death, and her determination to secure for him a proper, and final, resting place. Using her business connections at city hall, she'd collaborated with George Freeman and Harriet Ardle to transport Great-Grandfather's body from the backyard of his boardinghouse to the Maybury Mortuary as a John Doe. He couldn't be buried under his name because they feared the police would try to dispose of his body to protect the detective from the allegations against him. Alvarez later paid for his plot in the private cemetery of Evangelist Baptist Church, where Mr. Maybury was a deacon, and two months later paid for the headstone.

The next section of the affidavit has, perhaps, the most incendiary information. Clarita Alvarez and Mrs. Ardle conspired to get even with Detective Simenon. Ardle had sent for Anna Kate's family to transport Grandma and her mother back to the safety of St. Pete, but soon there was also another plan at work. When Great-Grandma's brothers arrived in Birmingham, the older one, with Alvarez's help, lured the detective to his death.

He deserved it. The pain he had caused so many in our community was an injustice he would never pay for. Jim Crow would see to that. Now we have justice for my husband's death, my rape, George Freeman's beating, and Bobby's murder. A man like that is fated to perish alone in an alley. We buried the knife that killed him with Bobby's body. Please, do not think badly of me for this deed. It is something I will live with for the rest of my life.

If you are reading this letter, I hope you will understand why I want to repay Bobby for his kindness. He was a great comfort to me during my illness, and to my boy, Paulo. He offered my fatherless son a man's attention at a time when he needed it the most. Bobby was a good man. May he rest in ever-lasting peace.

I look up from the letter with no tears. I don't have any more to give. The others at the table have sat quietly while I read. Now they stare at me with anticipation.

"Does the note have the answers you wanted?" Kristen finally asks.

I nod. "Mrs. Robinson, why didn't you give me this letter when I first came to you? The day you walked me to my great-grandfather's grave."

"I wanted to, but I couldn't. Although, as you'll recall, I tried to point you in the right direction with the visit to Mr. Griggs's grave, and the letters. The church was legally bound from disclosing any information about the unnamed grave Clarita Alvarez had paid for. Only Mr. Hazen here could do that."

"I see. One more question, please. I visited Mrs. Alvarez's son at his nursing home. Does the estate also ensure his care?"

"It does," Hazen says. "For as long as he lives. Mrs. Alvarez became quite a wealthy businesswoman in her own right following her husband's death."

"May I read the note?" Robinson asks.

"Yes. Of course. In fact, please read it aloud so the others can hear." I stand from the table. "I'm going to visit Great-Grandfather's grave."

"I think you know the way. It's the marker with the pine tree."

"Yes, I remember."

As I step through the side door into the church cemetery I hear Mrs. Robinson reading the note with her clipped enunciations.

It's a pleasant day. Cool under the mature trees, and the light shimmers where the sun pierces the changing leaves. The far corner of the graveyard, even at the height of the sun, is shadowy, and a chill lifts from the nubs of grass between the pavers.

I squat when I reach the spot where the gray headstone lies flush with the ground. Someone has cleaned the mildew from the marker. There is no name. I'll arrange to change that. I squint to read the date: November 1929 is carved into the stone. The month Alvarez paid for the marker. Since I still don't know the exact date of Great-Grandpa's death, maybe we'll leave it as is, or maybe add today's date. I'll see what Grandma thinks.

Above the date is etched a single pine tree, and I let my fingers linger in the grooves of the engraving. I expect the stone to be cold, but it feels warm. A stick lies across the corner of the marker, and as I brush it away I realize it's something else. I lift the piece of wood above my head so I can catch it in the light. It's smooth, cylindrical, the width of a thin cigar. I've seen something like it before. Then I remember. The old man at the funeral wore one like it around his neck. It's a whistle.

FORTY-NINE

———————◆———————

2019

I'm leaving Birmingham tomorrow. My story was as much a report about our contemporary crisis of racial enmity as it was a historical narrative of my great-grandfather's short life.

Saxby called to say my last blog had received the highest number of comments of any on the paper's website in five years. Following the publication of my three-part investigative piece, Simenon's grandson, the state senator, dropped out of the governor's race. The *Free Press* has already received reprint requests from a dozen papers and online news platforms. *Time, 60 Minutes*, and MSNBC are interested in following up on the story.

It wasn't a difficult choice for me to reveal that one of my grandmother's uncles was responsible for killing the policeman who murdered my great-grandfather. Grandma supposes it was one of the secrets whispered when they thought she was out of earshot.

Mama was worried how that information would make the family look, but Grandma laid my indecision to rest when she said, "Let the chips fall where they may." I think her carpenter father would have appreciated the analogy.

Captain Masterson's thumb drive, and the Alvarez affidavit, confirmed the information in the letters. Carl Simenon was a very bad cop with a dozen formal complaints in his file for excessive force, reckless discharge of a firearm, receipt of kickbacks, and more than one sexual assault. He had been the leader of a small group of rogue cops who used their badges for illicit gain and to harass anyone they didn't take a liking to. I guess my great-grandfather was one of them. But Saxby was right. Simenon's personal crusade against Black citizens in their own neighborhoods had put him at odds with the mayor's office, and with white owners who counted on the business of Black residents. There were several letters of reprimand from Simenon's supervisors about his overzealous actions.

According to Masterson's note that accompanied the thumb drive, when the detective was murdered, a few of his cronies, and then Chief of Police Pruitt, vowed revenge for his death. But by that time Simenon was a disgraced officer. "That's why he isn't on the memorial website," Masterson wrote. His note goes on to say he's now busy trying to excise the current department of hate-group members and sympathizers.

Kristen is still devastated. She hasn't spoken again to her mother or father, and she's received death threats. The original records she'd uncovered listing the Klan membership of dozens of prominent Birmingham businesspeople, politicians, clergy, and police officers figured prominently in my story. Kristen's boss suggested she take a sabbatical, and Darius will drive the two of us, plus Zach, who has asked to see us off, to the airport tomorrow afternoon for my return flight to Detroit, and Kristen's flight to Paraguay. We'll be accompanied by a police protection unit.

I've sent flowers to Carrie Mae Freeman, Cecile Clarke, Mattie Robinson, and the Rankin family. The flowers aren't nearly enough thanks to these generous people who have helped me reveal the truth about Great-Grandpa's death. I also sent a bouquet to Pauli Griggs at the nursing home. He won't understand it's from me, but I think he'll enjoy the flowers.

One of the upsides of the dramatic turn of events this story has caused is a new cooperative spirit between Monique Hendricks and Captain Masterson. What had been an arm's-length acquaintance has grown into mutual respect and a working partnership. Monique describes it as détente; Masterson says he's "walking the talk."

The captain has turned out to be an enigma. The day after I visited the cemetery, he asked me to come to police headquarters, and we spent a couple of hours in an on-the-record interview. It's also when he confidentially informed me that he had already known my great-great-uncle Cressman Smith, of Pinellas County, was the assailant in the Simenon murder.

"How did you find out? It wasn't in the file you gave me, and I only read about it in a sealed, private record."

"Well, the account is true, Ms. McKenzie. The detective yanked out some of his attacker's hair. A few strands were in the original case folder, sitting there for nine decades. I sent it to the lab as soon as I got my hands on it. We were able to make a DNA match to your relative using Veterans Affairs records. Frankly, I was surprised you revealed that fact in your story."

"I'm interested in reporting the truth, Captain. Will the police pursue some kind of investigation or file charges?"

"No. What would be the point? Smith is dead, and it would just mean displaying a whole lot more of the department's historical dirty laundry, wouldn't it?"

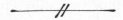

Tonight, I'm cooking one last dinner for Kristen, Monique, and Darius. Baked chicken, mashed potatoes, brussels sprouts, and sweet potatoes. I've also baked a Bundt cake.

Although a police patrol car has been on duty outside Kristen's house since the story broke two days ago, Darius has insisted on sleeping on her couch. Tonight, with her permission, I intend for him to join me in the guest bedroom.

The mood at dinner is mostly festive. We're all aware of Kristen's emotional conflict, and we're worried for her safety. Her world has been turned upside down, but she's trying to put on a good face. I give her mad props for that.

I know I've fallen in love with Darius. He and I had a frank, but sweet, conversation about our budding romance last night as he made up the sofa for sleeping.

"I knew the time would come for you to leave. I thought I'd have my feelings under control about it, but damn it, Meg, I don't want you to go."

"I have to. I have my work. My life is in Detroit."

We'd left the conversation at that, but now I catch him looking at me with a sadness that I feel with equal intensity. After I've cleared the dinner dishes, and bring the lemon-iced Bundt cake to the table, I propose another toast.

"To the miraculous surprise and joy of new friendships," I say, raising my glass.

THAT EVENING, JUST PAST MIDNIGHT, WHEN I REACH FOR DARius's hand and we close the bedroom door behind us, I turn to give him a gift. It's in a small box I bought from a street vendor near the library.

"Open it," I say.

He lifts the piece of whittled wood from the box and turns it in his fingers. "What is it? A whistle?"

"It's from someone very important to me. I'm leaving it in your care, but I'll be back for it. I promise."

FIFTY

Time's Undoing

2019

I've swirled in and out of the lives of loved ones when they think of me or need me. Anna Kate called to me for years, and Mae many years more. I filled my daughter's dreams with the comfort of my presence. She giggled in delight when I visited, but after a while my presence began to frighten her mother, who thought somehow I would take her daughter away from her.

Anna Kate worked hard to raise our two girls alone, putting in long hours as a laundress and seamstress, bringing her sense of order and cleanliness to benefit other people's families. Mae had to become a second mother to her sister, Barbara Ann.

Anna Kate and the girls later moved to Detroit for better opportunities. Mae had five children, Barbara three, and both built lives of their own away from the South. Anna Kate remarried and returned to St. Pete, where her heart attacked her at the age of fifty-five. I wonder how many more of her years were taken by toil, fear, and grief.

Sometimes family secrets are best kept until all those with

even a sliver of memory are gone, when there is no more blame to assign, or guilt to claim. But pain doesn't dim with memory. It resides deep in the marrow and lasts for generations.

I feel the pull of eternity as Meghan moves toward my grave site. I won't show myself to her again, but I've left a present, a thank-you gift, really. I watch from above as she squats before the headstone. Her tears seep deep into the earth, mingling with the cold soil until they warm my hurting bones. Now it's time to be free.

ACKNOWLEDGMENTS

———◆———

I began writing this book in rage, but by the time the final words were placed on the page, I had a gratifying sense of order and love. *Time's Undoing* is a novel about one family's tragic loss—my family's. But I believe the "souls of Black folk" are entwined in a common experience that crosses the borders of time and place. So, this story is offered on behalf of many unnamed Black families who have persevered.

Any book is always made better by the energizing grace and encouragement of good relationships. There are many friends, supporters, and family members to thank.

Thank you to AJ Head, Arli Christian, my Saturday Sister-Friends, Peggy O'Brien, and Renee Bess for your ongoing support. When I've asked, you've answered.

Thank you to my writing group, who critiqued and affirmed my first drafts: Celeste Crenshaw, Melanie Hatter, Tracy Tait, and Dottye Williams. The story got better and better through your feedback.

I'm grateful to my neighbor, Shawn Freeman, a Birmingham

native. She was an early reader who provided helpful comments and wrangled runaway commas.

A huge thank-you to my agent, Lori Galvin, of Aevitas Creative. How did I ever get along without you in my life? You saw this novel as an important story right away and asked all the hard questions. You advocated, edited, and supported me through the hand-wringing, doubts, joy, and fear. Plus, you get my humor. That's so important to me.

I can't say enough about my editor at Dutton, Lindsey Rose. She is a lover of books and a master at refining them. Her commitment to this book and her belief in this story freed me to take her gentle guidance and make this book the best it could be. She read each iteration with renewed excitement. You are a marvel.

I am grateful to the experts at Dutton/PRH who managed the birth of this book. Cover designer Sarah Oberrender—thank you for your creativity and patience. Thanks for the out-of-the-box thinking of the publicity and marketing teams, especially Sarah Thegeby, Amanda Walker, Nicole Jarvis, and Stephanie Cooper. A tip of the hat to Patricia Clarke, Alice Dalrymple, Daniel Brount, Hannah Dragone, Susan Schwartz, Ryan Richardson, and Charlotte Peters. Much appreciation to the copy editor and proofreaders who whipped this book into shape: Eileen Chetti, Amy Schneider, and Janine Barlow. And I can't forget the honchos who have championed this novel: editor in chief John Parsley and publisher Christine Ball. Thank you!

There is community:

What an immeasurable uplift to belong to Crime Writers of Color (CWoC). I'm proud to be a member and I hope I give as much as I get from this group. In particular, I owe a debt to Kellye Garrett, one of the cofounders of CWoC, who answered my frantic text with a phone call that was both soothing and sensible.

ACKNOWLEDGMENTS

A shout-out, also, to Sisters in Crime and Mystery Writers of America.

Then there is family:

Thank you to my siblings: Robert McGarrah, Tamara McGarrah Schwarz, and James McGarrah (and Wadiya Nyala in heaven) for sharing a childhood comprising equal parts care and dysfunction, which has transformed into our adult connection of love and solidarity.

I was back in touch with my first cousins over the course of writing and revising this book. I'm grateful to Scarlett Dawson for the family records and recollections she provided; and hugs to Marcus and Latisha as well. Some of my fondest childhood memories are of your mother, my aunt Barbara. She was a gentle and kind woman.

And there is home:

Thanks, Teresa Scott Rankin, for putting up with my moody writer ways. I love you. And I love our dogs, Abby and Frisby, who give unconditional love and keep me humble with their feeding demands and poop-scooping requirements.

Finally, thanks to the good people of Birmingham, Alabama. There are a lot of you!

ABOUT THE AUTHOR

Cheryl A. Head is an award-winning writer, television producer, broadcast executive, and media funder. When not writing fiction, Head consults on a wide range of diversity issues. She is a senior associate at Livingston Associates and a member of Crime Writers of Color, Mystery Writers of America, Sisters in Crime, and the Bouchercon Board of Directors.